# NEMESIS

FICTION BY ISAAC ASIMOV

Nemesis (*1989*)
Norby Down to Earth (*1988*) (*with Janet Asimov*)
Azazel (*1988*)
Prelude to Foundation (*1988*)
Other Universes of Isaac Asimov (*1987*)
Norby Finds a Villain (*1987*) (*with Janet Asimov*)
Fantastic Voyage II: Destination Brain (*1987*)
Norby and the Queen's Necklace (*1986*) (*with Janet Asimov*)
Robot Dreams (*1986*)
Foundation and Earth (*1986*)
The Best Science Fiction of Isaac Asimov (*1986*)
The Best Mysteries of Isaac Asimov (*1986*)
Science Fiction by Asimov (*1986*)
The Alternate Asimovs (*1986*)
Norby and the Invaders (*1985*) (*with Janet Asimov*)
It's Such a Beautiful Day (*1985*)
Robots and Empire (*1985*)
The Disappearing Man and Other Mysteries (*1985*)
The Edge of Tomorrow (*1985*)
Norby and the Lost Princess (*1985*) (*with Janet Asimov*)
Banquets of the Black Widowers (*1984*)
Norby's Other Secret (*1984*) (*with Janet Asimov*)
The Robots of Dawn (*1983*)
Norby, the Mixed-Up Robot (*1983*) (*with Janet Asimov*)
The Union Club Mysteries (*1983*)
The Winds of Change and Other Stories (*1983*)
Foundation's Edge (*1982*)
The Complete Robot (*1982*)
The Casebook of the Black Widowers (*1980*)
The Key Word and Other Mysteries (*1977*)
More Tales of the Black Widowers (*1976*)
The Bicentennial Man and Other Stories (*1976*)
Good Taste (*1976*)
Murder at the ABA (*1976*)

The Heavenly Host (*1975*)
Buy Jupiter and Other Stories (*1975*)
Tales of the Black Widowers (*1974*)
Have You Seen These? (*1974*)
The Best of Isaac Asimov (*1973*)
The Early Asimov (*1972*)
The Gods Themselves (*1972*)
The Best New Thing (*1971*)
Nightfall and Other Stories (*1969*)
Asimov's Mysteries (*1968*)
Through a Glass, Clearly (*1967*)
Fantastic Voyage (*1966*)
The Rest of the Robots (*1964*)
Nine Tomorrows (*1959*)
The Death Dealers (A Whiff of Death) (*1958*)
Lucky Starr and the Rings of Saturn (*1958*)
Earth Is Room Enough (*1957*)
Lucky Starr and the Moons of Jupiter (*1957*)
The Naked Sun (*1957*)
Lucky Starr and the Big Sun of Mercury (*1956*)
The End of Eternity (*1955*)
The Martian Way and Other Stories (*1955*)
Lucky Starr and the Oceans of Venus (*1954*)
The Caves of Steel (*1954*)
Lucky Starr and the Pirates of the Asteroids (*1953*)
Second Foundation (*1953*)
The Currents of Space (*1952*)
Foundation and Empire (*1952*)
David Starr: Space Ranger (*1952*)
Foundation (*1951*)
The Stars, Like Dust— (*1951*)
I, Robot (*1950*)
Pebble in the Sky (*1950*)

# ISAAC ASIMOV
# NEMESIS

A FOUNDATION BOOK

**DOUBLEDAY**

NEW YORK · LONDON · TORONTO · SYDNEY · AUCKLAND

A Foundation Book
Published by Doubleday, a division of
Bantam Doubleday Dell Publishing Group, Inc.
666 Fifth Avenue, New York, New York 10103

FOUNDATION, DOUBLEDAY, and the portrayal of the letter F
are trademarks of Doubleday, a division of
Bantam Doubleday Dell Publishing Group, Inc.

Library of Congress Cataloging-in-Publication Data

Asimov, Isaac, 1920–
Nemesis / Isaac Asimov.—1st ed.
p.  cm.
"A Foundation book."
I. Title.
PS3551.S5N46   1989
813'.54—dc20      89-32938
CIP


ISBN 0-385-24792-3
ISBN 0-385-26619-7 (Limited Edition)
Copyright © 1989 by Nightfall, Inc.
All Rights Reserved
Printed in the United States of America
October 1989
First Edition
BG

To Mark Hurst,
my valued copy editor,
who, I think, works over
my manuscripts
harder than I do

# CONTENTS

# C O N T E N T S

This book is not part of the Foundation Series, the Robot Series, or the Empire Series. It stands independently. I just thought I'd warn you of that to avoid misapprehension. Of course, I might someday write another novel tying this one to the others, but, then again, I might not. After all, for how long can I keep flogging my mind to make it work out these complexities of future history?

Another point. I made up my mind long ago to follow one cardinal rule in all my writing—to be *clear*. I have given up all thought of writing poetically or symbolically or experimentally, or in any of the other modes that might (if I were good enough) get me a Pulitzer prize. I would write merely clearly and in this way establish a warm relationship between myself and my readers, and the professional critics— Well, they can do whatever they wish.

However, my stories write themselves, I'm afraid, and in this one, I was rather appalled to find out that I was writing it in two strands. One set of events was taking place in the story's present, and another set was taking place in the story's past, but steadily approaching the present. I am sure you will have no trouble following the pattern, but since we are all friends, I thought I would let you know.

N E M E S I S

# PROLOGUE

He sat there alone, enclosed.

Outside were the stars, and one particular star with its small system of worlds. He could see it in his mind's eye, more clearly than he would see it in reality if he merely de-opacified the window.

A small star, pinkish-red, the color of blood and destruction, and named appropriately.

Nemesis!

Nemesis, the Goddess of Divine Retribution.

He thought again of the story he had once heard when he was young—a legend, a myth, a tale of a worldwide Deluge that wiped out a sinful degenerate humanity, leaving one family with which to start anew.

No flood, this time. Just Nemesis.

The degeneration of humanity had returned and the Nemesis that would be visited upon it was an appropriate judgment. It would not be a Deluge. Nothing as simple as a Deluge.

Even for the remnant who might escape— Where would they go?

Why was it he felt no sorrow? Humanity could not continue as it was. It was dying slowly through its own misdeeds. If it exchanged a slow excruciating death for a much faster one, was that a cause for sorrow?

Here, actually circling Nemesis, a planet. Circling the planet, a satellite. Circling the satellite, Rotor.

That ancient Deluge carried a few to safety in an Ark. He had only the vaguest idea of what the Ark was, but Rotor was its equivalent. It carried a sampling of humanity who would remain safe and from which a new and far better world would be built.

But for the old world—there would be only Nemesis!

He thought of it again. A red dwarf star, moving on its inexorable path. Itself and its worlds were safe. Not so Earth.

Nemesis was on its way, Earth!

Wreaking its Divine Retribution!

# ONE

## MARLENE

1.

Marlene had last seen the Solar System when she was a little over one year old. She didn't remember it, of course.

She had read a great deal about it, but none of the reading had ever made her feel that it could ever have been part of her, nor she a part of it.

In all her fifteen years of life, she remembered only Rotor. She had always thought of it as a large world. It was eight kilometers across, after all. Every once in a while since she was ten—once a month when she could manage it—she had walked around it for the exercise, and sometimes had taken the low-gravity paths so she could skim a little. That was always fun. Skim or walk, Rotor went on and on, with its buildings, its parks, its farms, and mostly its people.

It took her a whole day to do it, but her mother didn't mind. She said Rotor was perfectly safe. "Not like Earth," she would say, but she wouldn't say *why* Earth was not safe. "Never mind," she would say.

It was the people Marlene liked least. The new census, they said, would show sixty thousand of them on Rotor. Too many. Far too many. Every one of them showing a false face. Marlene hated seeing those false faces and knowing there was something different inside. Nor could she say anything about it. She had tried sometimes when she had been younger, but her mother had grown angry and told her she must never say things like that.

As she got older, she could see the falseness more clearly, but it bothered her less. She had learned to take it for granted and spend as much time as possible with herself and her own thoughts.

Lately, her thoughts were often on Erythro, the planet they had been orbiting almost all her life. She didn't know why these thoughts were coming to her, but she would skim to the observation deck at odd hours and just stare at the planet hungrily, wanting to be there—right there on Erythro.

Her mother would ask her, impatiently, why she should want to be on an empty barren planet, but she never had an answer for that. She didn't know. "I just want to," she would say.

She was watching it now, alone on the observation deck. Rotorians hardly ever came here. They had seen it all, Marlene guessed, and for some reason they didn't have her interest in Erythro.

There it was; partly in light, partly dark. She had a dim memory of being held to watch it swim into view, seeing it every once in a while, always larger, as Rotor slowly approached all those years ago.

Was it a real memory? After all, she had been getting on toward four then, so it might be.

But now that memory—real or not—was overlaid by other thoughts, by an increasing realization of just how large a *planet* was. Erythro was over twelve thousand kilometers across, not eight kilometers. She couldn't grasp that size. It didn't look that large on the screen and she couldn't imagine standing on it and seeing for hundreds—or even thousands—of kilometers. But she knew she wanted to. Very much.

Aurinel wasn't interested in Erythro, which was disappointing. He said he had other things to think of, like getting ready for college. He was seventeen and a half. Marlene was only just past fifteen. That didn't make much difference, she thought rebelliously, since girls developed more quickly.

At least they should. She looked down at herself and thought, with her usual dismay and disappointment, that somehow she still looked like a kid, short and stubby.

She looked at Erythro again, large and beautiful and softly red where it was lit. It was large enough to be a planet but actually, she knew, it was a satellite. It circled Megas, and it was Megas (much larger still) that was really the planet, even though everyone called Erythro by that name. The two of them together, Megas and Erythro, *and* Rotor, too, circled, the star Nemesis.

"Marlene!"

Marlene heard the voice behind her and knew that it was Aurinel. She had grown increasingly tongue-tied with him of late, and the reason for it embarrassed her. She loved the way he pronounced her name. He pronounced it correctly. Three syllables—Mar-LAY-nuh—with a little trill to the "r." It warmed her just to hear it.

She turned and mumbled, "Hi, Aurinel," and tried not to turn red.

He grinned at her. "You're staring at Erythro, aren't you?"

She didn't answer that. Of course that's what she would be doing. Everyone knew how she felt about Erythro. "How come you're here?" (Tell me you were looking for me, she thought.)

Aurinel said, "Your mother sent me."

(Oh well.) "Why?"

"She said you were in a bad mood and every time you felt sorry for yourself, you came up here, and I was to come and get you because she said it would just make you grumpier to stay here. So why are you in a bad mood?"

"I'm not. And if I am, I have reasons."

"What reasons? Come on, now. You're not a little kid any more. You've got to be able to express yourself."

Marlene lifted her eyebrows. "I am quite articulate, thank you. My reasons are that I would like to travel."

Aurinel laughed. "You've traveled, Marlene. You've traveled more than two light-years. No one in the whole history of the Solar System has ever traveled even a small fraction of a light-year. —Except us. So you have no right to complain. You're Marlene Insigna Fisher, Galactic Traveler."

Marlene suppressed a giggle. Insigna was her mother's maiden name and whenever Aurinel said her three names in full, he would salute and make a face, and he hadn't done that in a long time. She guessed it was because he was getting close to being a grown-up and he had to practice being dignified.

She said, "I can't remember that trip at all. You know I can't, and not being able to remember it means it doesn't matter. We're just here, over two light-years from the Solar System, and we're never going back."

"How do you know?"

"Come on, Aurinel. Do you ever hear anyone talk about going back?"

"Well, even if we don't, who cares? Earth is a crowded world and the whole Solar System was getting crowded and used up. We're better off out here—masters of all we survey."

"No, we're not. We survey Erythro, but we don't go down there to be its masters."

"Sure we do. We have a fine working Dome on Erythro. You know that."

"Not for us. Just for some scientists. I'm talking about *us*. They don't let us go down there."

"In time," said Aurinel cheerfully.

"Sure, when I'm an old woman. Or dead."

"Things aren't that bad. Anyway, come on out of here and into the world and make your mother happy. I can't stay here. I have things to do. Dolorette—"

Marlene felt a buzzing in her ears and she didn't hear exactly what Aurinel said after that. It was enough to hear—Dolorette!

Marlene *hated* Dolorette, who was tall and—and *vacuous*.

But what was the use? Aurinel had been hanging around her, and Marlene knew, just by looking at him, exactly how he felt about Dolorette. And now he had been sent to find her and he was just wasting his time. She could tell that was how he felt and she could also tell how anxious he was to get back to that—to that Dolorette. (Why could she always tell? It was so hateful sometimes.)

Quite suddenly, Marlene wanted to hurt him, to find words to give him pain. True words, though. She wouldn't lie to him. She said, "We're never going back to the Solar System. I *know* why not."

"Oh, why's that?" When Marlene, hesitating, said nothing, he added, "Mysteries?"

Marlene was caught. She was not supposed to say this. She mumbled, "I don't want to say. I'm not supposed to know." But she *did* want to say. At the moment she wanted *everyone* to feel bad.

"But you'll tell me. We're friends, aren't we?"

"Are we?" Marlene asked. She said, "Okay, I'll tell you. We're not ever going back because Earth is going to be destroyed."

Aurinel didn't react as she had expected. He burst into a loud squawk of a laugh. It took him a while to settle down, and she glared at him indignantly.

"Marlene," he said, "where did you hear that? You've been viewing thrillers."

"I have *not!*"

"But what makes you say anything like that?"

"Because I know. I can tell. From what people say, but don't say, and what they do, when they don't know they're doing it. And from things the computer tells me when I ask the right questions."

"Like what things it tells you?"

"I'm not going to tell *you.*"

"Isn't it possible? Just *barely* possible"—and he held up two fingers very closely together—"that you're imagining things?"

"No, it isn't possible. Earth won't be destroyed right away—maybe not for thousands of years—but it's going to be destroyed." She nodded solemnly, her face intense. "And nothing can stop it."

Marlene turned and walked away, angry at Aurinel for doubting her. No, not doubting her. It was more than that. He thought she was out of her mind. And there it was. She had said too much and had gained nothing by it. *Everything* was wrong.

Aurinel was staring after her. The laughter had ceased on his boyishly handsome face and a certain uneasiness was creasing the skin between his eyebrows.

2.

Eugenia Insigna had grown middle-aged during the trip to Nemesis, and in the course of the long stay after arrival. Over the years she had periodically warned herself: This is for life; and for our children's lives into the unseen future.

The thought always weighed her down.

Why? She had known this as the inevitable consequence of what they had done from the moment Rotor had left the Solar System. Everyone on Rotor—volunteers all—had known it. Those who had not had the heart for eternal separation had left Rotor before takeoff, and among those who had left was—

7

Eugenia did not finish that thought. It often came, and she tried never to finish it.

Now they were here on Rotor, but was Rotor "home"? It was home for Marlene; she had never known anything else. But for herself, for Eugenia? Home was Earth and Moon and Sun and Mars and all the worlds that had accompanied humanity through its history and prehistory. They had accompanied life as long as there had been life. The thought that "home" was not here on Rotor clung to her even now.

But, then, she had spent the first twenty-eight years of her life in the Solar System and she had done graduate work on Earth itself in her twenty-first to twenty-third years.

Odd how the thought of Earth periodically came to her and lingered. She hadn't liked Earth. She hadn't liked its crowds, its poor organization, its combination of anarchy in the important things and governmental force in the little things. She hadn't liked its assaults of bad weather, its scars over the land, its wasteful ocean. She had returned to Rotor with an overwhelming gratitude, and with a new husband to whom she had tried to sell her dear little turning world—to make its orderly comfort as pleasant to him as it was to her, who had been born into it.

But he had only been conscious of its smallness. "You run out of it in six months," he had said.

She herself hadn't held his interest for much longer than that. Oh well—

It would work itself out. Not for her. Eugenia Insigna was lost forever between worlds. But for the children. Eugenia had been born to Rotor and could live without Earth. Marlene had been born—or almost born—to Rotor alone and could live without the Solar System, except for the vague feeling that she had originated there. Her children would not know even that, and would not care. To them, Earth and the Solar System would be a matter of myth, and Erythro would have become a rapidly developing world.

She hoped so. Marlene had this odd fixation on Erythro already, though it had only developed in the last few months and might leave just as quickly as it had come.

Altogether, it would be the height of ingratitude to complain. No one could possibly have imagined a habitable world in orbit about Nemesis. The conditions that created habitability were remarkable. Estimate those probabilities and throw in the nearness of Nemesis to the Solar System and you would have to deny that it could possibly have happened.

She turned to the day's reports, which the computer was waiting, with the infinite patience of its tribe, to give her.

Yet before she could ask, her receptionist signaled and a soft voice came from the small button-speaker pinned to the left shoulder of her garment, "Aurinel Pampas wishes to see you. He has no appointment."

Insigna grimaced, then remembered that she had sent him after Marlene. She said, "Let him come in."

She cast a quick look at the mirror. She could see that her appearance was reasonable. To herself, she seemed to look younger than her forty-two years. She hoped she looked the same way to others.

It seemed silly to worry about her appearance because a seventeen-year-old boy was about to enter, but Eugenia Insigna had seen poor Marlene looking at that boy and she knew what that look portended. It didn't seem to Insigna that Aurinel, who was so fond of his own appearance, would ever think of Marlene, who had never been able to rid herself of her childhood pudginess, in any way other than as an amusing child. Still, if Marlene had to face failure in this, let her not feel that her mother had contributed to that failure in any way and had been anything but charming to the boy.

She'll blame me anyway, thought Insigna with a sigh, as the boy walked in with a smile that had not yet outgrown its adolescent shyness.

"Well, Aurinel," she said. "Did you find Marlene?"

"Yes, ma'am. Right where you said she'd be, and I told her you wanted her out of there."

"And how is she feeling?"

"If you want to know, Dr. Insigna—I can't tell if it's depression or something else, but she has a rather funny idea in her head. I don't know that she'd like my telling you about it."

"Well, I don't like setting spies on her either, but she frequently has strange ideas and she worries me. Please tell me what she said."

Aurinel shook his head. "All right, but don't tell her I said anything. This one is *really* crazy. She said that Earth was going to be destroyed."

He waited for Insigna to laugh.

She did not. Instead, she exploded. *"What?* What made her say that?"

9

"I don't know, Dr. Insigna. She's a very bright kid, you know, but she gets these funny ideas. Or she may have been putting me on."

Insigna cut in. "She may have been doing exactly that. She has a strange sense of humor. So listen, I don't want you to repeat this to anyone else. I don't want silly stories to get started. Do you understand?"

"Certainly, ma'am."

"I'm serious. Not a word."

Aurinel nodded briskly.

"But thanks for telling me, Aurinel. It was important to do so. I'll speak to Marlene and find out what's bothering her—and I won't let her know you told me."

"Thank you," said Aurinel. "But just one thing, ma'am."

"What's that?"

"*Is* Earth going to be destroyed?"

Insigna stared at him, then forced a laugh. "Of course not! You may go now."

Insigna looked after him and wished earnestly that she could have managed a more convincing denial.

3.

Janus Pitt made an impressive appearance, which had helped him in his rise to power as Commissioner of Rotor. In the early days of the formation of the Settlements, there had been a push for people of no more than average height. There had been thoughts of having a smaller per capita requirement for room and resources. Eventually, the caution had been deemed unnecessary and had been abandoned, but the bias was still there in the genes of the early Settlements and the average Rotorian remained a centimeter or two shorter than the average citizens of later Settlements.

Pitt was tall, though, with iron gray hair, and a long face, and deep blue eyes, and a body that was still in good shape, despite the fact that he was fifty-six.

Pitt looked up and smiled as Eugenia Insigna entered, but felt the usual small surge of uneasiness. There was something always uneasy-making about Eugenia, even wearying. She had these Causes (capital C) that were hard to deal with.

"Thank you for seeing me, Janus," she said, "on such short notice."

Pitt placed his computer on hold, and leaned back in his chair, deliberately producing an air of relaxation.

"Come," he said, "there's no formality between us. We go back a long way."

"And have shared a great deal," said Insigna.

"So we have," said Pitt. "And how is your daughter?"

"It's about her I wish to speak, as a matter of fact. Are we shielded?"

Pitt's eyebrows arched. "Why shielded? What is there to shield and from whom?"

The very question activated Pitt's realization of the odd position in which Rotor found itself. To all practical purposes, it was alone in the Universe. The Solar System was more than two light-years away, and no other intelligence-bearing worlds might exist within hundreds of light-years or, for all anyone knew, billions of light-years in any direction.

Rotorians might have fits of loneliness and uncertainty, but they were free of any fear of outside interference. Well, almost any fear, thought Pitt.

Insigna said, "You know what there is to shield. It was you who have always insisted on secrecy."

Pitt activated the shield and said, "Are we to take that up again? Please, Eugenia, it's all settled. It was settled when we left fourteen years ago. I know that you brood about it now and then—"

"Brood about it? Why not? It's *my* star," and her arm flailed outward as if in the direction of Nemesis. "It's *my* responsibility."

Pitt's jaw tightened. Do we have to go through all this again? he thought.

Aloud, he said, "We're shielded. Now, what's bothering you?"

"Marlene. My daughter. Somehow she knows."

"Knows what?"

"About Nemesis and the Solar System."

"How could she know? Unless you've told her?"

Insigna spread her arms helplessly. "Of course I didn't tell her, but I don't have to. I don't know how it is, but somehow Marlene seems to hear and see everything. And from the little things she hears and sees, she works things out. She's always been able to do it, but in the last year it's grown much worse."

"Well then, she guesses, and sometimes she makes lucky guesses. Tell her she's wrong, and see that she doesn't talk about it."

11

"But she's already told a young man, who came to tell me. That's how I know. Aurinel Pampas. He's a friend of the family."

"Ah yes. I'm aware of him—somewhat. Simply tell him not to listen to fantasies made up by a little girl."

"She's not a little girl. She's fifteen."

"To him, she's a little girl, I assure you. I said I'm aware of the young man. I'm under the impression he's pushing adulthood very hard and I remember, when I was his age, that fifteen-year-old girls were beneath contempt, especially if they were—"

Insigna said bitterly, "I understand. Especially if they are short, plump, and plain. Does it matter that she's highly intelligent?"

"To you and to me? Certainly. To Aurinel, certainly not. If necessary, I'll talk to the boy. You talk to Marlene. Tell her the idea is ridiculous, that it isn't true, and that she must not spread disturbing fairy tales."

"But what if it *is* true?"

"That's beside the point. Look, Eugenia, you and I have concealed this possibility for years, and it would be better if we continued to conceal it. If it gets around, it will be exaggerated, and there will be rising sentiment about the matter—useless sentiment. It will only distract us from the job that has occupied our time ever since we left the Solar System, and which will continue to occupy us for generations, perhaps."

She looked at him—shocked, unbelieving.

"Have you really no feeling for the Solar System, for Earth, the world on which humanity originated?"

"Yes, Eugenia, I have all sorts of feelings. But they're visceral and I can't let them sway me. We left the Solar System because we thought it was time for humanity to spread outward. Others, I'm sure, will follow; maybe they are already doing so. We have made humanity a Galactic phenomenon and we mustn't think in terms of a single planetary system any more. Our job is *here*."

They stared at each other, then Eugenia said, with a touch of hopelessness, "You'll talk me down again. You've talked me down for so many years."

"Yes, but next year I'll have to again, and the year after. You won't stay down, Eugenia, and you tire me. The first time should have been enough." And he turned away, back to his computer.

# TWO

## NEMESIS

4.

The first time he had talked her down had been sixteen years ago in the year 2220, that exciting year in which the possibilities of the Galaxy had opened up for them.

Janus Pitt's hair was a dark brown then, and he was not yet Commissioner of Rotor, though everyone spoke of him as the up-and-coming man. He did head the Department of Exploration and Commerce, however, and the Far Probe was his responsibility, and, to a large extent, the result of his actions.

It was the first attempt to push matter through space with a hyper-assisted drive.

As far as was known, only Rotor had developed hyper-assistance and Pitt had been the strongest proponent of secrecy.

He had said at a meeting of the Council. "The Solar System is crowded. There are more space Settlements than can easily be found room for. Even the asteroid belt is only an amelioration. It will be

13

uncomfortably crowded soon enough. What's more, each Settlement has its own ecological balance and we are drifting apart in that respect. Commerce is being throttled for fear of picking up someone else's strains of parasites or pathogens.

"The only solution, fellow Councillors, is to leave the Solar System —without fanfare, without warning. Let us leave and find a new home, where we can build a new world, with our own brand of humanity, our own society, our own way of life. This can't be done without hyper-assistance—which we have. Other Settlements will eventually learn the technique and will leave, too. The Solar System will be a dandelion gone to seed, its various components drifting in space.

"But if we go first, we will find a world, perhaps, before others follow. We can establish ourselves firmly, so that when others do follow and, perhaps, come across us in our new world, we will be strong enough to send them elsewhere. The Galaxy is large and there are bound to be elsewheres."

There had been objections, of course, and fierce ones. There were those who argued out of fear—fear of leaving the familiar. There were those who argued out of sentiment—sentiment for the planet of birth. There were those who argued out of idealism—the desire to spread knowledge so that others might go, too.

Pitt had scarcely thought he would win out. He had done so because Eugenia Insigna had supplied the winning argument. What an incredible stroke of luck it was that she had come to him first.

She was quite young then, only twenty-six, married but not yet pregnant. She was excited, flushed, and laden down with computer sheets.

Pitt had frowned, he recalled, at her intrusion. He was Secretary of the Department and she—well, she was nobody although, as it happened, this was the very last moment when she would be nobody.

At the time, he didn't realize this, of course, and he was annoyed that she had forced her way in. He cringed at the obvious excitement of the young woman. She was going to make him go through the infinite complexities of whatever it was she was holding in her hand, and do so with an enthusiasm that would quickly exhaust him.

She should give a brief summary to one of his assistants. He decided to say so. "I see you have data there, Dr. Insigna, that you wish to bring to my attention. I'll be glad to look at it in due course. Why don't you leave it with one of my people?" And he indicated the door,

14

hoping ardently that she would about-face and move in that direction. (Sometimes, in idle moments in later years, he would wonder what would have happened if she had, and his blood would run cold at the thought.)

But she said, "No no, Mr. Secretary. I must see you and no one else." Her voice trembled as she spoke, as though her inner excitement was unbearable. "It's the greatest discovery anyone has made since—since—" She gave up. "It's the *greatest.*"

Pitt looked dubiously at the sheets she was holding. They were quivering, but he felt no answering excitement of his own. These specialists always thought some micro-advance in their micro-field was system-shattering.

He said, resigned, "Well, Doctor, can you explain it simply?"

"Are we shielded, sir?"

"Why do we have to be shielded?"

"I don't want anyone else to hear till I'm sure—sure— I have to check again and recheck, till there's no doubt. But, really, I have no doubt. I'm not making sense, am I?"

"No, you're not," said Pitt coldly, placing his hand on a contact. "We're shielded. Now tell me."

"It's all here. I'll show it to you."

"*No.* First tell me. In words. Briefly."

She drew a deep breath. "Mr. Secretary, I've discovered the nearest star." Her eyes were wide and she was breathing rapidly.

Pitt said, "The nearest star is Alpha Centauri and that's been known for four centuries."

"It's the nearest star we've known, but it isn't the nearest we can know. I have discovered one that is closer. The Sun has a distant companion. Can you believe it?"

Pitt considered her carefully. It was rather typical. If they were young enough, enthusiastic enough, inexperienced enough, they would explode prematurely every time.

He said, "Are you sure?"

"I am. Really. Let me show you the data. It's the most exciting thing that has happened in astronomy since—"

"*If* it's happened. And don't show me the data. I'll look at it later. *Tell* me. If there's a star much closer than Alpha Centauri, why hasn't it been discovered before now? Why was it left to you to do so, Dr. Insigna." He knew he was sounding sarcastic, but she didn't seem to pay attention to his tone. She was far too excited.

"There's a reason. It's behind a cloud, a dark cloud, a puff of dust that just happens to be between the companion star and ourselves. Without the absorption of the dust, it would be an eighth-magnitude star, and it would certainly have been noticed. The dust cuts down the light and makes it nineteenth-magnitude, lost among many millions of other faint stars. There was no reason to notice it. No one looked at it. It's in Earth's far southern sky, so that most of the telescopes in pre-Settlement days couldn't even point in that direction."

"And if so, how is it you've noticed it?"

"Because of the Far Probe. You see, this Neighbor Star and the Sun are changing positions relative to each other, of course. I assume it and the Sun are revolving about a mutual center of gravity very slowly in a period of millions of years. Some centuries ago, the positions may have been such that we could have seen the Neighbor Star to one side of the cloud in its full brightness, but we would still have needed a telescope to see it and telescopes are only six centuries old—less old than that in those places on Earth from which the Neighbor Star would be visible. Some centuries from now, it will be seen clearly again, shining from the other side of the dust cloud. But we don't have to wait for centuries. The Far Probe did it for us."

Pitt could feel himself igniting, a distant core of warmth arising within him. He said, "Do you mean that the Far Probe took a picture of that section of the sky containing this Neighbor Star and that the Far Probe was far enough out in space to see around the cloud and detect the Neighbor Star at full brightness?"

"Exactly. We had an eighth-magnitude star where no eighth-magnitude star ought to be, and the spectrum was that of a red dwarf. You can't see red dwarf stars far away, so it had to be pretty close."

"Yes, but why closer than Alpha Centauri?"

"Naturally, I studied the same area of the sky as seen from Rotor and the eighth-magnitude star wasn't there. However, fairly near it was a nineteenth-magnitude star that wasn't present in the photograph taken by the Far Probe. I assumed that the nineteenth-magnitude star was the eighth-magnitude star, obscured, and the fact that they weren't *exactly* in the same place had to be the result of parallactic displacement."

"Yes, I understand about that. A nearby objects appears to be in different places against the distant background as one views it from different spots."

16

"That's right, but the stars are so distant that even if the Far Probe went out a big fraction of a light-year that change in position wouldn't produce a noticeable shift in distant stars, but it would in nearby stars. And for this Neighbor Star, it produced a huge shift; I mean, comparatively. I checked the sky for different positions of the Far Probe on its journey outward. There were three photographs taken during those intervals when it was in normal space, and the Neighbor Star was progressively brighter as the Probe viewed it farther and farther toward the edge of the cloud. From the parallactic displacement, the Neighbor Star turns out to be at a distance of just over two light-years. It's at half the distance of Alpha Centauri."

Pitt looked at her thoughtfully and, in the long silence that followed, she grew restless and uncertain.

"Secretary Pitt," she said, "do you want to see the data now?"

"No," he said. "I'm satisfied with what you've told me. Now I must ask you some questions. It seems to me, if I understand you correctly, that the chance that someone would concentrate on a nineteenth-magnitude star, and try to get its parallax and determine its distance, is negligible."

"Just about zero."

"Is there any other way of noticing that an obscure star must be very near to us?"

"It may have a large proper motion—for a star. I mean that if you watch it steadily, its own motion would change its place in the sky in a more or less straight line."

"Would that be noticed in this case?"

"It might be, but not all stars have a large proper motion, even if they are close to us. They are moving in three dimensions and we see the proper motion only in a two-dimensional projection. I can explain—"

"No, I'm continuing to take your word for it. Has this star got a large proper motion?"

"That would take some time to determine. I do have a few older pictures of that part of the sky and I could detect an appreciable proper motion. That would need more work."

"But do you think it has the kind of proper motion that would force itself on astronomers, if they just happened by accident to note the star?"

"No, I don't."

"Then is it possible that we on Rotor are the only ones who know

17

about this Neighbor Star, since we're the only ones who've sent out a Far Probe. This is your field, Dr. Insigna. Do you agree that we're the only ones who've sent out a Far Probe?"

"The Far Probe isn't entirely a secret project, Mr. Secretary. We've accepted experiments from the other Settlements and discussed that part of it with everyone, even Earth, which isn't too interested in astronomy these days."

"Yes, they leave it to the Settlements, which is sensible. But have any other Settlements sent out a Far Probe that they *have* kept secret?"

"I doubt that very much, sir. They would need hyper-assistance for that, and we have kept the technique of hyper-assistance *entirely* secret. If they had hyper-assistance, we'd know. They'd have to perform experiments in space that would give the fact away."

"According to the Open Science Agreement, all data obtained by the Far Probe is to be published generally. Does that mean that you have already informed—"

Insigna interrupted indignantly. "Of course not. I would have to find out a good deal more before I publish. What I have now is only a preliminary result that I'm telling you in confidence."

"But you are not the only astronomer working on the Far Probe. I presume you've shown the results to the others."

Insigna flushed and looked away. Then she said defensively, "No, I haven't. I noticed this datum. I followed it up. I worked out its significance. *I.* And I want to make sure I get the credit for it. There is only one star that is nearest to the Sun and I want to be in the annals of science as its discoverer."

"There might be a still closer one," and now Pitt permitted himself the first smile of the interview.

"It would have been long known. Even my star would be known but for the very unusual existence of that tiny obscuring cloud. To have another—and closer—star is quite out of the question."

"Then it boils down to this, Dr. Insigna. You and I are the only ones to know of the Neighbor Star. Am I right? No one else?"

"Yes, sir. Just you and I, so far."

"Not just so far. It must remain a secret to us until I am prepared to tell certain specific others."

"But the agreement—the Open Science Agreement—"

"Must be ignored. There are always exceptions to everything. Your discovery involves Settlement security. If Settlement security is involved, we are not required to make the discovery an open one. We don't make hyper-assistance open, do we?"

"But the existence of the Neighbor Star has nothing to do with Settlement security."

"On the contrary, Dr. Insigna, it does. Perhaps you don't realize it, but you have come upon something that can change the destiny of the human species."

### 5.

She stood there, frozen, staring at him.

"Sit down. We are conspirators, you and I, and we must be friendly. From now on, you are Eugenia to me when we're alone, and I am Janus to you."

Insigna demurred. "I don't think that's proper."

"It will have to be, Eugenia. We can't conspire on frigid, formal terms."

"But I don't want to conspire with anyone about anything, and that's all there is to it. And I don't see the point about keeping secret the facts concerning the Neighbor Star."

"I suppose you are afraid of losing the credit."

Insigna hesitated the merest moment, then said, "You can bet your last computer chip I am, Janus. I want my credit."

"For the moment," he said, "forget that the Neighbor Star exists. You know that I've been arguing for quite a while that Rotor ought to leave the Solar System. Where do you stand on that? Would you like to leave the Solar System?"

She shrugged. "I'm not sure. It would be nice to see some astronomical object close up for the first time—but it's a little frightening, too, isn't it?"

"You mean, leaving home?"

"Yes."

"But you wouldn't be leaving home. This is home. Rotor." His arm flipped from side to side. "It would come with you."

"Even so, Mr. Sec— Janus, Rotor isn't all there is to home. We have a neighborhood, the other Settlements, the planet Earth, the whole Solar System."

"It's a crowded neighborhood. Eventually, some of us will have to go, whether we want to or not. On Earth there was once a time when some people had to cross mountain ranges and oceans. Two centuries ago, people on Earth had to leave their planet for Settlements. This is just another step forward in a very old story."

"I understand, but there are some people who never went. There are people who are still on Earth. There are people who've lived in one small region of Earth for countless generations."

"And you want to be one of these nonmovers."

"I think my husband Crile does. He's quite outspoken about your views, Janus."

"Well, we have freedom of speech and thought on Rotor, so he can disagree with me if he pleases. Now here's something else I'd like to ask you. When people generally, on Rotor or elsewhere, think of moving away from the Solar System, where do they think of going?"

"Alpha Centauri, of course. It's the star everyone believes is closest. Even with hyper-assistance, we can't end up going faster than the speed of light on the average, so it would take us four years. Anywhere else, it would take much longer, and four years is long enough to travel."

"Suppose it were possible to travel even faster, and suppose you could reach much farther than Alpha Centauri, where would you go then?"

Insigna paused in thought awhile, then said, "I suppose—still Alpha Centauri. It would still be in the old neighborhood. The stars at night would still seem quite the same. That would give us a comfortable feeling. We would be closer to home, if we wanted to return. Besides, Alpha Centauri A, which is the largest of the three-star Alpha Centauri system, is practically a twin of the Sun. Alpha Centauri B is smaller, but not too small. Even if you ignore Alpha Centauri C, a red dwarf, you would still have two stars for the price of one, so to speak, two sets of planets."

"Suppose a Settlement has left for Alpha Centauri and found decent habitability there and settled down to build a new world, and back in the Solar System, it was known that this had happened. Where would the next Settlements go, once they decided to leave the Solar System?"

"To Alpha Centauri, of course," said Insigna without hesitation.

"So the human species would tend to go to the obvious place, and if one Settlement succeeds, others would follow quickly, until the new world was as crowded as the old, until there were many people with many cultures, and eventually many Settlements with many ecologies."

"Then it will be time to move on to other stars."

"But always, Eugenia, success in one place will draw other Settlements. A salubrious star, a good planet, will bring others flocking."

"I suppose so."

"But if we go to a star that is only a little over two light-years away, only half the distance of Alpha Centauri, and no one knows about it except us, who will follow us?"

"No one, until they find out about the Neighbor Star."

"But that might take a long time. For that long time, they would all flock to Alpha Centauri, or to any of a few other obvious choices. They would never notice a red dwarf star at their doorstep, or if they did notice it, they would dismiss it as unfit for human life—if they didn't know that human beings had already made it a going concern."

Insigna stared at Pitt uncertainly. "But what does all this mean? Suppose we go to the Neighbor Star and no one knows about it. What is the advantage?"

"The advantage is that we can fill the world. If there is a habitable planet—"

"There won't be. Not around a red dwarf star."

"Then we can use whatever raw material that exists there to build any number of Settlements."

"You mean there would be more room for us."

"Yes. Much more room than if they came flocking in after us."

"So we would have a little more time, Janus. Eventually we would fill the room available for us at the Neighbor Star, even if we were alone. So it would take us five hundred years instead of two hundred. What difference would that make?"

"All the difference you can imagine, Eugenia. Let the Settlements crowd in as they wish and we will have a thousand different cultures, bringing with them all the hatreds and misfittings of Earth's dismal history. Give us time to be here alone and we can build a system of Settlements that will be uniform in culture and ecology. It will be a far better situation—less chaotic, less anarchic."

"Less interesting. Less variegated. Less alive."

"Not at all. We'll diversify, I'm sure. The different Settlements will have their differences, but there will, at least, be a common base from which those differences will spring. It will be a far better group of Settlements for that. And even if I am wrong, surely you see that it's an experiment that must be tried. Why not devote one star to such a reasoned development and see if it works? We can take one star, a red

21

dwarf throwaway that no one would be ordinarily interested in, and use it to see if we can build a new kind of society and possibly a better one.

"Let us see what we can do," he went on, "if we don't have our energies worn out and broken by useless cultural differences, and our overall biology constantly perverted by alien ecological inroads."

Insigna felt herself moved. Even if it didn't work, humanity would have learned something—that this wouldn't work. And if it *did* work?

But then she shook her head. "It's a useless dream. The Neighbor Star will be independently discovered, no matter how we try to keep it secret."

"But how much of your own discovery, Eugenia, was accidental? Be truthful now. You just happened to notice the star. You just happened to compare it with what you could see on another map. Might you not have missed it altogether? And might not others have missed it under similar circumstances?"

Insigna did not answer, but the expression on her face was satisfactory to Pitt.

His voice had grown softer, almost hypnotic. "And if there is a delay of only a hundred years. If we are given only a hundred years to ourselves to build our new society, we would be large enough and strong enough to protect ourselves and make the others pass by and go on to other worlds. We won't have to hide any longer than that."

Again Insigna did not answer.

Pitt said, "Have I convinced you?"

She seemed to shake herself. "Not entirely."

"Then think about it, and I'll ask you just one favor. While you think about it, don't say a word to anyone about the Neighbor Star and let me have all the data in connection with it for safekeeping. I won't destroy it. My promise. We will need it if we are going to go to the Neighbor Star. Will you go that far at least, Eugenia?"

"Yes," she said at last in a small voice. Then she fired up. "One thing, though. I must be able to name the star. If I give it a name, then it's my star."

Pitt smiled briefly. "What do you want to call it? Insigna's Star? Eugenia's Star?"

"No. I'm not *that* foolish. I want to call it Nemesis."

"Nemesis? N-E-M-E-S-I-S?"

"Yes."

"But why?"

"There was a brief period of speculation back in the late twentieth century about the possibility of a Neighbor Star for the Sun. It came to nothing at that time. No Neighbor Star was found, but it had been referred to as 'Nemesis' in the papers devoted to it. I would like to honor those daring thinkers."

"Nemesis? Wasn't there a Greek goddess of that name? An unpleasant one?"

"The Goddess of Retribution, of Justified Revenge, of Punishment. It entered the language as a rather flowery word. The computer called it 'archaic' when I checked."

"And why would those old-timers have called it Nemesis?"

"Something to do with the cometary cloud. Apparently, Nemesis, in its revolution about the Sun, passed through the cloud and induced cosmic strikes that killed off large portions of Earth life every twenty-six million years."

Pitt looked astonished. "Really?"

"No, not really. The suggestion didn't survive, but I want Nemesis to be the name just the same. And I want it to go on record that I named it."

"I promise you that, Eugenia. It's your discovery and that will enter our records. Eventually, when the rest of humanity discovers the Nemesian region—would that be the right way of putting it?—they will then learn who made the discovery and how it came about. Your star, *your* Nemesis, will be the first star, other than the Sun itself, to shine over a human civilization; and the first, without exception, to shine over a human civilization that originated elsewhere."

Pitt watched her leave and felt, on the whole, confident. She would fall in line. His letting her name the star was the perfect touch. Surely she would want to go to her own star. Surely she would feel the attraction of building a logical and orderly civilization about *her* star, one from which civilizations all over the Galaxy might descend.

And then, just as he might have relaxed in the glow of a golden future, he was shaken by a faint touch of horror that was utterly alien to him.

Why Nemesis? Why should it have occurred to her to name it for the Goddess of Retribution?

He was almost weak enough to think of it as an evil omen.

# THREE

## MOTHER

### 6.

It was dinnertime, and Insigna was in one of those moods when she was just a little afraid of her own daughter.

Those moods had become more pronounced lately, and she didn't know why. Perhaps it was Marlene's increasing tendency to silence, to being withdrawn, to be always seeming to commune with thoughts too deep for speech.

And sometimes the uneasy fear in Insigna was mixed with guilt: guilt because of her lack of motherly patience with the girl; guilt because of her too-great awareness of the girl's physical shortcomings. Marlene certainly didn't have her mother's conventional prettiness or her father's wildly unconventional good looks.

Marlene was short and—*blunt*. That was the only word that Insigna could find that exactly fit poor Marlene.

And *poor*, of course. It was the adjective she almost always used in her own mind and could just barely keep out of her speech.

Short. Blunt. Thick without being fat, that was Marlene. Nothing graceful about her. Her hair was dark brown, rather long, and quite straight. Her nose was a little bulbous, her mouth turned down just a bit at the ends, her chin small, her whole attitude passive and turned in upon itself.

There were her eyes, of course, large and lustrously dark, with meticulous dark eyebrows that curved above them, long eyelashes that looked almost artificial. Still, eyes alone could not make up for everything else, however fascinating they might be at odd moments.

Insigna had known since Marlene was five that she was unlikely ever to attract a man on the physical plane alone, and that had become more obvious with each year.

Aurinel had kept a languid eye on her during her preteen years, obviously attracted to her precocious intelligence and her almost luminous understanding. And Marlene had been shy and pleased in his presence, as though dimly realizing that there was something about an object called a "boy" that was somehow endearing, but not knowing what it might be.

In the last couple of years, it seemed to Insigna that Marlene had finally clarified in her mind what "boy" meant. Her omnivorous reading of books and viewing of films too old for her body, if not her mind, undoubtedly helped her in this, but Aurinel had grown older, too, and as his hormones began to exert their sway over him, it was no longer badinage he was in search of.

At dinner that night, Insigna asked, "What kind of day did you have, dear?"

"A quiet one. Aurinel came looking for me and I suppose he reported to you. I'm sorry you have to take the trouble to hunt me down."

Insigna sighed. "But, Marlene, I can't help but think sometimes that you're unhappy and isn't it natural for me to be concerned about that? You're alone too much."

"I like to be alone."

"You don't act it. You show no signs of happiness at being alone. There are many people who would like to be friendly and you would be happier if you allowed them to be. Aurinel is your friend."

"Was. He's all busy these days with other people. Today that was obvious. It infuriated me. Imagine him getting all wrapped up because he was thinking about Dolorette."

25

Insigna said, "You can't quite blame Aurinel, you know. Dolorette is his age."

"Physically," said Marlene. "What a bubblehead."

"Physically counts a great deal at his age."

"He shows it. It makes a bubblehead out of him, too. The more he slobbers over Dolorette, the emptier his head gets. I can tell."

"But he'll keep on getting older, Marlene, and when he's a little older, he might find out what the really important things are. And you'll be getting older, too, you know—"

Marlene stared at Insigna quizzically. Then she said, "Come on, Mother. You don't believe what you're trying to imply. You don't believe it for a minute."

Insigna flushed. It suddenly occurred to her that Marlene wasn't guessing. She *knew*—but how did she know? Insigna had made her remark as sincerely as she could, had tried to *feel* it. But Marlene had seen through it without effort. It wasn't the first time either. Insigna had begun to feel that Marlene weighed the inflections, the hesitations, the motions, and always knew what you didn't want her to know. It must be this quality that made Insigna increasingly frightened of Marlene. You don't want to be glass to another's scornful glance.

What had Insigna said, for instance, that had led Marlene to believe the Earth was doomed to destruction? That would have to be taken up and discussed.

Insigna suddenly felt tired. If she couldn't ever fool Marlene, why try? She said, "Well, let's get down to it, dear. What is it you want?"

Marlene said, "I see you really want to know, so I'll tell you. I want to get away."

"Get away?" Insigna found herself unable to understand the simple words her daughter had used. "Where is there to get away to?"

"Rotor isn't all there is, Mother."

"Of course not. But it's all there is within more than two light-years."

"No, Mother, that's not so. Less than two thousand kilometers away is Erythro."

"That scarcely counts. You can't live there."

"There *are* people living there."

"Yes, but under a Dome. A group of scientists and engineers live there because they are doing necessary scientific work. The Dome is

26

much smaller than Rotor. If you feel cramped here, what will you feel there?"

"There's a whole world on Erythro outside the Dome. Someday people will spread out and live all over the planet."

"Maybe. It's by no means a certain thing."

"I'm sure it is a certain thing."

"Even if it is, it would take centuries."

"But it has to begin. Why can't I be part of the beginning?"

"Marlene, you're being ridiculous. You've got a very comfortable home here. When did all this start?"

Marlene pressed her lips together, then said, "I'm not sure. A few months ago, but it's getting worse. I just can't stand it here on Rotor."

Insigna looked at her daughter, frowning. She thought: She feels she has lost Aurinel, she is heartbroken forever, she will leave and punish him by doing so. She will send herself into exile on a barren world, and he will be sorry—

Yes, that line of thought was entirely possible. She remembered when she herself was fifteen. Hearts are so fragile then that a slight tap will crack them. Teenagers heal quickly, but no fifteen-year-old would or could believe that at the time. Fifteen! It is later, *later* that—

No use thinking about it!

She said, "What is it that attracts you about Erythro, Marlene?"

"I'm not sure. It's a large world. Isn't it natural to want a large world"—she hesitated, before adding the last two words, but she gulped them out somehow—"like Earth?"

"Like Earth!" Insigna spoke with vehemence. "You've never been on Earth. You don't know anything about Earth!"

"I've seen a great deal about it, Mother. The libraries are full of films about Earth."

(Yes, they were. Pitt had felt for some time now that such films ought to be sequestered—or even destroyed. He maintained that to break away from the Solar System meant to *break away;* it was wrong to maintain an artificial romanticism about Earth. Insigna had disagreed strongly, but now she suddenly thought that she could see Pitt's point.)

She said, "Marlene, you can't go by those films. They idealize things. They talk about the long past for the most part, when things on Earth were better, and, even so, it was never as good as they picture things to have been."

"Even so."

"No, not 'even so.' Do you know what Earth is like? It's an unlivable slum. They's why people have left it to form all the Settlements. People went from the large dreadful world of Earth to small civilized Settlements. No one wants to go in the other direction."

"There are billions of people who still live on Earth."

"That's what makes it an unlivable slum. Those who are there leave as soon as they can. That's why so many Settlements have been built and are so crowded. That's why we left the Solar System for *here*, darling."

Marlene said in a lower voice, "Father was an Earthman. He didn't leave Earth, even though he might have."

"No, he didn't. He stayed behind." She frowned, trying to keep her voice level.

"Why, Mother?"

"Come, Marlene. We've talked about this. Many people stayed home. They didn't want to leave a familiar place. Almost every family on Rotor had stay-on-Earths. You know that very well. Do you want to return to Earth? Is that it?"

"No, Mother. Not at all."

"Even if you wanted to go, you're over two light-years away and you can't go. Surely you understand that."

"Of course I understand that. I was just trying to point out that we have another Earth right here. It's Erythro. *That's* where I want to go; that's where I *long* to go."

Insigna couldn't stop herself. It was almost with horror that she heard herself say, "So you want to break away from me, as your father did."

Marlene flinched, then recovered. She said, "Is it really true, Mother, that he broke away from you? Perhaps things might have been different if you had behaved differently." Then she added quietly, just as though she were announcing that she was done with dinner. "You drove *him* away, didn't you, Mother?"

# FOUR

## FATHER

7.

Odd—or perhaps stupid—that she was still capable of hurting herself unbearably with thoughts of that kind after fourteen years.

Crile was 1.8 meters tall where, on Rotor, the average height for men was a bit under 1.7 meters. That alone (as in the case of Janus Pitt) gave him a commanding aura of strength that persisted well after the time when she came to recognize, without ever quite admitting it to herself, that she could not rely on his strength.

He had a craggy face, too; a prominent nose and cheekbones, a strong chin—a look, somehow, of hunger and wildness. Everything about him spoke of strong masculinity. She could almost smell it when she met him, and was struck with fascination at once.

Insigna was still a graduate student in astronomy at the time, completing her stint on Earth, looking forward to returning to Rotor so that she could qualify for work on the Far Probe. She dreamed of the wide advances the Far Probe would make possible (and never dreamed that she herself would make the most astonishing one).

And then she met Crile and found herself, to her own confusion, madly in love with an Earthman—an *Earthman*. Overnight she felt herself abandoning the Far Probe in her mind, becoming ready to remain on Earth just to be with him.

She could still remember the way he had looked at her in astonishment and said, "Remain here with me? I'd rather come to Rotor with you." She could not have imagined that *he* would want to abandon his world for *her*.

How Crile managed to obtain permission to come to Rotor, Insigna did not know and had never found out.

The immigration rules were strict, after all. Once any Settlement had a sizable population, it clamped down on immigration—first, because it could not exceed a certain definite limit on the number of people it could support comfortably, and, second, because it made a desperate effort to keep its ecological balance stable. People who came on important business from Earth—or even from other Settlements—had to undergo tedious decontamination procedures, a certain degree of isolation, and an enforced departure as soon as possible.

Yet here was Crile from Earth. He complained to her once of the weeks of waiting that had been part of the decontamination, and she was secretly pleased at the way he had persisted. Clearly, he must have wanted her very badly to submit to it.

Yet there were times when he seemed withdrawn and inattentive and she would wonder then what had really driven him to Rotor over such obstacles. Perhaps it was not she, but the need to escape Earth that had been the motivating force. Had he committed a crime? Made a murderous enemy? Fled a woman he had grown tired of? She had never dared ask.

And he had never offered information.

Even after he had been allowed to enter Rotor, there was a question as to how long he might be able to remain. The Bureau of Immigration would have to grant a special permit to make him a full citizen of Rotor and that was not ordinarily likely.

Insigna had found all the things that made Crile Fisher unacceptable to Rotorians additional inducements for fascination. She found that his being Earth-born lent him a difference and a glamour. True Rotorians would be bound to despise him as an alien—citizen or not

—but she found even that a source of erotic excitement. She would fight for him, and triumph, against a hostile world.

When he tried to find some sort of work that would enable him to earn money and occupy a niche in the new society, it was she who pointed out to him that if he married a Rotorian woman—Rotorian for three generations—that would be a powerful inducement for the Bureau of Immigration to grant him full citizenship.

Crile seemed surprised at that, as though it hadn't occurred to him, and then pleased. Insigna had found it a little disappointing. It would be much more flattering to be married for the sake of love than for the sake of citizenship, but then she thought to herself: Well, if that's what it takes—

So, after a typical long Rotorian engagement, they were married.

Life went on without much change. He was not a passionate lover, but he had not been that before the marriage either. He had offered her an absent affection, an occasional warmth that kept her constantly near happiness if not altogether immersed in it. He was never actively cruel and unkind, and he *had* given up his world for her and gone through considerable inconvenience to be with her. Surely that might be counted in his favor, and Insigna counted it so.

Even as a full citizen, which he had been granted after their marriage, there remained a kernel of dissatisfaction within him. Insigna was aware of this and could not entirely blame him. He might be a full citizen, yet he was still not a native-born Rotorian and many of the most interesting activities on Rotor were closed to him. She did not know what his training had been, for he never mentioned how much of an education he had had. He didn't *sound* uneducated, and there was no disgrace in being self-educated, but Insigna knew that on Earth the population did not take higher education as a given, the way that Settlement populations did.

The thought bothered her. She didn't mind Crile Fisher being an Earthman and facing down her friends and colleagues where that was concerned. She didn't know, though, if she could quite handle his being an *uneducated* Earthman.

But no one ever suggested he was, and he listened to the tales of her work on the Far Probe with patience. She never tested his education by discussing the technical details, of course. Yet sometimes he asked questions or made comments that reflected on such things and she valued them, when they came, for she always managed to convince herself that they were intelligent questions and comments.

31

Fisher had a job on one of the farms, a perfectly respectable job, even an essential one, but a job that was not high on the social scale. He did not complain or make a fuss about that—she'd give him that—but he never talked about it, or showed any pleasure in it. And there was always that air of discontent about him.

Insigna learned, therefore, to attempt no cheery "And what happened to you at work today, Crile?"

The few times she had asked, just at first, the answer had been a flat "Nothing much." And that would be all, except for a short annoyed look.

Eventually, she grew nervous about talking to him even of petty office politics and annoying errors. That, too, might serve as an unwelcome comparison of her work with his.

Insigna had to admit that her fears went against the evidence there, an example of her own insecurity rather than his. Fisher didn't show signs of impatience when she did find herself forced to discuss the day's work. Sometimes he even asked, with a pallid interest, about hyper-assistance, but Insigna knew little or nothing about that.

He was interested in Rotorian politics and showed an Earthman's impatience with the smallness of its concerns. She fought with herself not to show displeasure at that.

Eventually, there fell a silence between them, broken only by indifferent discussions concerning the films they had viewed, the social engagements they undertook, the small change of life.

It didn't lead to active unhappiness. Cake had quickly changed to white bread, but there were worse things than white bread.

It even had a small advantage. Working under tight security meant talking to *no one* about one's work, but how many managed to whisper partial confidences to wife or husband? Insigna had not done so, for she had little in the way of temptation, since her own work required little in the way of security.

But when her discovery of the Neighbor Star was suddenly placed under tight wraps, without warning, could she have managed? Surely it would have been the natural thing to do—to tell her husband of the great discovery that was bound to put her name into the astronomy texts for as long as humanity existed. She might have told him even before she told Pitt. She might have come bouncing in: "Guess what! Guess what! You'll never guess—"

But she hadn't. It didn't occur to her that Fisher would be interested. He might talk to others about their work, even to farmers or sheet-metal workers, but not to her.

So it was no effort to mention nothing to him of Nemesis. The matter was dead between them, was not missed, did not exist, until that dreadful day when their marriage came to an end.

8.

When did she move over wholeheartedly to Pitt's side?

At the start, Insigna had been horrified at the thought of keeping the Neighbor Star a secret, profoundly uneasy at the prospect of moving away out of the Solar System to a destination concerning which they knew nothing but the location. She found it ethically wrong and indecently dishonorable to set about building a new civilization by stealth, one which excluded all the rest of humanity.

She had given in on the grounds of Settlement security, but she had intended to fight Pitt privately, to bring up points of argument. She had rehearsed them in her own mind till they were foolproof and irrefutable and then, somehow, she never presented them.

Always—always—he took the initiative.

Pitt said to her, early on, "Now remember, Eugenia, you discovered the companion star more or less by accident, and one of your colleagues may do so as well."

"It's not likely—" she began.

"No, Eugenia, we're not going to depend on unlikelihood. We're going to make certain. You're going to see to it that no one looks in that direction, that no one wants to study the particular computer sheets that would give away the location of Nemesis."

"How can I possibly do that?"

"Very easily. I have spoken to the Commissioner and, as of now, you are in complete charge of the Far Probe research."

"But that would mean I've been moved over the head—"

"Yes. It means an advance in responsibility, in pay, in social stature. To which of these do you object?"

"I don't object to any of this," said Insigna, her heart beginning to pound.

"I'm sure you can fulfill the job of Chief Astronomer more than adequately, but your chief aim will be to see to it that the work done can be of the highest possible quality and significance, provided that what is done has nothing to do with Nemesis."

"But, Janus, you can't keep it completely secret forever."

"I don't intend to. Once we move out of the Solar System, we will all know where we're going. Till then, as few as possible will know, and those few will learn as late as possible."

Her promotion, Insigna noted with a little shame, cooled her objections.

On another occasion, Pitt said to her, "What about your husband?"

"What about my husband?" Insigna was immediately on the defensive.

"He is an Earthman, I understand."

Insigna's lips pressed together. "He is of Earth origin, but he is a Rotorian citizen."

"I understand. I assume you have told him nothing of Nemesis."

"Absolutely nothing."

"Has this husband of yours ever told you why he left Earth and worked so hard to become a Rotorian citizen?"

"No, he hasn't. And I haven't asked him."

"But don't you ever wonder?"

Insigna hesitated and then told the truth. "Yes, I have, sometimes."

Pitt smiled. "I should tell you, perhaps."

And he did, little by little. Never in any overly obtrusive manner. It was never a bludgeon, it was rather the dripping of water at every conversation. It brought her out of her intellectual shell. To live on Rotor, after all, made it entirely too easy to consider only things Rotorian.

But thanks to Pitt, to what he told her, to the films he suggested she view, she became aware of Earth and its billions, of its endemic starvation and violence, its drugs and alienation. She began to understand it as an abysmal pit of misery, something to flee from. She did not wonder any longer why Crile Fisher had left. She wondered why so few Earthmen followed his example.

Nor were the Settlements so much better off. She became aware of how they closed in on themselves, how people were prevented from moving freely from one to another. No Settlement wanted the microscopic flora and fauna of any other. Trade dwindled slowly, and was increasingly carried on by automated vessels with carefully sterilized loads.

The Settlements quarreled and found each other hateful. The circum-Martian Settlements were almost as bad. Only in the asteroid zone were the Settlements multiplying freely, and even those were growing suspicious of all the inner Settlements.

Insigna could feel herself begin to agree with Pitt, even to grow enthusiastic over a flight from intolerable misery and the beginning of a system of worlds where the seeds of suffering had been eradicated. A new start, a new chance.

And then she found that a baby was on the way and her enthusiasm began to wither. To risk herself and Crile on the long journey seemed worthwhile. To risk an infant, a child—

Pitt was unperturbed. He congratulated her. "It will be born here and you will have a little time to accustom yourself to the situation. It will be at least a year and a half before we're ready to go. And by then you will realize how fortunate you will be not to have to wait any longer. The child will have no memory of the misery of a ruined planet and a desperately divided humanity. It will know only a new world with a cultural understanding among its members. Lucky child. Fortunate child. My son and daughter are already grown, already marked."

And again Insigna began to think in that fashion, and by the time Marlene was born, she had indeed begun to dread delay, to fear that before they left, the child would be imprinted with the crowded failure that was the Solar System.

She was entirely on Pitt's side by this time.

Fisher seemed fascinated by Marlene, to Insigna's great relief. She had not thought that he would make much of a father. Yet he hovered over Marlene and took on his share of the duties involved in bringing her up. He seemed actually to grow cheerful as a result.

During the time Marlene was approaching her first birthday, rumors grew throughout the Solar System that Rotor intended to leave. It produced what was almost a system-wide crisis, and Pitt, who was now clearly in line for Commissionerhood, was grimly amused.

"Well, what can they do?" he said. "There's no way they can stop us, and all the outcries of disloyalty, together with their own display of Solar System chauvinism, will only serve to inhibit their investigations into hyper-assistance, which will serve us well."

Insigna said, "But how did it get out, I wonder, Janus?"

"I saw to it that it did." He smiled. "At this point, I don't any longer object to their learning the *fact* of our leaving, as long as they don't know our destination. It would, after all, be impossible to hide our leaving for much longer. We must take a vote on the matter, you know, and once all Rotorians know of our leaving, all the rest of the system will know, in any case."

"A vote?"

"Why, of course. Think it through. We can't take off with a Settlement-load of people who are too fearful or too homesick for their own Sun. We'd never make it. We want only those with us who are willing, even eager."

He was completely right. The campaign to win approval for leaving the Solar System began almost at once and the fact that the news had already leaked out served as a cushion to ease the reaction outside Rotor—and within it as well.

Some Rotorians were excited at the prospect; some were afraid.

Fisher reacted with thunderous brow, and one day he said, "This is crazy."

"It's inevitable," said Insigna with careful neutrality.

"Why? There's no reason to start wandering among the stars. Where would we go? There's nothing out there."

"There are billions of stars out there."

"How many planets? We don't know of any habitable planets anywhere, and very few of any other kind. Our Solar System is the only home we know."

"Exploration is in the blood of humanity." It was one of Pitt's phrases.

"That's romantic nonsense. Does anyone think that people are actually going to vote to separate themselves from humanity and vanish into space?"

Insigna said, "My understanding, Crile, is that sentiment on Rotor is rather in favor of it."

"That's just Council propaganda. You think people will vote to leave the Earth? Leave the Sun? Never. If it comes to that, we'll be going to Earth."

She felt something clutch at her heart. She said, "Oh no. Do you want one of those simoons, or blizzards, or mistrals, or whatever you call them? Do you want lumps of ice and falling water and blowing, whistling air?"

He lifted his eyebrows at her. "It's not that bad. There are storms occasionally, but they can be predicted. Actually, they're interesting —when they're not too bad. It's fascinating—a little cold, a little heat, a little precipitation. It makes for variation. It keeps you alive. And then, think of the variety of cuisines."

"Cuisines? How can you say that? Most people on Earth are starving. We're always collecting food shipments to send to Earth."

"*Some* people go hungry. It's not universal."

"Well, you certainly can't expect Marlene to live under such conditions."

"Billions of children do."

"And mine won't be one of them," said Insigna fiercely.

All her hopes lay in Marlene now. She was going on ten months of age, had two small teeth in the upper gum, two in the lower, could shamble about holding onto the rods of her playpen, and looked at the world with those wondering intelligent eyes.

Fisher was still clearly fond of his unpretty daughter; more fond than ever, in fact. When he wasn't dandling her, he was staring at her and remarking fondly on her beautiful eyes. He stressed her one lovely feature and it seemed to make up to him for everything else that was lacking.

Surely Fisher would not go back to Earth if it meant leaving Marlene forever. Insigna, somehow, lacked any confidence that he would choose her, the woman he had loved and married, over Earth, but surely Marlene would be the sticking point.

Surely?

9.

The day after the vote, Eugenia Insigna found Fisher white with rage. He said, or choked out, "It was a fixed vote."

She said, "Sh! You'll wake the baby."

And for a moment, he grimaced and visibly held his breath.

Insigna relaxed just a bit and said in a small voice, "There's no question that the people want to go."

"Did *you* vote to go?"

She considered. There was no use trying to placate him by lying. She had made her feelings obvious enough. She said, "I did."

He said, "Pitt ordered you to, I suppose."

That caught her by surprise. "No! I'm capable of making my own decisions."

"But you and he—" He let it trail off.

She felt her blood pressure rise suddenly. "What do you mean?" she said, angry now in her turn. Was he going to accuse her of infidelity?

"That—that politician. He's heading for Commissioner at any price. Everyone knows that. And you're planning to rise with him. Political loyalty will get you someplace, too, won't it?"

"Where will it get me? There's no place I want to get. I'm an astronomer, not a politician."

"You've been promoted, haven't you? You've been pushed over the head of older, more experienced people."

"Through hard work, I like to think." (How was she going to defend herself now, without being able to tell him the truth?)

"I'm sure you do like to think that. But it was through Pitt."

Insigna drew a deep breath. "Where is this leading us?"

"Listen!" His voice was low, as it had been since she had reminded him that Marlene was sleeping. "I cannot believe that a whole Settlement of people are going to risk traveling with hyper-assistance. How do you know what will happen? How do you know it will work? It could kill us all."

"The Far Probe worked well."

"Were there living things on this Far Probe? If not, how do you know how living things will react to hyper-assistance? What do you know about hyper-assistance?"

"Not a thing."

"Why not? You're working right there in the laboratory. You're not working on the farms, as I am."

(He *is* jealous, thought Insigna.) Aloud, she said, "When you say *the* laboratory, you seem to imply we're all piled together in one room. I told you. I'm an astronomer and I know nothing about hyper-assistance."

"You mean that Pitt never tells you anything about it?"

"About hyper-assistance? He doesn't know himself."

"Are you telling me no one knows?"

"Of course I'm not telling you that. The hyperspatialists know. Come on, Crile. Those who are supposed to know, know. Others don't."

"To all except the specialist few, it's a secret, then."

"Exactly."

"Then you don't really know that hyper-assistance is safe. Only the hyperspatialists know. How do you suppose they know?"

"I assume they've experimented."

"You *assume.*"

"It's a reasonable assumption. They assure us it's safe."

"And they never lie, I suppose."

"They'll be going, too. Besides, I'm *sure* they experimented."

He looked at her out of narrowed eyes, "Now you're *sure*. The Far Probe was *your* baby. Did they have life-forms aboard?"

"I was not involved with the actual procedures. I only dealt with the astronomical data that was gained."

"You're not answering my question about the life-forms."

Insigna lost her patience. "Look, I don't feel like being grilled endlessly, and the baby is beginning to be restless. I have a question or two myself. What do *you* plan to do? Are you coming along?"

"I don't have to. The terms of the vote are that anyone who doesn't want to come along doesn't have to."

"I know you don't have to, but *will* you? Surely you don't want to break up the family."

She tried to smile as she said this, but it didn't feel convincing.

Fisher said, slowly and a little grimly, "I also don't want to leave the Solar System."

"You would rather leave me? And Marlene?"

"Why would I have to leave Marlene? Even if you want to risk yourself on this wild scheme, must you risk the child?"

She said tightly, "If I go, Marlene goes. Get that through your head, Crile. Where would you take her? To some half-finished asteroidal Settlement?"

"Of course not. I'm from Earth and I can return there if I wish."

"Return to a dying planet? Great."

"It's got some years of life left to it, I assure you."

"Then why did you leave it?"

"I thought I'd be improving myself. I didn't know that coming to Rotor would mean a one-way ticket to nowhere."

"Not to nowhere," Insigna burst out, tormented past endurance. "If you knew where we were going, you wouldn't be so ready to turn back."

"Why? Where is Rotor going?"

"To the stars."

"To oblivion."

They stared at each other, and Marlene, opening her eyes, emitted a soft mew of wakefulness. Fisher looked down at the baby and, with a softening of his tone, said, "Eugenia, we don't have to split up. I certainly don't want to leave Marlene. Or you either. Come with me."

"To Earth?"

"Yes. Why not? I have friends there. Even now. As my wife and child, you'll have no trouble getting in. Earth doesn't worry much about ecological balance. We'll be on a whole giant planet out there; not on a little stinking bubble in space."

"Just on a whole giant bubble, enormously stinking. No no, never."

"Let me take Marlene, then. If you find the voyage worth the risk because you are an astronomer and want to study the Universe, that's your business, but the baby should stay here in the Solar System, and be safe."

"Safe on Earth? Don't be ridiculous. Is that what this whole thing has been for? A device to take my baby?"

"*Our* baby."

"*My* baby. You leave. I *want* you to leave, but you can't touch my baby. You tell me I know Pitt, and, yes, I do. That means I can arrange to have you sent to the asteroids whether you want to go or not, and then you can find your own way back to your decomposing Earth. Now get out of my quarters and find your own place to sleep till you are sent away. When you let me know where you'll be, I'll send along your personal possessions. And don't think you can come back. This place will be under guard."

At the moment that Insigna said this, with the bitterness in her heart overflowing, she meant it. She might have pled with him, cajoled him, begged, argued. But she hadn't. She had turned a harsh, unforgiving eye upon him and had sent him away.

And Fisher *did* leave. And she *did* send along his things. And he *did* refuse to come with Rotor. And he *was* sent away. And she supposed he *had* gone to Earth.

He was gone forever from her and from Marlene.

She had sent him away and he was gone forever.

# FIVE

## GIFT

10.

Insigna sat there, deeply surprised at herself. She had never told the story to anyone, though she had lived with it almost every day for fourteen years. She had never dreamed of telling it to anyone. She had assumed that she would take it to the grave with her.

Not that it was disgraceful in any way—merely private.

And here she had told it—at length and without reserve—to her adolescent daughter, to someone who, until the moment she had begun talking, she had considered a child—a peculiarly hopeless child.

And that child now looked at her solemnly, out of her dark eyes—unblinking, owlishly adult, somehow—and finally said, "Then you did drive him away, didn't you?"

"In a way, yes. But I was furious. He wanted to take *you*. To *Earth*." She paused, then said tentatively, "You understand?"

Marlene asked, "Did you want me so much?"

Insigna said indignantly, "Certainly!" And then, under the calm

41

gaze of those eyes, she stopped to think the unthinkable. Had she really wanted Marlene?

But then she calmly said, "Of course. Why wouldn't I?"

Marlene shook her head and, for a moment, there was that sullen look on her face. "I think I probably wasn't a charming baby. Perhaps *he* wanted me. Were you unhappy because he wanted me more than he wanted you? Did you keep me just because *he* wanted me?"

"What horrible things you're saying. That's not it at all," said Insigna, not at all sure whether she believed that or not. There was getting to be no comfort in discussing these things with Marlene. More and more, Marlene was developing this dreadful way of cutting under the skin. Insigna had noticed this before and had put it down to the occasional lucky blows of an unhappy child. But it was happening more and more often, and Marlene now seemed to be wielding the scalpel deliberately.

Insigna said, "Marlene. What made you think I had driven your father away? I had never said so, surely, or given you any reason to think so, have I?"

"I don't really know how I know things, Mother. Sometimes you mention Father to me, or to someone else, and you always sound as though there's something you regret, something you wish you could do over."

"There is? I never feel that."

"And little by little, as I get these impressions, they get clearer. It's the way you talk, the way you look—"

Insigna gazed at her daughter intently, then said very suddenly, "What am I thinking?"

Marlene jumped slightly and then gave a short giggle. She was not a laugher, and that giggle was as far as ever she went—usually. She said, "That's easy. You're thinking that I know what you're thinking, but you're wrong. I don't read minds. I just tell from words and sounds and expressions and movements. People just can't keep what they think hidden. And I've watched them so long."

"Why? I mean, why have you felt it necessary to watch them?"

"Because when I was a kid, everyone lied to me. They told me how sweet I was. Or they told you that when I was listening. They always had a look plastered all over them that said, 'I don't really think that at all.' And they didn't even know it was there. I couldn't believe at first they didn't know. But then I said to myself, 'I guess it's more comfortable for them to make believe they're telling the truth.' "

Marlene paused and then abruptly asked her mother, "Why didn't you tell Father where we were going?"

"I couldn't. It was not my secret."

"Perhaps if you had, he would have come with us."

Insigna shook her head vigorously. "No, he wouldn't. He had made up his mind to return to Earth."

"But if you had told him, Mother, Commissioner Pitt wouldn't have let him leave, would he? Father would have known too much."

"Pitt wasn't Commissioner then," said Insigna with absent irrelevance. Then, with sudden vigor, "I wouldn't have wanted him on those terms. Would you?"

"I don't know. I can't tell how he would have been if he had stayed."

"But I can tell." Insigna felt as though she were burning again. Her mind went back to that last conversation and her last wild shout telling Fisher to go, that he *must* go. No, it had been no mistake. She wouldn't have wanted him as a prisoner, an enforced member of Rotor. She hadn't loved him *that* much. For that matter, she hadn't hated him that much either.

And then she changed the subject quickly, allowing no time for her expression to give her away. "You upset Aurinel this afternoon. Why did you tell him Earth would be destroyed? He came to me about that and was very concerned."

"All you had to do was to tell him that I was just a kid and no one listens to what a kid says. He would have believed that right away."

Insigna ignored that. Maybe it was a good idea to say nothing in order to avoid the truth. "Do you really think Earth will be destroyed?"

"I do. You talk about Earth sometimes. You say, 'Poor Earth.' You almost always say, 'Poor Earth.'"

Insigna felt herself flush. Did she really speak of Earth in those terms? She said, "Well, why not? It's overcrowded, worn-out, full of hatred and famines and miseries. I'm sorry for the world. Poor Earth."

"No, Mother. You don't say it that way. When you say it—" Marlene held up her hand in a groping gesture, feeling for something, her fingertips just missing it.

"Well, Marlene?"

"It's clear in my mind, but I don't know how to put it in words."

"Keep on trying. I must know."

"The way you say it, I can't help but think you feel guilty—as though it were your fault."

"Why? What do you think I've done?"

"I heard you say it once when you were in the view room. You looked at Nemesis, and it seemed to me, then, that Nemesis was mixed up in it. So I asked the computer what Nemesis meant and it told me. It's something that relentlessly destroys, something that inflicts retribution."

"That wasn't the reason for the name," cried Insigna.

"You named it," said Marlene quietly, inexorably.

That was no secret, of course, any longer, once they had left the Solar System behind them. Insigna had then taken the credit for the discovery and for the name.

"It's because I named it that I know that that wasn't the reason for the name."

"Then why do you feel guilty, Mother?"

(Silence—if you don't want to tell the truth.)

Insigna said at last, "How do you think Earth will be destroyed?"

"I don't know, but I think *you* know, Mother."

"We're speaking at cross-purposes, Marlene, and let's let it go for now. What I want, though, is to make sure you understand that you are not to talk about any of this to anyone—not about your father, and not about this nonsense of Earth's destruction."

"If you don't want me to, of course I won't, but the destruction bit is not nonsense."

"I say it is. We'll define it as nonsense."

Marlene nodded. "I think I'll go view for a while," she said with seeming indifference. "Then I'll go to bed."

"Good!" Insigna watched her daughter leave.

Guilty, thought Insigna. I feel guilty. I wear it on my face like a bright banner. Anyone who looks can see it.

No, not anyone. Just Marlene. She has the gift of doing so.

Marlene had to have something to compensate for all she didn't get. Intelligence wasn't enough. It didn't make up sufficiently, so she had this gift of reading expression, intonation, and otherwise invisible bodily twitches, so that no secret was safe from her.

How long had she kept this dangerous attribute to herself? How long had she known about it? Was it something that grew stronger with age? Why did she allow it to emerge now, to peep out from

44

behind the curtain she seemed to have drawn over it, and to use it as something with which to beat her mother?

Was it because Aurinel had rejected her, finally and definitely, according to what she had seen in him? Was she striking out blindly in consequence?

Guilty, thought Insigna. Why shouldn't I feel guilty? It is all my fault. I should have known from the start, from the instant of discovery—but I didn't want to know.

# SIX

## APPROACH

### 11.

How early had she known? From the moment she had named the star
Nemesis? Had she felt what it was and what it meant, and had she
named it appropriately without conscious thought?

When she had first spotted the star, it had been only the act of
finding it that counted. There had been no room in her mind for
anything but immortality. It was her own star, Insigna's Star. She
had been tempted to call it that. How glorious that had sounded, even
as she had reluctantly avoided it with a hollow internal grimace of
mock modesty. How unbearable it would have been now if she had
fallen into that trap.

After the discovery, there had come the shock of Pitt's demand for
secrecy, and then the furious preparation for the Leaving. (Would
that be what it would be called in the history books someday? The
Leaving? Capitalized?)

Then, after the Leaving, there were two years in which the ship skipped steadily and barely into and out of hyperspace—and the endless calculations that were involved in that hyper-assistance, for which astronomical data was constantly required, with herself supervising the supply. The density and composition of interstellar matter alone—

At no time in those four years had she been able to think of Nemesis in detail; not once could she zero in on the obvious.

Was that possible? Or did she simply turn away from what she did not want to see? Had she deliberately sought refuge in all the secrecy and scurry and excitement that presented itself to her?

But there came a time when the last hyperspatial period was behind them; when, for a month, they would be decelerating through an initial hail of hydrogen atoms, which they struck with such speed that those atoms were converted into cosmic ray particles.

No ordinary space vehicle could have endured that, but Rotor had a thick layer of soil around it that had been thickened for the trip, and the particles were absorbed.

There would come a time, she had been assured by one of the hyperspatialists when one would enter and leave hyperspace at ordinary speeds. "Given hyperspace in the first place," he had said, "no new conceptual breakthrough is required. It's just engineering."

Maybe! The remaining hyperspatialists, however, considered the notion so much star exhaust.

Insigna hurried in to see Pitt when the appalling truth descended upon her. He had had little time for her in the last year, and she had understood. There was a certain tension that became more and more evident as the excitement of the trip wound down, as people realized that in a matter of months they would be in the neighborhood of another star. They would then have the constant problem of having to survive over a long period in the vicinity of a strange red dwarf star without any guarantee of reasonable planetary material to serve as a supply source, let alone a living place.

Janus Pitt no longer looked like a young man, although his hair was still dark, his face unlined. Only four years had passed since she had come to him with the news of Nemesis' existence. There was, however, a harried look in his eyes, a sense of having had his joy rubbed away and his cares left naked to the world.

He was Commissioner-elect now. Perhaps that might account for a great deal of what might be troubling him, but who could tell? Insigna had never known true power—or the responsibility that accompanied it—but something told her it might have the capacity for souring one who did.

Pitt smiled at her absently. They had been forced to be close when they had shared a secret that at first no one—and then almost no one —had shared with them. They could then talk unguardedly with each other, when they could not do so with anyone else. After the Leaving, however, when the secret was revealed, they had grown apart again.

"Janus," she said, "there is something eating away at me and I had to come to you with it. It's Nemesis."

"Is there anything new? You can't say you've found out it isn't where you thought it was. It's right out there, less than sixteen billion kilometers away. We can see it."

"Yes, I know. But when I first found it, at a distance of two-plus light-years, I took it for granted that it was a companion star, that Nemesis and the Sun were circling a common center of gravity. Something that close would almost have to be. It would be so dramatic."

"All right. Why shouldn't things be dramatic now and then?"

"Because as close as it is, it is clearly too far away to be a companion star. The gravitational attraction between Nemesis and the Sun is terribly weak, so weak that the gravitational perturbations of nearby stars would make the orbit unstable."

"But Nemesis is there."

"Yes, and more or less between ourselves and Alpha Centauri."

"What has Alpha Centauri got to do with it?"

"The fact is that Nemesis is not much farther from Alpha Centauri than it is from the Sun. It's just as likely to be a companion star of Alpha Centauri. Or, more likely, whichever system it belongs to, the presence of the other star is now disrupting it, or has already disrupted it."

Pitt looked at Insigna thoughtfully and tapped his fingers lightly on the arm of his chair. "How long does it take Nemesis to go around the Sun—assuming it's the Sun's companion?"

"I don't know. I'd have to work out its orbit. That's something I should have done before the Leaving, but there were so many other things occupying me then, and now, too—but that's no excuse."

"Well, make a guess."

Insigna said, "If it's a circular orbit, it would take Nemesis just over fifty million years to make a circuit about the Sun, or, more properly, about the center of gravity of the system, with the Sun making a similar circuit. The line between the two, as they moved, would always pass through that center. On the other hand, if Nemesis is following a highly elliptical orbit and is now at its farthest—as it must be, for if it ventured farther still, it would certainly not be a companion star—then perhaps as little as twenty-five million years."

"Last time, then, that Nemesis was in this position, more or less between Alpha Centauri and the Sun, Alpha Centauri must have been in a much different position than it is now. Twenty-five to fifty million years would move Alpha Centauri, wouldn't it? How much?"

"A good fraction of a light-year."

"Would that mean that this is the first time Nemesis is being fought over by the two stars? Till now, would it have been circling peacefully?"

"Not a chance, Janus. Even if you count out Alpha Centauri, there are other stars. One star may have arrived now, but there had to be another star in interfering distance at some other part of its orbit in the past. The orbit just isn't stable."

"What's it doing here in our neighborhood, then, if it isn't orbiting the Sun?"

"Exactly," said Insigna.

"What do you mean, 'exactly'?"

"If it were orbiting the Sun, it would be moving at a speed, relative to the Sun, of somewhere between eighty and one hundred meters a second, depending on Nemesis' mass. That's very slow motion for a star, so it would seem to stay in the same place for a long time. It would therefore remain behind the cloud for a long time, especially if the cloud is moving in the same direction relative to the Sun. With such a slow motion and its light dimmed, it's no wonder it's never been noticed till now. However—" She paused.

Pitt, who made no effort to seem devouringly interested, sighed and said, "Well? Can you get to the point?"

"Well, if it's *not* in orbit about the Sun, then it is in independent motion and it should be moving relative to the Sun at a hundred kilometers a second or so, a thousand times as fast as if it were in orbit. It just happens to be in our neighborhood now, but it is moving on, will pass the Sun, and will never return. But, just the same, it stays behind the cloud, scarcely budging from its position."

"Why should that be?"

"There's one way it can be moving at a good clip, and yet not *seem* to be moving from its position in the sky."

"Don't tell me it's vibrating back and forth."

Insigna's lip curled. "Please don't try to make jokes, Janus. This isn't funny. Nemesis might be moving more or less straight toward the Sun. It wouldn't be shifting either to the right or left, so that it would not seem to be changing position, but it would be coming right toward us; that is, right toward the Solar System."

Pitt stared at her in surprise. "Is there evidence for that?"

"Not yet. There was no reason to take the spectrum of Nemesis when it was first spotted. It was only after I had noticed the parallax that a spectral analysis would have made sense, and then I never got around to it. If you remember, you put me at the head of the Far Probe project, and told me to direct everyone's attention *away* from Nemesis. I couldn't have arranged a close spectral analysis at that time, and since the Leaving—well, I haven't. But I will investigate the matter now, you can be sure."

"Let me ask you a question. Wouldn't it produce the same effect of motionlessness, if Nemesis were moving directly *away* from the Sun? It's a fifty-fifty chance whether it's moving toward the Sun or away from it, isn't it?"

"Spectral analysis will tell us. A red shift of the spectral lines will mean there's a recession; a violet shift, an approach."

"But it's too late now. If you take its spectrum, it will tell you it's approaching us, because we're approaching *it.*"

"Right now, I wouldn't take the spectrum of Nemesis. I'd take it of the Sun. If Nemesis is approaching the Sun, then the Sun will be approaching Nemesis, and we can allow for our own motion. Besides, we're slowing and, in a month or so, we will be moving so slowly that our motion won't be affecting the spectroscopic results appreciably."

For the space of half a minute, Pitt seemed lost in thought, staring at his uncluttered desk, his hand slowly stroking the computer terminal. Then he said, without bothering to look up, "No. These are observations that need not be made. I don't want you worrying yourself about it any more, Eugenia. It's a nonproblem, so just forget it."

The wave of his hand made it clear that she was to leave.


12.


Insigna's breath made a whistling sound as it was forced out of angrily tightened nostrils. She said in a low husky voice, "How dare you, Janus? How dare you?"

"How dare I what?" Pitt frowned.

"How dare you order me out of here as though I were a computer-puncher? If I hadn't found Nemesis, we wouldn't be here. You wouldn't be Commissioner-elect. Nemesis is mine. I have a *say* in it."

"Nemesis isn't yours. It's Rotor's. So please leave now and let me get on with the business of the day."

"Janus," she said, raising her voice. "I tell you again that, in all likelihood, Nemesis is moving toward our Solar System."

"And I tell you again that it is only a fifty-fifty chance that it is. And even if it were heading toward the Solar System—not *our* Solar System any longer, by the way, but *their* Solar System—don't tell me it's going to hit the Sun. I won't believe you if you do. In its whole nearly five-billion-year history, the Sun has never been struck by a star, or even come close. The odds against stellar collisions even in relatively crowded parts of the Galaxy are enormous. I may not be an astronomer, but I know that much."

"Odds are just odds, Janus, not certainties. It's *conceivable*, however unlikely, that Nemesis and the Sun might collide, but I recognize that it's very unlikely they will. The trouble is that a close approach, even without collision, might be fatal to Earth."

"How close is a close approach?"

"I don't know. It will take a great deal of computation."

"All right, then. You suggest that we take the trouble to make the necessary observations and computations and, if we find out that the situation is indeed fraught with danger to the Solar System, then what? Do we warn the Solar System?"

"Well yes. What choice would we have?"

"And how would we warn them? We have no means of hypercommunication and, even if we had, they have no system for receiving hypermessages. If we sent out a luminal message of some sort—light, micro-waves, modulated neutrinos—it would take over two years to reach Earth, assuming we have a beam powerful enough, or sufficiently coherent. And even then, how would we know if they had received it? If they had and bothered to answer, that answer would take another two years to return. And what will be the final result of the warning? We will have to tell them where Nemesis is and they will see that the information is coming from that direction. The whole point of our secrecy, the whole plan for establishing a homogeneous civilization around Nemesis, free of interference, would be lost."

51

"Whatever the cost, Janus, how could you consider *not* warning them?"

"Where's your concern? Even if Nemesis is moving toward the Sun, how long would it take for it to reach the Solar System?"

"It could reach the neighborhood of the Sun in five thousand years."

Pitt sat back in his chair and regarded Insigna with a kind of wry amusement. "Five thousand years. Only five thousand years? Look, Eugenia, two hundred and fifty years ago, the first Earthman stood on the Moon. Two and a half centuries have passed and here we are at the nearest star. Where will we be in another two and a half centuries, at this rate? At any star we wish. And in five thousand years, *fifty* centuries, we will be all over the Galaxy, barring the presence of other intelligent forms of life. We will be reaching out to other galaxies. Within five thousand years, technology will have advanced to the point where, if the Solar System were really in trouble, all its Settlements and its entire planetary population could take off for deep space and other stars."

Insigna shook her head. "Don't think that technological advance means that you can empty the Solar System by a mere wave of the hand, Janus. To remove billions of people without chaos and without tremendous loss of life would require long preparation. If they are in mortal danger five thousand years from now, they must know *now*. It is not too soon to begin to plan."

Pitt said, "You have a good heart, Eugenia, so I'll offer a compromise. Suppose we take a hundred years in which to establish ourselves here, to multiply, to build a cluster of Settlements that will be strong enough and stable enough to be secure. *Then* we can investigate Nemesis' destination and—if necessary—warn the Solar System. They will still have nearly five thousand years in which to prepare. Surely a small delay of a century will not be fatal."

Insigna sighed. "Is that your vision of the future? Humanity squabbling endlessly over the stars? Each little group trying to establish itself as supreme over this star or that? Endless hatred, suspicion, and conflict, of the kind we had on Earth for thousands of years, expanded into the Galaxy for thousands more?"

"Eugenia, I have no vision. Humanity will do as it pleases. It will squabble as you say, or it will perhaps set up a Galactic Empire, or do something else. I can't dictate what humanity will do, and I don't intend to try to shape it. For myself, I have only this one Settlement to care for, and this one century in which to establish it at Nemesis. By then, you and I will be safely dead, and our successors will handle the problem of warning the Solar System—if that should be necessary. I'm trying to be reasonable, not emotional, Eugenia. You are a reasonable person, too. Think about it."

Insigna did. She sat there, looking somberly at Pitt, while he waited with almost exaggerated patience.

Finally she said, "Very well. I see your point. I will get on with analyzing Nemesis' motion relative to the Sun. Perhaps we can forget the whole thing."

"No." Pitt raised an admonishing finger. "Remember what I said earlier. These observations will not be made. If it turns out that the Solar System is not in danger, we will have gained nothing. We will then merely do what I insist we do in any case—spend a century strengthening the civilization of Rotor. If, however, you find that there *is* danger, then your conscience will hurt and you will be consumed with apprehensions and fears and guilt. The news will somehow get out and it will weaken the resolve of Rotorians, many of whom may be as sentimental as you are. We would then lose a great deal. Do you understand me?"

She was silent, and he said, "Good. I see you do." Again, the wave of his hand made it clear that she was to leave.

This time she left, and Pitt, looking after her, thought: She is really becoming insupportable.

# SEVEN

---

# DESTRUCTION?

### 13.

Marlene watched her mother owlishly. She was careful to keep her expression flat and meaningless, but within herself she was both pleased and surprised. Her mother was finally telling her of the events involving her father and Commissioner Pitt. She was being treated as a grown-up.

Marlene said, "I would have checked Nemesis' motions regardless of what Commissioner Pitt said, Mother, but I see you didn't. Your guilt makes it plain."

Insigna said, "I can't get used to the notion that I wear my guilt like a label on my forehead."

"No one hides their feelings," said Marlene. "If you really watch, you can always tell."

(Others couldn't. Marlene had learned that only slowly, and with difficulty. People just didn't look, they didn't sense, they didn't care.

54

They didn't watch faces, and bodies, and sounds, and attitudes, and little nervous habits.)

"You shouldn't really *watch* like that, Marlene," said Insigna, as though their thoughts had taken parallel paths. She put her arm around the girl's shoulder to prevent her words from sounding like a scolding. "People get nervous when those large dark eyes of yours fix on them soulfully. Respect people's privacy."

"Yes, Mother," said Marlene, noting without effort that her mother was trying to protect herself. She was nervous about herself, wondering how much she gave away at each moment.

Then Marlene said, "How is it that despite all your guilty feelings about the Solar System, you did nothing?"

"A number of reasons, Molly."

(Not "Molly," thought Marlene with anguish. Marlene! Marlene! Marlene! Three syllables. Accent on the second. Grown up!)

"Like what reasons?" asked Marlene sulkily. (Couldn't her mother detect the wave of hostility that swept over Marlene each time a kid name was used? Surely it twisted her face, smoldered her eyes, convulsed her lips. Why didn't people notice? Why didn't people look?)

"For one thing, Janus Pitt was very convincing. However odd the points he makes, however hostile you feel toward them at the time, he always makes you see that he has good reasons for his viewpoints."

"If that's true, Mother, he's awfully dangerous."

Insigna seemed to break away from her thoughts to glance curiously at her daughter. "Why do you say that?"

"Every point of view can have good reasons behind it. If someone can seize those reasons quickly, and present them convincingly, he can argue anyone into anything, and that's dangerous."

"Janus Pitt has those abilities, I'll admit. I'm surprised you understand these things."

(Marlene thought: Because I'm only fifteen, and you're used to thinking I'm a child.)

Aloud, she said, "You learn a lot watching people."

"Yes, but remember what I told you. Control the watching."

(Never.) "So Mr. Pitt persuaded you."

"He made me see there'd be no harm in waiting awhile."

"And you weren't even curious to study Nemesis and see exactly where it was going? You would have to be."

"I was, but it's not as easy as you think. The Observatory is in constant use. You have to wait your turn to use the instruments. Even if I'm the head, I can't use them freely. Then, too, when someone does use them, there's no secret about it. We know what it's being used for and why. There was very little chance I would be able to develop a really detailed spectrum of Nemesis and of the Sun, or to use the Observatory computer on the necessary calculations, without people knowing at once what I was doing. I suspect that Pitt had a few people in the Observatory watching me, too. If I had stepped out of line, he would have known at once."

"He couldn't do anything to you about it, could he?"

"He couldn't have me shot for treason if that's what you mean—not that he'd dream of doing such a thing—but he could relieve me of my Observatory duties and put me to work in the farms. I wouldn't want that. It wasn't long after I'd had that little talk with Pitt that we discovered that Nemesis had a planet—or a companion star. To this day, we're not sure what to call it. They were only separated by a distance of four million kilometers and the companion object didn't radiate in visible light at all."

"You're talking about Megas, aren't you, Mother?"

"Yes, I am. It's an old word meaning 'big' and, for a planet, it's very big, considerably bigger than the Solar System's largest planet, Jupiter. But it's very small for a star. Some think of Megas as a brown dwarf." She broke off and eyed her daughter narrowly, as though suddenly uncertain as to her capacity to absorb matters. "Do you know what a brown dwarf is, Molly?"

"Marlene is my name, Mother."

Insigna flushed slightly. "Yes. I'm sorry if I forget now and then. I can't help it, you know. I had a very dear little girl once whose name was Molly."

"I know. And next time I'm six, you can call me Molly all you want."

Insigna laughed. "Do you know what a brown dwarf is, Marlene?"

"Yes, I do, Mother. A brown dwarf is a small starlike body, with too little mass to develop the temperatures and pressures to bring about hydrogen fusion in its interior, but enough mass to bring about secondary reactions that keep it warm."

"That's right. Not bad. Megas is on the borderline. It's either a very warm planet or a very dim brown dwarf. It gives off no visible light, but emits richly in the infrared. It's not quite like anything we've ever studied. It was the first extrasolar planetary body—that is, the first planet outside the Solar System—that we have been able to study in detail, and the Observatory was totally immersed in it. I wouldn't have had a chance to work on Nemesis' motion even if I had wanted to, and, to tell you the truth, I forgot about it for a time. I was as interested in Megas as everyone else was, you see?"

"Um," said Marlene.

"It turned out it was the only sizable planetary body circling Nemesis, but it was enough. It was five times the mass—"

"I know, Mother. It's five times the mass of Jupiter, and one thirtieth the mass of Nemesis. The computer taught me that long ago."

"Of course, dear. And it's no more habitable than Jupiter is; less, if anything. That was disappointing at first, even though we didn't really expect to find a habitable planet circling a red dwarf star. If a planet were close enough to a star like Nemesis to keep water liquid, tidal influences would force it to face one side to Nemesis at all times."

"Isn't that what Megas does, Mother? I mean, one side always faces Nemesis?"

"Yes, it does. That means it has a warm side and cold side, with the warm side quite warm. It would be at red heat, if it weren't that the circulation of its dense atmosphere tends to equalize temperatures somewhat. Because of this and because of Megas' own inner warmth, even the cold side is quite warm. There are many things about Megas that were unique in astronomical experience. And then we discovered that Megas had a satellite or, if you want to consider Megas a very small star, it had a planet—Erythro."

"Which Rotor orbits, I know. But, Mother, it's been over eleven years since there was all that fuss about Megas and Erythro. In all that time, haven't you managed to sneak a look at the spectra of Nemesis and the Sun? Haven't you done a little figuring?"

"Well—"

Marlene said hastily, "I know you have."

"By my expression?"

"By everything about you."

"You can be a very uncomfortable person to have around, Marlene. Yes, I have."

"And?"

"Yes, it's heading for the Solar System."

There was a pause. Then Marlene said in a low voice, "Is it going to hit?"

"No, as far as my figures are concerned. I'm quite sure it's not going to hit the Sun, or the Earth, or any significant part of the Solar System, for that matter. But it doesn't have to, you see. Even if it misses, it will probably destroy the Earth."

14.

It was quite clear to Marlene that her mother did not like to talk about Earth's destruction, that there was internal friction inhibiting her discourse, that if she were left to herself, she would stop talking. Her expression—the way she pulled away a little from Marlene, as though anxious to leave; the way she licked her lips very delicately, as though she were trying to remove the taste of her words—was clarity itself to Marlene.

But she did not want her mother to stop. She had to know more.

She said gently, "If Nemesis misses, how will it destroy the Earth?"

"Let me try to explain. The Earth goes around the Sun, just as Rotor goes around Erythro. If all there were in the Solar System were the Earth and the Sun, then the Earth would go around in the same path almost eternally. I say 'almost' because, as it turns, it radiates gravitational waves that bleed the Earth's momentum, and that causes it very, very slowly to spin into the Sun. We can ignore that.

"There are other complicating factors because Earth isn't alone. The Moon, Mars, Venus, Jupiter, every object in the neighborhood pulls at it. The pulls are very minor compared to that of the Sun, so Earth remains in its orbit more or less. However, the minor pulls, which are shifting in direction and intensity in a complicated way, as the various objects themselves move, introduce minor changes in Earth's orbit. Earth moves in and out slightly, its axial tilt veers and changes its slant a bit, the eccentricity alters somewhat, and so on.

"It can be shown—it *has* been shown—that all these minor changes are cyclic. They don't progress in one direction, but move back and forth. What it amounts to is that the Earth, in its orbit about the Sun, quivers slightly in a dozen different ways. All the bodies in the Solar System quiver in this way. Earth's quiver doesn't prevent it from supporting life. At the worst, it may get an ice age or an ice disappearance and a rise and fall in sea level, but life has survived everything for well over three billion years.

"But now let us suppose Nemesis dashes by and misses, that it doesn't approach closer than a light-month or so. That would be less than a trillion kilometers. As it passes—and it would take a number of years to pass—it would give a gravitational push to the system. It would make the quivering worse, but then, when it was gone, the quivers would settle down again."

Marlene said, "You look as though you think it would be a lot worse than you make it sound. What's so bad about Nemesis giving the Solar System a little extra quiver—if it all settles down again afterward?"

"Well, will it settle down again in quite the same place? That's the problem. If Earth's equilibrium position is a little different—a little farther from the Sun, a little nearer, if its orbit is a little more eccentric or its axis a little more tilted, or less—how will that affect Earth's climate? Even a small change might make it an uninhabitable world."

"Can't you calculate it out in advance?"

"No. Rotor isn't a good place to calculate from. It quivers, too, and a great deal. It would take considerable time and considerable calculation to deduce from my observations here *exactly* what path Nemesis is taking—and we just won't be sure till it gets considerably closer to the Solar System, long after I am dead."

"So you can't tell exactly just how closely Nemesis will pass the Solar System."

"It is almost impossible to calculate. The gravitational field of every nearby star within a dozen light-years has to be taken into account. After all, the tiniest uncalculated effect may build up to such a deviation in over two light-years as to make a passage that is calculated as a near-hit come out, actually, to be a total miss. Or vice versa."

"Commissioner Pitt said everyone in the Solar System will be able to leave if they want to by the time Nemesis arrives. Is he right?"

"He might be. But how can one tell what will happen in five thousand years? What historical twists will take place and how that will affect matters? We can *hope* everyone will get off safely."

"Even if they're not warned," said Marlene, feeling rather diffident at pointing out an astronomical truism to her mother, "they'll find out for themselves. They've got to. Nemesis will come closer and closer and it will be unmistakable after a while and they can calculate its path much more accurately as it comes closer."

"But they will have that much less time to make their escape—if one is necessary."

Marlene stared at her toes. She said, "Mother, don't be angry with me. It seems to me as though you'd be unhappy even if everyone got away from the Solar System safely. Something else is wrong. Please tell me."

Insigna said, "I don't like the thought of everyone leaving Earth. Even if it is done in orderly fashion, with plenty of time and with no casualties to speak of, I still don't like the thought. I don't want Earth to be abandoned."

"Suppose it must be."

"Then it will be. I can bow to the inevitable, but I don't have to like it."

"Are you sentimental about Earth? You studied there, didn't you?"

"I did my graduate work in astronomy there. I didn't like Earth, but that doesn't matter. It's the place where human beings originated. Do you know what I mean, Marlene? Even if I didn't think much of it when I was there, it's still the world where life developed over the eons. To me it's not only a world but an idea, an abstraction. I want it to exist for the sake of the past. I don't know if I can make that clear."

Marlene said, "Father was an Earthman."

Insigna's lips tightened a bit. "Yes, he was."

"And he went back to Earth."

"The records say he did. I suppose he did."

"I'm half an Earthperson, then. Isn't that so?"

Insigna frowned. "We're all Earthpeople, Marlene. My great-great-grandparents lived on Earth all their lives. My great-grandmother was born on Earth. Everyone, without exception, is descended from Earthpeople. And not just human beings. Every speck of life on every Settlement, from a virus to a tree, is descended from Earth life."

Marlene said, "But only human beings know it. And some are closer than others. Do you think about Father, sometimes, even now?" Marlene looked up briefly at her mother's face and winced. "It's none of my business. That's what you're going to tell me."

"That's the feeling I just had, but I don't have to be guided by my feelings. After all, you're his daughter. Yes, I think about him now and then." She shrugged her shoulders slightly.

Insigna said, "Do *you* think about him, Marlene?"

"I have nothing to think of. I don't remember him. I've never seen any holograms, or anything."

"No, there was no point in—" Her voice trailed off.

"But when I was littler, I used to wonder why some fathers stayed with their children when the Leaving happened, and some fathers didn't. I thought that maybe the ones who left didn't like their children, and that Father didn't like me."

Insigna stared at her daughter. "You never told me that."

"It was a private thought when I was little. When I got older, I knew that it was more complicated than that."

"You should never have had to think so. It's not true. I would have assured you of that, if I had had the slightest idea—"

"You don't like to talk about those times, Mother. I understand."

"I would have anyway, if I had known about that thought of yours; if I could read your face as you read mine. He *did* love you. He would have taken you with him if I had allowed it. It's my fault, really, that you two are separated."

"His, too. He might have stayed with us."

"Well, he might have, but now that the years have passed, I can see and understand his problems a little better than I could then. After all, I wasn't leaving home; my world was coming with me. I may be over two light-years from Earth, but I'm still at home on Rotor where I was born. Your father was different. He was born on Earth and not on Rotor, and I suppose he couldn't bear the thought of leaving Earth altogether, and forever. I think about that now and then, also. I hate the thought of Earth being deserted. There must be several billion people there whose hearts would break to leave it."

There was silence between them for a moment, then Marlene said, "I wonder what Father is doing back on Earth right now."

"How can we possibly tell, Marlene? Twenty trillion kilometers is a long, long way, and fourteen years is a long, long time."

"Do you suppose he's still alive?"

"We can't even know that," said Insigna. "Life can be very short on Earth." Then, as though suddenly aware she wasn't talking to herself, she said, "I'm sure he's alive, Marlene. He was in excellent health when he left, and he's only just approaching fifty now." Then softly, "Do you miss him, Marlene?"

Marlene shook her head. "You can't miss what you've never had."

(But *you* had him, Mother, she thought. And *you* miss him.)

61

# EIGHT

## AGENT

### 15.

Oddly enough, Crile Fisher found it necessary to become accustomed to Earth—or reaccustomed to it. He had not thought that Rotor had become so much a part of him in a matter of not quite four years. It had been the longest period during which he had been away from Earth, but surely it had not been long enough to make Earth seem strange to him.

There was now the sheer size of Earth, the distant horizon ending sharp against the sky instead of turning up mistily. There were the crowds, the unchanging gravity, the sense of wild and willful atmosphere, of temperature soaring and diving, of nature out of all control.

It was not that he had to experience any of this to feel it. Even when he was in his own quarters, he knew it was all out there and the ferality of it all pervaded his spirit, somehow invaded it. Or it might be that the room was too small, too full, that the drift of sound was

62

too unmistakable, as though he were being pressed in on by a crowded and decaying world.

Strange that he had missed Earth so intensely in those years on Rotor; and that, now that he was back on Earth, he missed Rotor so intensely. Was he to spend his life wanting to be where he was not?

The signal light flashed and he heard the buzz. It flickered—things on Earth tended to flicker, while on Rotor everything was constant with an almost aggressive efficiency. "Enter," he said in a low voice, but it was loud enough to activate the de-locking mechanism.

Garand Wyler entered (Fisher knew it would be he) and looked at the other with an amused expression. "Have you budged since I left, Crile?"

"Here and there. I've eaten. Spent some time in the bathroom."

"Good. You're alive, then, even if you don't look it." He was grinning broadly, his skin smooth and brown, his eyes dark, his teeth white, his hair thick and crisp. "Brooding about Rotor?"

"I think of it now and then."

"I kept meaning to ask, but never got around to it. It was Snow White without the Seven Dwarfs, wasn't it?"

"Snow White," said Fisher. "I never saw one black person there."

"In that case, good riddance to them. Did you know that they're gone?"

Fisher's muscles tightened and he nearly got to his feet, but he resisted the impulse. He said, nodding, "They said they would be."

"They meant it. They drifted away. We watched as far as we could; eavesdropped their radiation. They pumped up speed with this hyper-assistance of theirs and, in a split second, while we could still make them out loud and clear, they were gone. Everything cut off."

"Did you pick them up when they got back into space?"

"Several times. Each time weaker. They were traveling at the speed of light after they had really flexed their muscles, and after three blips, into hyperspace and back into space, they were too far to be picked up."

Fisher said bitterly, "Their choice. They kicked out the nays—like me."

"I'm sorry you weren't there. You should have been. It was interesting to watch. You know there were some hard-liners who insisted to the very end that hyper-assistance was a fraud, that it was all faked up, for some reason."

"Rotor had the Far Probe. They couldn't have it sent as far away as they did without hyper-assistance."

"Faked! That's what the hard-liners said."

"It was genuine."

"Yes, now they know it was. All of them. When Rotor just vanished off the instruments, there was no other explanation. Every Settlement was watching. No mistake. It vanished on every set of instruments at the same second. The irritating thing is, we can't tell where it's going."

"Alpha Centauri, I suppose. Where else?"

"The Office keeps thinking that it might not be Alpha Centauri and that you might know that."

Fisher looked annoyed. "I've been debriefed all the way to the Moon and back. I haven't held back anything."

"Sure. We know that. It's nothing you know about. They want me to talk to you, friend to friend, and see what you may know that you *don't* know about. Something may turn up that you haven't thought of. You were there four years, married, had a kid. You couldn't have missed everything."

"How could I? If there were the slightest notion that I was after anything, I'd have been kicked off. Just being from Earth made me completely suspect. If I hadn't married—given that kind of proof that I planned to stay Rotorian—I would have been kicked off anyway. And as it was, they kept me far away from anything critical or sensitive."

Fisher looked away. "And it worked. My wife was just an astronomer. I didn't have my pick, you know. I couldn't put an ad on holovision announcing that I was in the market for a young lady who was a hyperspatialist. If I had met one, I would have done my best to hook on to her even if she looked like a hyena, but I never met one in all my time there. The technology was so sensitive, I think they kept the key people in complete isolation. I think they must all have worn masks in the laboratories and used code names. Four years—and I never got a hint, never found out a thing. And I knew it would mean I was through with the Office."

He turned to Garand and said with sudden passion, "Things got so bad that I turned into some kind of lout. The sense of failure was just overpowering."

Wyler was sitting across the table from Fisher in the cluttered room, teetering back on the rear legs of his chair, but carefully holding the table lest he teeter too far.

He said, "Crile, the Office can't afford to be delicate, but it isn't totally unfeeling. They regret having to approach you like this, but they must. And I regret being given the job, but I must. We are concerned that you've failed and brought us nothing. If Rotor hadn't left, we might have felt there was nothing to bring. But they did leave. They did have hyper-assistance, and yet you've brought us nothing."

"I know that."

"But that doesn't mean we want to throw you out or—get rid of you. We hope we can still use you. So I have to make sure that your failure was an honest one."

"What does that mean?"

"I have to be able to tell them that you didn't fail because of any personal weakness. After all, you married a Rotorian woman. Was she pretty? Were you fond of her?"

Fisher snarled, "What you're really asking is whether, out of love for a Rotorian woman, I deliberately protected Rotor and helped them keep their secret."

"Well," said Wyler, unmoved. "Did you?"

"How can you ask that? If I had decided to be a Rotorian, I would have left with them. By now I would be lost in space and you might never find me. But I didn't do that. I got off Rotor and returned to Earth, even though I knew my failure would probably destroy my career."

"We appreciate your loyalty."

"There's more loyalty in this than you think."

"We recognize that you probably loved your wife and that, as a matter of duty, you had to leave her. That would count in your favor, if we could be sure—"

"Not so much my wife. It was my daughter."

Wyler viewed Fisher thoughtfully. "We know you have a one-year-old daughter, Crile. Under the circumstances, perhaps you shouldn't have given that particular hostage to fortune."

"I agree. But I can't treat myself as though I were a well-oiled robot. Things happen against one's will sometimes. And once the child was born and I had had her for a year—"

"That is understandable, but it was *only* a year. Scarcely time, really, to build a relationship—"

Fisher grimaced. "You may think it understandable, but you *don't* understand."

"Explain, then. I'll try."

"It was my sister, you see. My younger sister."

Wyler nodded. "There's mention of that in your compufile. Rose, I think."

"Roseanne. She died in the San Francisco riots eight years ago. She was only seventeen."

"I'm sorry."

"She wasn't a participant on either side. She was one of those innocent bystanders who is so more apt to get hurt than the ringleaders or the officers. At least we found her body and I had something to cremate."

Wyler maintained a half-embarrassed silence.

Fisher said finally, "She was only seventeen. Our parents died"— he brushed his hand to one side, as though indicating it was not something he wished to discuss—"when she was four and I was fourteen. I worked after school and I saw to it that she was fed, and clothed, and comfortable, even when I was not. I taught myself programming—not that I ever made a decent living out of that either— and then, when she was seventeen, when she had never hurt a soul, when she didn't even know what all the fighting and shouting was about, she was simply trapped—"

Wyler said, "I can see why you volunteered for Rotor."

"Oh yes. For a couple of years I was just numb. I joined the Office partly to keep my mind occupied and partly because I thought there would be danger in it. I rather looked forward to death for a while—if I could manage to do something useful en route. When the problem of placing an agent on Rotor was discussed, I volunteered for it. I wanted to get off Earth."

"And now you're back. Do you regret that?"

"A little bit, yes, but Rotor choked me. With all its faults, Earth has *room*. If only you could have seen Roseanne, Garand. You have no idea. She wasn't pretty, but she had such eyes." Fisher's own eyes were focused on the past, a slight pucker between his brows as though he were peering hard to clearly focus. "Beautiful eyes, but frightening ones. It seemed to me that I could never meet them without feeling nervous. She could look right into you—if you know what I mean."

"Actually, I don't," said Wyler.

Fisher paid no attention. "She always knew when you were lying or hiding the truth. You couldn't be silent without her guessing what the trouble was."

"You're not going to tell me she was a telepath?"

"What? Oh no. She used to say she read expressions and listened to intonations. She said no one could hide what they were thinking. No matter how you laughed, you could not hide the tragic undercurrent; no smile sufficed to hide bitterness. She tried to explain, but I could never grasp what it was she did. She was something special, Garand. I was in *awe* of her. And then my child was born. Marlene."

"Yes?"

"She had the same eyes."

"The baby had your sister's eyes?"

"Not immediately, but I watched them develop. When she was six months old, those eyes made me flinch."

"Your wife flinched, too?"

"I never noticed her being affected, but then, she never had a sister Roseanne. Marlene hardly cried at all; she was *peaceful*. I remember Roseanne was like that as a baby. And Marlene didn't show any signs that she was going to be particularly pretty either. It was as though Roseanne had come back to me. So you see how hard it turned out to be."

"Coming back to Earth, you mean."

"Doing that and leaving them behind. It was like losing Roseanne a second time. I'll never see her now. Never!"

"But you came back anyway."

"Loyalty! Duty! But if you want the truth, I almost didn't. I was standing there, torn. Torn *apart*. I was *desperately* wanting not to leave Roseanne—Marlene. You see, I confuse the names. And Eugenia—my wife—said to me in a heartbroken way, 'If you knew where we were going, you wouldn't be so ready to turn back.' And at that moment I didn't want to leave. I asked her to come to Earth with me. She refused. I asked her to let me take Ro—Marlene, at least. She refused. And then, when I might have given in and stayed, she went wild and ordered me out. And I went."

Wyler stared at Fisher reflectively. " 'If you knew where we were going, you wouldn't be so ready to turn back.' Is that what she said?"

"Yes, that's what she said. And when I said, 'Why? Where is Rotor going?', she said, 'To the stars.' "

"That can't be right, Crile. You *knew* they were planning to go to the stars, but she said, '*If* you knew where we were going—' There was something you didn't know. What was it you didn't know?"

"What are you talking about? How can anyone know what he doesn't know?"

Wyler shrugged it off. "Did you tell this to the Office during the debriefing?"

Fisher considered. "I guess not. I didn't even think of it till I started telling you the story about how I nearly stayed." He closed his eyes, then said slowly, "No, this is the first time I've talked about that. It's the first time I've let myself think about it."

"Very well, then. Now that you think about it—where was Rotor going? Did you hear any speculations on Rotor about that? Any rumors? Any guesses?"

"The assumption was that it would be to Alpha Centauri. Where else? It's the nearest star."

"Your wife was an astronomer. What did she say about it?"

"Nothing. She never discussed it."

"Rotor sent out the Far Probe."

"I know."

"And your wife was involved—as an astronomer."

"She was, but she never discussed it either, and I was careful not to do so. My mission would have been aborted, and perhaps I might have been imprisoned—or executed, for all I know—if I displayed an unhealthy curiosity too openly."

"But as an astronomer, she would know the destination. She as much as said so. 'If *you* knew—' You see? She knew and if you knew, too—"

Fisher didn't seem interested. "Since she didn't tell me what she knew, I can't tell you."

"Are you sure? No casual remarks whose significance you didn't note at the time? After all, you're *not* an astronomer and she might have said something you didn't quite get. Do you remember anything at all she said that set you to puzzling?"

"I can't think of anything."

"Think! Is it possible that the Far Probe located a planetary system around one or both of the Sun-like stars of Alpha Centauri?"

"I can't say."

"Or planets about any star?"

Fisher shrugged.

"Think!" said Wyler urgently. "Is there any reason for you to think that she meant, 'You think we're going to Alpha Centauri, but there are planets circling it and we're heading for those.' Or could she have meant, 'You think we're going to Alpha Centauri, but we're going to another star where we're sure there will be a useful planet.' Something like that?"

"I couldn't possibly guess."

Garand Wyler's generous lips compressed themselves tightly for a moment. Then he said, "I'll tell you what, Crile, my old friend. There are three things that are going to happen now. First, you're going to have to undergo another debriefing. Second, I suspect we're going to have to persuade the Ceres Settlement to allow us the use of their asteroid telescope, and use it to inspect, very closely, every star within a hundred light-years of the Solar System. And, third, we'll have to whip our hyperspatialists into jumping a little higher and farther. You watch and see if that's not what happens."

# NINE

---

# ERYTHRO

### 16.

There were times, once in a while, once in an ever longer while as the years passed (or so it seemed to him), when Janus Pitt found time to sit back in his chair, alone and silent, and just allow his mind to relax. Those were moments when there were no orders to give, no information to absorb, no immediate decisions to make, no farms to visit, no factories to inspect, no regions in space to penetrate, no one to see, no one to listen to, no one to foil, no one to encourage—

And always when such times came, Pitt allowed himself the final and least exhaustible luxury—that of self-pity.

It was not that he would have anything different than what it was. He had planned for all his adult life to be Commissioner because he thought that no one could run Rotor as he could; and now that he was Commissioner, he still thought so.

But why, among all the fools of Rotor, could he find no one who could see long-range as he could? It was fourteen years since the

70

Leaving, and still no one could really see the inevitable; not even after he had explained it carefully.

Someday, back in the Solar System, sooner rather than later, someone would develop hyper-assistance as the hyperspatialists on Rotor had—perhaps even in a better form. Someday humanity would set out in its hundreds and thousands of Settlements, in its millions and billions of people, to colonize the Galaxy, and that would be a brutal time.

Yes, the Galaxy was enormous. How often had he heard that? And beyond it were other galaxies. But humanity would not spread out evenly. Always, always, there would be some star systems that, for one reason or another, were better than other star systems, and they would be the ones snarled and fought over. If there were ten star systems and ten colonizing groups, all ten would zero in on one of the star systems, and one only.

And sooner or later, they would discover Nemesis and the colonizers would appear. How would Rotor survive then?

Only if Rotor gained as much time as possible, built up a strong civilization, and expanded reasonably. If they had enough time, they might expand their hold over a group of stars. If not, Nemesis alone would be enough—but it must be made impregnable.

Pitt did not dream of universal conquest, of conquest of any kind. What he wanted was an island of tranquillity and security against the days when the Galaxy would be aflame and in chaos as a result of conflicting ambitions.

But he alone could see this. He alone bore the weight of it. He might live another quarter century and might remain in power through all that time, either as actual Commissioner or as an elder statesman whose word would be decisive. Yet, eventually, he would die—and to whom could he then bequeath his far-sightedness?

Then Pitt felt a twinge of self-pity. He had labored for so many years, would labor for so many more, yet was appreciated—truly appreciated—by none. And it would all come to an end anyway, because the Idea would be drowned in the ocean of mediocrity that constantly lapped at the ankles of those few who could see beyond the years.

It was fourteen years since the Leaving and when, at any time, had he been able to be quietly confident? He went to sleep each night with the fear that he would be awakened before morning with the news that another Settlement had arrived—that Nemesis had been *found.*

He passed through every day with some hidden part of him paying no attention to what was immediately on the agenda, but listening— listening for the fatal words.

Fourteen years and they were still not safe. One additional Settlement had been built—New Rotor. There were people living on it, but it was a new world, of course. It still smelled of paint, as the old saying had it. Three more Settlements were in various stages of construction.

Soon—within the decade, at any rate—the number of Settlements under construction would increase, and they would be given that oldest of all commands: Be fruitful and multiply!

With the example of Earth before them, with the knowledge that each Settlement had a narrow and unexpandable capacity, procreation had always been under strict control in space. There the immovable needs of arithmetic met the possibly irresistible force of instinct and immovability won. But as the number of Settlements grew, there would come a time when more people would be needed—many more—and the urge to produce them could be unleashed.

It would be temporary, of course. No matter how many Settlements there were, they could be filled without effort by any population that could easily double its numbers every thirty-five years, or less. And when the day came when the rate of Settlement formation passed through its inflection point and began to diminish, it might be far harder to stuff the djinn back into its bottle than it had been to release it.

Who would see this well in advance, and prepare for it once Pitt himself was gone?

And there was Erythro, the planet that Rotor orbited in such a way that huge Megas and ruddy Nemesis rose and set in an intricate pattern. Erythro! That had been a question from the beginning.

Pitt remembered well the early days of their entry into the Nemesian System. The limited intricacy of the planetary family of Nemesis had exposed itself little by little, as Rotor raced toward the red dwarf star.

Megas had been discovered at a distance of four million kilometers from Nemesis, only one fifteenth the distance of Mercury from the Sun of the Solar System. Megas obtained about the same amount of energy as Earth got from its Sun, but with a lesser intensity of visible light and a higher intensity of infrared.

Megas, however, was clearly not habitable, even at first glance. It was a gas giant, with one side always facing Nemesis. Both its rotation and revolution were twenty days long. The perpetual night on half of Megas cooled it only moderately, since its own interior heat rose to the surface. The perpetual day on the other half was unendurably hot. That Megas kept its atmosphere under this heat was entirely because, with its mass higher and its radius smaller than that of Jupiter, its surface gravity was fifteen times that of Jupiter, and forty times that of Earth.

Nor did Nemesis have any other sizable planet.

But then, as Rotor drew closer, and Megas could be seen more clearly, the situation was altered again.

It was Eugenia Insigna who brought Pitt the news. It was not that she had made the discovery herself. It had merely showed up on the computer-enhanced photographs, and had been brought to Insigna's attention since she was Chief Astronomer. With considerable excitement, she had brought it to Pitt in his Commissioner's chambers.

She had begun simply enough, keeping her voice level, though it was shaking with emotion.

"Megas has a satellite," she said.

Pitt had lifted his eyebrows ever so slightly, but then he said, "Isn't that to be expected? The gas giants of the Solar System have anywhere up to a score of satellites."

"Of course, Janus, but this is not an ordinary satellite. It's large."

Pitt kept his cool. "Jupiter has four large satellites."

"I mean, really large, with almost Earth's size and mass."

"I see. Interesting."

"More than that. Much more than that, Janus. If this satellite revolved about Nemesis directly, tidal influences would cause only one side to face Nemesis, and it would be uninhabitable. Instead, only one side faces Megas, which is much cooler than Nemesis. Furthermore, the satellite's orbit is tilted substantially to Megas' equator. This means that in the satellite's sky, Megas is seen from only one hemisphere and it moves north and south with a cycle of about one day, while Nemesis moves across the sky, rising and setting, again with a cycle of one day. One hemisphere has twelve hours of darkness and twelve hours of light. The other hemisphere has the same but during its daytime, Nemesis is frequently in eclipse for up to half an hour at a time, with the cooling made up for by Megas' mild warmth. During the dark hours, in that hemisphere, the darkness is ameliorated by Megas' reflected light."

"The satellite has an interesting sky, then. How fascinating for astronomers."

"It's not just an astronomical lollipop, Janus. It's possible that the satellite has an equable temperature at the right range for human beings. It may be a habitable world."

Pitt smiled. "Even more interesting, but it wouldn't have our kind of light, though, would it?"

Insigna nodded. "That's true enough. It would have a ruddy sun and a dark sky because there would be no short-wave light to be scattered. And there would be a reddish landscape, I suppose."

"In that case, since you named Nemesis, and one of your people named Megas, I'll take the privilege of naming the satellite. Call it Erythro, which if I recall correctly, is related to the Greek word for 'red.' "

The news remained good for quite some time thereafter. An asteroid belt of respectable size was located beyond the orbit of the Megas-Erythro system, and those asteroids would clearly be an ideal source of material for building more Settlements.

And as they approached Erythro, the nature of its habitability seem to grow ever more favorable. Erythro was a planet of sea and land, though its seas, from preliminary estimates of its cloud cover as made out in visible light and the infrared, seemed shallower than Earth's oceans, and really impressive mountains on the land were very few. Insigna, on the basis of further calculations, insisted that the climate on the planet as a whole would be entirely suitable for human life.

And then when the inflight had brought them to a distance from which Erythro's atmosphere could be studied spectroscopically with precision, Insigna said to him, "Erythro's atmosphere is a little denser than Earth's and it contains free oxygen—16 percent of it, plus 5 percent argon and the rest nitrogen. There must be small quantities of carbon dioxide, but we haven't detected it yet. The point is, it's a breathable atmosphere."

"Sounds better and better," said Pitt. "Who could have imagined this when you first spotted Nemesis?"

"Better and better for the biologist. Maybe not very good for Rotor on the whole, though. A sizable content of free oxygen in the atmosphere is a sure indication of the presence of life."

"Life?" said Pitt, momentarily stupefied at the thought.

"Life," said Insigna, boring in, taking an apparent perverse pleasure in stressing the possibilities. "And if life, then possibly intelligent life, perhaps even a high civilization."

### 17.

What followed was a nightmare for Pitt. He had not only to live with the terrible apprehension of his own Earthpeople pursuing and overtaking him, superior in number certainly, and in technology possibly —but there was an accompanying fear now that was, if anything, greater. They might be approaching and infringing on an old and advanced civilization capable of eradicating them in a moment of absent-minded annoyance as a human being might, without thinking, crush a mosquito that buzzed too near his ear.

As they continued to approach Nemesis, Pitt said to Insigna with a deeply troubled air, "Need oxygen truly imply the existence of life?"

"It's a thermodynamic inevitability, Janus. In an Earth-like planet —and, as nearly as we can tell, Erythro is Earth-like—free oxygen cannot exist, any more than in any Earth-like gravitational field, a rock can be suspended in open air of its own accord. Oxygen, if present in the atmosphere to begin with, would spontaneously combine with other elements in the soil, giving off energy. It would only continue to exist in the atmosphere if some process were to supply energy and continually regenerate free oxygen."

"I understand that, Eugenia, but why need the energy-supply process necessarily involve life?"

"Because nothing has ever been encountered in nature that would do the job, except the photosynthetic action of green plants that make use of solar energy to release oxygen."

"When you say 'nothing has ever been encountered in nature,' you mean in the Solar System. This is another system with a different sun and a different planet under different conditions. The laws of thermodynamics may still hold, but what if there is some chemical process that we haven't encountered in the Solar System and that is forming the oxygen here?"

"If you're a betting man," said Insigna, "don't bet on it."

What was needed was evidence, and Pitt had to wait for the evidence to appear.

To begin with, Nemesis and Megas turned out to have extremely weak magnetic fields. This created no particular stir for it had been expected, since both star and planet rotated very slowly. Erythro, with a rotational period of twenty-three hours and sixteen minutes (equal to the period of its revolution about Megas), had a magnetic field that was similar, in intensity, to Earth's.

Insigna expressed her satisfaction. "At least we don't have to worry about dangerous radiation effects from intense magnetic fields, especially since Nemesis' stellar wind is bound to be much less intense than that of the Sun. That's good, because it means we might be able to detect the presence or absence of life on Erythro at a distance. Technological life, anyway."

"Why's that?" asked Pitt.

"It's not at all likely that a high level of technology can be reached without copious use of radio-wave radiation, which would be speeding away from Erythro in all directions. We ought to be able to differentiate between it and any random radio-wave radiation from the planet itself, when such natural radiation is minor, considering that its magnetic field is weak."

Pitt said, "I've been thinking that this may not be necessary; that we can reason out Erythro's lifelessness, even though it does have an oxygen atmosphere."

"Oh? I'd like to hear how that might be done."

"I've thought this out. Listen! Didn't you say that tidal influences slow the rotations of Nemesis, Megas, and Erythro? And didn't you say that, as a result, Megas has moved farther from Nemesis, and Erythro has moved farther from Megas?"

"Yes."

"Therefore, if we look into the past, Megas was once closer to Nemesis and Erythro was closer to Megas and to Nemesis, too. That means that Erythro was far too warm for life to begin with, and may only have become hospitable to life recently. There might not have been enough time for a technological civilization to develop."

Insigna laughed gently. "Good point. I mustn't underestimate your astronomical ingenuity—but not good enough. Red dwarf stars have a long life and Nemesis might easily have been formed in the very youth of the Universe—say, fifteen billion years ago. The tidal influence would have been very strong at first, when the bodies were closer together, and most of the driving apart may have taken place in the first three or four billion years. The tidal influence decreases as the cube of the distance and, in the last ten billion years or so, there would not have been much change and that would be *plenty* of time for several technological civilizations to be built up, one after the other. No, Janus, let's not speculate. Let's wait and see if we can detect radio-wave radiation, or not."

—Closer still to Nemesis.

It was a tiny red orb now to the unaided eye, but its dimness could be looked at without trouble. To one side, Megas was visible as a ruddy dot. In the telescope, it showed at something less than half-phase as a result of the angle it made with Rotor and with Nemesis. Erythro could be made out in the telescope, too, as a dimmer crimson dot.

It grew brighter with time, and Insigna said, "It's good news for you, Janus. No suspicious radio-wave radiation of possibly technological origin has yet been detected."

"Wonderful." Pitt felt the wave of relief as though it were a physical warmth washing over him.

"Don't leap, though," said Insigna. "They might use less radio-wave radiation that we might expect. They might shield it very well. They might even use something else in place of radio waves."

Pitt's mouth quirked into a small half-smile. "Are you suggesting that seriously?"

Insigna shrugged uncertainly.

Pitt said, "Because if you're a betting woman, don't bet on it."

—Closer still to Nemesis, and Erythro was now a large orb to the unaided eye, with bloated Megas near it, and Nemesis on the other side of the Settlement. Rotor had adjusted its velocity to keep pace with Erythro, which, through the telescope, showed drifting broken clouds in the familiar spiral shapes of a planet of Earth-type temperature and atmosphere, and, therefore, it should be counted on as possessing an at least vaguely Earth-like climate.

Insigna said, "There are no signs of light on the nightside of Erythro. That should please you, Janus."

"The absence of light is not consistent with a technological civilization, I suppose."

"It certainly isn't."

"Let me play devil's advocate, then," said Pitt. "With a red sun and dim light, wouldn't a civilization produce a dim artificial light as well?"

"It might be dim in the visible region, but Nemesis is rich in the infrared and we would expect artificial light to be similarly rich.

What infrared we detect, however, is planetary. It appears, more or less equally, over the entire land surface, whereas artificial light would have patterns, coming off richly in population concentrations, sparsely elsewhere."

"Then forget it, Eugenia," said Pitt buoyantly. "There is no technological civilization. It might make Erythro less interesting in some ways, but you can't want us to face our equals, or, perhaps, our superiors. We would have to leave and go elsewhere, and we have nowhere else to go, and perhaps an insufficient energy supply to get there if we did. As it is, we can stay."

"There's still copious oxygen in the atmosphere, so there's still certain to be life on Erythro. It's only a technological civilization that's lacking. It means we'll have to go down and study its life-forms."

"Why?"

"How can you ask, Janus? If we have another sample of life here, one that is altogether independent of the life developed on Earth, what a bonanza it would be for our biologists!"

"I see. You're talking about scientific curiosity. Well, the life-forms won't go away, I suppose. There will be time enough for that later. First things first."

"What can come ahead of a study of a totally new form of life?"

"Eugenia, be reasonable. We must establish ourselves here. We must build other Settlements. We must create a large and well-ordered society, one far more homogeneous, self-understanding, and peaceful than ever existed in the Solar System."

"For that we'll need material supplies, which takes us down to Erythro again, where we'll have to study the life-forms—"

"No, Eugenia. To land on Erythro and to take off again in the face of its gravitational field would be too costly at the present moment. The intensity of the gravitational fields of Erythro and of Megas— don't forget Megas—is great enough, even out here in space. One of our people calculated it for me. We'll have a problem getting our supplies even from the asteroid belt, but it will be less of a problem than getting them from Erythro. In fact, if we station ourselves in the asteroid belt, matters would be even more price-effective. The asteroid belt will be where we build our Settlements."

"Are you proposing to ignore Erythro?"

"For a while, Eugenia. When we are strong, when our energy supply is much greater, when our society is stable and growing, time enough then to investigate Erythro's life-forms or, perhaps, its unusual chemistry."

Pitt smiled soothingly, understandably, at Insigna. The side issue of Erythro, he knew, had to be delayed as long as possible. If it bore no technological society, then whatever other life-forms and resources it had could wait. The pursuing hordes from the Solar System were the true enemy.

Why couldn't others see what had to be done? Why were others so easily diverted into useless side paths?

How would he ever dare to die and leave the fools unprotected?

# TEN

---

# PERSUASION

18.

So now, twelve years after the discovery that no technological civilization existed on Erythro, and twelve years during which no Settlements from Earth had suddenly appeared to ruin the new world that was gradually being constructed, Pitt could appreciate these rare moments of rest. And yet, even in these rare moments, doubts crept in. He wondered whether Rotor would not have been better off, if he had clung to that original resolve of his—if they had not remained in orbit about Erythro, and if the Dome on Erythro had never been built.

He was leaning back in his soft chair, the restraining fields cushioning him, the aura of peace lulling him almost into sleep, when he heard the soft buzz that drew him back, reluctantly, into reality.

He opened his eyes (he had not realized they were closed) to look at the small viewpatch on the opposite wall. A touch of a contact magnified it into holovision.

It was Semyon Akorat, of course.

There he was with his bald bullethead. (Akorat shaved off the dark fringe that would otherwise show, feeling, quite rightly, that a few fugitive hairs would but make the desert in the center look the more pathetic, whereas a shapely skull, unmarred by interruption, could look almost stately.) There he was, also, with his worried eyes, which always looked worried even when there was no cause for worry.

Pitt found him unpleasant, not because of any failure in loyalty or efficiency (he could not be improved on, either way) but simply because of conditioned response. Akorat always announced an invasion of Pitt's privacy, an interruption of his thoughts, a necessity for doing what he would rather not do. In short, Akorat was in charge of Pitt's appointments and said who could see him and who could not.

Pitt frowned slightly. He could not recall that he had an appointment, but he often forgot and relied on Akorat not to.

"Who is it?" he said resignedly. "No one important, I hope."

"No one at all of any real significance," said Akorat, "but perhaps you had better see her."

"Is she within earshot?"

"Commissioner," said Akorat reproachfully, as though he were being accused of dereliction of duty. "Of course not. She is on the other side of the screen." He had an enormous precision of speech, which Pitt found soothing. There was never any question of mistaking his words.

Pitt said, "She? I presume it Dr. Insigna, then. Well, stick to my instructions. *Not* without an appointment. I've had enough of her for a while, Akorat. Enough of her for the last twelve years, in fact. Make up an excuse. Say I'm in meditation—no, she won't believe that— say—"

"Commissioner, it's not Dr. Insigna. I would not have disturbed you if it were. It's—it's her daughter."

"Her daughter?" For a moment, he fumbled over her name. "You mean Marlene Fisher?"

"Yes. Naturally, I told her you were busy, and she said that I ought to be ashamed of myself for telling a lie, for my expression showed it was a lie, up and down, and that my voice was too tense to be telling the truth." He recited this with baritone indignation. "In any case, she won't leave. She insists you will see her if you know she is waiting. Would you see her, Commisioner? Those eyes of hers rattle me, frankly."

"It seems to me I've heard of her eyes, too. Well, send her in, send her in, and I'll try to survive her eyes. Come to think of it, she has some explaining to do."

She entered. (Remarkably self-possessed, Pitt thought, though properly demure and with no sign of defiance.)

She sat down, her hands loosely in her lap, and clearly waited for Pitt to speak first. He let her wait a little, while he considered her in a rather absent fashion. He had seen her occasionally when she was younger, but not for a while, now. She had not been a pretty child and she wasn't any prettier now. She had broad cheekbones, and a certain gracelessness about her, but she did have remarkable eyes, and shapely eyebrows and long eyelashes, too.

Pitt said, "Well, Miss Fisher, I'm told you wanted to see me. May I ask why?"

Marlene looked up at him, her eyes cool, and seemed entirely at ease. She said, "Commissioner Pitt, I think my mother must have told you that I told a friend of mine that the Earth was going to be destroyed."

Pitt's eyebrows hunched down over his own rather ordinary eyes. He said, "Yes, she did. And I hope she told you that you must not speak of such matters in so foolish a way again."

"Yes, she did, Commissioner, but not speaking about it doesn't mean it isn't so; and calling it foolish doesn't make it so."

"I am Commissioner of Rotor, Miss Fisher, and it is my function to concern myself with such matters, and therefore you must leave it entirely to me, whether it is so or not so, whether it is foolish or not foolish. How did you get the idea that the Earth was going to be destroyed? Is this something your mother told you?"

"Not directly, Commissioner."

"But indirectly. Is that it?"

"She couldn't help that, Commissioner. Everyone speaks in all sorts of ways. There's the choice of words. There's intonation, expression, the flicker of eyes and eyelids, little tricks of clearing the throat. A hundred things. Do you know what I mean?"

"I know exactly what you mean. I watch for those things myself."

"And you feel very proud of that, Commissioner. You feel you're very good at it and that that's one of the reasons you're Commissioner."

Pitt looked startled. "I didn't say that, young woman."

"Not in words, Commissioner. You didn't have to." Her eyes were fixed on his. There was no trace of a smile on her face, but her eyes seemed amused.

"Well then, Miss Fisher, is that what you came to tell me?"

"No, Commissioner. I came because my mother has found it difficult to see you recently. No, she didn't tell me so. I just gathered it. I thought you might see me, instead."

"All right, you're here. Now what is it you came to tell me?"

"My mother is unhappy about the chance that Earth may be destroyed. My father's there, you know."

Pitt felt a small spasm of anger. How could a purely personal matter be allowed to interfere with the welfare of Rotor and all that it might become in the future? This Insigna, for all her usefulness in having found Nemesis in the first place, had long been an albatross about his neck with her unfailing way of heading down every wrong path. And now, when he would see her no more, she sent her mad daughter.

He said, "Are you under the impression that this destruction you speak of will happen tomorrow, or next year?"

"No, Commissioner, I know that it will happen in just a little bit less than five thousand years."

"If that is the case, your father will be long gone by then, as will your mother, and I, and you. And when we're all gone, it will still be nearly five thousand years before destruction for Earth and possibly other planets of the Solar System—if that destruction happens at all, which it won't."

"It's the idea of it, Commissioner, whenever it happens."

"Your mother must have told you that long before the time comes, the people of the Solar System will be aware of—of whatever you think will happen, and will deal with it. Besides, how can we complain of planetary destruction? Every world faces it eventually. Even if there are no cosmic collisions, every star must pass through a red giant stage and destroy its planets. Just as all human beings will die someday, so will all planets. Planetary lifetimes are a little longer, but that's all. Do you understand all that, young lady?"

"Yes, I do," said Marlene seriously. "I have a good relationship with my computer."

(I'll bet she does, thought Pitt, and then—too late—tried to wipe out the small sardonic smile that had twitched into existence on his face. She had probably used it to understand his attitude.)

He said with a note of finality, "Then we come to the end of our conversation. The talk of destruction is foolish, and even if it weren't, it has nothing to do with you, and you must never speak of it again, or not only you, but your mother as well, will be in trouble."

"We're not at the end of our conversation yet, Commissioner."

Pitt felt himself losing patience, but he said, quite calmly, "My dear Miss Fisher, when your Commissioner says it's the end, it *is*—regardless of what you think."

He half-rose, but Marlene sat where she was. "Because I want to offer you something you would dearly like to have."

"What?"

"The good riddance of my mother."

Pitt sank back into his chair, truly puzzled. "What do you mean by that?"

"If you will listen to me, Commissioner, I will tell you. My mother can't live like this. She's concerned about Earth and the Solar System and—and she thinks about my father sometimes. She thinks that Nemesis may be the nemesis of the Solar System and since she gave it the name, she feels responsible. She's an emotional person, Commissioner."

"Yes? You've noticed that, have you?"

"And she bothers you. She reminds you every once in a while about matters that she feels strongly about, and you don't want to hear about, and so you refuse to see her, and you wish she'd go away. You *can* send her away, Commissioner."

"Indeed? We've got one other Settlement. Shall I send her to New Rotor?"

"No, Commissioner. Send her to Erythro."

"Erythro? But why should I send her there? Just because I want to get rid of her?"

"That would be your reason. Yes, Commissioner. It would not be my reason, though. I want her on Erythro because she can't really work at the Observatory. The instruments always seem to be in use and she feels she's being watched all the time. She feels your annoyance. And besides, Rotor isn't a good base for delicate measurements. It turns too rapidly and too unevenly for good measurements."

"You have it all at your fingertips. Did your mother explain this to you? No, you don't have to tell me. She didn't tell you directly, did she? Only indirectly."

"Yes, Commissioner. And there's my computer."

"The one you have friendly relations with?"

"Yes, Commissioner."

"And so you think she will be able to work better on Erythro."

"Yes, Commissioner. It will be a stabler base, and she might make the kind of measurements that will convince her that the Solar System will survive. Even if she finds out otherwise, it will take a long time for her to be sure of that and for that time, at least, you'll be rid of her."

"I see that you want to be rid of her, too, is that it?"

"Not at all, Commissioner," said Marlene with composure. "I would go with her. You'd be rid of me, too, which would please you even more than being rid of her."

"What makes you think I want to get rid of you, too?"

Marlene fixed her gaze on him, somber, unblinking. "Now you do, Commissioner, since you now know that I have no trouble in interpreting your inner feelings."

Suddenly, Pitt found himself desperately wanting to get rid of this monster. He said, "Let me think about this," and turned his head. He felt that he was being childish in looking away, but he did not want this horrible youngster to read his face like the open book it was.

It was, after all, the truth. He *did* now want to get rid of mother and daughter alike. Where the mother was concerned, he had indeed thought, on several occasions, of exiling her to Erythro. But since she would scarcely have wanted to go, there would have been a most unappetizing fuss and he had no stomach for that. Now, though, her daughter had given him a reason why she might indeed want to go to Erythro, and that, of course, changed things.

He said slowly, "If your mother really wants this—"

"She really does, Commissioner. She hasn't mentioned it to me, and it may be she hasn't even thought of it yet, but she will want to go. I know that. Trust me."

"Do I have a choice? And do *you* want to go?"

"Very much, Commissioner."

"Then I will arrange for it at once. Does that satisfy you?"

"Yes, it does, Commissioner."

"Then shall we *now* consider the interview at an end?"

Marlene rose and ducked her head in a graceless bow, presumably one that was intended to be repsectful. "Thank you, Commissioner."

She turned and left, and it wasn't till she had been gone for several

85

minutes that Pitt dared unclench the grip that had kept his face in place till it was aching.

He dared not have allowed her to deduce from anything he said or did or seemed, the final item that he, and only one other person, knew about Erythro.

# ELEVEN

## ORBIT

### 19.

Pitt's quiet time was over, but he did not wish it to be over. Quite arbitrarily, he canceled his afternoon appointments. He wanted more thinking time.

Specifically, he wanted to think about Marlene.

Her mother, Eugenia Insigna Fisher, was a problem, and had, in fact, grown to be more of one over the last dozen years. She was emotional and jumped far ahead of anything reason would allow. Yet she was a human being; she could be led and controlled; she could be pent-up within the comfortable walls of logic; and though she might be restless at times, she could be made to remain there.

Not so with this Marlene. Pitt had no doubt that she was a monster, and he could only be grateful that she had foolishly revealed herself in order to help her mother on so trivial an occasion. But then she was inexperienced and lacked the wisdom to have kept her abilities hidden until she could use them in a truly devastating fashion.

But she would only grow more dangerous as she grew older, so she would have to be stopped now. And she *would* be stopped by that other monster, Erythro.

Pitt gave himself credit. He had recognized Erythro as a monster from the start. It had its own expression to read—the reflection of the bloody light of its star, an expression that was ominous and menacing.

When they had reached the asteroid belt, a hundred million miles outside the orbit in which Megas and Erythro circled Nemesis, Pitt had said, with full confidence, "This is the place."

He had expected no difficulty. The rational view admitted nothing else. Among the asteroids, Nemesis cast little heat and light. The loss of natural heat and light was nothing, since Rotor had fully functional micro-fusion. In fact, it was actually a benefit. With its red light dimmed to almost nothing, it did not weigh down the heart, darken the mind, and shiver the soul.

Then, too, a base in the asteroidal belt would place them in an area where the gravitational effects of Nemesis and Megas would be weak, and where maneuverability would, in consequence, be less energy-expensive. The asteroids would be more easily mined, and considering the feeble light of Nemesis, there should be plenty of volatiles on those little bodies.

Ideal!

And yet the people of Rotor made it clear that, by an overwhelming majority, they wanted to move the Settlement into orbit around Erythro. Pitt labored to point out that they would be bathed in angrily depressing red light, that they would be held firmly in the grip of Megas as well as Erythro, and that they might still have to go to the asteroids for raw materials.

Pitt discussed it angrily with Tambor Brossen, the ex-Commissioner, to whose post he had succeeded. The rather weary Brossen openly enjoyed his new role as elder statesman far more than he had ever enjoyed being Commissioner. (He had been known to say that he lacked Pitt's pleasure in making decisions.)

Brossen had laughed at Pitt's concern over the matter of Settlement location—not outright, to be sure, but gently, with his eyes. He said, "There's no need, Janus, to feel that you must educate Rotor into absolute agreement with you. Let the Settlement have its own way once in a while; they will be all the readier to let you have your way at other times. If they want to orbit Erythro, let them orbit Erythro."

"But it makes no sense, Tambor. Don't you understand that?"

"Of course I understand that. I also understand that Rotor has been in orbit around a sizable world all its existence. That's what seems right to Rotorians and that's what they want to have again."

"We were in orbit about Earth. Erythro is not Earth; it is nothing like Earth."

"It is a world and is about the same size as Earth. It has land and sea. It has an atmosphere with oxygen in it. We could travel thousands of light-years before finding a world this much like Earth. I tell you again. Let the people have it."

Pitt had followed Brossen's advice, though something within him muttered dissension every step of the way. New Rotor was also in orbit around Erythro and so were the two others in process of construction. Of course, Settlements in the asteroid belt were on the drawing boards, but the public clearly lacked eagerness to put them through.

Of all that had happened since the discovery of Nemesis, it was this orbiting of Erythro that Pitt considered Rotor's greatest mistake. It should not have happened. And yet—and yet—could even he have forced it on Rotor? Might he have tried harder? And would that merely have led to a new election and his displacement?

It was nostalgia that was the great problem. People tended to look back and Pitt could not always make them turn their head and look forward. Consider Brossen—

He had died seven years ago and Pitt had been at his deathbed. Pitt alone had happened to catch the old man's dying words. Brossen had beckoned to Pitt, who had leaned close to him. Brossen had reached out a feeble hand, the skin dry as paper. Clutching feebly at Pitt, he had whispered, "How bright the Sun of Earth was," and had died.

So because Rotorians could not forget how bright the Sun had once been, and how green the Earth had once been, they cried out in exasperation against Pitt's logic and demanded that Rotor orbit a world that was not green, and that circled a sun that was not bright.

It meant the loss of ten years in the rate of progress. They would have been ten years farther ahead had they been located in the asteroid belt from the start. Pitt was convinced of that.

That alone was enough to poison Pitt's feelings toward Erythro, but there was, in connection with it, matters that were worse—much worse.

# TWELVE

## ANGER

### 20.

As it happened, Crile Fisher, having given Earth its first hint that there was something peculiar about Rotor's destination, gave it its second hint as well.

He had been back on Earth two years now, with Rotor growing dimmer in his mind. Eugenia Insigna was a rather perplexing memory (what had he felt for her?), but Marlene remained a bitterness. He found he could not separate her from Roseanne in his mind. The one-year-old daughter he remembered and the seventeen-year-old sister he also remembered fused into one personality.

Life was not hard. He drew a generous pension. They had even found work for him to do, an easy administrative position in which he was required to make decisions on occasion that were guaranteed to affect nothing of importance. They had forgiven him, at least in part, he thought, because he had remembered that one remark of Eugenia's, "If you knew where we were going—"

Yet he had the impression that he was kept under watch, anyway, and he had grown to resent it.

Garand Wyler appeared now and then, always friendly, always inquisitive, always returning the subject to Rotor in one way or another. He had, in fact, made his appearance now, and the subject of Rotor came up, as Fisher expected it would.

Fisher scowled, and said, "It's been nearly two years. What do you people want of me?"

Wyler shook his head. "I can't say I know, Crile. All we have is that remark of your wife's. It's obviously not enough. She must have said something else in the years you spent with her. Consider the conversations you have had; the talk that bounced back and forth between the two of you. Is there nothing there?"

"This is the fifth time you've asked that, Garand. I have been questioned. I have been hypnotized. I have been mind-probed. I have been squeezed dry, and there is nothing in me. Let me go and find something else to tackle. Or put me back to work. There are a hundred Settlements out there, with friends confiding in each other and enemies spying on each other. Who knows what one of them may know —and may not even know that he knows."

Wyler said, "To be truthful, old man, we've been moving in that direction, and we've also been concentrating on the Far Probe. It stands to reason that Rotor must have found something the rest of us don't know. We've never sent out a Far Probe. Neither has any other Settlement. Only Rotor had the capacity for it. Whatever Rotor found must be in the Far Probe data."

"Good. Look through that data. There must be enough there to keep you busy for years. As for me, leave me alone. All of you."

Wyler said, "As a matter of fact, there is enough there to keep us busy for years. Rotor supplied a great deal of data in line with the Open Science Agreement. In particular, we have their stellar photography at every range of wavelength. The Far Probe cameras were able to reach almost every part of the sky, and we've been studying it in detail and have found nothing in it of interest."

"Nothing?"

"So far, nothing, but, as you say, we can continue to study it for years. Of course, we already have any number of items the astronomy people are delighted with. It keeps them happy and busy, but not a single item, not the sniff of one seems to help us decide where they went. Not so far. I gather that there is absolutely nothing, for instance, to lead us to think that there are planets orbiting either large star of the Alpha Centauri system. Nor are there are any unexpected Sun-like stars we don't know about in our neighborhood. Personally, I wouldn't expect to find much anyway. What could the Far Probe see that we couldn't see from the Solar System? It was only a couple of light-months away. It should make no difference. Yet some of us feel that Rotor must have seen *something* and rather quickly, too. Which brings us back to you."

"Why me?"

"Because your ex-wife was the head of the Far Probe project."

"Not really. She became Chief Astronomer after the data had been collected."

"She was the head afterward and certainly an important part during. Did she never say anything to you about what they had found in the Far Probe?"

"Not a word. Wait, did you say that the Far Probe cameras were able to reach almost every part of the sky?"

"Yes."

"How much is 'almost every part?' "

"I'm not in their confidence to the point where I can give you exact figures. I gather it's at least 90 percent."

"Or more?"

"Maybe more."

"I wonder—"

"What do you wonder?"

"On Rotor, we had a fellow named Pitt running things."

"We know that."

"But I think I know how he would do things. He would hand out the Far Probe data a little at a time, living up to the Open Science Agreement, but just barely. And somehow, by the time Rotor left, there would have been some of the data—10 percent or less—that he would not have had time to get to you. And that would be the important 10 percent or less."

"You mean the part that tells us where Rotor went."

"Maybe."

"Only we haven't got it."

"Sure, you have it."

"How do you make that out?"

"Just a little while ago you wondered why you should expect to see anything in the Far Probe photographs that you couldn't see in the

Solar System records. So why are you wasting your time on what they gave you? Map out the part of the sky they *didn't* give you and study that part on your *own* maps. Ask yourself if there's anything there that might look different on a Far Probe map—and why. That's what I would do." His voice suddenly rose to a formidable shout. "You go back there. Tell them to look at the part of the sky they don't have."

Wyler said thoughtfully, "Topsy-turvy."

"No, it isn't. Perfectly straightforward. Just find someone in the Office who does more with his brain than sit on it, and you may get somewhere."

Wyler said, "We'll see." He held out his hand to Fisher. Fisher scowled and wouldn't take it.


It was months before Wyler made an appearance again, and Fisher didn't welcome him. He had been in a quiet mood on this off-day from work, and had even been reading a book.

Fisher was not one of those people who felt that a book was a twentieth-century abomination, that only viewing was civilized. There was something, he thought, about holding a book, about the physical turning of pages, about the ability to lose one's self in thought over what one has read, or even to drowse off, without coming to, and finding the film a hundred pages beyond, or flickering at its close. Fisher was rather of the opinion that the book was the more civilized of the two modes.

He was all the more annoyed at being roused out of his pleasant lethargy.

"Now, what, Garand?" he said ungraciously.

Wyler did not lose his urbane smile. He said, between his teeth, "We've found it, just exactly as you said we would."

"Found what?" said Fisher, not remembering. Then, realizing what this must refer to, he said hastily, "Don't tell me anything I'm not supposed to know. I won't be tangled with the Office anymore."

"Too late, Crile. You're wanted. Tanayama himself wants you in front of him."

"When?"

"As soon as I can get you there."

"In that case, tell me what's going on. I don't want to face him cold."

"That's what I intend to do. We studied every portion of the sky that the Far Probe did not report on. Apparently those who did so asked themselves, as you advised, what it was that a Far Probe camera could see that a Solar System camera could not. The obvious answer was a displacement of the nearer stars, and once that was in their heads, the astronomers found an astonishing thing, something they couldn't have predicted."

"Well?"

"They found a very dim star with a parallax of well over one second of arc."

"I'm not an astronomer. Is that unusual?"

"It means that the star is at only half the distance of Alpha Centauri."

"You said 'very dim.' "

"It's behind a small dust cloud, they tell me. Listen, if you're not an astronomer, your wife on Rotor was. Perhaps she discovered it. Did she ever say anything to you about it."

Fisher shook his head. "Not a word. Of course—"

"Yes?"

"In the last few months, there was an excitement about her. A kind of brimming over."

"You didn't ask why?"

"I assumed it was the imminent departure of Rotor. She was excited about going and that drove me mad."

"On account of your daughter?"

Fisher nodded.

"The excitement may have been over the new star, too. It all fits. Naturally, they'd go to this new star. And if your wife had discovered it, they would be going to *her* star. That would account for some of her eagerness to go. Doesn't it make sense?"

"Maybe. I can't say it doesn't."

"All right, then. That's what Tanayama wants to see you about. And he's angry. Not at you, apparently, but he's angry."


21.


It was later that same day, for there was no delay on this occasion, that Crile Fisher found himself in the office of the Terrestrial Board of Inquiry, or, as it was far better known to its employees, simply the Office.

Kattimoro Tanayama, who had directed the Office for over thirty years, was getting quite elderly. The holographs shown of him (there weren't many) had been recorded years before, when his hair was still smooth and black, his body straight, his expression vigorous.

Now his hair was gray, his body (never tall) was slightly bent, and possessed an air of frailty. He might, thought Fisher, be reaching the point where he was considering retiring, if it were conceivable that he intended to do anything but die in harness. His eyes, Fisher noted, were, between their narrowed lids, as keen and as sharp as ever.

Fisher had a little trouble understanding him. English was as nearly universal a language on Earth as it was possible for a language to be, but it had its varieties, and Tanayama's was not the North American variety Fisher was accustomed to.

Tanayama said coldly, "Well, Fisher, you failed us on Rotor."

Fisher saw no point in arguing the matter; and no point in arguing with Tanayama, in any case.

"Yes, Director," he said tonelessly.

"Yet you may still have information for us."

Fisher sighed silently, then said, "I have been debriefed over and over."

"So I have been told, and so I know. You have not been asked everything, however, and I have a question to which I—I—want an answer."

"Yes, Director?"

"In your stay on Rotor, have you been aware of anything that would lead you to believe that the Rotorian leadership hated Earth?"

Fisher's eyebrows climbed. "Hate? It was clear to me that the people on Rotor, as on all Settlements, I think, looked down on Earth, despised it as decadent, brutal, and violent. But hatred? I don't think they thought enough of us, frankly, to feel hatred."

"I talk of the leadership, not of the multitude."

"So do I, Director. No hatred."

"There's no other way of accounting for it."

"Accounting for what, Director? If that is a question I may ask?"

Tanayama looked up at him sharply (the force of his personality made one rarely aware of just how short he was). "Do you know that this new star is moving in our direction? Quite in our direction?"

Fisher, startled, looked quickly toward Wyler, but Wyler sat in comparative shadow, well out of range of the sunlight from the window, and was not, in appearance, looking at anything.

Tanayama, who was standing, said, "Well, sit down, Fisher, if it will help you think. I will sit down, too." He sat down on the edge of his desk, his short legs dangling.

"Did you know about the motion of the star?"

"No, Director. I didn't know of the existence of the star at all till Agent Wyler told me."

"You didn't? Surely it was known on Rotor."

"If so, no one told me."

"Your wife was excited and happy in the last period before Rotor left. So you told Agent Wyler. What was the reason?"

"Agent Wyler had thought it might be because she had discovered the star."

"And perhaps she knew of the star's motion and was pleased at the thought of what would happen to us."

"I can't see why that thought should make her happy, Director. I must tell you that I do not actually know that she knew of the star's motion or even that it existed. I do not, of my own knowledge, know that anyone on Rotor knew that the star existed."

Tanayama looked at him thoughtfully, rubbing one side of his chin lightly, as though relieving a slight itch.

He said, "The people on Rotor were all Euros, I believe, weren't they?"

Fisher's eyes widened. He hadn't heard that vulgarism in a long time—never from a government functionary. He remembered Wyler's comment soon after he had returned to Earth about Rotor being "Snow White." He had dismissed it as a piece of lighthearted sarcasm, and had given no heed to it.

He said resentfully, "I don't know, Director. I didn't study them all. I don't know what their ancestries may be."

"Come, Fisher. You don't have to study them. Judge by their appearances. In all your stay on Rotor, did you encounter one face that was Afro, or Mongo, or Hindo? Did you encounter a dark complexion? An epicanthic fold?"

Fisher exploded. "Director, you're being twentieth-century." (If he had known a stronger way of putting it, he would have.) "I don't give these things thought, and no one on Earth should. I'm surprised you do, and I don't think it would help your position if it were known that you do."

"Don't indulge in fairy tales, Agent Fisher," said the Director, moving one gnarled finger from side to side in admonition. "I am talking about what is. I know that on Earth we ignore all variation among ourselves, at least outwardly."

"Just outwardly?" said Fisher in indignation.

"Just outwardly," said Tanayama coldly. "When Earth's people go out to the Settlements, they sort themselves out by variation. Why should they do that, if they ignored all variation? On any Settlement, all are alike, or, if there is some admixture to begin with, those who are well outnumbered feel ill-at-ease, or are made to feel ill-at-ease, and shift to another Settlement where they are not outnumbered. Isn't that so?"

Fisher found he could not deny this. It was so, and he had somehow taken it for granted without questioning it. He said, "Human nature. Like clings to like. It set up a—neighborhood."

"Human nature, of course. Like clings to like, because like hates and despises unlike."

"There are M—Mongo Settlements, too." Fisher stumbled over the word, and realized full well that he might be mortally offending the Director—an easy and dangerous man to offend.

Tanayama did not blink. "I know that well, but it's the Euros who most recently dominated the planet, and they cannot forget it, can they?"

"The others, perhaps, cannot forget that either, and they have more cause to hate."

"But it's Rotor that went flying off to escape from the Solar System."

"It happened to be they who had discovered hyper-assistance."

"And they went to a nearby star that only they knew of, one which is heading toward our Solar System and may pass closely enough to disrupt it."

"We don't know they know that, or that they even know the star."

"Of course they know it," said Tanayama with what was almost a snarl. "And they left without warning us."

"Director—with respect—this is illogical. If they are going to establish themselves on a star that will, on its approach, disrupt our Solar System, the star's own system will also be disrupted."

"They can easily escape, even if they build more Settlements. We have an entire world of eight billion people to evacuate—a much more difficult task."

"How much time do we have?"

Tanayama shrugged. "Several thousand years, they tell me."

"That's a great deal of time. It might not have occurred to them, just conceivably, that it was necessary to warn us. As the star approaches, it will surely be discovered without warning."

"And by that time, we will have less time to evacuate. Their discovery of the star was accidental. We would not have discovered it for a long time, but for your wife's indiscreet remark to you, and but for your suggestion—a good one—that we look closely at the part of the sky that had been omitted. Rotor was counting on our discovery being as belated as possible."

"But, Director, why should they want such a thing? Sheer motiveless hate?"

"Not motiveless. So that the Solar System, with its heavy load of non-Euros, might be destroyed. So that humanity can make a new start on a homogenous basis of Euros only. Eh? What do you think of that?"

Fisher shook his head helplessly. "Impossible. Unthinkable."

"Why else should they have failed to warn us?"

"Might it not be that they did not themselves know of the star's motion?"

"Impossible," said Tanayama ironically. "Unthinkable. There is no other reason for what they have done but their willingness to see us destroyed. But we will discover hyperspatial travel for ourselves, and we will move out to this new star and find them. And we will even the score."

# THIRTEEN

# DOME

### 22.

Eugenia Insigna greeted her daughter's statement with a half-laugh of disbelief. How does one go about doubting a young daughter's sanity as an alternative to doubting one's own hearing capacity?

"What did you say, Marlene? What do you mean I'm going to Erythro?"

"I asked Commissioner Pitt, and he said he would arrange it."

Insigna looked blank. "But why?"

Betraying a bit of irritation, Marlene answered, "Because you say you want to make delicate astronomical measurements and you can't do it delicately enough from Rotor. You can do it from Erythro. But I see I'm not answering your real question."

"You're right. What I meant was why should Commissioner Pitt have said he would arrange it? I've asked several times before this, and he has always refused. He's unwilling to let *anyone* go to Erythro —except for some specialists."

"I just put it to him in a different way, Mother." Marlene hesitated a moment. "I told him that I knew he was anxious to get rid of you and this was his chance."

Insigna drew in her breath so sharply that she choked slightly and had to cough. Then, eyes watering, she said, "How could you *say* that?"

"Because it's true, Mother. I wouldn't have said it if it weren't true. I've heard him speak to you, and I've heard you speak about him, and it's just so clear that I know you see it, too. He's *annoyed* with you, and wishes you'd stop bothering him about—about whatever you bother him about. You know that."

Insigna pressed her lips together and said, "You know, darling, I'm going to have to take you into my confidence from now on. It really embarrasses me to have you worm these things out."

"I know, Mother." Marlene's eyes dropped. "I'm sorry."

"But I still don't understand. You didn't have to explain to him that he's annoyed with me. He must know he is. Why, then, didn't he send me to Erythro when I asked him to do so in the past?"

"Because he hates having anything to do with Erythro, and just getting rid of you wasn't enough to overcome his dislike of the world. Only this time it's not just you going. It's you and I. Both of us."

Insigna leaned forward, placing her hands flat on the table between them. "No, Molly—Marlene. Erythro is not the place for you. I won't be there forever. I'll take my measurements and come back and you'll stay right here and wait for me."

"I'm afraid not, Mother. It's clear that he's only willing to let you go because that's the only way we can get rid of *me*. That's why he agreed to send you when I asked that we *both* go, and wouldn't agree when you asked that just you go. Do you see?"

Insigna frowned. "No, I don't. I really don't. What do *you* have to do with it?"

"When we were talking, and I explained that I knew he would like to get rid of both of us, his face froze—you know, so he could wipe out all expression. He knew I could understand expressions and little things like that, and he didn't want me to guess what he was feeling, I suppose. But that's also a giveaway, you see, and tells me a lot. Besides, you can't suppress everything. Your eyes flicker, and I guess you don't even know it."

"So you knew he wanted to get rid of you, too."

"Worse than that. He's *scared* of me."

"Why should he be scared of you?"

"I suppose because he hates having me know what he doesn't want me to know." She added with a dour sigh, "Lots of people get upset with me for that."

Insigna nodded. "I can understand that. You make people feel naked—mentally naked, I mean, like a cold wind is blowing across their minds."

Her eyes focused on her daughter. "Sometimes I feel that way myself. Looking back, I think you've disturbed me since you were a small child. I told myself often enough that you were simply unusually intelli—"

"I think I am," said Marlene quickly.

"That, too, yes, but it was clearly something more than that, though I didn't see it very clearly. Tell me—do you mind talking about this?"

"Not to you, Mother," said Marlene, but there was a note of cau tion in her voice.

"Well then, when you were younger and found out that you could do this and other children couldn't—and even other grown-ups couldn't—why didn't you come and tell me about it?"

"I tried once, actually, but you were impatient. I mean, you didn't say anything, but I could tell you were busy and couldn't be bothered with childish nonsense."

Insigna's eyes widened. "Did I *say* it was childish nonsense?"

"You didn't *say* it, but the way you looked at me and the way you were holding your hands said it."

"You should have insisted on telling me."

"I was just a little kid. And you were unhappy most of the time—about Commissioner Pitt, and about Father."

"Never mind about that. Is there anything else you can tell me now?"

"There's only one thing," said Marlene. "When Commissioner Pitt said we could go, there was something about the way he said it that made me think he left out something—that there was something he didn't say."

"And what was it, Marlene?"

"That's just it, Mother. I can't read *minds,* so I don't know. I can only go by outside things and that leaves things hazy, sometimes. Still—"

"Yes?"

"I have the feeling that whatever it was he didn't say was rather unpleasant—maybe even evil."

## 23.

Getting ready for Erythro took Insigna quite a while, of course. There were matters on Rotor that could not be left at midpoint. There had to be arrangements in the astronomy department, instructions to others, appointment of her chief associate to the position of Chief Astronomer pro-tem, and some final consultations with Pitt, who was oddly noncommunicative on the matter.

Insigna finally put it to him during her last report before leaving.

"I'm going to Erythro tomorrow, you know," she said.

"Pardon me?" He looked up from the final report she had handed him, and which he had been staring at, though she was convinced he wasn't reading it. (Was she picking up some of Marlene's tricks and not knowing how to handle it? She mustn't begin to believe that she was penetrating below the surface when, in fact, she was not.)

She said patiently, "I'm going to Erythro tomorrow, you know."

"Is it tomorrow? Well, you'll be coming back eventually, so this is not good-bye. Take care of yourself. Look upon it as a vacation."

"I intend to be working on Nemesis' motion through space."

"That? Well—" He made a gesture with both hands as though pushing something unimportant away. "As you wish. A change of surroundings is a vacation even if you continue working."

"I want to thank you for allowing this, Janus."

"Your daughter asked me to. Did you know she asked me to?"

"I know. She told me the same day. I told her she had no right to bother you. You were very tolerant of her."

Pitt grunted. "She's a very unusual girl. I didn't mind obliging her. It's only temporary. Finish your calculations and return."

She thought: That's twice he mentioned my return. What would Marlene make out of that if she were here? Something evil, as she says? But what?

She said evenly, "We'll come back."

He said, "With the news, I hope, that Nemesis will prove harmless —five thousand years from now."

"That's for the facts to decide," she said grimly, then left.

### 24.

It was strange, Eugenia Insigna thought. She was over two light-years from the spot in space where she was born and yet she had only been on a spaceship twice and then for the shortest possible journeys—from Rotor to Earth and then back to Rotor again.

She still had no great urge to travel in space. It was Marlene who was the driving force behind this trip. It was she who, independently, had seen Pitt and persuaded him to succumb to her strange form of blackmail. And it was she who was truly excited, with this odd compulsion of hers to visit Erythro. Insigna could not understand that compulsion and viewed it as another part of her daughter's unique mental and emotional complexity. Still, whenever Insigna quailed at the thought of leaving safe, small, comfortable Rotor for the vast empty world of Erythro, so strange and menacing, and fully six hundred and fifty thousand kilometers away (nearly twice as far away as Rotor had been from Earth), it was Marlene's excitement that reinvigorated her.

The ship that would take them to Erythro was neither graceful nor beautiful. It was serviceable. It was one of a small fleet of rockets that acted as ferries, blasting up from the stodgy gravitational pull of Erythro, or coming down without daring to give in to it by even a trifle, and, either way, working one's way through the cushiony, windy, unpredictability of an untamed atmosphere.

Insigna didn't think the trip would be pleasurable. Through most of it they would be weightless and two solid days of weightlessness would, no doubt, be tedious.

Marlene's voice broke into her reverie. "Come on, Mother, they're waiting for us. The baggage is all checked and everything."

Insigna moved forward. Her last uneasy thought as she passed through the airlock was—predictably—But why was Janus Pitt so willing to let us go?

### 25.

Siever Genarr ruled a world as large as Earth. Or, to be more accurate perhaps, he ruled, *directly,* a domed region that covered nearly three square kilometers and was slowly growing. The rest of the world, however, nearly five hundred million square kilometers of

103

land and sea, was unoccupied by human beings. It was also occupied by no other living things above the microscopic scale. So if a world is considered as being ruled by the multicellular life-forms that occupied it, the hundreds who lived and worked in the domed region were the rulers, and Siever Genarr ruled over them.

Genarr was not a large man, but his strong features gave him an impressive look. When he was young, this had made him look older than his age—but that had evened itself out now that he was nearly fifty. His nose was long and his eyes somewhat pouchy. His hair was in the first stages of grizzle. His voice, however, was a musical and resonant baritone. (He had once thought of the stage as a career, but his appearance doomed him to occasional character roles, and his talents as an administrator took precedence.)

It was those talents—partly—that had kept him in the Erythro Dome for ten years, watching it grow from an uncertain three-room structure to the expansive mining and research station it had now become.

The Dome had its disadvantages. Few people remained long. There were shifts, since almost all those who came there considered themselves in exile and wished, more or less constantly, to return to Rotor. And most found the pinkish light of Nemesis either threatening or gloomy, even though the light inside the Dome was every bit as bright and homelike as that on Rotor.

It had its advantages, too. Genarr was removed from the hurly-burly of Rotorian politics, which seemed more ingrown and meaningless each year. Even more important, he was removed from Janus Pitt, whose views he generally—and uselessly—opposed.

Pitt had been strenuously opposed to any settlement on Erythro from the start—even to Rotor orbiting around Erythro. Here, at least, Pitt had been defeated by overwhelming public opinion, but he saw to it that the Dome was generally starved for funds and that its growth was slowed. If Genarr had not successfully developed the Dome as a source of water for Rotor—far cheaper than it could be obtained from the asteroids—Pitt might have crushed it.

In general, though, Pitt's principle of ignoring the Dome's existence as far as possible meant that he rarely attempted to interfere with Genarr's administrative procedures—which suited Genarr right down to Erythro's damp soil.

It came as a surprise to him, then, that Pitt should have bothered to inform him personally of the arrival of a pair of newcomers, instead of allowing the information to show up in the routine paperwork. Pitt had, indeed, discussed the matter in detail, in his usual clipped and arbitrary manner that invited no discussion, or even comment, and the conversation had been shielded, too.

It came as an even greater surprise that one of the people coming to Erythro was Eugenia Insigna.

Once, years before the Leaving, they had been friends, but then, after their happy college days (Genarr remembered them wistfully as rather romantic), Eugenia had gone to Earth for her graduate studies and had returned to Rotor with an Earthman. Genarr had scarcely seen her—except once or twice, at a distance—since she had married Crile Fisher. And when she and Fisher had separated, just before the Leaving, Genarr had had work of his own and so had she—and it never occurred to either to renew old ties.

Genarr had, perhaps, thought of it occasionally, but Eugenia was quite apparently sunk in sorrow, with an infant daughter to raise, and he was reluctant to intrude. Then he was sent to Erythro and that ended even the possiblility of renewal. He had periodic vacation time on Rotor, but he was never at ease there any longer. Some old Rotorian friendships remained, but only in lukewarm fashion.

Now Eugenia was coming with her daughter. Genarr, at the moment, didn't remember the girl's name—if he had ever known it. Certainly, he had never seen her. The daughter should be fifteen by now, and he wondered, with a queer little interior tremble, if she was beginning to look anything like the young Eugenia had.

Genarr looked out his office window with an almost surreptitious air. He had grown so used to Erythro Dome that he no longer saw it with a critical eye. It was the home of working people of both sexes—adults, no children. Shift workers, signed up for a period of weeks or possibly months, sometimes returning eventually for another shift, sometimes not. Except for himself and four others who, for one reason or another, had learned to prefer the Dome, there were no permanents.

There was no one to take pride in it as an ordinary abode. It was kept clean and orderly as a matter of necessity, but there was also an air of artificiality about it. It was too much a matter of lines and arcs, planes and circles. It lacked irregularity, lacked the chaos of permanent life, where a room, or even just a desk, had adjusted itself to the hollows and waverings of a particular personality.

There was himself, of course. His desk and his room reflected his own angular and planar person. That, perhaps, might be another reason he was at home in the Erythro Dome. The shape of his inner spirit matched its spare geometry.

But what would Eugenia Insigna think of it? (He was rather pleased she had resumed her maiden name.) If she were as he remembered her, she would revel in irregularity, in the unexpected touch of frippery, for all she was an astronomer.

Or had she changed? Did people ever change, essentially? Had Crile Fisher's desertion embittered her, twisted her—

Genarr scratched the hair at his temple where it had gone distinctly gray and thought that these speculations were useless and time-wasting. He would see Eugenia soon enough, for he had left word that she was to be brought to him as soon as she had arrived.

Or should he have gone to greet her in person?

No! He had argued that with himself half a dozen times already. He couldn't look too anxious; it wouldn't suit the dignity of his position.

But then Genarr thought that that wasn't the reason at all. He didn't want to make her uneasy; he didn't want her to think he was still the same uncomfortable and incompetent admirer who had retreated in so shambling a manner before the tall and brooding good looks of the Earthman. And Eugenia had never looked at him again after she had seen Crile—never seriously looked at him.

Genarr's eyes scanned the message from Janus Pitt—dry, condensed, as his messages always were, and with that indefinable feel of authority behind it, as though the possibility of disagreement were not merely unheard of—but actually unthought of.

And he now noted that Pitt spoke more forcefully of the young daughter than of the mother. There was especially Pitt's statement that the daughter had expressed a deep interest in Erythro, and if she wished to explore its surface, she was to be allowed to.

Now why was that?

## 26.

And there she was. Fourteen years older than at the time of the Leaving. Twenty years older than she was in her pre-Crile youth, the day they had gone into Farming Area C and climbed the levels into low gravity, and she had laughed when he tried a slow somersault and had turned too far and had come down on his belly. (Actually, he could easily have hurt himself, for though the sensation of weight decreased, mass and inertia did not, and damage could follow. Fortunately, he had not suffered *that* humiliation.

Eugenia *looked* older, too, but she had not thickened very much, and her hair—shorter now, and straight—was more matter-of-fact somehow, but was still a lively dark brown.

And when she advanced toward him, smiling, he could feel his traitor heart speed a bit. She held out both hands and he took them.

"Siever," she said, "I have betrayed you, and I'm so ashamed."

"Betrayed me, Eugenia? What are you talking about?" What *was* she talking about? Surely not her marriage to Crile.

She said, "I should have thought of you every day. I should have sent you messages, given you the news, insisted on coming to visit you."

"Instead, you never thought of me at all!"

"Oh, I'm not *that* bad. I thought of you every once in a while. I never really *forgot* you. Don't think that for a moment. It's just that my thoughts never really prompted me to do anything."

Genarr nodded. What was there to say? He said, "I know you've been busy. And I've been here—out of sight and, therefore, out of mind."

"Not out of mind. You've scarcely changed at all, Siever."

"That's the advantage of looking old and craggy when you're twenty. After that, you never change, Eugenia. Time passes and you just look a trifle older and a trifle craggier. Not enough to matter."

"Come now, you make a profession of being cruel to yourself so that soft-hearted women will leap to your defense. That hasn't changed at all."

"Where's your daughter, Eugenia? I was told she would be coming with you."

"She came. You can be sure of that. Erythro is her idea of Paradise, for no reason I can possibly think of. She went to our quarters to straighten them out and unpack for the two of us. She's that kind of young woman. Serious. Responsible. Practical. Dutiful. She possesses what someone once described to me as all the unlovable virtues."

Genarr laughed. "I'm quite at home with them. If you only knew how hard I've tried, in my time, to cultivate at least one charming vice. I've always failed."

"Oh well, as one grows older, I suspect one needs more unlovable virtues and fewer charming vices. But why did you retreat permanently to Erythro, Siever? I understand that Erythro Dome has to be administered, but surely you're not the only one on Rotor who can do the job."

Genarr said, "Actually, I like to think I am. In a way, though, I enjoy it here and I do get to Rotor on occasion for a short vacation."

"And never come to see me?"

"Just because I have a vacation doesn't mean you do. I suspect you're far busier than I am, and have been ever since you discovered Nemesis. But I'm disappointed. I wanted to meet your daughter."

"You will. Her name's Marlene. Actually, it's Molly in my heart, but she won't allow that. At the age of fifteen, she has become remarkably intolerant and insists on being called Marlene. But you'll meet her, never fear. Actually, I didn't want her here the first time. How could we reminisce freely with her present?"

"Do you want to reminisce, Eugenia?"

"About some things."

Genarr hesitated. "I'm sorry Crile didn't join the Leaving."

Insigna's smile became fixed. "About *some* things, Siever." She turned away and walked to the window, staring out. "This is an elaborate place you have here, by the way. Just the little I've seen of it is impressive. Bright lights. Actual streets. Sizable buildings. And yet the Dome is hardly ever spoken of or referred to back on Rotor. How many people live and work here?"

"It varies. We have our slow and busy times. We've had as many as nearly nine hundred people here. At the moment, the number is five hundred and sixteen. We know every individual present. It's not easy. Each day sees some come, some go."

"Except you."

"And a few others."

"But why the Dome, Siever? After all, Erythro's atmosphere is breathable."

Genarr pushed out his lower lip and, for the first time, he did not meet her eyes. "Breathable, but not really comfortable. The light level is wrong. When you get outside the Dome, you're bathed in a pinkish light, tending to orange when Nemesis is high in the sky. It's bright enough. You can read. Still, it doesn't seem natural. Then, too, Nemesis itself doesn't look natural. It looks too large, and most people think it looks threatening and that its reddish light makes it seem angry—and they get depressed. Nemesis is dangerous in actual fact, too, at least in a way. Because it isn't blindingly bright, there is a tendency to gaze at it and watch for sunspots. The infrared can easily harm the retina. People who must go out in the open wear a special helmet for that reason—among other things."

"Then the Dome is more of a device to keep normal light in, so to speak, rather than to keep anything out."

"We don't even keep air out. The air and water that circulates in the Dome is drawn from Erythro's planetary supply. Naturally, though, we're careful to keep something out," said Genarr. "We keep out the prokaryotes. You know, the little blue-green cells."

Insigna nodded thoughtfully. That had turned out to be the explanation for the oxygen content in the air. There *was* life on Erythro, even all-pervasive life, but it was microscopic in nature, only equivalent to the simplest forms of cellular life in the Solar System.

She said, "Are they really prokaryotes? I know that's what they're called, but that's what our bacteria are also called. Are they bacteria?"

"If they're equivalent to anything in the history of Solar System life, it is to the cyanobacteria, those that photosynthesize. You're right to ask the question, though. No, they're not *our* cyanobacteria. They possess nucleoprotein, but with a structure fundamentally different from that which prevails in our form of life. They also have a kind of chlorophyll that lacks magnesium and works on infrared so that the cells tend to be colorless rather than green. Different enzymes, trace minerals in different proportions. Still, they resemble Earth cells sufficiently in outer appearance to be called prokaryotes. I understand that biologists are pushing for the word 'erythryotes' but for nonbiologists like ourselves, prokaryotes is good enough."

"And they're efficient enough in their workings to account for the oxygen in Erythro's atmosphere?"

"Absolutely. Nothing else could possibly explain its existence there. By the way, Eugenia, you're the astronomer, so what's the latest thinking on how old Nemesis might be?"

Insigna shrugged. "Red dwarfs are next to being immortal. Nemesis can be as old as the Universe and still go on for another hundred billion years or so without visible change. The best we can do is judge by the contents of the minor elements making up its structure. Supposing that it's a first-generation star and didn't begin with anything beyond hydrogen and helium, it is a bit over ten billion years old—a little more than twice the age of the Sun of the Solar System."

"Then Erythro is ten billion years old, too."

"Absolutely. A stellar system is formed all at once and not piece-meal. Why are you asking?"

"It just strikes me as odd that in ten billion years, life hasn't got past the prokaryote stage."

"I don't think that's surprising, Siever. On Earth, for somewhere between two and three billion years after life first appeared, it remained strictly prokaryote, and here on Erythro the energy concentration in sunlight is far less than it is on Earth. It takes energy to form more complicated life-forms. This sort of thing has been pretty well discussed among the Rotorians."

"I'm sure of it," said Genarr, "but it doesn't seem to reach us here at the Dome. Our minds are too fixed, I suppose, on our local duties and problems—though you'd think anything to do with the prokaryotes would come under that heading."

"For that matter," said Insigna, "we don't hear much about the Dome on Rotor."

"Yes, things tend to compartmentalize. But then, of course, there's nothing glamorous about the Dome, Eugenia. It's just a workshop, so I'm not surprised it gets lost in the press of events on Rotor. It's the new Settlements that are being built that get all the attention. Are you going to move to one of them?"

"Never. I'm a Rotorian, and I intend to stay one. I wouldn't even be here—if you'll pardon my saying so—if it weren't an astronomical necessity. I've got to make a number of observations from a base that is more stable than Rotor."

"So I have been informed by Pitt. I am instructed to give you my full cooperation."

"Good. I'm sure you will. Incidentally, you mentioned earlier that the Dome would like to keep the prokaryotes out. Do you succeed in doing so? Is the water here safe to drink?"

Genarr said, "Obviously, since we drink it. There are no prokaryotes in the Dome. Any water that comes in—anything at all that comes in—is bathed in blue-violet light that destroys the prokaryotes in a matter of seconds. The short-wave photons in the light are too energetic for the little things and break down key components of the cells. And even if some of them come in, they're not poisonous, as far as we can tell, or harmful in any way. We've tested them on animals."

"That's a relief."

"It works the other way, too. Our own microorganisms can't compete with Erythro's prokaryotes under Erythrotic conditions. At least when we seed Erythro's soil with our own bacteria, they don't succeed in growing and multiplying."

"What about multicellular plants?"

"We've tried it, but with very poor results. And it must be due to the quality of Nemesis' light because we can grow plants perfectly well inside the Dome, using Erythro's soil and water. We report these things back to Rotor, of course, but I doubt that the information gets widely publicized. As I said, Rotor isn't interested in the Dome. Certainly the fearsome Pitt isn't interested in us, and he's really all that counts on Rotor, isn't he?"

Genarr said that with a smile, but the smile seemed strained. (What would Marlene have said about it? Insigna wondered.)

She said, "Pitt isn't fearsome. He's sometimes *tiresome*, but that's a different thing. You know, Siever, I always thought when we were young that *you* might be Commissioner someday. You were enormously bright, you know."

"Were?"

"Still are, I'm sure, but in those days you were so politically oriented, had such ideas. I used to listen to you, entranced. In some ways, you would have been a better Commissioner than Janus is. You would have listened to people. You wouldn't have insisted on getting your own way as much."

"Which is precisely why I would have made a very poor Commissioner. You see, I don't have any precise goals in life. I just have the desire to do what seems to me to be the right thing at the moment, in the *hope* that it will end up with something bearable. Now, Pitt knows what he wants and intends to get there by any means."

"You're misjudging him, Siever. He's got strong views, but he's a very reasonable man."

"Of course, Eugenia. That's his great gift, his reasonableness. Whatever course he pursues, he always has a perfectly good, a perfectly logical, a perfectly human reason for it. He can make one up at any given moment, and is so sincere about it, he convinces even himself. I'm sure if you've had any dealings with him, you've managed to let him talk you into doing what you at first didn't want to do, and that he won you over not by orders and threats but by very patient, very rational arguments."

Insigna said weakly, "Well—"

At that, Genarr added sardonically, "I see you have indeed suffered from his reasonableness. You can see for yourself, then, what a good Commissioner he is. Not a good person, but a good Commissioner."

"I wouldn't go so far as to say he wasn't a good person, Siever," said Insigna, shaking her head slightly.

"Well, let's not argue about it. I want to meet your daughter." He rose to his feet. "Why don't I visit your quarters after dinner?"

"That would be delightful," said Insigna.

Genarr looked after her with a fading smile as she left. Eugenia had wanted to reminisce, and his own first reaction was to mention her husband—and she had frozen.

He sighed inwardly. He still had that extraordinary faculty of ruining his own chances.

27.

Eugenia Insigna said to her daughter, "His name is Siever Genarr, and he is properly addressed as Commander, because he's the head of the Erythro Dome."

"Of course, Mother. If that's his title, I'll call him that."

"And I don't want you to embarrass him—"

"I wouldn't do that."

"You would do so all too easily, Marlene. You know that. Just accept his statements without correcting them on the ground of body language. Please! He was a good friend of mine at college and for a while afterward. And even though he's been here in the Dome for ten years and I haven't seen him in all that time, he's *still* an old friend."

"I think he must have been a boyfriend."

"Now that's just what I mean," said Insigna. "I don't want you watching him and telling him what he really means or thinks or feels. And for your information, he was *not* my boyfriend, exactly, and we were certainly not lovers. We were friends and we liked each other— as friends. But after your father—" She shook her head, and gestured vaguely. "And be careful what you say about Commissioner Pitt—if that subject comes up. I get the feeling Commander Genarr distrusts Commissioner Pitt—"

Marlene bestowed one of her rare smiles on her mother. "Have you been studying Commander Siever's subliminal behavior? Because what you have is more than a feeling."

Insigna shook her head. "You see? You can't stop for a moment. Very well, it's not a feeling. He actually *said* he didn't trust the Commissioner. And you know," she added, half to herself, "he may have reason—"

She turned to Marlene and said suddenly, "Let me repeat, Marlene. You are perfectly free to watch the Commander and find out all you can, but don't say anything to him about it. Tell *me!* Do you understand?"

"Do you think there's danger, Mother?"

"I don't know."

"I do," said Marlene matter-of-factly. "I've known there was danger as soon as Commissioner Pitt said we could go to Erythro. I just don't know what the danger is."

28.

Seeing Marlene for the first time was a shock to Siever Genarr, one that was made worse by the fact that the girl looked at him with a sullen expression that made it seem that she knew perfectly well that he had received a shock, and just why.

The fact was that there was not a thing about her that seemed to indicate she was Eugenia's daughter, none of the beauty, none of the grace, none of the charm. Only those large bright eyes that were now boring into him, and they weren't Eugenia's either. They were the one respect in which she exceeded her mother, rather than fell short.

Little by little, though, he revised his first impression. He joined them for tea and dessert, and Marlene behaved herself with perfect propriety. Quite the lady, and obviously intelligent. What was it that Eugenia had said? All the unlovable virtues? Not quite that bad. It seemed to him that she ached for love, as plain people sometimes do. As he himself did. A sudden flood of fellow feeling swept over him.

And after a while, he said, "Eugenia, I wonder if I might have a chance to speak to Marlene alone."

Insigna said with an attempt at lightness, "Any particular reason, Siever?"

Genarr said, "Well, it was Marlene who spoke to Commissioner Pitt and it was she who persuaded the Commissioner to allow the two of you to come to the Dome. As Commander of the Dome, I'm pretty much dependent on what Commissioner Pitt says and does, and I would value what Marlene can tell me of the meeting. I think she would speak more freely if it were just the two of us."

Genarr watched Insigna leave and then turned to Marlene, who was now sitting in a large chair in a corner of the room, almost lost in its soft capaciousness. Her hands were clasped loosely in her lap and her beautiful dark eyes regarded the Commander gravely.

Genarr said with a hint of humor in his voice, "Your mother seemed a little nervous about leaving you here with me. Are you nervous, too?"

"Not at all," said Marlene. "And if my mother was nervous, it was on your behalf, not on mine."

"On *my* behalf. Why?"

"She thinks I might say something that would offend you."

"Would you, Marlene?"

"Not deliberately, Commander. I'll try not to."

"And I'm sure you'll succeed. Do you know why I want to see you alone?"

"You told my mother you want to find out about my interview with Commissioner Pitt. That's true, but you also want to see what I'm like."

Genarr's eyebrows drew together just a trifle. "Naturally, I would want to get to know you better."

"It's not that," said Marlene quickly.

"What is it, then?"

Marlene looked away. "I'm sorry, Commander."

"Sorry about what?"

Marlene's face twitched unhappily and she was silent.

Genarr said softly, "Now, Marlene, what is wrong? You must tell me. It is important to me that we talk frankly. If your mother told you to watch what you say, please forget that. If she implied that I was sensitive and easily offended, please forget that, too. In fact, I command you to speak to me freely and not to worry a bit about offending me, and you must obey my command because I'm the Commander of the Erythro Dome."

Marlene laughed suddenly. "You're really anxious to find out about me, aren't you?"

"Of course."

"Because you're wondering how I can look the way I do, when I'm my mother's daughter."

Genarr's eyes opened wide. "I never said anything of the sort."

"You didn't have to. You're an old friend of my mother's. She told me that much. But you were in love with her, and you haven't quite gotten over it, and you were expecting me to look the way she did when she was young, so when you saw me, you winced and drew back."

"I did? It was noticeable?"

"It was a very small gesture because you're a polite man and you tried to repress it, but it was there. I saw it easily. And then your eyes turned to my mother and back to me. And then there was the tone of your first words to me. It was all very plain. You were thinking I didn't look at all like my mother and you were disappointed."

Genarr leaned back in his chair and said, "But this is marvelous."

And a great gladness lit up Marlene's face. "You mean it, Commander. You *mean* it. You're not offended. You're not uncomfortable. It makes you happy. You're the first one, the *first* one. Even my mother doesn't like it."

"Liking or not liking it doesn't matter. That is totally irrelevant when it's a question of coming up against the extraordinary. How long have you been able to read body language in this way, Marlene?"

"Always, but I've gotten better at it. I think anyone must be able to do it, if they only watch—and think."

"Not so, Marlene. It can't be done. Don't think it. And you say I love your mother."

"No doubt about it, Commander. When you're near her, you give it away with every look, every word, every twitch."

"Do you suppose she notices?"

"She suspects you do, but she doesn't want you to."

Genarr looked away. "She never did."

"It's my father."

"I know."

Marlene hesitated. "But I think she's wrong. If she could see you the way I do right now—"

"But she can't, unfortunately. It makes me so happy that you do, though. You're beautiful."

Marlene flushed. Then she said, "You mean that!"

"Of course I do."

"But—"

"I can't lie to you, can I? So I won't try. Your face isn't beautiful. Your body isn't beautiful. But *you* are beautiful and that's what's important. And you can tell I really believe that."

"Yes, I do," said Marlene, smiling with such genuine happiness that even her face had a sudden distant cast of beauty.

Genarr smiled, too, and said, "Shall we now talk about Commissioner Pitt? Now that I know what an uncommonly shrewd young woman you are, it is all the more important I do so. Are you willing?"

Marlene clasped her hands lightly in her lap, smiled demurely, and said, "Yes, Uncle Siever. You don't mind if I call you that, do you?"

"Not at all. In fact, I'm honored. Now—tell me all about Commissioner Pitt. He has sent me instructions that I'm to give your mother all possible cooperation and that I am to make freely available to her all our astronomical equipment. Why do you suppose that is?"

"My mother wants to make delicate measurements of Nemesis' motion relative to the stars, and Rotor is too unsteady a base for those measurements. Erythro will do much better."

"Is this project of hers a recent one?"

"No, Uncle Siever. She's been trying to get the necessary data for a long time, she told me."

"Then why didn't your mother ask to come here a long time ago?"

"She did, but Commissioner Pitt refused."

"Why did he agree now?"

"Because he wanted to get rid of her."

"I'm sure of that—if she kept bothering him with her astronomical problems. But he must have been tired of her a long time ago. Why does he send her *now?*"

Marlene's voice was low. "He wanted to get rid of *me.*"

# FOURTEEN

# FISHING

29.

Five years had now passed since the Leaving. Crile Fisher found that hard to believe since it seemed so much longer than that, infinitely longer. Rotor was not in the past, but in another life altogether, one that he could only view with gathering incredulity. Had he really lived there? Had he had a wife?

He remembered only his daughter clearly, and even that had its element of confusion, for sometimes it seemed to him he remembered her as a teenager.

Of course, the problem was compounded by the fact that his life in the last three years, ever since Earth had discovered the Neighbor Star, had been a hectic one. He had visited seven different Settlements.

All of these were inhabited by Settlers of his own skin shade who spoke more or less his language and shared more or less his cultural orientation. (That was the advantage of Earth's variety. Earth could

117

supply an agent similar in appearance and culture to the general population of any Settlement.)

Of course, there was a limit to how closely he could melt into any Settlement. No matter how he matched its population superficially, he still had a distinctive accent of speech, he could not remain as graceful as they under changes of gravitational pull, he could not skim along as they did in low gravity. In a dozen ways, he betrayed himself on each Settlement he visited, and always they withdrew from him just slightly, even though, in each case, he had gone through quarantine and medical treatment before being allowed to even enter the Settlement proper.

Of course, he remained on each Settlement only a few days to a few weeks. Never was he expected to remain on a Settlement on a semipermanent basis or to build himself a family there as he had done on Rotor. But then Rotor had had hyper-assistance, and since then Earth had been looking for items of narrower importance, or at least he had been sent on tasks of narrower importance.

He had been back now for three months. There was no word of a new assignment and he was not anxious for one. He was tired of the uprooting, tired of not fitting in, tired of the pretense of being a tourist.

And there was Garand Wyler, his old friend and colleague, fresh from a Settlement of his own and staring at him with tired eyes. The dark skin of his graceful hand glimmered in the light as he raised his sleeve to his nose for a moment, then let it drop.

Fisher half-smiled. He knew the gesture, had gone through it himself. Each Settlement had its own characteristic odor, depending on the crops it grew, the spices it used, the perfumes it affected, the very nature of the machinery and lubricants it used. It quickly went unnoticed, but on the return to Earth, the Settlement odor clung to one quite detectably. And though the person might be bathed, and the clothing washed so that others did not notice, one still noticed the smell on himself.

Fisher said, "Welcome back. How was your Settlement this time?"

"As always—terrible. Old Man Tanayama is correct. What all the Settlements fear and hate most is variety. They don't want differences in appearance, tastes, ways, and life. They select themselves for uniformity and despise everything else."

Fisher said, "You're right. And it's too bad."

Wyler said, "That's a mild, unfeeling way of putting it. 'Too bad.'

'Oops, I dropped the dish. Oh, too bad.' 'Whoops, my contact seal is out of line. Oh, too bad.' We're talking humanity here. We're talking about Earth's long struggle to find a way of living together, all cultures, all appearances. It isn't perfect yet, but compare it to how it was even a century ago, and it's heaven. Then, when we get a chance to move into space, we shuck it all off and move right back into the Dark Ages. And you say, 'Too bad.' That's some reaction to something that's an enormous tragedy."

"I agree," said Fisher, "but unless you can tell me something practical I can do about it, what does it matter how eloquently I denounce it? You were at Akruma, weren't you?"

"Yes," said Wyler.

"Did they know about the Neighbor Star?"

"Certainly. As far as I know, the news has now reached every Settlement."

"Were they concerned?"

"Not a bit. Why should they be? They've got thousands of years. Long before the Neighbor Star is anywhere near, and if it should seem to be dangerous, which isn't absolutely certain, you know, they can wander off. They can all wander off. They admire Rotor, and only wait for a chance to get away themselves." Wyler was frowning, his tone bitter.

He went on, "They'll all leave, and we'll be stuck. How are we going to build enough Settlements for eight billion human beings and get them all away?"

"You sound just like Tanayama. What good will it do us to chase them down and punish them, or destroy them? We'll still be here and we'll still be stuck. If they all stayed behind like good kids and faced the Neighbor Star with us, would we be better off?"

"You're cold about this, Crile. Tanayama is hot, and I'm on his side. He's hot enough to pull the Galaxy apart if necessary to find hyper-assistance on our own. He wants it so we can chase after Rotor and blow them out of space, but even if that does no good, we're going to need hyper-assistance to get as many people off Earth as possible if it turns out that the Neighbor Star will make it necessary. So what Tanayama is doing is right, even if his motives are wrong."

"And suppose we have hyper-assistance and then we find we only have the time and the resources to get a billion people off. Which is the billion that goes? And what happens if those who are in charge start saving only their own kind?"

Wyler growled, "It doesn't bear thinking of."

"It doesn't," agreed Fisher. "Let's be glad we'll be long gone before even the barest beginning can be made."

"If it comes to that," said Wyler, his voice suddenly dropping. "The barest beginning may already have been made. I suspect we have hyper-assistance now, or just about have it."

Fisher's expression was one of deep cynicism. "What makes you think that? Dreams? Intuition?"

"No. I know a woman whose sister knows someone on the Old Man's staff. Will that do you?"

"Of course not. You'll have to give me more than that."

"I'm not in a position to. Look, Crile, I'm your friend. You know I helped you get back your status in the Office."

Crile nodded. "I do and I appreciate it. And I've tried to make an adequate return now and then."

"You have done so and I appreciate that. Now what I want to do is give you some information which is supposed to be confidential and which I think you will find useful and important. Are you ready to accept it and keep me clear?"

"Always ready."

"You know what we've been doing, of course."

Fisher said, "Yes." It was the kind of useless, rhetorical question that required no other answer.

For five years agents of the Office (for the last three years, Fisher among them) had been rummaging in the informational garbage heaps of the Settlements. Scavenging.

Every Settlement was working on hyper-assistance, just as Earth itself was, ever since the word had leaked out that Rotor had it, and *certainly* ever since Rotor had proved the fact by leaving the Solar System.

Presumably most Settlements, perhaps all, had obtained some scrap of what it was that Rotor had done. By the Open Science Agreement, each one of those scraps should have been laid on the table and if all were then put together, it might have meant practical hyper-assistance for all. That, however, was clearly too much to ask in this particular case. There was no telling what useful side effects might be born of the new technique and no Settlement could abandon the hope that it might be first in the field and, in this way, gain an important lead on the others in one way or another. So each hoarded what it had —if it had anything—and not one of them had enough.

And Earth itself, with its vastly elaborate Terrestrial Board of Inquiry, sniffed at all the Settlements indiscriminately. Earth was fishing, and Fisher, appropriately enough, was one of the fishermen.

Wyler said slowly, "We've put what we've got together and I gather it's enough. We'll be able to have hyper-assisted travel. And I'm thinking we'll go out to the Neighbor Star. Wouldn't you want to be on that trip when it goes out there?"

"Why do I want to be on it, Garand? If there's going to be such a trip, which I doubt."

"I'm pretty sure there will be. I can't give you my source, but take my word for it, it's reliable. And, of course, you'll want to make the trip. You might see your wife. Or if not her—your kid."

Fisher moved restlessly. It seemed to him he spent half his days now trying not to think of those eyes. Marlene would be six years old now, talking in a quiet deliberate way—like Roseanne. Seeing through people—like Roseanne.

He said, "You're talking nonsense, Garand. Even if there were such a flight, why would they let me be on it? They would send specialists of one sort or another. Besides, if there's one person the Old Man will keep off, it's me. He may have let me get back into the Office and given me assignments, but you know how he is about failures, and I certainly failed him on Rotor."

"Yes, but that's the very point. That's what makes you a specialist. If he's going after Rotor, how can he fail to include the one Earthman who lived on Rotor for four years? Who would understand Rotor better and who would know better how to deal with them? Ask to see him. Point this out, but remember, you're not supposed to know that we have hyper-assistance. Just talk possibilities, make use of the subjunctive. And don't drag me into it in any way. I'm not supposed to know about it either."

Fisher's brow furrowed in thought. Was it possible? He dared not hope.

### 30.

The next day, while Fisher was still wondering whether to risk asking for an interview with Tanayama, the decision was taken out of his hands. He was summoned.

A simple agent is rarely summoned by the Director. There are plenty of deputies to grind away at them. And if an agent *is* summoned by the Old Man, it is almost never good news. So Crile Fisher prepared himself with grim resignation for an assignment as an inspector of the fertilizer factories.

Tanayama looked up at him from behind his desk. Fisher had seen him only rarely and briefly in the three years since Earth's discovery of the Neighbor Star, and he seemed unchanged. He had been small and shriveled for so long that there seemed no room for any further physical change. The sharpness of his eyes had not abated either, nor the withered grim set of his lips. He might even be wearing the same garments he had worn three years before. Fisher could not tell.

But if the harsh voice, too, was the same, the tone was surprising. Apparently, in the face of astronomical odds, the Old Man had called him in for the purpose of praising him.

Tanayama said in his queer, and not altogether unpleasant, distortion of Planetary English, "Fisher, you have done well. I want you to hear that from me."

Fisher, standing (he had not been invited to sit down), managed to suppress his small start of surprise.

The Director said, "There can be no public celebration of this, no laser-beam parade, no holographic procession. It is not in the nature of things. But I tell you this."

"That is quite enough, Director," said Fisher. "I thank you."

Tanayama stared fixedly at Fisher out of his narrow eyes. Finally, he said, "And is that all you have to say? No questions?"

"I presume, Director, you will tell me what I need to know."

"You are an agent, a capable man. What have you found out for yourself?"

"Nothing, Director. I do not seek to find out anything but what I am instructed to find out."

Tanayama's small head nodded very slightly. "An appropriate answer, but I seek inappropriate ones. What have you guessed?"

"You seem pleased with me, Director, and it may therefore be that I have brought in some information that has proved useful to you."

"In what respect?"

"I think nothing would prove more useful to you than having obtained the technique of hyper-assistance."

Tanayama's mouth made a noiseless: "Ah-h-h." He said, "And next? Assuming this to be so, what are we to do next?"

"Travel to the Neighbor Star. Locate Rotor."

"Nothing better than that? That is all there is to do? You see no farther?"

And at this point, Fisher decided it would be foolish not to gamble. He could not possibly be handed a better opportunity. "One thing better; that, when the first Earth vessel goes out of the Solar System by means of hyper-assistance, I be on it."

Fisher had scarcely said that when he knew his gamble was lost—or at least not won. Tanayama's face darkened. He said in a sharply imperative tone, "Sit down!"

Fisher could hear the soft movement of the chair behind him, rolling toward him at the words of Tanayama, words that its primitive computerized motor could understand.

Fisher sat down, without looking behind him to make certain the chair was there. To have done so would have been insulting and, at the present moment, there was no room to insult Tanayama.

Tanayama said, "Why do you want to be on the vessel?"

With an effort, Fisher kept his voice level. "Director, I have a wife on Rotor."

"A wife you abandoned five years ago. Do you think she would welcome you back?"

"Director, I have a child."

"She was one year old when you left. Do you think she knows she has a father? Or cares?"

Fisher was silent. These were points that he had thought about himself, over and over.

Tanayama waited briefly, then said, "But there will be no flight to the Neighbor Star. There will be no vessel for you to be on."

Again, Fisher had to suppress surprise. He said, "Forgive me, Director. You did not say we had hyper-assistance. You said, 'Assuming this to be so—' I should have noted your choice of words."

"So you should have done. So you should always do. Nevertheless, we do have hyper-assistance. We can now move through space, just as Rotor has done; or at least we will, once we build a vehicle and are sure the design is adequate, and all its features workable—which may take a year or two. But then what? Are you seriously suggesting we take it to the Neighbor Star?"

Fisher said cautiously, "Surely that is an option, Director."

"A useless one. Think it out, man. The Neighbor Star is over two light-years away. No matter how skillfully we make use of hyper-assistance, it will take us more than two years to arrive there. Our

123

theoreticians now tell me that while hyper-assistance will allow a ship to go faster than light for brief periods of time—the faster, the briefer—the end result is always that it cannot reach any point in space faster than a ray of light would have, if the two had started from the same point of origin."

"But if that is so—"

"If that is so, you would be forced to remain on a spaceship in close quarters with several other crewpeople for over two years. Do you think you can endure that? You know very well that small ships have never made long trips. What we need is a Settlement, a structure large enough to provide a reasonable environment—like Rotor. How long will that take?"

"I couldn't say, Director."

"Perhaps ten years if all works well—if there are no hitches or mishaps. Remember, we haven't built a Settlement in nearly a century. All the recent Settlements have been built by other Settlements. If, suddenly, we begin building one, we will attract the attention of all the Settlements that already exist, and that must be avoided. Then, too, if such a Settlement can be built, and outfitted with hyper-assistance, and sent to the Neighbor Star in over a two-year flight, what will it do when it gets there? As a Settlement, it will be vulnerable and easy to destroy if Rotor has warships, as it certainly will have. Rotor will have more warships than we could possibly carry on our traveling Settlement. After all, they have been there for three years already, and may be there for twelve more years before we get there. They will blow our Settlement out of space on sight."

"In that case, Director—"

"No further guessing, Agent Fisher. In that case, we must have true hyperspatial travel, so that we may move any distance we like in as short a period as we like."

"Pardon me, Director, but is that possible? Even in theory?"

"That is not for you or me to say. We need scientists to concentrate on the matter, and we don't have them. For a century or more, Earth has suffered a brain drain to the Settlements. So now we must reverse that. We must raid the Settlements, after a fashion, and persuade the best physicists and engineers to come to Earth. We can offer them a great deal, but it will have to be done carefully. We can't be too open, you understand, or the Settlements will certainly forestall us. Now—"

He paused, and studied Fisher thoughtfully.

Fisher stirred uneasily and said, "Yes, Director?"

"The physicist I have my eye on is one T. A. Wendel, who, I'm told, is the best hyperspatialist in the Solar System—"

"It was the hyperspatialists on Rotor who discovered hyper-assistance." Fisher could not resist allowing a certain dryness to enter his voice.

Tanayama ignored that. He said,   "Discoveries can be made by happy accident, and an inferior mind can stumble ahead while a superior one is taking the time to lay a firm foundation. That has frequently happened in history. Besides, Rotor only has what proved, in the end, to be merely hyper-assistance, a speed-of-light drive. I want a superluminal drive, one that is far beyond the speed of light. And I want Wendel."

"And do you wish me to get him for you?"

"Her. She's a woman. Tessa Anita Wendel of Adelia."

"Oh?"

"That is why we want you for the job. Apparently"—and here Tanayama seemed to radiate a quiet amusement, although nothing in his facial expression seemed to indicate that—"you are irresistible to women."

Fisher's expression grew wooden. "I ask pardon for contradicting you, Director, but I do not find it so. I have never found it so."

"The reports are persuasive, just the same. Wendel is a middle-aged woman, in her forties, twice-divorced. She should not be hard to persuade."

"To be honest, sir, I find the assignment distasteful and, under those circumstances, it is possible another agent would be better suited for the task."

"But I want you just the same. If you fear that you would not be your flirtatious and maddeningly attractive self if you approached her with face averted and nose wrinkled, I will sweeten matters for you, Agent Fisher. You failed on Rotor, but your service since has, in part, made up for it. You can now completely make up for it. If, however, you do not bring back this woman, that will be a far greater failure than Rotor was, and you will never have the chance to make up for *that*. Still, I don't want you governed by apprehension alone. I will throw in a bit of anticipation. Bring back Wendel and when a superluminal vessel is built and heads out toward the Neighbor Star, you will be on it if you wish."

"I will do my best," said Fisher, "and I would have done my best even if there were no occasion for either apprehension or anticipation."

"An excellent answer," said Tanayama, allowing himself the thinnest of smiles, "and undoubtedly well rehearsed."

And Fisher left, fully realizing that he had been sent out on his most crucial fishing expedition yet.

# FIFTEEN

# PLAGUE

31.

Eugenia Insigna smiled at Genarr over dessert. "You seem to lead a pleasant life here."

Genarr smiled, too. "Pleasant enough, but claustrophobic. We live on a huge world, but I'm bounded by the Dome. The people here tend to be ingrown. When I do meet someone interesting, they leave in a couple of months, at most. Generally, the people here in the Dome bore me most of the time, though probably not as much as I bore them. That's why the arrival of you and your daughter would have been a holovision item, even if you were anyone else. Of course, since it's you—"

"Flatterer," said Insigna sadly.

Genarr cleared his throat. "Marlene warned me, for my own good, you understand, that you have not quite gotten over—"

But Insigna overrode him suddenly. "I can't say I've noticed any holovision attention."

Genarr gave up. He said, "Just a manner of speaking. We're planning a little party tomorrow evening, and you'll then be formally introduced and everyone will get a chance to know you."

"And discuss my appearance, and choice of costume, and chew over whatever is known about me."

"I'm sure of it. But Marlene will be invited, too, and that means, I suppose, that you will know a great deal more about all of us than we will about you. Your information will be more reliable, too."

Insigna looked uneasy, "Did Marlene act up?"

"You mean, did she read my body language? Yes, ma'am."

"I told her not to."

"I don't think she can help it."

"You're right. She can't. But I told her not to *tell* you about it. I take it she did tell you."

"Oh yes. I ordered her to do so. Actually, I commanded her to do so in my role as Commander."

"Well, I'm sorry. It can be so annoying."

"But it wasn't. Not to me. Eugenia, please understand this. I like your daughter. I like her very much. I have the idea that she has had a miserable life being someone who knows too much and whom no one likes. That she has turned out full of what you referred to as the unlovable virtues is little short of a miracle."

"I warn you. She'll tire you out. And she's only fifteen."

Genarr said, "There's some law, I think, that prevents mothers from ever remembering when they themselves were fifteen. She casually mentioned a boy, and you may know that the pangs of unrequited love hurt as deeply at fifteen as at twenty-five, maybe even more so. Though *your* teenage years may well have been sunny ones, considering your appearance. Remember, too, that Marlene is in a particularly bad position. She knows she's plain and she knows she's intelligent. She feels that intelligence should much more than make up for lack of beauty and she also knows that it doesn't, so she rages helplessly and knows that that does no good either."

"Well, Siever," said Insigna, trying to sound light, "you're quite the psychologist."

"No, not at all. It's just this one thing I understand. I've been through it myself."

"Oh—" Insigna seemed at a loss.

"It's all right, Eugenia. I have no intention of being sorry for myself, and I wasn't trying to lure you into sympathy for a poor, broken soul—because I'm not. I'm forty-nine, not fifteen, and I've made my peace with myself. Had I been handsome and stupid when I was fifteen, or twenty-one, as, at that time in life, I wished I had been, I would undoubtedly now no longer be handsome—but I'd still be stupid. So, in the long run, I've won out, and so, I'm positive, will Marlene—if there *is* a long run."

"And what do you mean by that, Siever?"

"Marlene tells me that she talked to our good friend Pitt, and that she deliberately antagonized him in order to make him willing to send you to Erythro because that meant getting rid of her, too."

"I don't approve of that," said Eugenia. "I don't mean about manipulating Pitt, because I don't think Pitt is that easy to manipulate. I mean *trying* to do it. Marlene is getting to the point where she thinks she can pull puppet strings, and this may get her into serious trouble."

"Eugenia, I do not wish to frighten you, but I think Marlene *is* in serious trouble right now. At least, it may be Pitt's hope that she will be."

"Now, Siever, that's impossible. Pitt may be opinionated and overbearing, but there's nothing vicious about him. He's not going to strike out at a teenage girl just because she played foolish games with him."

The dinner was over, but the lights were still somewhat lowered in Genarr's rather elegant quarters, and Insigna reacted with a slight frown as Genarr leaned over to close the contact that activated the shield.

"Secrets, Siever?" she said with a forced laugh.

"Yes, as a matter of fact, Eugenia. I'm going to have to play the psychologist again. You don't know Pitt as I do. I've *competed* with him, and that's why I'm out here. He wanted to get rid of me. In my case, however, separation is enough. It may not be enough in Marlene's case."

Another forced laugh. "Come, Siever. What are you saying?"

"Listen, and you'll understand. Pitt is secretive. He has a fixed aversion to anyone knowing what he intends. It gives him a sense of power to be moving down a hidden road and dragging others, all unwitting, with him."

"You may be right. He kept Nemesis secret, and forced the secrecy on me, too."

"He's got many secrets, more than you and I know, I'm sure. But

129

here's Marlene, to whom a person's hidden motives and thoughts are as clear as day. No one likes that—Pitt, least of all. So he's sent her out here—and you, too, since he couldn't send her without you."

"All right. What of that?"

"You don't suppose he wants her back, do you? Ever?"

"That's paranoid, Siever. You can't really believe Pitt would intend to keep her in permanent exile."

"He can, in one way. You see, Eugenia, you don't know the early history of the Dome as I do, and as Pitt does, and as hardly anyone else does. You know Pitt's penchant for secrecy and it works here, too. You have to understand why we remain in the Dome and make no effort to colonize Erythro."

"You explained. The character of the light—"

"That is the official explanation, Eugenia. Accept the light; it is something we can grow accustomed to. Consider what else we have: a world with a normal gravity, a breathable atmosphere, a pleasant temperature range, weather cycles reminiscent of Earth, no life-forms above the prokaryote stage, and with those prokaryotes not infectious in any way. Yet we make no move to colonize the world, even in a limited fashion."

"Well, then, why not?"

"In the early days of the Dome, people went out freely to explore outside. They took no special precautions, breathed the air, drank the water."

"Yes?"

"And some of them fell ill. Mentally. Permanently. Not violently insane, but—divorced from reality. Some have improved with time, but none, as far as I know, has recovered completely. It is, apparently, not contagious, and they are taken care of on Rotor—quietly."

Eugenia frowned. "Are you making this up, Siever? I haven't heard a word of it."

"I remind you again of Pitt's penchant for secrecy. This was not something you had a need to know. It was not your department. It was something *I* had a need to know because I was sent here to deal with it. If I failed, we might have had to abandon Erythro altogether, and a pall of fear and discontent would have fallen over us all."

He fell silent for a moment, then said, "I shouldn't be telling you this. I am, in a sense, violating my oath of office. Still, for Marlene's sake—"

A look of deepest apprehension crossed Eugenia's face. "What are you saying? That Pitt—"

"I'm saying that Pitt may have thought that Marlene might come down with what we called 'Erythrotic Plague.' It wouldn't kill her. It wouldn't even make her ill in the ordinary sense, but it would sufficiently disorder her brain to put her peculiar gift out of action, perhaps, and that is what Pitt would want."

"But that is horrible, Siever. Unthinkable. To subject a child—"

"I'm not saying it will happen, Eugenia. What Pitt wants is not necessarily what Pitt will get. Once I got here, I introduced drastic methods of protection. We don't go out in the open, except in the equivalent of protective suits, and we don't stay out longer than need be. The filtration procedures of the Dome have been improved, too. Since I instituted those measures, we've only had two cases, both rather light."

"But what causes it, Siever?"

Genarr laughed briefly but not lightly. "We don't know. That's the worst of it. We can't sharpen our defenses any further. Careful experiments indicate that there is nothing in either air or water that would seem to account for it. Nor in the soil—after all, we have the soil here in the Dome; we can't divorce ourselves from it. We have the air and water, too, properly filtered. Still, many people have breathed raw Erythrotic air and drunk raw Erythrotic water and have done so with complete impunity and no consequences."

"Then it must be the prokaryotes."

"It can't be. We've all ingested them or breathed them inadvertently, and we've used them in animal experiments. Nothing happens. Besides, if it were the prokaryotes, the Plague would be expected to be contagious and, as I said, it isn't. We've experimented with the radiation from Nemesis and that seems to do no harm. What's more, once—only once—someone who'd never been outside got it inside the Dome. It's a mystery."

"You have no theories?"

"I? No. I'm just content that it has virtually stopped. Still, as long as we are so ignorant of the nature and cause of the Plague, we can never be sure that it won't start up again. There was one suggestion—"

"What was that?"

"A psychologist reported this suggestion to me and I passed it on to Pitt. He claimed that those who came down with the disorder were more imaginative than those who did not, more out of the ordinary, mentally speaking. More intelligent, more creative, more unusual. He suggested that whatever the cause, the more remarkable brains were less resistant, more easily upset."

"Do you think that might be so?"

"I don't know. The trouble is that there is no other distinction. Both sexes were hit, roughly equally, and no clear bias as far as age, education, or gross physical characteristics could be found. Of course, the Plague victims make up a relatively small sample, so the statistics aren't compelling. Pitt thought we might go along with the out-of-the-usual bit, and in recent years, no one has come to Erythro who hasn't been a pretty dull clod—not unintelligent, you understand, but a plodder. Like myself. I'm the ideal subject for immunity from the Plague, an ordinary brain. Right?"

"Come, Siever, you aren't—"

"On the other hand," said Genarr, not waiting for her protest, "I would say that Marlene's brain was remarkably out of the ordinary."

"Oh yes," began Eugenia. "I see what you're getting at."

"It's possible that when Pitt discovered that Marlene had this ability and that she was asking to go to Erythro, he saw at once that by merely acceding to her request, he might possibly get rid of a mind he instantly recognized as dangerous."

"Obviously, then, we ought to leave—go back to Rotor."

"Yes, but I'm quite sure Pitt can prevent that for a while. He can insist that these measurements you wish to make are vital and must be completed and you won't be able to use the Plague as an excuse. If you even try, he will have you held for mental examination. I would suggest that you complete those measurements as quickly as you can, and, as for Marlene, we will take all possible precautions. The Plague *has* died down, and the suggestion that out-of-the-ordinary brains are particularly vulnerable is just that, a suggestion, and no more. There's no real reason to think we can't get away with it. We can keep Marlene safe and do Pitt in the eye. You'll see."

Insigna stared at Genarr, not quite seeing him, her stomach tying itself into a knot.

# SIXTEEN

# HYPERSPACE

32.

Adelia was a pleasant Settlement, much more pleasant than Rotor had been.

Crile Fisher had now been on six Settlements other than Rotor and all had been more pleasant than Rotor. (Fisher paused momentarily to go over the list of names and sighed. There were seven, not six. He was losing track. Perhaps it was all getting to be too much for him.)

Whatever the number, Adelia was the most pleasant Settlement Crile had visited. Not perhaps physically. Rotor had been an older Settlement, one that had managed to work itself into an assembly of traditions, so to speak. There was an efficiency about it, a sense of each person knowing his place exactly, being satisfied with it, and working away at it successfully.

Of course, Tessa was here on Adelia—Tessa Anita Wendel. Crile had not pursued matters there yet, perhaps because Tanayama's characterization of him as irresistible to women had shaken him. How-

133

ever much it might have been meant as humor (or as sarcasm), it forced him, almost against his will, to go slowly. Producing a fiasco would seem doubly bad in the eyes of someone who believed him, however insincerely, to have a way with women.

It was two weeks after Fisher had settled himself into the Settlement before he managed to see her. It was always a source of wonder to him that on any Settlement one could always manage to arrange to get a view of *anyone*. Not all his experience had accustomed him to the smallness of a Settlement, to the fewness of its population, to the manner in which everyone knew everyone else in his or her social circle—*everyone* else—and almost everyone else outside that circle, too.

When he did see her, however, Tessa Wendel turned out to be rather impressive. Tanayama's description of her as middle-aged and as twice-divorced—the quirk of his aged lips as he said so, as though he were knowingly setting Fisher an unpleasant task—had built a picture in Fisher's mind of a harsh woman, hard-faced, with a nervous twitch, perhaps, and an attitude toward men that was either cynical or hungry.

Tessa did not seem at all like this from the moderate distance at which he first saw her. She was almost as tall as he was and brunette, with her hair sleeked down. She looked quite alert and she smiled easily—he could tell that. Her clothes were refreshingly simple, as though she went out of her way to eschew ornament. She had kept herself slim and her figure was still surprisingly youthful.

Fisher found himself wondering why she was twice-divorced. He was ready to assume that she had tired of the men, rather than the other way around, even though common sense told him that incompatibility could strike against all odds.

It was necessary to be at some social function at which she would also be present. His being an Earthman interposed a small difficulty, but there were people on every Settlement who were, to some extent or other, in Earth's pay. One of them would surely see to it that Fisher would be "launched," to use the term most Settlements applied to the ritual.

The time came, then, when he and Wendel were facing each other and she gazed at him thoughtfully, her eyes making a slow sweep downward, then upward again, followed by the inevitable, "You're from Earth, aren't you, Mr. Fisher."

"Yes, I am, Dr. Wendel. And I regret that exceedingly—if it offends you."

"It doesn't offend me. I presume you've been decontaminated."

"Indeed. To death, just about."

"And why have you dared the decontamination process in order to come here?"

And Fisher said, without staring at her too directly, but keen to detect the effect, "Because I was told that Adelian women were particularly beautiful."

"And now, I suppose, you will go back and deny the rumor."

"On the contrary, it has just been confirmed."

She said, "You're a fetcher, you know that?"

Fisher didn't know what a "fetcher" was in Adelian slang, but Wendel was smiling, and Fisher decided the first exchange had gone well.

Was it because he was irresistible? He suddenly remembered that he had never tried to be irresistible to Eugenia. He had merely wanted a way of being launched into the difficult Rotorian society.

The Adelian society was not so difficult, Fisher decided, but he had better not belabor his irresistibility. Yet to himself, he smiled sadly.

33.

A month later, Fisher and Wendel were sufficiently at ease with each other to spend some time together in a low-G gym. Fisher had almost enjoyed the workout—but only almost, because he had never grown sufficiently acclimated to gymnastics at low-G to avoid a certain amount of space sickness. On Rotor, there had been less attention to such things, and he had usually been excluded from them because he was not a native Rotorian. (That was not legal, but custom often has a habit of being stronger than legality.)

They took an elevator to a higher-G level, and Fisher felt his stomach settling down. Both he and Wendel were wearing a minimum of clothing, and he had the feeling that she was as aware of his body as he was of hers.

After their showers, they had both robed and retired to one of the Privacies, where they could order a small meal.

Wendel said, "You're not bad at low-G for an Earthman, Crile. Are you enjoying yourself on Adelia?"

"You know I am, Tessa. An Earthman can never get entirely used to a small world, but your presence would overbalance a great many disadvantages."

"Yes. That's exactly what a fetcher would say. How does Adelia compare to Rotor?"

"To Rotor?"

"Or to the other Settlements you've been on? I can name them all, Crile."

Fisher felt discomfited. "What did you do? Investigate me?"

"Of course."

"Am I that interesting?"

"I find anyone interesting who is clearly going out of his way to be interested in me. I want to know why. Excluding the possibility of sex, of course. That's taken as a given."

"Why am I interested in you, then?"

"Suppose you tell me. Why were you on Rotor? You were there long enough to get married and have a child and then you got off in a hurry before it scooted away. Were you afraid of being stuck on Rotor all your life? Didn't you like it there?"

Fisher had gone from feeling discomfited to feeling harassed. He said, "Actually, I didn't like Rotor very much because they didn't like me—Earthmen, that is. And you're right. I didn't want to be stuck there as a second-class citizen all my life. Other Settlements are easier on us. Adelia is."

"Rotor had a secret, though, that it was trying to keep from Earth, didn't it?" Wendel's eyes seemed to glitter with amusement.

"A secret? You mean, I suppose, hyper-assistance."

"Yes, I suppose that *is* what I mean. And I suppose that that was what you were after."

"I?"

"Yes, of course you. Did you get it? I mean, that's why you married a Rotorian scientist, wasn't it?" She rested her face on her two fists, elbows on the table, and leaned toward him.

Fisher shook his head, and said guardedly, "She never said a word to me about hyper-assistance. You're all wrong about me."

Wendel ignored his remark, and said, "And now you want to get it from me. How do you plan to do that? Are you going to marry me?"

"Would I get it from you if I married you?"

"No."

"Then marriage seems to be out of the question, doesn't it?"

"Too bad," said Wendel, smiling.

Fisher said, "Are you asking me these questions because you're a hyperspatialist?"

"Where were you told that that was what I was? Back on Earth, before you came here?"

"You're listed in the *Adelian Roster.*"

"Ah, you've investigated me, too. What a curious pair we are. Did you notice that I was listed as a theoretical physicist?"

"It also lists your papers, and when quite a few of the titles have the word 'hyperspatial,' it makes you sound like a hyperspatialist to me."

"Yes, but I'm a theoretical physicist just the same, so I approach the whole matter of hyperspatialism in a theoretical way. I've never tried to put it into practice."

"But Rotor did. Did that bother you? I wonder. After all, someone on Rotor got ahead of you."

"Why should it bother me? The theory is interesting, but the application isn't. If you were to read more of my papers than the titles, you would discover that I say, quite flatly, that hyper-assistance isn't worth the effort."

"Rotorians were able to get a vessel far into space and studied the stars."

"You're talking about the Far Probe. That enabled Rotor to get parallax measurements for a number of comparatively distant stars, but is that worth the expense they went to? How far did the Far Probe go? Just a few light-months. That's not really very far. As far as the Galaxy is concerned, the Far Probe's extreme position and that of Earth and the imaginary line that can be drawn between them all amounts to a point in space."

"They did more than send out the Far Probe," said Fisher. "The entire Settlement left."

"They certainly did. That was in '22, so they've been gone six years now. And all we know is that they left."

"Isn't that enough?"

"Of course not. Where did they go? Are they still alive? *Can* they still be alive? Human beings have never been isolated on a Settlement. They have always had Earth in the vicinity, and other Settlements, too. Can a few tens of thousands of human beings survive, alone in the Universe, on a small Settlement? We have no idea if that is a psychological possibility. My guess is that it isn't."

"I imagine their purpose would be to find a world they could live on. They wouldn't remain on a Settlement."

"Come, what world will they find? They've been gone six years. There are exactly two stars they could have reached by now since hyper-assistance can only move them at an average speed equal to that of light. That's Alpha Centauri, a three-star system, four-point-three light-years away, one of the three being a red dwarf. Then there's Barnard's star, a single red dwarf, five-point-nine light-years away. Four stars: a Sun-like star, a near-Sun-like star, and two red dwarfs. The two Sun-likes are part of a moderately close binary and therefore unlikely to have an Earth-like planet in stable orbit. Where do they go next? They won't make it, Crile. I'm sorry. I know that your wife and child were on Rotor, but they won't make it."

Fisher kept calm. He knew something she didn't. He knew about the Neighbor Star—but that was a red dwarf, too.

He said, "Then you think that interstellar flight is impossible?"

"In a practical sense, yes, if hyper-assistance is all there is."

Fisher said, "You make it sound as though hyper-assistance *isn't* all there is, Tessa."

"It may *be* all there is. It wasn't long ago when we thought that even that much was impossible and to go further yet— Still, we can at least dream of true hyperspatial flight and true superluminal velocities. If we could go as quickly as we wished for as long as we wished, then the Galaxy, perhaps the Universe, would become one large Solar System, so to speak, and we could have it all."

"That's a nice dream, but is it possible?"

"We've had three All-Settlement Conferences on the matter since Rotor's flight."

"Just All-Settlement? What about Earth?"

"There were Earth observers present, but Earth is not a physicists' paradise these days."

"What conclusions did the conferences reach?"

Wendel smiled. "You're not a physicist."

"Leave out the hard parts. I'm curious."

She merely smiled at him.

Fisher clenched his fist on the table before him. "Forget this theory of yours that I'm some sort of secret agent after your information. I have a child out there somewhere, Tessa. You say she's probably dead. What if she's alive? Is there a chance—"

Wendel's smile disappeared. "I'm sorry. I did not think of that. But be practical. Finding a Settlement somewhere in a volume of space that is represented by a sphere that, at the present time, is six light-years in radius and is growing ever larger with time is an impossible task. It took us over a century to find the tenth planet, and that was enormously larger than Rotor and a much smaller volume of space had to be combed."

Fisher said, "Hope springs eternal. Is true hyperspatial flight possible? You can say yes or no."

"Most say no—if you want the truth. There may be a few who say they can't say, but they tend to mumble."

"Does anyone say yes right out loud?"

"One person that I know of does. I do."

"You think it's *possible?*" said Fisher with an astonishment he did not have to fake. "Do you say that openly, or is it something you tell yourself in the dark of the night."

"I've published on the subject. One of those articles you only read the title of. No one dares agree with me, of course, and I've been wrong before, but I think I'm right now."

"Why do the others all think you're wrong?"

"That's the hard part. It's a matter of interpretation. Hyper-assistance on the Rotorian model, the techniques of which are by now understood in the Settlements generally, by the way, depends on the fact that the product of the ratio of ship speed to light speed, multiplied by time, is a constant, where the ratio of ship speed to light speed is greater than one."

"What does that mean?"

"That means that when you go faster than light, the faster you go, the shorter the time you can maintain that speed, and the longer the time you must go more slowly than light before you can get a boost over it again. The result is that, in the end, your average speed over a particular distance is no greater than the speed of light."

"Well?"

"That makes it sound as though the uncertainty principle is involved, and the uncertainty principle, all of us are convinced, can't be fooled with. If the uncertainty principle *is* involved, then true hyperspatial flight would seem to be theoretically impossible, and most physicists have come down on that side of the argument, while the rest of them waffle. My view, however, is that what's involved merely *seems* like the uncertainty principle but isn't, and that true hyperspatial flight is, therefore, not eliminated."

"Can the matter be settled?"

"Probably not," said Wendel, shaking her head. "The Settlements are definitely not interested in wandering off with mere hyper-assistance. No one is going to repeat the Rotorian experiment and voyage for years to probable death. On the other hand, neither is any Settlement going to invest an incredible amount of money, resources, and effort in order to try to work out a technique that the vast majority of experts in the field are convinced is theoretically impossible."

Fisher leaned forward. "Doesn't that bother you?"

"Of course it bothers me. I'm a physicist and I'd like to prove that my view of the Universe is the correct one. However, I've got to accept the limits of the possible. It will take enormous sums and the Settlements will give me nothing."

"But, Tessa, even if the Settlements are not interested, Earth is—and to any amount."

"Really?" Tessa smiled in what seemed mild amusement and she reached out to stroke Fisher's hair, slowly and sensually. "I thought we'd get to Earth eventually."

34.

Fisher seized Wendel's wrist and gently drew her hand away from his head. He said, "You've been telling me the truth about your opinions of hyperspatial flight, haven't you?"

"Completely."

He said, "Then Earth wants you."

"Why?"

"Because Earth wants hyperspatial flight, and you're the one important physicist who thinks it can be done."

"If you knew that, Crile, why the cross-examination?"

"I didn't know it until you told me so. The only information I had been given was that you were the most brilliant physicist alive today."

"Oh, I am, I am," said Wendel mockingly. "And you were sent to get me?"

"I was sent to *persuade* you."

"Persuade me to do what? To come to Earth? Overcrowded, filthy, impoverished, wracked by uncontrolled weather. What an enticing thought."

"Listen to me, Tessa. Earth is not all of a piece. It may have all those faults, but there are parts that are beautiful and peaceful and that is all *you* would see. You don't really know what Earth is like. You've never been there, have you?"

"Never. I'm Adelian, born and bred. I have been to other Settlements, but I've never been to Earth, thank you."

"Then you *can't* know what Earth is like. You can't know what a large world is. A real world. You live here enclosed, in a toy box, with a few square kilometers of surface, with a handful of people. You're living in a miniature that you've used up long ago and that has nothing more to offer you. Earth, on the other hand, is over six hundred million square kilometers of surface. It is eight billion human beings. It is infinite variety—lots of it very bad, but lots of it very good."

"And all of it very poor. And you have no science."

"Because scientists—and with them science—have moved out to the Settlements. That's why we need you and others. Come back to Earth."

"I still don't see why."

"Because we have goals, ambitions, desires. The Settlements have only self-satisfaction."

"What good are all those goals and ambitions and desires? Physics is an expensive pursuit."

"And Earth's per capita wealth is low, I admit it. Individually, we are poor, but eight billion people, each contributing something out of poverty, can amass a vast sum. Our resources, misused as they are and have been, are still enormous, and we can find more money and more labor than all the Settlements together—if it is for something we feel an absolute need. I assure you that Earth feels an absolute need for hyperspatial flight. Come to Earth, Tessa, and you will be treated as that rarest of resources, a brilliant brain we must have—and the one thing we can't supply on our own."

Wendel said, "I'm not at all sure that Adelia would be willing to let me go. It may be a self-satisfied Settlement, but it knows the value of brains, too."

"They can't object to your attending a scientific meeting on Earth."

"And once there, you mean, I needn't return?"

"You will have no complaint with regard to treatment. You will be more comfortable there than you are here. Your every desire, your every wish— More than that, you can head the hyperspatial project and you will have an unlimited budget to devise tests of any kind, run experiments, make observations—"

"Well! What a princely bribe you offer me!"

141

NEMESIS

Fisher said earnestly, "Is there anything more you can ask for?"

"I wonder," said Wendel. "Why were you sent? An attractive man like you? Were they expecting you to bring back an elderly female physicist—susceptible—frustrated—drawn by your body like a fish by a hook?"

"I don't know what was in the mind of those who sent me, Tessa, but that was not in my mind. Not after one look at you. You are not elderly, as you well know. I don't for a minute believe that you are either susceptible or frustrated. Earth is offering you a physicist's dream. That has nothing to do with whether you are male or female, elderly or youthful."

"What a shame! Suppose I proved recalcitrant and didn't wish to go to Earth? What were you to do as a last measure of persuasion? Suppress your distaste for the process and make love to me?"

Wendel crossed her arms over her magnificent breasts and looked at him quizzically.

Fisher said carefully, choosing his words, "Again, I cannot say what was in the mind of those who sent me. Making love was not part of my explicit instructions, nor was it part of my intentions, though if it had been, I assure you that I would feel no distaste at the prospect. I felt, however, that you would see the advantages from a physicist's point of view and I would not denigrate you by supposing that you would need anything more."

"How wrong you are," said Wendel. "I see the advantages from a physicist's point of view, and I am anxious to accept the offer and to pursue the butterfly of hyperspatial flight down the corridors of the possible—but I do not wish to give up your best efforts at persuasion either. I want it all."

"But—"

"In short, if you want me, you must pay me. Persuade me as though I were recalcitrant, as best as ever you can, or I won't go to Earth. Come, why do you suppose we are here in a Privacy? What do you think Privacies are for? Once we have exercised, showered, eaten a bit, drank a little, conversed, experienced some pleasure in all these things, there is opportunity to experience others. I insist. Persuade me to come to Earth."

And at the touch of her finger, the light within the Privacy dimmed seductively.

# SEVENTEEN

# SAFE?

### 35.

Insigna felt uneasy. It was Siever Genarr who had insisted that Marlene be consulted in the matter.

He said, "You're her mother, Eugenia, and you can't help but think of her as a little girl. It takes a while for a mother to realize she is not an absolute monarch, that her daughter is not a piece of property."

Eugenia Insigna avoided his mild eye. She said, "Don't lecture me, Siever. You have no children of your own. It's easy to be pompous about other people's children."

"Do I sound pompous? I'm sorry. Let us say, I'm not as emotionally bound as you are to the memory of an infant. I *like* the girl a great deal, but I have no picture of her in my mind except that of a burgeoning young woman with a very remarkable mind. She's *important*, Eugenia. I have a peculiar feeling that she is much more important than either you or I. She must be consulted—"

"She must be kept *safe*," Insigna countered.

"I agree, but she must be consulted as to how best to keep her safe. She is young, she is inexperienced, but she may possibly know better than we do what must be done. Let us talk among ourselves as though we were three adults. Promise me, Eugenia, that you won't try to make use of maternal authority."

Insigna said bitterly, "How can I promise that? But we'll talk to her."

So now the three were together in Genarr's office, the room shielded, and Marlene, looking quickly from one to the other, pressed her lips tightly together and said unhappily, "I'm not going to like this."

Insigna said, "I'm afraid it *is* bad news. Here it is—bluntly. We're considering a return to Rotor."

Marlene looked astonished. "But your important work, Mother. You can't abandon that. But I see you don't intend to. I don't understand, then."

"Marlene," Insigna spoke slowly and with emphasis. "We're considering that *you* return to Rotor. Only *you.*"

At that, there were a few moments of silence, while Marlene searched both of their faces. Then she said, almost in a whisper, "You're serious. I can't believe it. I *won't* return to Rotor. I don't want to. *Ever.* Erythro is my world. Right here is where I want to be."

"Mar*lene*—" began Insigna, her voice shrill.

Genarr held up his hand in Insigna's direction, shaking his head slightly. She fell silent, and Genarr said, "Why are you so anxious to be here, Marlene?"

And Marlene answered flatly, "Because I am. You can be hungry for some particular food sometimes—just feel like eating it. You can't explain why. You just want it. I'm hungry for Erythro. I don't know why, but I want it. I don't have to explain that."

Genarr said, "Let your mother tell you what we know."

Insigna took Marlene's cold and unresponsive hand in hers and said, "Do you remember, Marlene, before we left for Erythro, when you were telling me about your conversation with Commissioner Pitt—"

"Yes?"

"You told me then that when he said we could go to Erythro, he left out something. You didn't know what that something was, but you said it was rather unpleasant—sort of evil."

"Yes, I remember."

Insigna hesitated and Marlene's large penetrating eyes grew hard. She whispered, as though she was talking to herself and wasn't entirely aware that her inner thoughts were being voiced. "Optic flicker at head. Hand nearly at temple. Moves away." The sound died, though her lips continued to move.

Then, in loud outrage, she said, "Are you under the impression there's something wrong with my mind?"

"No," said Insigna quickly. "Quite the reverse, dear. We know that your mind is an excellent one, and we want it to stay that way. Here's the story—"

Marlene listened to the tale of the Erythro Plague with what seemed to be the deepest suspicion, and finally said, "I see you believe what you are telling me, Mother, but it could be that someone told you a lie."

"She heard it from me," said Genarr, "and I tell you, of my personal experience, that it's all the truth. Now you tell me if I am telling the truth right now."

Marlene clearly accepted that and moved onward. "Why am I in particular danger, then? Why am I in danger more than you or Mother?"

"As your mother said, Marlene— The Plague is thought to strike more readily at people who are more imaginative, more fanciful. There is evidence that leads some to believe that unusual minds are more susceptible to the Plague, and since yours is the most unusual I have ever encountered, it seems to me possible that you are dangerously susceptible. The Commissioner has sent instructions that you are to have a free hand on Erythro, that we're to make it possible for you to see and experience whatever you wish, that we are even to allow you to explore outside the Dome—if that is your desire. It sounds very kind of him, but might he not want to expose you to the outside in the wish, in the *hope*, of increasing your chance at coming down with the Plague?"

Marlene considered this with no sign of emotion.

Insigna said, "Don't you see, Marlene? The Commissioner doesn't want to kill you. We're not accusing him of that. He just wants to put your mind out of action. It is inconvenient to him. You can easily find out things about him and about his intentions that he doesn't want you to know, and he won't have that. He's a man of secrets."

"If Commissioner Pitt is trying to do me harm," said Marlene at length, "then why are you trying to send me back to him?"

Genarr raised his eyebrows. "We've explained it. You're in danger here."

"I'd be in danger there, with him. What might he do next—if he really wants to destroy me? If he thinks I'm going to be destroyed here, then he'll forget about me. He'll leave me alone, won't he? At least for as long as I'm here?"

"But the Plague, Marlene. The *Plague.*" She reached out to hug her.

Marlene evaded the embrace. "I'm not worried about the Plague."

"But we explained—"

"It doesn't matter what you explained. I'm not in danger here. Not at all. I know my mind. I've lived with it all my life. I understand it. It's not in danger."

Genarr said, "Be reasonable, Marlene. However stable you feel your mind to be, it's subject to disease and deterioration. You might get meningitis, epileptic symptoms, a brain tumor, or, eventually, senescence. Can you hold any of those things at bay just by being sure none of it will happen to you?"

"I'm not talking about any of those things. I'm talking about the Plague. That won't happen to me."

"You can't possibly be sure, dear. We don't even know what the Plague is."

"Whatever it is, it won't happen to me."

"How can you tell, Marlene?" asked Genarr.

"I just know."

Insigna felt her patience break. She caught Marlene by both elbows. "Marlene, you *must* do as you're told."

"No, Mother. You don't understand. On Rotor, I've felt a pull toward Erythro. It pulls me more strongly than ever, now that I'm on it. I want to stay on it. I'll be safe here. I don't want to go back to Rotor. I'll be less safe there."

Genarr raised his hand, stopping whatever it was that Insigna was about to say. "I suggest a compromise, Marlene. Your mother is here to make certain astronomical observations. It will take her some time. Promise that, while she is busy at it, you will be content to stay inside the Dome and take such precautions as I think will make sense, and that you submit to periodic tests. If we detect no change in your mental functioning, you can wait here in the Dome till your mother is done and then we can discuss it again. Agreed?"

Marlene bent her head in thought. Then she said, "All right. But, Mother, don't think of pretending to be finished when you're not finished. I will know. And don't think of doing a quick job instead of a good one. I will know that, too."

Insigna frowned and said, "I won't play games, Marlene, and don't think I will ever deliberately do bad science—even for your sake."

Marlene said, "I'm sorry, Mother. I know that you find me irritating."

Insigna sighed heavily. "I don't deny that, but, irritating or not, Marlene, you are my daughter. I love you, and I want to keep you safe. As far as that goes, am I lying?"

"No, Mother, you are not lying, but please believe me when I say I *am* safe. Since I've been on Erythro, I've been happy. I never was happy on Rotor."

Genarr said, "And why are you happy?"

"I don't know, Uncle Siever. But being happy is enough, even when you don't know why, isn't it?"

36.

"You look tired, Eugenia," said Genarr.

"Not physically, Siever. Just tired inside after two months of calculations. I don't know how it was possible for astronomers in prespatial times to do what they did with nothing more than primitive computers. For that matter, Kepler worked out the laws of planetary motion with nothing more than logarithms, and had to consider himself fortunate that they had just been invented."

"Pardon a nonastronomer, but I thought that these days, astronomers simply gave their instruments their directions, then went to sleep and, after a few hours, woke up and found everything printed up neatly and waiting at the desk."

"I wish. But this job was different. Do you know how precisely I had to calculate the actual velocity of Nemesis and the Sun relative to each other, so that I could know exactly where and when the two made their closest approach? Do you know how tiny an error would be sufficient to make it seem that Nemesis would do Earth no harm when it would really destroy it—and vice versa?

"It would be bad enough," Insigna went on intensely, "if Nemesis and the Sun were the only two bodies in the Universe, but there are nearby stars, all of them moving. At least a dozen of them are massive enough to have a tiny effect on Nemesis or the Sun or both. Tiny, but large enough to mount up to an error of millions of kilometers one way or another, if ignored. And in order to get it right, you have to know the mass of each star with considerable precision, and its position, and its velocity.

"It's a fifteen-body problem, Siever, enormously complicated. Nemesis will go right through the Solar System and have a perceptible effect on several of the planets. A lot depends on the actual position of each planet in its orbit as Nemesis passes through, of course, and by how much it will shift under the influence of Nemesis' gravity, and how this shift will affect its pull on the other planets. And, by the way, the effect of Megas also has to be calculated."

Genarr listened gravely. "And what's the bottom line, Eugenia?"

"As it happens, I believe the effect will be to make Earth's orbit a trifle more eccentric than it is now and the semimajor axis a bit smaller than it is now."

"Which means?"

"Which means that Earth will become too hot to be habitable."

"And what will happen to Megas and Erythro?"

"Nothing measurable. The Nemetic System is much smaller than the Solar System and therefore is held together more tightly. Nothing here will budge significantly, but Earth will."

"When will this happen?"

"In five thousand and twenty-four years, plus or minus fifteen, Nemesis will reach the point of closest approach. The effect will spread itself out over twenty or thirty years as Nemesis and the Sun approach and separate."

"Are there going to be any collisions or anything like that?"

"Almost zero chance of anything significant. No collisions between any major bodies. Of course, a solar asteroid might strike Erythro, or a Nemetic asteroid might strike the Earth. There would be a very small chance of that, though it would be catastrophic for Earth if it happened. There's no chance of calculating that, however, until the stars are very close to each other."

"But, in any case, Earth will have to be evacuated. Is that it?"

"Oh yes."

"But they've got five thousand years to do it in."

"Five thousand years is none too long to arrange for the evacuation of eight billion people. They should be warned."

"Won't they find out for themselves, even if they aren't warned?"

"Who knows when? And even if they find out soon, we should give them the technique of hyper-assistance. They will have to have it."

"I'm sure they will have that on their own, too, and perhaps in not too long a time."

"And if they don't?"

"I'm also sure that within a century or less, communication will be established between Rotor and Earth. After all, if we have hyper-assistance for transportation, we will have it for communication eventually. Or we will send a Settlement back to Earth and there will still be time."

"You talk like Pitt."

Genarr chuckled. "He can't be wrong all the time, you know."

"He won't want to communicate. I know it."

"He can't always have his way either. We have a Dome here on Erythro, though he opposed it. And even if we don't beat him on that, he'll be dead eventually. Really, Eugenia, don't worry excessively about Earth at this moment. We have nearer concerns. Does Marlene know you are about done?"

"How can she fail to know? Apparently, the exact state of my progress is imprinted on the way I swish my sleeve or comb my hair."

"She's getting ever more perceptive, isn't she?"

"Yes. Have you noticed that, too?"

"Indeed I have. Just in the short time I've known her."

"I suppose part of it is due to her growing older. She's growing perception, perhaps, the way she's growing breasts. Then, too, she spent most of her life trying to hide her ability because she didn't know what to make of it, and because it got her into trouble. Now that she's not afraid, it's out and expanding, so to speak."

"Or because, for some reason, as she says, she likes being on Erythro and her pleasure extends her perceptions."

Insigna said, "I have had a thought about this, Siever. I don't wish to pester you with my follies. I do tend to accumulate worries about Marlene, about Earth, about everything— Do you suppose that Erythro *is* affecting her? I mean, adversely? Do you suppose that a touch of the Plague is taking the form of making her even more perceptive?"

"I don't know that that question can be answered, Eugenia, but if her heightened perception is the effect of the Plague, it doesn't seem to bother her mental balance at all. And I can tell you this—none of those who suffered from the Plague in all our stay here showed any symptoms remotely like Eugenia's gift."

149

Insigna heaved a sigh. "Thank you. You're comforting. And thank you, too, for being so gentle and friendly with Marlene."

Genarr's mouth quirked in a small lopsided smile. "It's easy. I'm very fond of her."

"You make that sound so natural. She's not a likable girl. I know that, even if I'm her mother."

"I find her likable. I've always preferred brains to beauty in women —unless I could get both, as in your case, Eugenia—"

"Twenty years ago, maybe," said Eugenia with another sigh.

"My eyes have aged with your body, Eugenia. They see no change. But it doesn't matter to me that Marlene is not beautiful. She's fearfully intelligent, even apart from her perception."

"Yes, there is that. It consoles me even when she is most burdensome."

"Well, as to that, I'm afraid Marlene will continue to be a burden, Eugenia."

Insigna looked up sharply. "In what way?"

"She has made it plain to me that being in the Dome is not enough. She wants to be out there, out on the soil of the world itself just as soon as you are done with your work. She insists!"

And Insigna stared at him in horror.

# EIGHTEEN

## SUPERLUMINAL

### 37.

Three years on Earth had aged Tessa Wendel. Her complexion had coarsened a bit. She had put on some weight. There was the beginning of jowls and dark patches under her eyes. Her breasts had grown a shade pendulous and her waist had thickened.

Crile Fisher knew that Tessa was in her late forties now, that she was five years older than he was. But she did not look older than her years. She was still a fine mature figure of a woman (as he had heard someone refer to her), but she would no longer pass for a woman in her thirties, as she might easily have done when he had first met her at Adelia.

Tessa was aware of it, too, and had spoken of it bitterly to him only the week before.

"It's you, Crile," she had said one night when they were in bed together (a time when, apparently, she was most conscious of aging). "The fault is yours. You sold me on Earth. 'Magnificent,' you said.

'Enormous,' you said. 'Variety. Always something new. Inexhaustible.' "

"And isn't it?" he said, knowing what she found objectionable, but willing to let her vent her feelings once again.

"Not where gravity is concerned. All over this entire bloated, impossible planet, you have the same gravitational pull. Up in the air, down in a mine, here, there, everywhere, one G—one G—one G. It should kill you all out of sheer boredom."

"We know no better, Tessa."

"*You* know better. You've been on Settlements. There you can pick your gravitational pull to suit yourself. You can exercise at low gravity. You can lighten the strain on your tissues now and then. How can you *live* without that?"

"We exercise here on Earth, too."

"Oh please—you do it with that pull, that eternal pull, yanking down on you. You spend all your time fighting it instead of letting your muscles interplay. You can't leap, you can't fly, you can't soar. You can't let yourself drop into the greater pull or rise into the lesser one. And that pull, pull, pull drags every bit of you down, so that you sag and wrinkle and age. Look at me! *Look* at me!"

"I look at you as often as I can," said Fisher solemnly.

"Don't look at me, then. If you do, you'll throw me over. And if you do *that*, I'll go back to Adelia."

"No, you won't. What will you do there after you've exercised at low gravity? Your research work, your laboratories, your team are all here."

"I'll start over and build a new team."

"And will Adelia support you in the style to which you are now accustomed? Of course not. You'll have to admit that Earth is not stinting you, that you are getting all you want. Wasn't I right?"

"Weren't you right? Traitor! You didn't tell me that Earth had hyper-assistance. You also didn't tell me that they had discovered the Neighbor Star. In fact, you let me pontificate on the uselessness of Rotor's Far Probe and never once told me that it had discovered anything more than a few parallaxes. You sat there and laughed at me, like the heartless wretch you are."

"I would have told you, Tessa, but what if you had decided not to come to Earth? It was not my secret to give you."

"But after I came to Earth?"

"As soon as you got to work, actually to work, we told you."

"*They* told me, and left me feeling stunned and foolish. You might have given me just a hint so that I wouldn't come off like such an idiot. I should have killed you, but what could I do? You're addictive. You knew you were when you heartlessly seduced me into coming to Earth."

That was a game she insisted on playing, and Fisher knew his role. He said, "Seduced you? You insisted. You wouldn't have it any other way."

"You liar. You forced yourself on me. It was rape—impure and complex. And you're going to do it again. I can see it in those dreadful lust-filled eyes."

It had been months since she had played that particular game and Fisher knew it came when she was satisfied with herself professionally. He said afterward, "Have you made progress?"

"Progress? I think you can call it that." She was panting. "I have a demonstration that I've set up for tomorrow for your decaying and ancient Earthman, Tanayama. He's been pushing for it mercilessly."

"He's a merciless fellow."

"He's a stupid fellow. You'd think that even if a society doesn't know science, they would know something *about* science, about how it works. If they give you a million global credits in the morning, they shouldn't expect anything definite by evening the same day. They should at least wait till the next morning and give you the whole night to work in. Do you know what he said to me last time we spoke, when I said I might have something to show him?"

"No, you hadn't told me. What did he say?"

"You'd think he'd say: 'It's amazing that in a mere three years you've worked out something so astonishing and new. We must give you enormous credit and the weight of gratitude we feel toward you is immeasurable.' That's what you would *think* he would say."

"No, not in a million years would I think that Tanayama would say anything like that. What *did* he say?"

"He said, 'So you have something finally, after three years. I should hope so. How long do you think I have to live? Do you think I have been supporting you, and paying for you and feeding you an army of assistants and workers in order to have you produce something after I'm dead and can't see it?' That's what he *did* say, and I tell you I would like to delay the demonstration till he is dead, for my own satisfaction, but I suppose that the work comes first."

"Do you really have something that will satisfy him?"

153

"Only superluminal flight. *True* superluminal flight, not that hyper-assistance nonsense. We now have something that will open the door to the Universe."

38.

The site where Tessa Wendel's research team labored, intent on shaking the Universe, had been prepared for her even before she had been recruited and come to Earth. It was inside a vast mountainous redoubt that was totally off-limits to Earth's teeming population, and in it a veritable city of research had been built.

And now Tanayama was there, seated in a motorized chair. Only his eyes, behind their narrowed lids, seemed alive—sharp, glancing this way and that.

He was by no means the highest figure in Earth's government, not even the highest figure then present, but he had been, and still was, the force behind the project and all automatically gave way to him.

Only Wendel seemed unintimidated.

His voice was a rustling whisper. "What will I see, Doctor? A ship?"

There was no ship in view, of course.

Wendel said, "No ship, Director. Ships are years away. I have only a demonstration, but it is an exciting one. You will see the first public demonstration of true superluminal flight, something that is far beyond hyper-assistance."

"How am I going to see that?"

"It was my understanding, Director, that you have been briefed."

Tanayama coughed wrackingly and had to pause to catch his breath. "They tried to talk to me," he said, "but I want it from you." His eyes, baleful and hard, were fixed on her. "You're in charge," he said. "It is your scheme. Explain."

"I can't explain the theory. That would take too long, Director. It would tire you."

"I want no theory. What am I going to *see?*"

"What you are going to see are two cubical glass containers. Both contain a hard vacuum."

"Why a vacuum?"

"Superluminal flight can only be initiated in a vacuum, Director. Otherwise the object made to move faster than light drags matter with it, increasing energy expenditures and decreasing controllabil-

154

ity. It must end in a vacuum, too, or else the results can be catastrophic because—"

"Never mind the 'because.' If this superluminal flight of yours must begin and end in a vacuum, how do we make use of it?"

"It is necessary, first, to move out into outer space by ordinary flight and then move into hyperspace and stay there. You arrive near your destination and move out into ordinary space, and then make the final move by ordinary flight."

"That takes time."

"Even superluminal flight can't be done instantaneously, but if you can move from the Solar System to a star forty light-years away in forty days rather than forty years, it would be ungrateful to grumble over the time lapse."

"All right, then. You have these two cubical glass containers. What of them?"

"They are holographic projections. Actually, they are three thousand kilometers apart through the body of the Earth, each in a mountain fastness. If light could travel from one to the other through unobstructed vacuum, it would take that light fully 1/1000th of a second—one millisecond—to make the passage. We're not going to use light, of course. Suspended in the middle of the cube at the left, held in space by a powerful magnetic field, is a small sphere, which is actually a tiny hyperatomic motor. Do you see it, Director?"

"I see something there," said Tanayama. "Is that all you have?"

"If you will watch carefully, you will see that it will disappear. The countdown is progressing."

It was a whisper in each person's ear, and, at zero, the sphere was gone from one cube and present in the other.

"Remember," said Wendel, "those cubes are really three thousand kilometers apart. The timing mechanism shows that the duration between the departure and the arrival was a little over ten microseconds, which means that the passage took place at almost a hundred times the speed of light."

Tanayama looked up. "How can I tell? The whole thing could be a trick designed to fool someone you believe to be a gullible old man."

"Director," said Wendel sternly. "There are hundreds of scientists here, all with reputations, a number of them Earthmen. They will show you anything you want to see, explain how the instruments work. You will find nothing here but honest science done well."

"Even if all is as you say, what does it mean? A little ball. A Ping-

Pong ball, traveling a few thousand kilometers. Is that what you have after three years?"

"What you have seen is perhaps more than anyone had a right to expect, Director, with all due respect. What you have seen may be the size of a Ping-Pong ball, and it may have traveled no more than three thousand kilometers, but it is true superluminal flight just as much as if we had moved a starship from here to Arcturus at a hundred times the speed of light. What you have seen is the first public demonstration of true superluminal flight in human history."

"But it's the starship I want to see."

"For that you will have to wait."

"I have no time. I have no time," rasped Tanayama in a voice that was nothing more than a hoarse whisper. A fit of coughing shook him again.

And Wendel said in a low voice that perhaps only Tanayama heard, "Even *your* will cannot move the Universe."

### 39.

The three days devoted to officialdom in what was unofficially known as Hyper City had passed grindingly, and now the interlopers were gone.

"Even so," said Tessa Wendel to Crile Fisher, "it will take two or three more days to recover and get back to work with full intensity." She looked haggard and intensely displeased as she said, "What a vile old man."

Fisher had no trouble divining the reference to be to Tanayama. "He's a sick old man."

Wendel shot an angry look at him. "Are you defending him?"

"Just stating a fact, Tessa."

She lifted a finger in admonishment. "I am quite certain that that miserable relic was as irrational and unreasonable in days past when he was not sick, or, for that matter, when he was not old. How long has he been Director of the Office?"

"He's a fixture. Over thirty years. And before that he was Chief Deputy for almost as long and probably the real power behind a succession of three or four figurehead Directors. And no matter how old or sick he gets, he'll stay Director till he dies—maybe for three days afterward, while people wait to make sure he doesn't rise from the dead."

"I gather you think this is funny."

"No, but what can you do but laugh at the spectacle of a man who, without open power, without even being known to the general public, has kept everyone in the government in fear and subjection for nearly half a century simply because he has firm control over everyone's disreputable secrets and would not hesitate to make use of them."

"And they endure him?"

"Oh yes. There's not a person in the government who has ever been willing to sacrifice his own career with certainty, merely on the chance of bringing down Tanayama."

"Even now when his hold on matters must be growing tenuous?"

"You're making a mistake. His grip may fail with death, but until his actual death that grip of his will never be tenuous. It will be the last that goes, sometime after his heart stops."

"What drives people so?" asked Wendel with distaste. "Is there no desire to let go early enough to have a chance to die in peace?"

"Not Tanayama. Never. I wouldn't say I'm an intimate of his, but in fifteen years or so, I have made contact with him now and then, never without being badly bruised in the process. I knew him when he was still vigorous, and I always knew he would never stop. To answer your earlier question, different things drive different people, but in Tanayama's case, it's hatred."

"I should think so," said Wendel. "It shows. No one that hateful can fail to hate. But who does Tanayama hate?"

"The Settlements."

"Oh, he does?" Wendel was obviously remembering that she was a Settler from Adelia. "I've never heard a Settler say a kind word for Earth either. And you know *my* feelings for anyplace without variable gravity."

"I'm not talking dislike, Tessa, or distaste or contempt. I'm talking blind scarlet hatred. Almost any Earthman dislikes the Settlements. They have all the latest. They're quiet, uncrowded, comfortable, middle-class. They have ample food, ample recreation, no bad weather, no poor. They have robots that are kept smoothly out of sight. It's only natural for people who consider themselves deprived to dislike those who seem to have everything. But with Tanayama, it's active boiling hatred. I think he would like to see the Settlements destroyed, every one."

"Why, Crile?"

"My own theory is that what gets him is none of the things I have listed. What he can't stand is the cultural homogeneity of the Settlements. Do you know what I mean?"

"No."

"The people of the Settlements select themselves. They select people like themselves. There's a shared culture, even, to some extent, a shared physical appearance on each Settlement. Earth, on the other hand, is, and through all of history has been, a wild mixture of cultures, all enriching each other, competing with each other, suspicious of each other. Tanayama and many other Earthmen—myself, for instance—consider such a mixture to be a source of strength, and feel that cultural homogeneity on the Settlements weakens them and, in the long run, shortens their potential life span."

"Well, then, why hate the Settlements for possessing something you consider a disadvantage to them? Does Tanayama hate us for being better off *and* for being worse off? It doesn't make sense."

"It doesn't have to. Who would bother hating, if it had to be reasoned out into sensibleness first? Perhaps—just perhaps—Tanayama is afraid that the Settlements will succeed too well and will prove cultural homogeneity to be a good thing after all. Or perhaps he thinks that the Settlements are as anxious to destroy the Earth as he himself is to destroy the Settlements. The matter of the Neighbor Star infuriated him."

"The fact that Rotor discovered the Neighbor Star and did not inform the rest of us?"

"More than that. They did not bother to warn us that it was speeding toward the Solar System."

"They might not have known, I suppose."

"Tanayama would never believe that. I'm sure that he feels that they knew and deliberately refused to warn us, hoping that we would be caught unprepared, and that Earth, or at least Earth's civilization, would be destroyed."

"Has it been decided that the Neighbor Star will approach closely enough to damage us? I haven't heard *that*. It's my understanding that most astronomers think it will pass at a great enough distance to leave us substantially untouched. Have you heard differently?"

Fisher shrugged. "No, I haven't, but I think it feeds Tanayama's hatred to believe that there is danger here. And from that, you move logically to the notion that superluminal flight is what we must have in order to locate an Earth-like world elsewhere. Then we can transfer as much of Earth's population as possible to that other world—if the worst comes to worst. You'll have to admit that's sensible."

"It is, but you don't have to imagine destruction, Crile. It is a natural feeling that humanity ought to spread outward even if Earth remains perfectly safe. We've moved out to the Settlements and reaching for the stars is a logical next step, and for that next step, we must have superluminal travel."

"Yes, but Tanayama would find that a cold view. The colonization of the Galaxy is something I'm sure he is willing to leave to generations to come. What he wants for himself is to find Rotor and punish it for having abandoned the Solar System without regard for the rest of the human community. He wants to live to see *that* and that's why he keeps pushing you, Tessa."

"He can push all he wants, and it won't help him. He's a dying man."

"I wonder. Modern medical procedures can perform marvels and I'm sure the doctors will go all out for Tanayama."

"Even modern medicine can only go so far. I asked the doctors."

"And they answered? I would have supposed that the question of Tanayama's health was a state secret."

"Not to me, under the circumstances, Crile. I went to the medical team that attended the Old Man here and told them that I was anxious to build an actual ship capable of carrying human beings to the stars, and that I wanted to do so before Tanayama died. I asked them how much time I had."

"And what did they say?"

"I had a year. That's what they said. At the most. They urged me to hurry."

"Can you do it in one year?"

"In one year? Of course not, Crile, and I'm glad of it. I find pleasure in the fact that that poisonous person won't live to see it. What are you making faces about, Crile? Does it bother you that I make so cruel a remark?"

"It's a petty remark, anyway, Tessa. That Old Man, however poisonous, has done all this. He's made Hyper City possible."

"Yes, but for his own purposes, not mine. And not Earth's or humanity's. And I'm allowed to have my pettiness, too. I am sure that Director Tanayama never once pitied anyone he considered his enemy or lightened the pressure of his foot on that enemy's throat by a dyne. And I imagine he doesn't expect pity or mercy from anyone

159

else. He would probably despise, as a weakling, anyone who offered it."

Fisher still looked unhappy. "How long *will* it take, Tessa?"

"How can anyone say? It might take forever. Even if everything broke reasonably well, I don't see how it could take less than five years at the least."

"But why? You already have superluminal flight."

Wendel sat up straight. "No, Crile. Don't be naïve. All I have is a laboratory demonstration. I can take a light object—a Ping Pong ball —in which a tiny hyperatomic motor makes up 90 percent of the mass, and move it superluminally. A ship, however, with people aboard, is a totally different thing. We'll have to be certain, and for that five years is optimistic. I tell you that before the days of modern computers and the kind of simulations they make possible, five years would be an unrealizable dream. Even fifty years might have been."

Crile Fisher shook his head, and said nothing.

Tessa Wendel watched him thoughtfully, then said, almost testily, "What's the matter with you? Are you in such a great hurry also?"

Fisher said soothingly, "I'm sure you're as anxious to get this done as anyone, but I do long for a practical hyperspatial ship."

"You, more than someone else?"

"I, quite a bit."

"Why?"

"I'd like to go to the Neighbor Star."

She glared at him. "Why? Are you dreaming of reuniting with the wife you abandoned?"

Fisher had never discussed Eugenia with Tessa Wendel in any detail, and he had no intention of being trapped into it now.

He said, "I have a daughter out there. I think you can understand that, Tessa. You have a son."

So she did. He was in his early twenties, attending Adelia University, and he occasionally wrote his mother.

Wendel's face softened. "Crile," she said, "you mustn't allow yourself false hopes in this. I'll grant you that since they knew about the Neighbor Star, that's where they went. With merely hyper-assistance, however, the trip must have taken over two years. We can't be sure that Rotor survived such a trip. And even if they did, the chances of finding a suitable planet around a red dwarf star is just about zero. Having survived that far, they might then have traveled on in search of a suitable planet. Where? And how would we find them?"

"I imagine they knew there was no hope for a suitable planet around the Neighbor Star. Wouldn't they have been prepared, therefore, simply to put Rotor into a suitable orbit around the star?"

"Even if they survived the flight, and even if they went into orbit around the star, it would be a sterile life, and there might be no possibility of continuing it for long in any form compatible with civilization. Crile, you've got to steel yourself. What if we manage to organize the expedition to the Neighbor Star and find nothing at all, or at most, the empty hulk of what is left of Rotor?"

Fisher said, "In that case, that would be that. But surely there must be a chance that they survived."

"And that you'll find your child? Dear Crile, is it safe to build your hopes on that? Even if Rotor survived and your child survived, she was only one year old when you left her and that was in '22. If she appeared before you right now as she now is, she'd be ten years old, and if we went out to the Neighbor Star at the earliest practical moment, she would be fifteen. She wouldn't know you. For that matter, you wouldn't know her."

"Ten years old, or fifteen, or fifty. If I saw her, Tessa, I would know her," said Fisher.

# NINETEEN

---

# REMAINING

40.

Marlene smiled hesitantly at Siever Genarr. She had grown used to invading his office at will.

"Am I interrupting you at a busy time, Uncle Siever?"

"No, dear, this is not really a busy job. It was devised so that Pitt could get rid of me, and I took it and kept it so that I could be rid of Pitt. It's not something I would admit to everyone, but I'm compelled to tell you the truth since you always spot the lie."

"Does that frighten you, Uncle Siever? It frightened Commissioner Pitt, and it would have frightened Aurinel—if I had ever let him see what I could do."

"It doesn't frighten me, Marlene, because I've given up, you see. I've just made up my mind that I'm made of glass as far as you're concerned. Actually, it's restful. Lying is hard work when you stop to think about it. If people were really lazy, they'd never lie."

Marlene smiled again. "Is that why you like me? Because I make it possible for you to be lazy?"

"Can't you tell?"

"No. I can tell you like me, but I can't tell *why* you like me. The way you hold yourself shows you like me, but the *reason* is hidden inside your mind and all I can get about that are vague feelings sometimes. I can't quite reach in there." She thought for a while. "Sometimes I wish I could."

"Be glad you can't. Minds are dirty, dank, uncomfortable places."

"Why do you say that, Uncle Siever?"

"Experience. I don't have your natural ability, but I've been around people for much longer than you have. Do you like the inside of your own mind, Marlene?"

Marlene looked surprised. "I don't know. Why shouldn't I?"

"Do you like everything you think? Everything you imagine? Every impulse you have? Be honest, now. Even though I can't read you, be honest."

"Well, sometimes I think silly things, or mean things. Sometimes I get angry and think of doing things I wouldn't really do. But not often, really."

"Not often? Don't forget that you're used to your own mind. You hardly sense it. It's like the clothes you wear. You don't feel the touch of them because you're so used to their being there. Your hair curls down the back of your neck, but you don't notice. If someone else's hair touched the back of your neck, it would itch and be unbearable. Someone else's mind might think thoughts no worse than yours, but they would be someone *else's* thoughts and you wouldn't like them. For instance, you might not like my liking you—if you knew why I liked you. It is much better and more peaceful to accept my liking you as something that exists, and not scour my mind for reasons."

And inevitably, Marlene said, "Why? What are the reasons?"

"Well, I like you because once I *was* you."

"What do you mean?"

"I don't mean I was a young lady with beautiful eyes and the gift of perception. I mean that I was young and thought I was plain and that everyone disliked me for being plain. And I knew I was intelligent, and I couldn't understand why everyone didn't like me for being intelligent. It seemed unfair to be scorned for a bad property while a good property was ignored.

"I was hurt and angry, Marlene, and made up my mind that I

would never treat others as people treated me, but I haven't had much chance to put that good resolution into practice. Then I met you, and you come close. You're not as plain as I was by far, and you're *much* more intelligent than I ever was, but I don't mind your being better than me." He smiled very broadly. "It's like giving myself a second chance—with advantages. But come, I don't think that is what you came to talk to me about. I may not be perceptive in your sense, but I can tell that much."

"Well, it's my mother."

"Oh?" Genarr frowned with a sudden obvious and almost painful increase in interest. "What about her?"

"She's just about finished her project here, you know. If she goes back to Rotor, she'll want me to go back with her. Must I?"

"I think so. Don't you want to?"

"No, I don't, Uncle Siever. I feel it's *important* that I stay here. So what I would like you to do is to tell Commissioner Pitt that you would like to keep us here. You can make up an excuse that sounds good. And the Commissioner, I'm pretty sure, will be quite glad to have us stay, especially if you explain that Mother has found out that Nemesis *will* destroy Earth."

"Has she told you *that*, Marlene?"

"No, she didn't, but she didn't have to. You can explain to the Commissioner that Mother will probably annoy him continually with her insistence that the Solar System be warned."

"Has it occurred to you that Pitt would not be keen on obliging me? If he gets the idea I want to keep Eugenia and you here in the Erythro Dome, he's liable to order you back to Rotor just to annoy me."

"I'm quite sure," said Marlene calmly, "that the Commissioner would much rather please himself by keeping us here, than displease you by taking us back. Besides, *you* want Mother here because you're —you're fond of her."

"Very fond of her. All my life, it seems. But your mother's not fond of *me*. You told me quite a while ago that your father still occupies her thoughts."

"She likes you more and more, Uncle Siever. She likes you a great deal."

"Liking is not loving, Marlene. I'm sure you've already discovered that."

Marlene reddened. "I'm talking about *old* people."

"Like me," and Genarr leaned his head back and laughed. Then he said, "I'm sorry, Marlene. It's just that old people always think young people haven't really learned about love; and young people think that old people have forgotten about love; and, you know, they're both wrong. And why do you think it's important to stay in the Erythro Dome, Marlene? Surely not just because you like me."

"Of course I like you," said Marlene seriously. "Very much. But I want to stay here because I like Erythro."

"I've explained that it's a dangerous world."

"Not for me."

"You're still certain that the Plague won't affect you?"

"Of course it won't."

"But how do you know?"

"I just *know.*" I've always *known* this, even when I was on Rotor. I had no reason not to."

"No, you didn't. But after you were told about the Plague?"

"That didn't change things. I feel completely safe here. Even more than on Rotor."

Genarr shook his head slowly. "I must admit that I don't understand this." He studied her solemn face, her dark eyes half-hidden by those magnificent lashes. "However, let me read *your* body language, Marlene—if I can. You mean to have your own way in this, at whatever cost, and to remain on Erythro."

"Yes," said Marlene flatly. "And I expect you to help me."

### 41.

Eugenia Insigna blazed quietly with anger. Her voice was not loud, but it was intense. "He can't do this, Siever."

"Of course he can, Eugenia," said Genarr just as quietly. "He's the Commissioner."

"But he's not an absolute ruler. I have my citizen's rights, and one of them is freedom of movement."

"If the Commissioner wishes to establish a state of emergency, either general, or, for that matter, confined to one person, then citizen's rights are suspended. That's more or less the gist of what the Enabling Act of '24 says."

"But it makes a mockery of all the laws and traditions we have, dating back to Rotor's establishment."

"I agree."

"And if I make an outcry over this, Pitt will find himself—"

"Eugenia, please. Listen to me. Let it go. For now, why don't you and Marlene simply stay here? You're more than welcome."

"What are you saying? This amounts to imprisonment without accusation, without trial, without judgment. We are compelled to stay in Erythro indefinitely by the arbitrary ukase—"

"Please do it without objection. It will be better."

"How better?" Insigna spoke with infinite contempt.

"Because Marlene, your daughter, is very anxious that you do so." Insigna looked blank. "Marlene?"

"Last week she came to me full of suggestions that I maneuver the Commissioner into ordering the two of you to remain here on Erythro."

Insigna half-rose from her seat, wildly indignant. "And you actually did it?"

Genarr shook his head vigorously. "No. Now listen to me. All I did was to inform Pitt that your work here was finished and that I was uncertain whether it was his intention to have you return to Rotor with Marlene or to stay here. It was a perfectly neutral statement, Eugenia. I showed it to Marlene before I sent it off and she was satisfied. She said, and I quote, 'If you give him the choice, he will keep us here.' And, apparently, he's doing that."

Insigna sank back. "Siever, are you really following the advice of a fifteen-year-old girl?"

"I don't think of Marlene as merely a fifteen-year-old girl. But tell me, why are you so anxious to go back to Rotor?"

"My work—"

"There is none. There will be none if Pitt doesn't want you. Even assuming he allows you to return, you'd find yourself replaced. Here, on the other hand, you'll find equipment you can use—that you *have* used. You came here, after all, to do what could not be done on Rotor."

"My work doesn't matter!" cried out Insigna with sweeping inconsistency. "Don't you see that I want to return for the same reason that he wants me to stay? He wants Marlene destroyed. If I had known, before I left, of this Erythro Plague, we'd never have come. I can't risk Marlene's mind."

"Her mind is the last thing I'd want to risk," said Genarr. "I would sooner risk myself."

"But it is at risk if we stay here."

"Marlene doesn't think so."

"Marlene! Marlene! You seem to think she's a goddess. What does she know?"

"Listen to me, Eugenia. Let's talk about this rationally. If it really seemed that Marlene was in danger, I would get you both back to Rotor somehow, but listen to me first. There's nothing megalomaniacal about Marlene, is there?"

Insigna was trembling. Her passion had not receded. "I don't know what you mean."

"Is she prone to making grandiose claims that are fanciful, that are patently ridiculous?"

"Of course not. She's a very sensible— Why do you ask these questions? You know that she makes no claims that aren't—"

"That aren't substantiated. I know. She never boasted about her perceptivity. It was more or less forced out of her by circumstance."

"Yes, but what is the purpose of all this!"

Genarr kept on, quietly. "Has she ever laid claim to having strange intuitive powers? Has she ever expressed herself as certain that something, some particular something, was sure to happen, or was sure not to happen, for no reason other than that she was certain?"

"No, of course not. She clings to evidence. She doesn't make wild claims without evidence."

"Yet in one respect, perhaps *only* in one respect, she does. She is certain that the Plague cannot touch her. She claims that she experienced this utter confidence, this certainty that Erythro cannot harm her, even on Rotor, and that it grew stronger when she reached the Dome. She is quite determined—*completely* determined—to remain here."

Insigna's eyes widened and her hand flew to her mouth. She made an inarticulate sound and then said, "In that case—" and remained staring at him.

"Yes," Genarr said in sudden alarm.

"Don't you see it? Isn't this the Plague striking? Her personality is changing. Her mind is being affected."

Genarr sat frozen at the thought for a moment, then he said, "No, it can't be. In all the cases of Plague, nothing like this has been detected. This is not the Plague."

"Her mind is different from those of others. It would be affected differently."

"No," said Genarr desperately. "I can't believe that. I won't believe

167

that. I believe that if Marlene says she is certain she is immune, that she *is* immune, and that her immunity will help us solve the puzzle of the Plague."

Insigna's face whitened. "Is that why you want her here on Erythro, Siever? To use her as a tool against the Plague?"

"No. I don't want her here only to use her. Nevertheless, she wants to stay and she may *be* a tool, quite apart from whether we want her to be one or not."

"And just because she wants to remain on Erythro, you are willing to allow her to do so? Just because she wants to stay out of some perverse desire she can't explain and in which you and I can see no reason or logic. You seriously think she should be allowed to remain here merely because she wishes to? Do you dare tell me that?"

Genarr said with an effort, "As a matter of fact, I am tempted in that direction."

"It is easy for you to be tempted. She is not your child. She is *my* child. She is the only—"

"I know," said Genarr. "She is the only thing you have left of— Crile. Don't stare at me like that. I know that you have never overcome your loss. I understand how you feel." He said this last softly, gently, and looked as if he wanted to reach out and touch Insigna's bowed head.

"Just the same, Eugenia, if Marlene really wants to explore Erythro, I think nothing will stop her from doing so in the end. And if she is absolutely convinced that the Plague will not touch her mind, perhaps that mental attitude will prevent it from doing so. Marlene's aggressive sanity and confidence may be her mental immune mechanism."

Insigna snapped her head up, her eyes smoldering. "You are speaking nonsense, and you have no right to give in to this sudden streak of romanticism in a mere child. She is a stranger to you. You do not love her."

"She is no stranger to me and I *do* love her. More important, I *admire* her. Love would not give me that depth of confidence that would permit the risk, but admiration would. Think about it."

And they sat there, staring at each other.

# TWENTY

# PROOF

## 42.

Kattimoro Tanayama, with his accustomed tenacity, lived out the year he had been allotted, and was well into another year before his long battle was over. When the time came, he left the field of battle without a word or sign, so that the instruments recorded death before any onlooker could see it had come.

It made little stir on Earth and none at all in the Settlements, for the Old Man had always done his work outside the public eye and had been all the stronger for it. It was those who dealt with him who knew his power, and those who most depended on his strength and policy who were the most relieved to see him go.

The news reached Tessa Wendel early, by the special channel set up between her headquarters and World City. Somehow, the fact that it had been expected for months did not ease the shock.

What would happen now? Who would succeed Tanayama and what changes would be made? She had been speculating on the matter for a long time, but it was only now that the questions seemed to have real meaning. Obviously, despite everything, Wendel (and perhaps all who were involved) had not really expected the Old Man to die.

She turned for comfort to Crile Fisher. Wendel was realistic enough to know that it was not her now clearly middle-aged body (in less than two months, she would be reaching an incredible fifty) that held Fisher. He was forty-three now and the bloom of youth had become somewhat overblown there, too, but it wasn't as obvious in a man. In any case, he was held, and she could still make herself feel that it was *she* who held him, figuratively, especially on those occasions when she held him, literally.

She said to Fisher, "Well, now what?"

Fisher said, "It's no surprise, Tessa. It should have happened before this."

"Granted, but it's happened now. It was his blind determination that kept this project going. Now what?"

Fisher said, "As long as he was alive, you were eager for him to die. Now you are concerned. But I don't think you need worry. The project will continue. Something this size has a life of its own and it can't be stopped."

"Have you ever tried to calculate how much this has cost, Crile? There'll be a new Director of the Terrestrial Board of Inquiry and the Global Congress will certainly pick someone they can control. There'll be no new Tanayama before whom they must all cower—not in the foreseeable future. And then they'll look at their budget and, without Tanayama's gnarled hand covering it, they will see it is meters deep in red ink, and they'll want to cut it back."

"How can they? They've spent so much already. Are they to stop with nothing to show for it? That would really be a fiasco."

"They can blame it on Tanayama. 'He was a madman,' they'll say, 'an egomaniac, driven by an obsession'—all of which is true to a considerable extent, as we both know—and now they, who were not responsible for any of this, can return Earth to sanity and abandon something the planet can't really afford."

Fisher smiled. "Tessa, my love, your penetration of the manner of political thinking is probably par for a first-class hyperspatialist genius. The Director of the Office is—in theory, and in public perception—an appointed official of narrow powers who is supposedly under the thorough control of the President-General and the Global

Congress. These supposedly powerful officials, who are elected, cannot make it plain that Tanayama ruled them all and had them cowering in corners, afraid to let their hearts beat without his permission. They would reveal themselves to be cowards and incapable weaklings, and they would risk losing their positions at the next election. They will have to continue the project. They will make cosmetic cuts only."

"How can you be so sure?" muttered Wendel.

"Long experience at watching elected officialdom, Tessa. Besides, if we stop short, we're just inviting all the Settlements to get it before we do—to move out into deep space and leave us behind the way Rotor did."

"Oh? How will they do that?"

"Given their knowledge of hyper-assistance, wouldn't you say that an advance to superluminal flight is inevitable?"

Wendel looked at Fisher sardonically. "Crile, my love, your penetration of hyperspatialism is probably par for a first-class wheedler of secrets. Is that what you think of my work? That it is an inevitable consequence of hyper-assistance? Haven't you grasped the fact that hyper-assistance is a natural consequence of relativistic thinking? It still doesn't allow travel faster than the speed of light. To move on to superluminal velocities requires a true leap in both thought and practice. It would not come naturally, and I have explained this to various people in the government. They complained about the slowness and the expense, and I had to explain the difficulties. They'll remember this now and they won't be afraid to stop us at this point. I can't whip them onward by suddenly telling them that we may be outraced."

Fisher shook his head. "Of course you can tell them that. And they'll believe you, too, because it will be true. We can be easily overtaken."

"Haven't you listened to what I've said?"

"I have, but you're leaving something out. Allow a little for common sense, especially from someone you've just called a first-class wheedler of secrets."

"What are you talking about, Crile?"

"This vast leap from hyper-assistance to superluminal flight is only a vast leap if one begins at the beginning, as you did. The Settlements, however, are not beginning at the beginning. Do you really think they know nothing at all about our project, about Hyper City? Do you think that I and my Earthly colleagues are the only wheedlers of secrets in the Solar System? The Settlers have their wheedlers, who work just as hard as we do and just as effectively. For one thing, they've known *you* were on Earth almost from the day you arrived here."

"What if they knew?"

"Just this. Do you think they don't have computers that will tell them you have written and published papers in the field? Do you think they don't have access to those papers? Do you think they haven't read them painstakingly and carefully and that they haven't found out you think that superluminal speeds are theoretically possible?"

Wendel bit her lip and said, "Well—"

"Yes, think about it. When you wrote your thoughts on superluminal velocity, you were merely speculating. You were virtually a minority of one in thinking it might be possible. No one took it seriously. But now you come to Earth and you stay there. You suddenly drop from sight and do not return to Adelia. They may not know all the details of what you're doing, for security on this project has been as tight as Tanayama's paranoia could make it. Still, the mere fact that you've disappeared is suggestive and there can't be any possible doubt, in the light of what you've published, as to what you're working on."

"Something like Hyper City can't be kept a total secret. The incredible sums of money being invested must leave a noticeable trace. So every Settlement is scrabbling for odds and ends they may be able to convert into bits of knowledge. And every bit gives them hints that will enable them to progress much more quickly than you were able to. You tell them all that, Tessa, if any question arises over ending the project. We can and *will* be overtaken in the race if we stop running. That thought will keep the new people as fired-up over the matter as ever Tanayama was, and it all has the merit of being true."

Wendel was silent for a considerable time while Fisher watched her carefully.

"You're right, my dear wheedler of secrets," she said at last. "I made a mistake in thoughtlessly considering you a lover rather than an adviser."

"Why should the two necessarily be mutually exclusive?" asked Fisher.

"Although," said Wendel, "I know very well that you have your own motivations in this."

"What does that matter," said Fisher, "even if it's true, provided mine run parallel with yours?"

43.

A delegation of Congressmen eventually arrived, along with Igor Koropatsky, the new Director of the Terrestrial Board of Inquiry. He had been in subordinate positions at the Office for years, so he was not completely unknown to Tessa Wendel.

He was a quiet man, with smooth, thinning gray hair, a rather bulbous nose, a comfortable double chin, who looked well-fed and good-natured. He was shrewd undoubtedly, but he obviously lacked Tanayama's almost diseased intensity. At a full kilometer, you could see that.

Congressmen were with him, of course, as though to show that this successor was their property and under their control. They must surely be hoping it would stay that way. Tanayama had been a long and bitter lesson.

No one suggested that the project be ended. Rather, the concern was that it be hastened—if possible. Wendel's cautious attempt to stress the possibility that the Settlements might overtake Earth, or be hot on its heels, was accepted without demur, almost dismissed as obvious on the face of it.

Koropatsky, who was allowed to be spokesman and to take the responsibility, said, "Dr. Wendel, I do not ask for a long, formal tour of Hyper City. I have been here before, and it is more important that I spend some time reorganizing the Office. I mean no disrespect to my distinguished predecessor, but any shifting of an important administrative body from one person to another requires a great deal of reorganization, especially if the predecessor's tenure has been a lengthy one. Now I am not, by nature, a formal man. Let us, therefore, speak freely and informally, and I will ask some questions which I hope you will answer in a way that a man of my own modest attainments in science will have no trouble in understanding."

Wendel nodded. "I will do my best, Director."

"Good. When do you expect to have a superluminal starship in operation?"

"You must realize, Director, that this is an essentially unanswerable question. We are at the mercy of unforeseen difficulties and accidents."

"Assume only reasonable difficulties and no accidents."

"In that case, since we have completed the science and need only the engineering, if we are fortunate we will have a ship in three years, perhaps."

"You will be ready in 2236, in other words."

"Certainly not sooner."

"How many persons will it carry?"

"Five to seven, perhaps."

"How far will it go?"

"As far as we wish, Director. That is the beauty of superluminal velocity. Because we are passing through hyperspace, where the ordinary laws of physics do not apply, not even the conservation of energy, it costs no more effort to go a thousand light-years than to go one."

The Director stirred uneasily. "I am not a physicist, but I find it difficult to accept an environment without constraints. Are there not things you cannot do?"

"There are constraints. We need a vacuum and a gravitational intensity below a certain point if we are to make the transition into and out of hyperspace. We will, with experience, undoubtedly find additional restraints which might have to be determined through test flights. The results might necessitate further delays."

"Once you have the ship, where will the first flight take you?"

"It might seem prudent to allow the first trip to go no farther than the planet Pluto, for instance, but that might well be considered an unbearable waste of time. Once we have the technology with which to visit the stars, the temptation to actually visit one would be overwhelming."

"Such as the Neighbor Star?"

"That would the logical goal. Ex-Director Tanayama wanted that visited, but I must point out that there are other stars far more interesting. Sirius is only four times as far away and it would give us a chance to observe a white dwarf star at close range."

"Dr. Wendel, I think that the Neighbor Star must be the goal, though not necessarily for Tanayama's reasons. Suppose you travel far out to some other star—any other star—and return. How would you prove that you had indeed been in the neighborhood of another star?"

Wendel looked startled. "Prove? I don't understand you?"

"I mean, how would you counter accusations that the supposed flight was actually a fake."

"A *fake?*" Wendel rose furiously to her feet. "That is insulting."

Koropatsky's voice suddenly grew dominating. "Sit down, Dr. Wendel. You are being accused of nothing. I am trying to foresee a situation and to guard against it. Humanity moved into space almost three centuries ago. It is a not-altogether-forgotten episode in history and my subdivision of the globe remembers it particularly well. When the first satellites went up in those dim days of terrestrial confinement, there were those who insisted everything presented by those satellites were fakes. The first photographs of the far side of the Moon were accused of having been faked. Even the first pictures of Earth from space were called fakes by some few who believed the Earth was flat. Now if Earth claims to have superluminal flight, we may run into similar trouble."

"Why, Director? Why should anyone think we would lie about a thing like that?"

"My dear Dr. Wendel, you are naïve. For over three centuries, Albert Einstein has been the demigod who invented cosmology. People, for generation after generation, have grown used to the concept of the speed of light as an absolute limit. They will not readily give it up. Even the principle of causality—and one can't think of anything more basic than that cause must precede effect—seems violated. That's one thing.

"Another, Dr. Wendel, is that the Settlements might find it politically useful to convince their peoples, and Earthmen, too, that we are lying. It will confuse us, involve us in polemics, waste our time, and give them more of a chance to catch up. So I ask you: Is there a simple proof that any flight you might make would be a truly legitimate one?"

Wendel said icily, "Director, we would permit scientists to inspect our ship once we return. We will undertake to explain the techniques used—"

"No no no. Please. Don't go any further. That would only convince scientists as knowledgeable as yourself."

"Well then, when we come back we will have photographs of the sky and the nearer stars will be positioned slightly differently with respect to each other. From the change in relative positions, it will be possible to calculate exactly where we were relative to the Sun."

"Also just for scientists. Completely unconvincing to the average person."

"We'll have close-up pictures of whatever star we visit. It will be quite different from our Sun in every respect."

"But this sort of thing is done in every trivial holovision program dealing with interstellar travel. It is the small change of the science fiction epic. It would be no more than a 'Captain Galaxy' program."

"In that case," said Wendel with teeth-clenching exasperation, "I don't know of any way. If people will not believe, then they will not believe. It is a problem you must handle. I am only a scientist."

"Now now, Doctor. Keep your temper, please. When Columbus returned from his first trip across the ocean seven and a half centuries ago, no one accused him of fakery. Why? Because he brought back with him native people from the new shores he had visited."

"Very good, but the chance of finding life-bearing worlds and bringing back specimens is very small."

"Perhaps not. Rotor, you know, is believed to have discovered the Neighbor Star with their Far Probe and to have left the Solar System soon after that. Since they never returned, it is possible that they traveled to the Neighbor Star and remained there and, in fact, are still there."

"So Director Tanayama believed. However, the trip, with hyper-assistance, would have taken over two years. It may be that through accident, through scientific failure, through psychological problems, they never completed the trip. That, too, would account for their never returning."

"Nevertheless," said Koropatsky, quietly insistent, "they may have arrived."

"Even if they have arrived, they are likely to have simply gone into orbit around the star, in the certain absence of any habitable world. In isolation, the psychological strains, which didn't stop them en route, would stop them then, and it is likely there is now only a dead Settlement whirling the Neighbor Star forever."

"Then you now see that it must be the goal because once you're there, you will seek out Rotor, alive or dead. Either way, you must bring back something unmistakably Rotorian and it would then be very easy for everyone to believe that you had indeed gone out to the stars and come back." He smiled broadly. "Even *I* would believe it, and that would answer my question as to how you would prove that you had made a superluminal trip. That will be your mission, then, and for that, never fear, Earth will continue to find you the money and resources and workers you will need."

And when after a dinner during which technical points were not raised, Koropatsky said to Wendel, in the friendliest possible tone, but with more than a hint of ice beneath, "Just the same, remember that you have only three years to do it in. At the *most.*"

44.

"So my clever ploy wasn't really needed," said Crile Fisher with a slight air of regret.

"No. They were determined to continue without the threat of being overtaken. The only thing that bothered them, and it was something that never seemed to bother Tanayama, was this matter of having to battle possible cases of fakery. I suppose Tanayama just wanted to destroy Rotor. As long as that was done, the world could yell 'Fake' all it wanted."

"They wouldn't. He would have had the ship bring back something to show *him* that Rotor was destroyed. That would prove it to the world, too. What kind of fellow is the new Director?"

"Quite the reverse of Tanayama. He seems soft, almost apologetic, but I have a feeling that the Global Congress is going to find him just as hard to handle as Tanayama was. He has to settle into his job, that's all."

"From what you've told me about the conversation, he seems more sensible than Tanayama."

"Yes, but it still steams me—that suggestion of fakery. Imagine thinking spaceflights would be faked. It's probably the result of Earthmen having no feel for space. No feel at all. It's you people having this endless world and, except in a microscopic fraction of cases, never leaving it."

Fisher smiled. "Well, I'm one of the microscopic fraction that has left it. Often. And you're a Settler. So neither one of us is planetbound."

"That's right," said Wendel, shooting him a sidelong glance. "Sometimes I think you don't remember that I'm a Settler."

"Believe me, I never forget it. I don't go about muttering to myself, 'Tessa is a Settler! Tessa is a Settler!' but, at all times, I know you are."

"Does anyone else, though?" She waved her hand around as though

177

to include an indefinite surrounding volume. "Here is Hyper City under unimaginably tight security and why? Against the Settlers. The whole point is to get out there with practical superluminal flight before the Settlers can even get started. And who is in complete charge of the project? A Settler."

"Is this the first time you've thought of that in the five years you've been on the project?"

"No, but I think of it periodically. I just don't understand it. Aren't they afraid to trust me?"

Fisher laughed. "Not really. You're a scientist."

"So?"

"So scientists are considered mercenaries without ties to any one society. Give a scientist a fascinating problem and all the money, equipment, and help that he or she needs to tackle that problem, and that scientist wouldn't care who the source of support was. Be truthful— You care neither for Earth, nor Adelia, nor for the Settlements as a whole, nor even for humanity as a whole. You just want to work out the details of superluminal flight, and you have no loyalties beyond that."

Wendel said haughtily, "That's a stereotype, and not every scientist will fit it. *I* may not fit it."

"I'm sure they realize that, too, so that you are probably under constant surveillance, Tessa. Some of your closest associates probably have, as an important aspect of their work, the constant monitoring of your activities, and the constant reporting to the government."

"You're not referring to yourself, I hope."

"Don't tell me you've never thought that I might be remaining near you entirely in my role as wheedler of secrets."

"As a matter of fact, the idea has occurred to me—now and then."

"But it's *not* my job. I suspect that I'm too close to you to be trusted. In fact, I'm quite sure that I'm reported on, too, and that my activity is carefully weighed. As long as I keep you happy—"

"You're a cold-blooded person, Crile. How can you find humor in something like that?"

"There's no humor there. I'm trying to be realistic. If you ever tire of me, I lose my function. An unhappy Tessa may be an unproductive Tessa, so I will be suddenly gotten out of your hair and the way will be smoothed for my successor. After all, your contentment is worth far more to them than mine is, and I recognize that it is only sensible that that be the case. You see my realism?"

Whereupon Wendel reached out suddenly to stroke Crile's cheek. "Don't worry. I think I've grown too used to you to tire of you now. In the hot blood of my youth, I could grow bored with my men and discard them, but now—"

"It's too much of an effort, eh?"

"If you choose to think of it that way. I might also finally be in love —in my way."

"I understand your meaning. Love in cool blood can be restful. But I suspect this is not the proper moment to prove it. You'll have to chew over this exchange with Koropatsky first, and get that poisonous feeling about fakery out of your system."

"I'll get over that someday. But there's another thing. I told you a little while ago about Earthpeople having no feel for space."

"Yes, I remember."

"Well, here's an example. Koropatsky has no feeling—no feeling at all—for the sheer size of space. He talked about going to the Neighbor Star and finding Rotor. Now how is that to be done? Every once in a while, we spot an asteroid and lose it before we can calculate its orbit. Do you know how long it takes to relocate that lost asteroid, even with all our modern devices and instruments? Years sometimes. Space is large, even in the near vicinity of a star, and Rotor is small."

"Yes, but we search for one asteroid among a hundred thousand. Rotor, on the other hand, will be the only object of its kind near the Neighbor Star."

"Who told you that? Even if the Neighbor Star doesn't have a planetary system in our sense, it is extremely unlikely that it won't be surrounded by debris of one sort or another."

"But it would be dead debris, like our dead asteroids. Since Rotor will be a functioning Settlement, it will be emitting a wide range of radiation, and that should be easy to detect."

"*If* Rotor is a functioning Settlement. What if it isn't? Then it's just another asteroid and finding it may prove an enormous task. We may not succeed at all in any reasonable period of time."

Fisher could not keep his face from falling into lines of misery.

Wendel made a small sound and moved closer to him, placing an arm around his unresponsive shoulder. "Oh, my dear, you *know* the situation. You must face it."

Fisher said in a choked voice, "I know. But they *may* have survived. Isn't that true?"

"They may," said Wendel with a slightly synthetic lilt to her voice, "and if they have, so much the better for us. As you pointed out, it would then be easy to locate them through their radiational output. And more than that—"

"Yes?"

"Koropatsky wants us to bring back something that will prove we encountered Rotor, feeling that would be the best evidence that we had indeed been in deep space and returned, covering several light-years in, at most, a few months. Except— What exactly could we bring back that would be convincing? Suppose we find some drifting bits of metal or concrete. Not any bit will do. A lump of metal with nothing to identify it as Rotorian would be something we might well have taken with us. Even if we manage to find a piece that is charac-teristic of Rotor—some artifact that could only exist on a Settlement —it might be considered a fake.

"If, however, Rotor were a working, living Settlement, we might be able to persuade some Rotorian to come back with us. A Rotorian can be identified as one. Fingerprints, retinal patterns, DNA analysis. There may even be people on other Settlements, or on Earth, who would be able to recognize the particular Rotorian we bring back. Koropatsky hinted heavily that we do this. He pointed out that Co-lumbus, returning from his first voyage, brought Native Americans with him.

"Of course"—and Wendel sighed heavily as she went on—"there is a limit to how much we can bring back, animate or inanimate. Some-day we may have starships as large as Settlements, but our first one is going to be a small and, by later standards, a primitive thing, I'm sure. We might be able to bring back one Rotorian; more than one would be more than we could handle, so we'll have to pick the right one."

"My daughter, Marlene," said Fisher.

"She might not want to come. We can only take someone who's willing to return. There's bound to be one among the thousands, perhaps even a large number, but if she doesn't want to come—"

"Marlene will be willing to come. You let me talk to her. Somehow I'll win her over."

"Her mother might not wish it."

"Somehow I'll talk her into it," said Fisher stubbornly. "Somehow I'll manage."

Wendel sighed again. "I can't let you live with that thought, Crile.

Don't you see that we can't take your daughter back, even if she is willing to come?"

"Why not? *Why not?*"

"She was one year old when she left. She has no memories of the Solar System. No one in the Solar System could identify her. There are very unlikely to have been any records that could be checked independently elsewhere in the system. No, we would have to have some middle-aged person at the least, and one who has visited other Settlements or, better yet, Earth."

She paused and then said tightly, "Your wife might be suitable. Didn't you once tell me that she took part of her education on Earth? There would be records and she would be identifiable. Though, to be honest, I would much rather take someone else."

Fisher was silent.

Wendel said, almost timidly, "I'm sorry, Crile. It's not as I would wish it."

And Fisher said bitterly, "Just let my Marlene be alive. We'll see what can be done."

# TWENTY-ONE

# BRAIN SCAN

## 45.

"I'm sorry," said Siever Genarr, looking down his long nose at mother and daughter with an expression that seemed to beg their pardon even without his words. "I had told Marlene that this job was not a very busy one and then almost immediately thereafter we had a kind of minicrisis with our power supply and I found I had to delay this conference of ours. The crisis is over, however, and wasn't much to begin with, now that we can view it in hindsight. Am I forgiven?"

"Of course, Siever," said Eugenia Insigna. She was clearly restless. "I won't say it's been an easy three days, though. I feel that every hour we stay here increases Marlene's danger."

Marlene said, "I don't fear Erythro at all, Uncle Siever."

Insigna said, "And I don't think Pitt can do anything against us on Rotor. He knows that, or he wouldn't have sent us here."

Genarr said, "And I will try to play the honest broker and satisfy you both. Whatever Pitt can or cannot do openly, there is a great deal he can do indirectly, so it's dangerous, Eugenia, for you to let your fear of Erythro lead you to underestimate Pitt's resolve and ingenuity. To begin with, if you return to Rotor, you will be doing so against his emergency ruling and he can imprison you or send you into exile on New Rotor or even send you back here.

"As for Erythro, we don't dare underestimate the danger of the Plague either, even though it seems to have died out in its virulent early form. I am as reluctant to risk Marlene as you are, Eugenia."

And Marlene whispered in exasperation, "There's no risk."

Insigna said, "Siever, I don't think we should carry on this discussion of Marlene in her presence."

"You're wrong. I want to do it in her presence. I suspect that she knows better than either of us what she ought to do. She is the caretaker of that mind of hers and it is our job to interfere with her as little as possible."

Insigna made an inarticulate sound in her throat, but Genarr went on, a quality of remorselessness entering his voice: "I want her in this discussion because I want her input. I want her opinion."

Insigna said, "But you *know* her opinion. She wants to go out there, and you're saying that we must let her do what she wants to do because she is somehow magical."

"No one said a word about magical, or about simply letting her go out. I would like to suggest we experiment, with all due precautions."

"In what way?"

"To begin with, I would like a brain scan." He turned to Marlene. "Do you understand, Marlene, that that's necessary? Do you have any objections?"

Marlene frowned slightly. "I've had brain scans. Everyone has had brain scans. They don't let you start school without a brain scan. Any time you have a complete medical examination—"

"I know," said Genarr gently. "I haven't completely wasted these last three days. I have here"—and his hand came to rest on a stack of computer strips at the left end of his desk—"the computerization of every single brain scan you've ever had."

"But you're not telling everything, Uncle Siever," said Marlene calmly.

"Ah," said Insigna with a touch of triumph. "What is he hiding, Marlene?"

"He's a little nervous about me. He doesn't entirely believe my feeling that I'm safe. He's uncertain."

Genarr said, "How can that be, Marlene? I feel quite certain about your safety."

But Marlene said with a glow of sudden enlightenment, "I think that's why you waited three days, Uncle Siever. You argued yourself into being certain so that I wouldn't see your uncertainty. But it didn't work. I can still see it."

Genarr said, "If that shows, Marlene, then it's only because I value you so highly that I find even the slightest risk unpleasant."

Insigna said angrily, "If you find even the slightest risk unpleasant, how do you suppose I feel, as a mother? So in your uncertainty, you obtain brain scans, violating Marlene's medical privacy."

"I had to find out. And I did. They're insufficient."

"Insufficient in what way?"

"In the early days of the Dome, when the Plague struck again and again, one of our concerns was to devise a more detailed brain scanner and a more efficiently programmed computer to interpret the data. This has never been transferred to Rotor. Pitt's exaggerated desire to hide the Plague led him to resist the sudden appearance of an improved brain scanner on Rotor. It might have given rise to inconvenient questions and rumors. Ridiculous, to my way of thinking, but in this, as in many other things, Pitt had his way. Therefore, Marlene, you have never been properly brain scanned and I want you to have one on *our* device."

Marlene shrank back, "No."

A look of hope crossed Insigna's face. "Why not, Marlene?"

"Because when Uncle Siever said that—he was suddenly much more uncertain."

Genarr said, "No, that's not—" He stopped himself, lifted his arms, and let them drop helplessly. "Why do I bother? Marlene, dear, if I seemed suddenly concerned, it's because we need as detailed a brain scan as possible to serve as a standard of mental normality. Then, if you are exposed to Erythro and suffer even the slightest mental distortion as a result, it can be detected by brain scan even when no one can tell by simply looking at you or talking to you. Well, as soon as I mention a detailed brain scan, I think of the possibility of detecting an otherwise indetectable mental change—and the thought itself sparks an automatic concern. *That's* what you detect. Come, Marlene, how much uncertainty do you detect? Be quantitative."

But Marlene said, "Not much, but it's there. The trouble is, I can only tell you're uncertain. I can't tell *why*. Maybe this special brain scan is dangerous."

"How can it be? It has been used so— Marlene, you *know* Erythro won't hurt you. Don't you also know that the brain scan won't hurt you?"

"No, I don't."

"Do you know that it *will* hurt you?"

A pause and then Marlene said reluctantly, "No."

"But how can you be sure about Erythro and not sure about the brain scan?"

"I don't know. I just know that Erythro won't hurt me, but I don't know that the brain scan won't. Or will."

A smile crossed Genarr's face. It did not take unusual abilities to see that he was enormously relieved.

Marlene said, "Why does that make you feel good, Uncle Siever?"

Genarr said, "Because if you were making up your intuitional feelings—out of a desire to be important, or out of general romanticism, or out of some sort of self-delusion—you would apply it to everything. But you don't. You pick and choose. Some things you know and some things you don't know. That makes me far more inclined to believe you when you claim to be sure Erythro won't hurt you and I no longer in the least fear that the brain scan will reveal anything disturbing."

Marlene turned to her mother. "He's right, Mother. He feels much better and so I feel much better. It's so obvious. Can't you see it, too?"

"It doesn't matter what I see," said Insigna. "*I* don't feel better."

"Oh, Mother," murmured Marlene. Then, more loudly to Genarr, "I'll take the scan."

46.

"This is not surprising," murmured Siever Genarr.

He was watching the computer graphics in their intricate, almost floral patterns, as they moved slowly in and out in false color. Eugenia Insigna, at his side, stared at it keenly, but understood nothing.

"What is not surprising, Siever?" she asked.

"I can't tell you properly because I don't have their jargon down pat. And if Ranay D'Aubisson, who's our local guru on this, were to explain it, neither you nor I would understand her. However, she did point this out to me—"

"It looks like a snail shell."

"The color makes it stand out. It's a measure of complexity rather than a direct indication of physical form, Ranay says. This part is atypical. We don't find it in brains generally."

Insigna's lip trembled. "You mean she's already affected?"

"No, of course not. I said atypical, not abnormal. Surely I don't have to explain *that* to an experienced scientific observer. You'll have to admit that Marlene *is* different. In a way, I'm glad that the snail shell is there. If her brain were completely typical, we'd have to wonder why she seems to be what she is; where the perceptivity is coming from. Is she cleverly faking it, or are we fools?"

"But how do you know it isn't something—something—"

"Diseased? How can that be? We have all of the brain scans collected over her lifetime from infancy. That atypicality was always there."

"It was never reported to me. No one ever remarked on it."

"Of course not. Those early brain scans were the usual fairly primitive type and it wouldn't show, at least not so that it would hit you in the face. *But*, once we have this proper brain scan and can see the detail clearly, we can go back to the early ones and make it out. Ranay has already done so. I tell you, Eugenia, this advanced brain scanning technique ought to be standard on Rotor. Pitt's suppression of it is one of his most foolish moves. It's expensive, of course."

"I'll pay," murmured Insigna.

"Don't be silly. I'm putting this one on the Dome budget. After all, this may be helpful in solving the Plague mystery. At least, that's what I'll claim if it's ever questioned. Well, there you are. Marlene's brain is recorded in greater complexity than ever before. If she should be even slightly affected, it will show on the screen."

"You have no idea how frightening this is," said Insigna.

"I don't blame you, you know. But she is so confident that I can't help going along with her. I'm convinced that this solid sense of security has meaning behind it."

"How can it?"

Genarr pointed to the snail shell. "You don't have that, and I don't have it, so neither of us is in a position to tell where and how she gets her sense of security. But she has it, so we must let her out on the surface."

"Why must we risk her? Can you possibly explain to me why we must risk her?"

"Two reasons. First, she does seem determined, and I have the feeling that she'll get whatever she's determined to get—sooner or later. In that case, we might as well be cheerful about it and send her off, since we won't be able to stop her for very long. Secondly, it's possible we'll learn something about the Plague as a result. What that might be, I can't say, but anything, however small, that will yield additional information concerning the Plague is worth a great deal."

"Not my daughter's mind."

"It won't come to that. For one thing, even though I have faith in Marlene and believe there's no risk, I will do what I can to minimize it for your sake. In the first place, we'll not let her out onto the surface itself for a while. I may take her out on a flight over Erythro, for instance. She'll see lakes and plains, hills, canyons. We might even go as far as the edge of the sea. It all has a stark beauty—I saw it once —but it is barren. There is no life anywhere that she can see—only the prokaryotes in the water, which are invisible, of course. It's possible that the uniform barrenness may repel her and she may lose interest in the outside altogether.

"If, however, she is still keen on going out, on feeling the soil of Erythro under her feet, we will see to it that she wears an E-suit."

"What is an E-suit?"

"An Erythro-suit. It's a straightforward affair—like a spacesuit, except that it doesn't have to hold in air pressure against a vacuum. It's an impermeable combination of plastic and textile that's very light and doesn't impede motion. The helmet with its infrared shielding is somewhat more substantial and there is an artificial air supply and ventilation. What it amounts to is that the person in an E-suit is not subjected to the Erythro environment. And on top of that, there'll be someone with her."

"Who? I would trust no one with her but myself."

Genarr smiled. "I couldn't imagine a less suitable companion. You know nothing about Erythro, really, and you're frightened of it. I wouldn't dare let you out there. Look, the only person we can trust is not you, but me."

"You?" Insigna stared at him, open-mouthed.

"Why not? No one here knows Erythro better than I do, and if Marlene is immune to the Plague, so am I. In ten years on Erythro, I haven't been affected in the slightest. What's more, I can fly an aircraft, which means we won't need a pilot. And then, too, if I go out with Marlene, I can watch her closely. If she does anything abnormal,

187

no matter how slightly, I'll have her back in the Dome and under the brain scan faster than light."

"By which time, of course, it will be too late."

"No. Not necessarily. You mustn't look upon the Plague as an all-or-nothing matter. There have been light cases, even very light cases, and people who are lightly affected can live reasonably normal lives. Nothing will happen to her. I'm sure of it."

Insigna sat in her chair, silent, seeming somehow small and defenseless.

Genarr impulsively placed his arm around her. "Come, Eugenia, forget this for a week. I promise she'll not go out for at least a week—longer than that if I can weaken her resolve by showing her Erythro from the air. And during the flight she will be enclosed in the aircraft and will be as safe there as she is here. As for right now, I'll tell you what—you're an astronomer, aren't you?"

She looked at him and said, wanly, "You know I am."

"Then that means that you never look at the stars. Astronomers never do. They only look at their instruments. It's night over the Dome now, so let's go up to the observation deck and observe. The night is absolutely clear, and there is nothing like just looking at the stars to make one feel quiet and at peace. Trust me."

47.

It was true. Astronomers did not look at the stars. There was no need. One gave instructions to the telescopes, the cameras, and the spectroscope by way of the computer, which received instructions in the way of programming.

The instruments did the work, the analyses, the graphic simulations. The astronomer merely asked the questions, then studied the answers. For that, one didn't have to look at the stars.

But then, she thought, how does one look at stars idly? Can one when one is an astronomer? The mere sight should make one uneasy. There was work to be done, questions to be asked, mysteries to be solved, and, after a while, surely one would return to one's workshop and set some instruments in motion while one distracted one's mind by reading a novel or watching a holovision spectacle.

She muttered this to Siever Genarr, as he went about his office, checking loose ends before leaving. (He was a confirmed loose-end checker, Insigna remembered from the ancient days when they were all young. It had irritated her then, but perhaps she ought to have admired it. Siever had so many virtues, she thought, and Crile, on the other hand—)

She dragged at her thoughts mercilessly and pointed them another way.

Genarr was saying, "Actually, I don't use the observation deck myself very often. There always seems to be something else to do. And when I do go, I almost always find myself alone up there. It will be pleasant to have company. Come!"

He led the way to a small elevator. It was the first time Insigna had been in an elevator in the Dome, and, for a fleeting moment, it was as though she were back on Rotor—except that she felt no change in pseudo-gravitation pull and did not feel herself pressed gently against one of the walls through a Coriolis effect, as she would have been on Rotor.

"Here we are," said Genarr, and motioned to Insigna to step out. She did so, curiously, into the empty chamber, and, almost at once, shrank back. She said, "Are we exposed?"

"Exposed?" Genarr asked, bewildered. "Oh, you mean, are we open to Erythro's atmosphere? No no. Have no fears about that. We are enclosed in a hemisphere of diamond-coated glass which nothing scratches. A meteorite would smash it, of course, but the skies of Erythro are virtually meteor-free. We have such glass on Rotor, you know, but"—and his voice took on a tone of pride—"not quite this quality, and not quite this size."

"They treat you well down here," said Insigna, reaching out gently to touch the glass again and assure herself of its existence.

"They must, to get people to come here." Then, reverting to the bubble, "It rains, of course, on occasion, but it's cloudy then anyway. And once the skies clear, it dries up quickly. A residue is left behind, and during the day, a special detergent mixture cleans the bubble. Sit down, Eugenia."

Insigna sat in a chair that was soft and comfortable and that reclined almost of its own accord, so that she found herself looking upward. She could hear another chair sigh softly as Genarr's weight pushed it backward. And then, the small night-lights, which had cast a glow sufficient to point out the presence and location of chairs and small tables in the room, went out. In the darkness of an uninhabited world, the sky, cloudless, and as dark as black velvet, burned with sparks.

Insigna gasped. She knew what the sky was like in theory. She had seen it on charts and maps, in simulations and photographs—in every shape and way except reality. She found herself *not* picking out the interesting objects, the puzzling items, the mysteries that demanded she get to work. She didn't look at any one object, but at the patterns they made.

In dim prehistory, she thought, it was the study of the patterns, and not of the stars themselves, that gave the ancients the constellations and the beginning of astronomy.

Genarr was right. Peace, like a fine, unfelt cobweb, settled down over her.

After a while, she said, almost sleepily, "Thank you, Genarr."

"For what?"

"For offering to go out with Marlene. For risking your mind for my daughter."

"I'm not risking my mind. Nothing will happen to either of us. Besides, I have a—a fatherly feeling toward her. After all, Eugenia, we go a long way back together, you and I, and I think—have always thought—highly of you."

"I know," said Insigna, feeling the stirrings of guilt. She had always known how Genarr had felt—he could never obscure it. It had inspired her with resignation before she met Crile, and with annoyance afterward.

She said, "If I've ever hurt your feelings, Siever, I am truly sorry."

"No need," said Genarr softly, and there was a long silence while peace deepened, and Insigna found herself earnestly hoping that no one would enter and break the strange spell of serenity that held her fast.

And then Genarr said, "I have a theory as to why people don't come up to the observation deck here. Or on Rotor. Did you ever notice that the observation deck isn't used much on Rotor either?"

"Marlene liked to go there on occasion," said Insigna. "She told me she was usually alone up there. In the last year or so, she would tell me that she liked to watch Erythro. I should have listened more closely—paid attention—"

"Marlene is unusual. I think what gets most people and keeps them from coming up here is that."

"What?" asked Insigna.

"That," said Genarr. He was pointing to some spot in the sky, but in the darkness she could not see his arm. "That very bright star; the brightest in the sky."

"You mean the Sun—our Sun—the Sun of the Solar System."

"Yes, I do. It's an interloper. Except for that bright star, the sky would be just about the same as the one we see from Earth. Alpha Centauri is rather out of place and Sirius is shifted slightly, but we wouldn't notice that. Barring such things, the sky you see is what the Sumerians saw five thousand years ago. All except for the Sun."

"And you think the Sun keeps people away from the observation deck?"

"Yes, perhaps not consciously, but I think the sight of it makes them uneasy. The tendency is to think of the Sun as far, far away, unreachable, part of an altogether different Universe. Yet there it is in the sky, bright, demanding our attention, stirring up our guilt for having run away from it."

"But then why don't the teenagers and children go to the observation deck? They know little or nothing of the Sun and the Solar System."

"The rest of us set a negative example. When we're all gone, when there's no one on Rotor to whom the Solar System is anything but a phrase, I think the sky will seem to belong to Rotor again, and this place will be crowded—if it still exists."

"Do you think it won't still exist?"

"We can't foresee the future, Eugenia."

"We seem to be flourishing and growing so far."

"Yes, we are, but it's that bright star—the interloper—that I'm worried about."

"Our old Sun. What can it do? It can't reach us."

"Sure it can." Genarr was staring at the bright star in the western sky. "The people we've left behind on Earth and on the Settlements are bound to discover Nemesis eventually. Maybe they already have. And maybe they've worked out hyper-assistance. I'm of the opinion they must have developed hyper-assistance soon after we left. Our disappearance must have stimulated them greatly."

"We left fourteen years ago. Why aren't they already here?"

"Perhaps they quail at the thought of a two-year flight. They know that Rotor attempted it, but they don't know that we succeeded at it. They may think that our wreckage is strewn through space all the way from the Sun to Nemesis."

"*We* didn't lack the courage to attempt it."

"Sure we did. Do you think that Rotor would have made the attempt if we hadn't had Pitt? It was *Pitt* who drove the rest of us, and I doubt that there's another Pitt anywhere in the Settlements, or on Earth for that matter. You know I don't like Pitt. I disapprove of his methods, of his morals, or the lack of them, of his deviousness, of his cold-blooded ability to send a girl like Marlene to what he clearly hopes will be her destruction, and yet if we go by results, he may go down in history as a great man."

"As a great leader," said Insigna. "*You* are a great man, Siever. There's a clear difference."

There was silence again, till Genarr said softly, "I keep waiting for them to come here after us. That's my biggest fear, and it seems to strengthen when the interloper shines down upon me. It's fourteen years now since we left the Solar System. What have they been doing in these fourteen years? Have you ever wondered about that, Eugenia?"

"Never," said Insigna, half-asleep. "My worries are more immediate."

# TWENTY-TWO

# ASTEROID

## 48

August 22, 2235! It meant something to Crile Fisher, for it was Tessa Wendel's birthday. To be precise, it was her fifty-third birthday. She made no reference to the day, or to its significance—perhaps because she had been so proud of her youthful appearance on Adelia, or perhaps because she was overconscious of Fisher's five years' advantage.

But their relative age difference didn't matter to Crile.

Even if Fisher had not been attracted to her intelligence and to her sexual vigor, Tessa held the key to Rotor and he knew it.

There were fine wrinkles around her eyes now, and a distinct flabbiness to her upper arms, but her unmentioned birthday was one of triumph for her, and she came swinging into the apartment, which had grown steadily more lavish with the years, and threw herself into her sturdy field-bottomed armchair with a smile of satisfaction on her face.

"It went as smoothly as interstellar space. Absolute perfection."

"I wish I had been there," said Crile.

"I wish you had, too, Crile, but we're on a strictly need-to-know basis, and I get you involved in more things than I should, as it is."

The goal had been Hypermnestra, an otherwise undistinguished asteroid that was in a convenient position, not too close to other asteroids at the moment, and, what was more important, not too close to Jupiter. It was also unclaimed by any Settlement, and unvisited by any. And, to top it off, there were the first two syllables of the name, which, however trivial, seemed to represent a proper target for a superluminal flight through hyperspace.

"I take it you got the ship there safely."

"Within ten thousand kilometers. We could easily have placed it closer, but we didn't want to risk an intensification of its gravitational field, feeble though it was. And back, of course, to the prearranged spot. It's being shepherded in by two ordinary vessels."

"I suppose the Settlements were on the lookout."

"Of course, but it's one thing to see that the ship vanishes instantaneously, and quite another to tell where it went; whether it went at or near light speed, or many multiples of it; and, most of all, how it was done. So what they do see means nothing."

"They had nothing in the neighborhood of Hypermnestra, did they?"

"They had no way of knowing what the destination was, barring a breakdown of security, and that *apparently* didn't happen. If they had known, or guessed, that alone still would not have helped them. All in all, Crile, very satisfactory."

"Obviously a giant step."

"With additional giant steps still facing us. It was the first ship, capable of carrying a human being, to attain superluminal velocity, but, as you know, it was staffed—if that's the word—by one robot."

"Did the robot operate successfully?"

"Completely, but that's not very significant, except that it shows we can transfer a fairly large mass there and back in one piece—at least in one piece on the macro-scale. It will take several weeks of inspection to make sure that no dangerous damage was done on the micro-scale. And, of course, that still leaves us the task of building larger ships, of making sure that life-support systems are incorporated and functioning well, and of multiplying safety provisions. A robot can take stresses that human beings cannot."

"And is the schedule holding up?"

"So far. So far. Another year or year and a half—if there are no disasters or unexpected accidents—and we ought to be able to surprise the Rotorians, assuming them to exist."

Fisher winced, and Wendel said, looking hangdog, "I'm sorry. I keep promising myself not to say things like that, but it does slip out once in a while."

"Never mind," said Fisher. "Is it definitely settled that I'll be going on the first trip to Rotor?"

"If anything can be definitely settled for something that won't take place for a year or more. There's no way of guarding against sudden shifts of needs."

"But so far?"

"Apparently, Tanayama had left behind a note to the effect that you were promised a berth—more decent of him than I would have expected. Koropatsky was kind enough to tell me about the note today, after the successful flight, when it seemed to me that it might be a good time to advance the possibility."

"Good! Tanayama promised it to me by word of mouth once. I am glad he put it on the record."

"Do you mind telling me why he made that promise? Tanayama always struck me as someone who gave nothing for nothing."

"You're right. I got the trip on condition that I brought you back to Earth to work on superluminal velocities. I think you'll recall I carried out that task triumphantly."

Wendel snorted. "I doubt that it was that alone that shook and moved your government. Koropatsky said that he would not consider himself bound by Tanayama's promises, ordinarily, but that you had lived on Rotor for some years and that your special knowledge might come in handy. My own feeling is that your special knowledge, after thirteen years, might have dimmed, but I didn't say that, because I was feeling good after the trial, and decided that, for the moment, I loved you."

Fisher smiled. "I feel relieved, Tessa. I hope you'll be on the first flight, too. Did you get *that* straightened out?"

Wendel pulled her head back an inch or two as though to get Fisher into better focus. "That was a lot harder, my boy. They were perfectly willing to send you into danger, but as for me, they said that I couldn't be spared. 'Who could carry on the project if anything happens to you?' they said. So I said: 'Only any one of about twenty of my subordinates who are as well up on superluminal flight as I am,

195

and whose minds are younger and nimbler.' A lie, of course, since there's no one quite like me, but it impressed them."

"There's something to what they say, you know. Should you take the risk?"

"Yes," said Wendel. "For one thing I want the credit of being captain of the first superluminal flight. For another I am curious to see another star, and resent that these Rotorians got there first, if—" She caught herself and said, "And finally, and most important, I believe, I want to get off Earth." She said that with a virtual snarl.

Afterward, as they lay in bed together, she said, "And when the time comes, and we finally get there, what a marvelous feeling it will be!"

Fisher did not answer. He was thinking of a child with strange large eyes, and of his sister, and the two seemed to fuse as drowsiness closed down over him.

# TWENTY-THREE

# AIRFLIGHT

49.

Long-distance travel through a planetary atmosphere was not something that Settlers accepted as part of their society. On a Settlement, distances were small enough so that elevators, legs, and an occasional electric cart were all that was necessary. As for inter-Settlement travel, that was by rocket.

Many Settlers—at least, back in the Solar System—had been in space so many times that progress through it was almost as common to them as walking. It was a rare Settler, however, who had traveled to Earth, where alone atmospheric travel existed, and which had made use of airflight.

Settlers who could face the vacuum as though it were a friend and brother felt unfathomable terror if expected to sense, somehow, the whistle of air past a vehicle without ground-support below.

Yet air travel, on occasion, was an obvious necessity on Erythro. Like Earth it was a large world, and like Earth it had a fairly dense

NEMESIS

(and breathable) atmosphere. There were reference books on airflight available on Rotor, and even several Earth immigrants with aeronautical experience.

So the Dome owned two small aircraft, somewhat clumsy, somewhat primitive, ungiven to large bursts of speed, or to headlong maneuverability—but serviceable.

In fact, Rotor's very ignorance of aeronautical engineering helped in one respect. The Dome's aircraft were far more computerized than any corresponding vessel on Earth. In fact, Siever Genarr liked to think of the vessels as intricate robots that happened to be built in the shape of aircraft. Erythro's weather was much milder than Earth's could possibly be, since the low intensity of the radiation from Nemesis was insufficient to power large and violent storms, so that an aircraft-robot was less likely to have to face an emergency. Far less likely.

As a result, virtually anyone could fly the raw and unpolished aircraft of the Dome. You simply told the plane what you wanted it to do and it was done. If the message was unclear, or seemed dangerous to the robotic brain of the vessel, it asked for clarification.

Genarr watched Marlene climb into the cabin of the plane with a certain natural concern, if not with the lip-biting terror of Eugenia Insigna, who stood well away from the scene. ("Don't come any closer," he had ordered Insigna sternly, "especially if you're going to look as though you were witnessing the sure beginning of calamity. You'll panic the girl.")

It seemed to Insigna that there were grounds for panic. Marlene was too young to remember a world where airflight was common. She had taken a rocket calmly enough to come to Erythro, but how would she react to this unheard of flight through air?

And yet Marlene climbed into the cabin and took her seat with a look of utter calm on her face.

Was it possible she did not grasp the situation? Genarr said, "Marlene, dear, you do know what we're going to be doing, don't you?"

"Yes, Uncle Siever. You're going to show me Erythro."

"From the air, you know. You'll be flying through the air."

"Yes. You said so before."

"Does the thought of it bother you?"

"No, Uncle Siever, but it's bothering you a lot."

"Only on your behalf, dear."

"I'll be perfectly all right." She turned her calm face toward him as

198

he climbed in after her and took his seat. She said, "I can understand Mother being concerned, but you're more concerned than she is. You're managing to show it less in any big way, but if you could see yourself licking your lips, you would be embarrassed. You feel that if something bad happens, it will be your fault, and you just can't stand the thought. Just the same, nothing's going to happen."

"Are you sure of that, Marlene?"

"Absolutely sure. Nothing will harm me on Erythro."

"You said that about the Plague, but we're not talking about that now."

"It doesn't matter what we're talking about. *Nothing* will harm me on Erythro."

Genarr shook his head slightly in disbelief and uncertainty, and then wished he hadn't, for he knew she read that as easily as though it were appearing in the largest block letters on the computer screen. But what was the difference? If he had repressed it all and had acted as if he were made of cast bronze, she would still have seen it.

He said, "We'll go into an airlock and stay there just a while, so that I can check the responsiveness of the vessel's brain. Then we will go through another door and the plane will then move up in the air. There'll be an acceleration effect, and you'll be pressed backward, and we'll be moving in the air, with nothing beneath us. You understand that, I hope?"

"I am not afraid," said Marlene quietly.

### 50.

The aircraft remained on its steady course across a barren landscape of rolling hills.

Genarr knew that Erythro was geologically alive and knew also that what geological studies had been made of the world indicated that there had been periods in its history when it had been mountainous. And there were still mountains here and there on the cis-Megan hemisphere, the hemisphere in which the bloated circle of the planet Megas, around which Erythro orbited, hung almost motionless in the sky.

Here on the trans-Megan side, however, plains and hills were the chief feature of the two large continents.

To Marlene, who had never seen a mountain in her life, even the low hills were exciting.

There were rivulets on Rotor, of course, and from the height at which they were viewing Erythro, these rivers looked no different.

Genarr thought: Marlene will be surprised when she sees them at a closer view.

Marlene look curiously at Nemesis, which had passed its noon-mark and had declined toward the west. She said, "It's not moving, is it, Uncle Siever?"

"It's moving," said Genarr. "Or, at least Erythro is turning relative to Nemesis, but it turns only once a day, while Rotor turns once every two minutes. In comparison, Nemesis, as seen from here on Erythro, is moving less than 1/700th as fast as it seems to be moving as seen from Rotor. It seems to be standing still here, by comparison, but it isn't standing entirely still."

Then, casting a quick glance at Nemesis, he said, "You've never seen Earth's Sun, the Sun of the Solar System, you know; or, if you have, you don't remember it, having been a baby at the time. The Sun was much smaller as seen from Rotor's position in the Solar System."

"Smaller?" said Marlene in surprise. "The computer told me that it was Nemesis that was smaller."

"In reality, yes. Still, Rotor is so much closer to Nemesis than it ever was to the Sun in the old days that Nemesis *seems* larger."

"We're four million kilometers from Nemesis, aren't we?"

"But we were a hundred fifty million kilometers from the Sun. If we were that far from Nemesis, we'd get less than 1 percent of the light and warmth we get now. If we were as close to the Sun as we are to Nemesis, we'd be vaporized. The Sun is much larger, brighter, and hotter than Nemesis."

Marlene wasn't looking at Genarr, but apparently his tone of voice was sufficient. "From the way you talk, Uncle Siever, I think you wish you were back near the Sun."

"I was born there, so I get homesick sometimes."

"But the Sun is so hot and bright. It must be dangerous."

"We didn't look at it. And you shouldn't look at Nemesis too long either. Look away, dear."

Genarr cast another quick glance at Nemesis, however. It hung in the western sky, red and vast, its apparent diameter at four degrees of arc, or eight times that of the Sun as seen from Rotor's old position. It was a quiet red circle of light, but Genarr knew that, on comparatively rare occasions, it would flare and, for a few minutes, there would be a white spot on that serene face that would be painful to look at. Mild sunspots, in darker red, were more common, but not as noticeable.

He murmured an order to the plane, which veered sufficiently to put Nemesis farther to the rear, out of direct view.

Marlene took a last, thoughtful glance at Nemsis, then turned her eyes to Erythro's vista stretched out below.

She said, "You get used to the pink color of everything. It doesn't look so pink after a while."

Genarr had noticed that himself. His eyes caught differences in tint and shade so that the world began to seem less monochromatic. The rivers and small lakes were ruddier and darker than the land surface, and the sky was dark. Little of the red light of Nemesis was scattered by Erythro's atmosphere.

The most hopeless thing about Erythro, however, was the barrenness of the land. Rotor, even on its tiny scale, had green fields, yellow grain, varicolored fruit, noise making animals, all the color and sound of human habitation and structures.

Here there was only silence and inanimation.

Marlene frowned. "There is life on Erythro, Uncle Siever."

Genarr couldn't tell whether Marlene was making a statement, asking a question, or answering his thought as revealed by his body language. Was she insisting on something or seeking reassurance?

He said, "Certainly. Lots of life. It's all-pervasive. It's not only in the water either. There are prokaryotes living in the water films about the soil particles, too."

After a while, the ocean made its appearance on the horizon ahead, first as simply a dark line, then a thickening band as the air vehicle approached it.

Genarr cast careful sidelong glances at Marlene, watching her reaction. She had read about Earth's oceans, of course, and must have seen images on holovision, but nothing can prepare anyone for the actual experience. Genarr, who had been on Earth once (once!) as a tourist, had seen the edge of an ocean. He had never been over one, out of sight of land, however, and he wasn't sure of his own reactions.

It rolled back below them and now the dry land shrank behind into a lighter line and, eventually, it was gone. Genarr looked down with a queer feeling in the pit of his stomach. He remembered a phrase from an archaic epic: "the wine-dark sea." Below them the ocean certainly did look like a vast rolling mass of red wine, with pink froth here and there.

There were no markings to identify in that vast body of water, and there was no place to land. The very essence of "location" was gone. Yet he knew that when he wanted to return, he need do no more than direct the plane to take them back to land. The plane's computer kept track of position in accurate reckoning of speed and direction and would know where land was—even where the Dome was.

They passed under a thick cloud deck and the ocean turned black. A word from Genarr, and the plane lifted through and above the clouds. Nemesis shone again, and the ocean could no longer be seen beneath them. There was, instead, a sea of pink water droplets, billowing and rising here and there, so that bits of fog moved, occasionally, past the window.

Then the clouds seemed to part and between their edges, glimpses of the wine-dark sea could again be seen.

Marlene watched, her mouth partly open, her breath shallow. She said in a whisper, "That's all water, isn't it, Uncle Siever?"

"Thousands of kilometers in every direction, Marlene—and ten kilometers deep in spots."

"If you fall into it, I suppose you drown."

"You needn't worry about that. This vehicle won't fall into the ocean."

"I know it won't," said Marlene matter-of-factly.

There was another sight, Genarr thought, to which Marlene could well be introduced.

Marlene broke in on his thought. "You're getting nervous again, Uncle Siever."

Genarr felt amused at the manner in which he was learning to take Marlene's penetration for granted. He said, "You've never seen Megas, and I was wondering if I ought to show it to you. You see, only one side of Erythro faces Megas, and the Dome was built on the side of Erythro that doesn't face it, so that Megas is never in our sky. If we continue to fly in this direction, however, we'll enter the cis-Megas hemisphere and we'll see it rise above the horizon."

"I would like to see that."

"You will, then, but be prepared. It's large. Really large. Nearly twice as wide as Nemesis and it looks almost like it's about to fall on us. Some people simply can't endure the sight. It won't fall, though. It can't. Try to remember that."

They moved along at a higher altitude and a heightened speed. The ocean lay below in wrinkled sameness, occasionally obscured by clouds.

Eventually, Genarr said, "If you'll look ahead and a little to the right, you'll see Megas beginning to show at the horizon. We'll turn toward it."

It looked like a small patch of light along the horizon at first, but grew like a slow upward swell. Then the widening arc of a deep red circle lifted itself above the horizon. It was distinctly deeper than Nemesis, which could still be seen to the right and in back of the plane, and somewhat lower in the sky.

As Megas loomed larger, it soon became apparent that what was being revealed was not a full circle of light, a bit more than a semicircle.

Marlene said with interest, "Now *that's* what they mean by 'phases,' isn't that right?"

"Exactly right. We only see the part that's lit by Nemesis. As Erythro goes around Megas, Nemesis seem to move closer to Megas and we see less and less of the lit half of the planet. Then when Nemesis skims just above or below Megas, we just see a thin curve of light at Megas' boundary; that's all we see of its lighted hemisphere. Sometimes Nemesis actually moves behind Megas. Nemesis is then eclipsed, and all the dim stars of night come out, not just the bright ones that show even when Nemesis is in the sky. During the eclipse, you can see a large circle of darkness with no stars in it at all, and that show you where Megas is. When Nemesis reappears on the other side, you began to see a thin curve of light again."

"How marvelous," said Marlene. "It's like a show in the sky. And look at Megas—all those moving stripes."

They stretched across the lighted portion of the globe, thick and reddish brown, interspersed with orange, and slowly writhing.

"They're storm bands," said Genarr, "with terrific winds that blow this way and that. If you watch closely, you'll see spots form and expand, drift along, then spread out and vanish."

"It *is* like a holovision show," said Marlene raptly. "Why don't people watch it all the time?"

"Astronomers do. They watch it through computerized instruments located on this hemisphere. I've seen it myself in our Observatory. You know, we had a planet like this back in the Solar System. It's called Jupiter, and it's even larger than Megas."

By now, the planet had lifted entirely above the horizon, looking like a bloated balloon that had, somehow, partially collapsed along its left half.

Marlene said, "It's lovely. If the Dome were built on this side of Erythro, *everyone* could watch it."

"Actually not, Marlene. It doesn't seem to work that way. Most people don't like Megas. I told you that some people get the impression that Megas is falling and it frightens them."

Marlene said impatiently, "Only a few people would have such a silly notion."

"Only a few to begin with, but silly notions can be contagious. Fears spread, and some people who wouldn't be afraid if left to themselves, become afraid because their neighbor is. Haven't you ever noticed that sort of thing?"

"Yes, I have," she said with a touch of bitterness. "If one boy thinks a bimbo is pretty, they all do. They start competing—" She paused, as if in embarrassment.

"The contagious fear is one reason we built the Dome on the other hemisphere. Another is that with Megas always in the sky, astronomic observations are more difficult to make in *this* hemisphere. But I think it's time we begin our return. You know your mother. She'll be in a panic."

"Call her and tell her we're all right."

"I don't have to. This ship is sending out signals continuously. She knows we're all right—physically. But that's not what she's worried about," he said, tapping his temple significantly.

Marlene slumped in her chair and a look of deep discontent crossed her face. "What a pain. I know everyone will say, 'It's just because she *loves* you,' but it's such a bother. Why can't she just take my word for it that I'll be all right?"

"Because she *loves* you," said Genarr, as he quietly instructed the aircraft to return home, "just as you love Erythro."

Marlene's face brightened at once. "Oh, I do."

"Yes yes. It's quite visible in your every reaction to the world."

And Genarr wondered how Eugenia Insigna would react to *that*.

### 51.

She reacted in fury. "What do you mean, she loves Erythro? How can she love a dead world? Is it possible you brainwashed her? Is there some reason you've talked her into loving it?"

"Eugenia, be reasonable. Do you really believe it is possible to brainwash Marlene into anything? Have you ever succeeded in doing so?"

"Then what happened?"

"Actually, I tried to subject her to situations that would displease or frighten her. If anything, I tried to 'brainwash' her into *disliking* Erythro. I know from experience that Rotorians, brought up in the tight little world of a Settlement, hate the endlessness of Erythro; they don't like the redness of the light; they don't like that enormous puddle of an ocean; they don't like darkening clouds; they don't like Nemesis; and, most of all, they don't like Megas. All these things tend to depress and frighten them. And I showed all these things to Marlene. I took her out over the ocean and then, far enough out to show her Megas entirely above the horizon."

"And?"

"And nothing bothered her. She said she got used to the red light, and it stopped looking so terribly red. The ocean didn't in the least frighten her, and, most of all, she found Megas interesting and amusing."

"I can't believe it."

"You must. It's true."

Insigna sank into thought, then said reluctantly, "Maybe it's a sign that she's already infected with the—the—"

"With the Plague. I arranged for another brain scan as soon as we got back. We still haven't got the complete analysis, but the preliminary inspection shows no change. The mind pattern changes markedly and noticeably even in a light case of the Plague. Marlene simply doesn't have it. However, an interesting thought just occurred to me. We know that Marlene is perceptive, that she can note all sorts of little things. Feelings flow from others to her. But have you ever detected anything that might seem the reverse? Do feelings flow from her to others?"

"I don't understand what you're getting at."

"She knows when I'm uncertain and a little anxious, no matter how I try to hide the fact, or that I'm calm and unafraid. Is there any way, though, that she can force me or encourage me to become uncertain and a little anxious—or calm and unafraid? If she detects, can she also impose?"

Insigna stared at him. "I think that's crazy!" she said, her voice choked in disbelief.

"Perhaps. But have you ever noticed that sort of effect with Marlene? Think about it."

"I don't have to think. I've never noticed any such thing."

"No," muttered Genarr, "I suppose you haven't. She would certainly love to make you feel less nervous about herself, and she certainly fails to bring that about. However— It is true, though, if we just cling to Marlene's perceptive ability, that it has strengthened since she has arrived on Erythro. Agreed?"

"Yes. Agreed."

"But it's more than that. She's now strongly intuitive. She *knows* that she is immune to the Plague. She is *certain* that nothing on Erythro will harm her. She stared down at the ocean in convinced knowledge that the aircraft wouldn't drop into it and drown her. Has she had this kind of attitude back on Rotor? Hasn't she felt uncertain and insecure on Rotor when there was reason to feel so, just as any other youngster might?"

"Yes! Certainly."

"But here she's a new girl. Totally sure of herself. Why?"

"I don't know why."

"Is Erythro affecting her? No no, I mean nothing like the Plague. Is there some other effect? Something completely different? I'll tell you why I ask. I felt it myself."

"Felt what yourself?"

"A certain optimism about Erythro. I didn't mind the desolation, or anything else. It's not that I was desperately put off by it before, that Erythro made me seriously uneasy, but I never *liked* the planet. On this trip with Marlene, however, I came nearer to liking it than ever before in my ten years of residence here. It was possible, I thought, that Marlene's delight was contagious, or that she might somehow be forcing it on me. Or else whatever it is about Erythro that is affecting her may be affecting me, too—in her presence."

Insigna said sarcastically, "I think, Siever, that you had better have a brain scan yourself."

Genarr raised his eyebrows. "Do you think I haven't? I've undergone a check periodically ever since I've been here. There've been no changes except those inseparable from the aging process."

"But have you checked your mind pattern since getting back from the plane trip?"

"Of course. First thing. I'm no fool. The complete analysis isn't back yet, but the preliminary work shows no change."

"Then what are you going to do next?"

"The logical thing. Marlene and I are going out of the Dome, and out upon Erythro's surface."

"No!"

"We'll take precautions. I've been out there before."

"You, perhaps," said Insigna stubbornly. "Not she. Never she."

Genarr sighed. He whirled in his chair, looking at the false window in the wall of his office as though he were trying to penetrate it and look out upon the redness beyond. Then he looked back at Insigna.

"Out there is a huge brand-new world," he said, "one that belongs to no one and nothing except ourselves. We can take that world and develop it with all the lessons we've learned from our foolish misman-agement of our original world. We can build a good world this time, a clean world, a decent world. We can get used to the redness. We can bring it to life with our own plants and animals. We can make sea and land flourish and start the planet on its own course of evolution."

"And the Plague? What of that?"

"We might eliminate the Plague, and make Erythro ideal for us."

"If we eliminate the heat and the gravity, and alter the chemical composition, we can make Megas ideal for us, too."

"Yes, Eugenia, but you must admit that the Plague is in a different category from heat, gravity, and global chemistry."

"But the Plague is just as deadly in its own way."

"Eugenia, I think I've told you that Marlene is the most important person we have."

"She certainly is to me."

"To you, she's important simply because she is your daughter. To the rest of us, she is important for what she can do."

"What can she do? Interpret our body language? Play tricks?"

"She is convinced she is immune to the Plague. If she is, that might teach us—"

"*If* she is. It's childish fantasy and you know it. Don't grasp at cobwebs."

"There's a world out there, and I want it."

"You sound like Pitt after all. For that world, will you risk my daughter?"

"In human history, much more has been risked for much less."

"More shame to human history. And in any case, it's up to me to decide. She's my daughter."

And Genarr said in a low voice that seemed to contain infinite sorrow, "I love you, Eugenia, but I lost you once. I have had this feeble dream of perhaps trying to undo that loss. But now I'm afraid I must lose you again, and permanently. Because, you see, I'm going to tell you that it's not up to you to decide. It is not even up to me to decide. It is up to Marlene. Whatever she decides, she will do, somehow. And because she may well have the ability to win humanity a world, I am going to help her do what she wants to do, despite *you*. Please, you must accept that, Eugenia."

# TWENTY-FOUR

## DETECTOR

52.

Crile Fisher studied the *Superluminal* with a frozen expression. It was the first time he had seen it, and a quick glance at Tessa Wendel made it quite plain that she was smiling with what he could only think of as proprietary pride.

It sat there in a huge cavern, inside a triple web of security barriers. There were human beings present, but most of the work force consisted of carefully computerized (nonhumanoid) robots.

Fisher had seen many spaceships in his time, and of a multiplicity of models used for a multiplicity of purposes, but he had never seen one like the *Superluminal*—never seen one as repulsive in appearance.

Had he seen it without knowing what it was, he might not have guessed, even, that it was a spaceship. What did he say then? On the one hand, he did not want to anger Wendel. On the other hand, she was clearly waiting for his opinion, and she just as clearly expected praise.

And so he said in a somewhat subdued voice, "It has an eerie kind of grace—rather wasplike."

She had smiled at the phrase "eerie kind of grace," and Fisher felt he had chosen well. But then she said, "What do you mean 'wasplike,' Crile?"

"It's an insect I'm referring to," said Crile. "I know you're not aware of insects much on Adelia."

"We know about insects," said Wendel. "We may not have Earth's chaotic profusion—"

"You probably don't have wasps. Stinging insects, shaped rather like—" He pointed to the *Superluminal.* "They, too, have a large bulge in front, another bulge in back, and a narrow connecting unit."

"Really?" She looked at the *Superluminal* with a sudden sparking of new interest. "Find me a picture of a wasp when you can. I might understand the ship design better in the light of the insect—or vice versa, for that matter."

Fisher said, "Why the shape, then, if it wasn't inspired by the wasp?"

"We had to find a geometry that would maximize the chance of the entire ship moving as a unit. The hyperfield has a tendency to extend outward cylindrically to infinity, actually, and you let it have its way, to some extent. On the other hand, you don't want to give in entirely. You can't, in fact, so you have to seal it off in the bulges. The field is just within the hull, maintained and enclosed by an intense and alternating electromagnetic field, and—you don't really want to hear all this, do you?"

"Not any more, I think," said Fisher, smiling slightly. "I've heard enough. But since I'm finally allowed to see this—"

"Now don't be hurt," said Wendel, putting her arm around his waist. "It was all strictly on a need-to-know basis. There were times when they hated having *me* around. They kept muttering, I imagine, about this suspicious Settler who was entirely too nosy, and wishing that I hadn't been the one who had designed the hyperfield, so they could kick me out. Now, however, things have lightened to the point where I could arrange to have you come and see it. You'll be on it eventually, after all, and I wanted you to admire it." She hesitated, then added, "And me."

He looked across at her and said, "You know that I admire you, Tessa, without any need for anything like this." And he put his arm around her shoulder.

"I'm continuing to get older, Crile," she said. "The process simply won't stop. And I'm also dismayingly satisfied with you. I've been with you seven years now, going on eight, and I haven't felt the old urge to see what other men might be like."

Fisher said, "Is that a tragedy? Perhaps it's just the fact that you've been so absorbed in the project. Now that the ship is completed, you'll probably have a feeling of release, and enough time to begin hunting again."

"No. I haven't the urge. I just haven't. But how about you? I know I neglect you at times."

"It's all right. When you neglect me for your work, that suits me. I want the ship as much as you do, dear, and one nightmare is that by the time it is finally ready, you and I will be too old to be allowed on." He smiled again, this time with distinct ruefulness. "In your awareness of oncoming age, Tessa, don't forget that I, too, am no longer a lad. In less than two years, I'll be fifty. But I have a question I'm reluctant to ask for fear of disappointment, but I'm going to, anyway."

"Ask away."

"You arranged to have me see the ship, to be allowed into this holy of holies. Somehow I don't think that Koropatsky would have allowed this if the project weren't near completion. He's almost as diseased on security as Tanayama was."

"Yes, as far as the hyperfield is concerned, the ship is ready."

"Has it flown?"

"Not yet. There are still things to do, but they don't involve the hyperfield itself."

"There have to be test flights, I suppose."

"With a crew aboard, of course. There's no way of doing it crewless and still feel that the life-support systems will work. Even animals won't give us the necessary assurance."

"Who will go on the first trip?"

"Volunteers chosen from among those on the project who qualify."

"How about you?"

"I'm the only one who won't be a volunteer. I *must* go. I could trust no one else to make decisions in an emergency."

"Then I go, too?" said Crile.

"No, not you."

Fisher's face instantly grew dark with anger. "The arrangement was—"

211

"Not on the test flights, Crile."

"When will they be over, then?"

"It's hard to say. It depends on what troubles may develop. If all goes as smoothly as possible, then two or three flights might suffice. A matter of months."

"When will the first test flight be?"

"That I don't know, Crile. We're still working on the ship."

"You said it was ready to go."

"Yes, as far as the hyperfield is concerned. But we're installing the neuronic detectors."

"What are those? I never heard you mention them."

Wendel did not answer directly. She looked around, quietly and thoughtfully, then said, "We're attracting attention, Crile, and I suspect that there are people here who feel nervous about your presence. Let's go home."

Fisher did not move. "I take it you refuse to discuss this with me. Even though it happens to be vital to me."

"We'll discuss it—at home."

### 53.

Crile Fisher was restless, his fury increasing. He refused to sit down and towered over Tessa Wendel, who had shrugged and taken a seat on the white modular couch and was now looking up at him, frowning.

"Why are you angry, Crile?"

Fisher's lips were trembling. He pressed them together and waited before answering, as though forcing himself to remain calm by sheer muscular effort.

He said finally, "Once a crew is made up without me, it will be a precedent. I won't *ever* get on. It must be understood from the beginning that I am on the ship every time until we reach the Neighbor Star—and Rotor. I don't want to be left out."

Wendel said, "Why do you jump at conclusions? You won't be omitted at the crucial time. The ship isn't even ready to go yet."

Fisher said, "You said the ship was ready. What are these neuronic detectors you're suddenly speaking of? It's a device to keep me quiet, to keep me distracted, and then sneak the ship away before I realize I'm left out. That's what they're doing. And you're playing along with it."

"Crile, you're mad. The neuronic detector is my idea, my insistence, my desire." She stared at him, unblinking, daring him to do something about it.

"Your idea!" he exploded. "But . . ."

She held out her hand as if to silence him. "It's something we've been working on concurrently with the ship. It's not something that falls within my expertise, but I have driven the neurophysicists onward rather mercilessly to have it. And the reason? Precisely because I want you on the ship when it leaves for the Neighbor Star. Don't you see?"

He shook his head.

"Figure it out, Crile. You would if you weren't blind with rage for no sane reason. It's perfectly straightforward. It's a 'neuronic detector.' It detects nerve activity at a distance. Complex nerve activity. In short, it detects the presence of intelligence."

Fisher stared at her. "You mean what doctors use in hospitals."

"Of course. It's a routine tool in medicine and in psychology to detect mental disorders early on—but at meter distances. I need it at *astronomical* distances. It's not something new. It's something old with a vastly increased range. Crile, if Marlene's alive, she'll be on the Settlement, on Rotor. Rotor will be there, somewhere, circling the star. I told you that it would not be easy to spot. If we don't find it quickly, can we be sure that it's not there—and not that we just somehow missed it, like missing an island in the ocean or an asteroid in space? Do we just continue searching for months, or years, to make sure that we haven't just missed it, that it's really not there?"

"And the neuronic detector—"

"Will find Rotor for us."

"Won't it be just as hard to detect—"

"No, it won't. The Universe is overrun with light and radio waves and all kinds of radiation, and we'll have to distinguish one source from a thousand others, or from a million others. It can be done, but it's not easy, and it may take time. However, to get the precise electromagnetic radiation associated with neurons in complex relationship is quite unique. We are not likely to have more than one source exactly like that—or if we do, it's because Rotor has built another Settlement. There you have it. I am as intent on finding your daughter for you as you are for finding her for yourself. And why would I do that if I weren't intent on having you on the flight with us? You'll be there."

Fisher looked overwhelmed. "And you forced the entire project to do this?"

"I have considerable power over them, Crile. And there's more to it as well. This is highly confidential; that's why I couldn't tell you at the ship."

"Oh? And what might that be?"

Wendel said, and there was a softness in her voice, "Crile, I spend more time thinking of you than you think. You don't know how strongly I want to spare you disappointment. What if we find nothing at the Neighbor Star? What if a sweep of the skies tells us definitely that there are no living intelligent life-forms anywhere in its vicinity? Do we go straight home and report that we found no sign of Rotor? Now, Crile, don't go into one of your moods. I'm not saying that failure to find intelligence at the Neighbor Star will necessarily imply that Rotor and its people have not survived."

"What else can it imply?"

"They might have been so dissatisfied with the Neighbor Star that they decided to move on elsewhere. Perhaps they stopped long enough to mine some asteroids for new materials they would need for construction and for refurbishing the micro-fusion motors. Then on they would go."

"And if that were so, how can we know where they would be?"

"They've been gone almost fourteen years. With hyper-assistance, they can travel only at the speed of light. If they have reached any star and settled in its neighborhood, it would have to be at a star within fourteen light-years distance of us. There are not very many of those. At superluminal velocity, we can visit each of those. With neuronic detectors, we can quickly decide whether Rotor is in the neighborhood of any of them."

"They might be wandering through space between stars at this very moment. How would we detect them then?"

"We wouldn't, but at least we increase our own chances just a bit if we investigate a dozen stars in six months with our neuronic detector, instead of spending that much time investigating one star in a futile search. And if we fail—and we have to face the fact that we might fail—then at least we will return with considerable data on a dozen different stars, a white dwarf, a blue-white hot star, a Solar look-alike, a close binary, and so on. We're not likely to make more than one trip in our lifetime, so why not make it a good one, and go down in history with a huge bang, eh, Crile?"

Crile said thoughtfully, "I suppose you're right, Tessa. To comb a dozen stars and find nothing will be bad enough, but to search a single star vicinity and return thinking that Rotor might have been somewhere else that was reachable but that we lacked the time to explore would be much worse."

"Exactly."

"I'll try to remember that," said Crile sadly.

"Another thing," said Wendel. "The neuronic detector might detect intelligence *not* of Earthly origin. We wouldn't want to miss it."

Fisher looked startled. "But that's not likely, is it?"

"Not at all likely, but if it happens, all the more reason not to miss it. Especially if it is within fourteen light-years of Earth. Nothing in the Universe can be as interesting as another intelligent life-form—or as dangerous. We'd want to know about it."

Fisher said, "What are the chances of detecting it at all if it is not of Earthly origin? The neuronic detectors are geared for human intelligence only. It seems to me that we wouldn't even recognize a really odd life-form as being alive, let alone as being intelligent."

Wendel said, "We may not be able to recognize life, but we can't possibly fail to recognize intelligence, in my view, and it's not life but intelligence that we're after. Whatever intelligence might be, however strange, however unrecognizable, it has to involve a complex structure, a very complex structure—at least as complex as the human brain. What's more, it's bound to involve the electromagnetic interaction. Gravitational attraction is too weak; the strong and weak nuclear interactions are too short-range. And as for this new hyperfield we're working with in superluminal flight, it doesn't exist in nature as far as any of us knows, but exists only when it is devised by intelligence.

"The neuronic detector can detect an elaborately complex electromagnetic field that will signify intelligence no matter the form or chemistry into which that intelligence may be molded. And we will be ready to either learn or run. As for unintelligent life, that is not at all likely to be dangerous to a technological civilization such as ourselves—though any form of alien life, even at the virus stage, would be interesting."

"And why must all this be kept secret?"

"Because I suspect—in fact, I *know*—that the Global Congress will want us back very quickly so that they can be sure the project is successful and so that they can learn to build better models of superluminal vessels based on our experience with this prototype. I, on the other hand, if things go well, would certainly want to see the Universe and let them wait. I don't say I'll definitely do it, but I want the option held open. If they knew I was planning that—even thinking it —I suspect they would try to crew the ship with others whom they would consider more amenable to orders."

Fisher smiled weakly.

Wendel said, "What's wrong, Crile? Suppose there's no sign of Rotor or its people. Would you then just want to go back to Earth in disappointment? The Universe at your fingertips, but given up?"

"No. I'm just wondering how long will it take to put in the detectors and all the other things you might dream up. In a little over two years, I'll be fifty. At fifty, agents working for the Office are routinely taken off field duty. They get desk jobs on Earth and are no longer allowed to take spaceflights."

"Well?"

"In a little over two years, I will no longer qualify for the flight. They'll tell me I'm too old, and the Universe won't be at my fingertips after all."

"Nonsense! They're going to let me go and I'm over fifty right now."

"You're a special case. It's your ship."

"You're a special case, too, since I will insist on you. Besides, they won't find it so easy to get qualified people to go on the *Superluminal.* It will be all we can do to persuade anyone to volunteer. And they'll have to volunteer; we can't risk placing the trip into the hands of unwilling and frightened draftees."

"Why wouldn't they volunteer?"

"Because they're Earthmen, my good Crile, and to almost all Earthmen, space is a horror. Hyperspace is a greater horror still and they're going to hang back. There is going to be you and me, and we're going to need three more volunteers and I tell you we'll have trouble getting them. I've sounded out many, and I have two good people with a halfway promise: Chao-Li Wu and Henry Jarlow. I haven't got my third yet. And even if, against all likelihood, there are as many as a dozen volunteers, they're not going to cut you out in favor of anyone else, for I will insist on your going with me as my ambassador to the Rotorians—if that becomes necessary. And if even that is not enough, I promise you that the ship will take off before you're fifty."

216

And now Fisher smiled with honest relief and said, "Tessa, I love you. You know, I really do."

"No," said Wendel, "I don't know that you really do, especially when you say it in that tone of voice, as though the admission has caught you by surprise. It's very odd, Crile, but in the almost eight years we've known each other, and lived together, and made love to each other, you've never once said that."

"Haven't I?"

"Believe me, I've listened. Do you know what else is odd? I've never said that I loved you, and yet, I love you. It didn't start that way. What do you suppose happened?"

Fisher said in a low voice, "It may be that we've fallen in love with each other so gradually that we never noticed. That may happen sometimes, don't you think?"

And they smiled at each other shyly, as though wondering what they ought to do about it.

# TWENTY-FIVE

## SURFACE

### 54.

Eugenia Insigna was apprehensive. More than that.

"I tell you, Siever, I haven't had a good night's sleep since you took her out in the aircraft." Her voice degenerated into what, in a woman of less firm character, might almost have been described as a whine. "Wasn't the flight through air—off to the ocean and back, and coming back after nightfall, too—wasn't that enough for her? Why don't you stop her?"

"Why don't *I* stop her?" said Siever Genarr slowly, as though he were tasting the question. "Why don't I stop *her?* Eugenia, we have gotten past the stage of being able to stop Marlene."

"That's ridiculous, Siever. It's almost cowardly. You're hiding behind her, pretending she's all-powerful."

"Isn't she? You're her mother. Order her to stay in the Dome."

Insigna's lips compressed. "She's fifteen. I don't like to be tyrannical."

"On the contrary. You would love to be tyrannical. But if you try, she'll look at you out of those clear extraordinary eyes of hers and say something like, 'Mother, you feel guilty of having deprived me of my father, so you feel that the Universe is conspiring to deprive you of me as punishment, and that's a silly superstition.'"

Insigna frowned. "Siever, that is the stupidest thing I've ever heard. I don't feel any such thing, and couldn't possibly."

"Of course you don't. I was just making something up. But Marlene won't be. She'll know, from the twitching of your thumb or the movement of your shoulder blade or *something*, just what is bothering you, and she'll tell you, and it will be so true, and so shameful, I suppose, that you will be too busy looking for ways to defend yourself, and you'll give in to her rather than have her keep peeling away the outer layers of your psyche."

"Don't tell me that's what's happened to you."

"Not much because she's fond of me, and I've tried to be very diplomatic with her. But if I cross her, I shudder to think what a shambles she'll make of me. Look, I've managed to delay her. Give me credit for that. She wanted to go out immediately after the plane trip. And I held her off to the end of the month."

"How did you do that?"

"Pure sophistry, I assure you. It's December. I told her that, in three weeks, the New Year would begin, at least if we go by Earth Standard time, and how best to celebrate the beginning of 2237, I asked her, than to begin the new era of the exploration and settlement of Erythro? You know, she views her own penetration of the planet in that light—as the beginning of a new age. Which makes it worse."

"Why worse?"

"Because she doesn't view it as a personal caprice, but as something of vital importance to Rotor, or even to humanity, perhaps. There's nothing like satisfying your personal pleasure and calling it a noble contribution to the general welfare. It excuses everything. I've done it myself, so have you, so has everyone. Pitt, more than anyone else whom I know, does it. He has probably convinced himself that he breathes only to contribute carbon dioxide to the plant life of Rotor."

"So, by playing on her megalomania, you had her wait."

"Yes, and it still gives us one more week to see if anything will stop her. I might say, though, that my plea didn't fool her. She agreed to wait, but she said, 'You think that if you delay me, you will win your way at least a little bit into the affections of my mother, don't you,

Uncle Siever? There's nothing about you that indicates you consider the coming of the new year of the slightest importance.' "

"How unbearably rude, Siever."

"Merely unbearably correct, Eugenia. Same thing, perhaps."

Insigna looked away. "My affections? What can I say—"

Genarr said quickly, "Why say anything? I've told you I loved you in the past, and I find that getting old—or getting older—hasn't much changed it. But that's *my* problem. You've never treated me unfairly. You never gave me reason to hope. And if I'm fool enough not to be able to take no for an answer, what concern is that of yours?"

"It concerns me that you're unhappy for any reason."

"That counts for a lot right there." Genarr managed a smile. "It's infinitely better than nothing."

Insigna looked away and, with obvious deliberation, returned to the topic of Marlene. "But, Siever, if Marlene saw your motivation, why did she agree to the delay?"

"You won't like this, but I'd better tell you the truth. Marlene said, 'I'll wait till the New Year, Uncle Siever, because perhaps that *will* please Mother, and I'm on your side.' "

"She said that?"

"Please don't hold it against her. I have obviously fascinated her with my wit and charm and she thinks she's doing you a favor."

"She's a matchmaker," said Insigna, obviously caught between annoyance and amusement.

"It *did* occur to me that if you could bring yourself to show an interest in me, we could use that to persuade her into all sorts of things that she would think would further encourage the interest— except that it would have to be real or she would see through it. And if it were real, she wouldn't feel it necessary to make sacrifices to bring about what was already so. Do you understand?"

"I understand," said Insigna, "that if it weren't for Marlene's perceptiveness, you would be positively Machiavellian in your approach to me."

"You've got me dead to rights, Eugenia."

"Well, why not do the obvious thing? Lock her up and, eventually, carry her onto the rocket back to Rotor."

"Bound hand and foot, I suppose. Aside from not thinking we could do such a thing, I've managed to catch Marlene's vision. I'm beginning to think of colonizing Erythro—a whole world for the taking."

"And breathing their alien bacteria, getting them into our food and water." Insigna's face curled into a grimace.

"What of it? We breathe, drink, and eat them—to an extent—right here. We can't keep them out of the Dome altogether. For that matter, there are bacteria on Rotor that we breathe, drink, and eat, too."

"Yes, but we're adapted to Rotor's life. These are *alien* bits of life."

"All the safer. If we're not adapted to them, neither are they to us. There are no signs they can possibly parasitize us. They would simply be so many innocuous dust particles."

"And the Plague."

"That's the real difficulty, of course, even in the case of something as simple as letting Marlene go outside the Dome. We will, of course, take precautions."

"What kind of precautions?"

"She would wear a protective suit, for one thing. For another, I'll go out with her. I'll serve as her canary."

"What do you mean, 'canary'?"

"It was a device they had on Earth some centuries back. Miners carried canaries—you know, little yellow birds—into mines. If the air went bad, the canary died before the men were affected, but the men, knowing there was a problem, would get out of the mine. In other words, if I begin to act queerly, we'll both be brought in at once."

"But what if it affects her before it affects you?"

"I don't think it will. Marlene feels immune. She's said that so many times that I have begun to believe her."

### 55.

Eugenia Insigna had never before watched the New Year approaching with such a painful concentration on the calendar. There had never been reason before. For that matter, the calendar was a vestigial hangover, twice removed.

On Earth, the year had begun by marking the seasons, and the holidays that related to the seasons—midsummer, midwinter, sowing, harvest—by whatever names they were called.

Crile (Insigna remembered) had explained the intricacies of the calendar to her, and had reveled in them in his dark and solemn way, as he did in everything that reminded him of Earth. She had listened to him with a mixture of ardor and apprehension; ardently because she wished to share his interest, as that might draw them closer together;

221

apprehensively because she feared his interest in Earth might drive him away from her, as eventually it did.

Strange that she still felt the pang—but was it dimmer now? It seemed to her that she could not actually remember Crile's face, that she remembered only the remembering now. Was it only the memory of a memory that stood between her and Siever Genarr now?

And yet it was the memory of a memory that held Rotor to the calendar now. Rotor had never had seasons. It had the year, of course, for it (and all the Settlements in the Earth-Moon system, which left out only those few that circled Mars or that were being built in the asteroid belt) accompanied Earth on its path around the Sun. Still, without seasons, the year was meaningless. Yet it was kept together with months and weeks.

Rotor had the day, too, fixed artificially at twenty-four hours during which sunlight was allowed to enter for half the time and blocked off for the other half. It could have been fixed for any length of time, but it was fixed at the length of an Earth day and divided into twenty-four hours of sixty minutes each, with each minute consisting of sixty seconds. (The days and nights were at least uniformly twelve hours long.)

There had been occasional movements among the Settlements to adopt a system of merely numbering days and grouping them into tens and multiples of tens; into dekadays, hectodays, kilodays, and, in the other direction, decidays, centidays, millidays; but that was really impossible.

The Settlements could not set up each their own system for that would have reduced trade and communications to chaos. Nor was any unified system possible save that of Earth, where 99 percent of the human population still lived, and to which ties of tradition still held the remaining 1 percent. Memory held Rotor and all the Settlements to a calendar that was intrinsically meaningless for them.

But now Rotor had left the Solar System and was a world that was isolated and alone. No day, or month, or year in the Earthly sense existed. It was not even sunlight that marked day from night, for Rotor gleamed with artificial daylight and darkened to a light whisper twelve hours on and twelve hours off. The harsh precision was not even broken by the gradual dimming and brightening at the boundaries that might simulate twilight and dawn. There seemed to be no need. And within this all-Settlement division, individual homes kept their illumination on and off to suit their whims or needs, but counted the days by Settlement time—which was Earth time.

Even here at the Erythro Dome, where there was a natural day and night that was casually used as such by those in occupation, it was the not-quite-matching Settlement day length, still tied to that of Earth (the memory of a memory) that was used in official calculations.

The movement was now stronger to leave the day as the only basic measure of time. Insigna knew for a fact that Pitt favored the decimalization of time measure, and yet even he hesitated to suggest it officially, for fear of rousing wild opposition.

But perhaps not forever. The traditional disorderly units of weeks and months seemed less important. The traditional holidays were more frequently ignored. Insigna, in her astronomical work, used days as the only significant units. Someday the old calendar would die, and, in the far unseen future, new methods of agreed-upon time marking would surely arise—a Galactic Standard calendar, perhaps.

But now she found herself marking off the time to a New Year that began arbitrarily. On Earth, at least, the New Year began at the time of a solstice—winter in the northern hemisphere, summer in the southern. It had a relationship to Earth's orbit around the Sun that only the astronomers on Rotor remembered clearly.

But now—even though Insigna was an astronomer—the New Year had to do only with Marlene's venture onto the surface of Erythro—a time chosen by Siever Genarr only because it involved a plausible delay, and accepted by Insigna only because she was officiously concerning herself with a teenager's notion of romance.

Insigna came out of her roaming through the depths of thought to find Marlene regarding her solemnly. (When had she entered the room so silently, or was Insigna so tied into an inner knot as to be unaware of footsteps?)

Insigna said in half a whisper, "Hello, Marlene."

Marlene said solemnly, "You're not happy, Mother."

"You don't have to be superperceptive to see that, Marlene. Are you still determined to step out on Erythro?"

"Yes. Entirely. Completely."

"Why, Marlene, why? Can you explain it so I can understand?"

"No, because you don't want to understand. It's calling me."

"*What's* calling you?"

"Erythro is. It wants me out there." Marlene's ordinarily glum face seemed suffused with a furtive happiness.

223

Insigna snapped, "When you talk like that, Marlene, you simply give me the impression that you are already infected by the—the—"

"The Plague? I'm not. Uncle Siever has just had another brain scan taken of me. I told him he didn't have to, but he said we had to have it for the record before we left. I'm perfectly normal."

"Brain scans can't tell you everything," said Insigna, frowning.

Marlene said, "Neither can a mother's fears." Then, more softly, "Mother, please, I know you want to delay this, but I won't accept a delay. Uncle Siever has promised. Even if it rains, even if it's bad weather, I'm going out. At this time of the year, there are never real storms or temperature extremes. There are almost never at any time of the year. It's a *wonderful* world."

"But it's barren—dead. Except for *germs,*" Insigna said spitefully.

"But someday we'll put life of our own upon it." Marlene looked away, her eyes lost in dreaming. "I'm sure of it," she said.

56.

"The E-suit is a simple suit," said Siever Genarr. "It doesn't have to withstand pressure. It's not a diving suit or a spacesuit. It has a helmet, and it has a compressed air supply that can be regenerated, and a small heat-exchange unit that keeps the temperature comfortable. And it's airtight, obviously."

"Will it fit me?" asked Marlene, looking at the display of thickish pseudo-textile material with distaste.

"Not fashionably so," said Genarr, his eyes twinkling. "It isn't made for beauty, but for use."

Marlene said in a slightly exasperated tone, "I'm not interested in looking beautiful, Uncle Siever, but I don't want to be slopping around in it. If it makes walking hard, it won't be worth it."

Eugenia Insigna interrupted. She had been watching, a little white-faced and pinch-lipped. "The suit is necessary to protect you, Marlene. I don't care how sloppy it is."

"But it doesn't have to be uncomfortable, Mother, does it? If it happens to fit, it would protect me just the same."

"This will fit fairly well, actually," said Genarr. "It's the best we could find. After all, we only have them in adult sizes." He turned his head toward Insigna. "We don't use them much these days. There was a time after the Plague died down that we did some exploring, but by

224

now we know the immediate surroundings quite well, and on the rare occasions we do go out, we tend to use enclosed E-cars."

"I wish you'd use an enclosed E-car now."

"No," said Marlene, obviously pained at the suggestion. I've been out in a vehicle. I want to walk. I want to—feel the ground."

"You're mad," said Insigna discontentedly.

Marlene fired back, "Will you stop implying—"

"Where's your perceptivity? I wasn't referring to the Plague. I mean just plain mad, just mad in the ordinary sense. I mean— Please, Marlene, you're driving me mad, as well."

She then said, "Siever, if these are old E-suits, how do you know they don't leak?"

"Because we've tested them, Eugenia. I assure you they're in good working order. Remember, I'm going out with her, and also in a suit."

Insigna was clearly seeking objections. "And suppose you suddenly have to—" She waved her hand meaninglessly.

"Urinate? Is that what you mean? That can be taken care of, though it's not comfortable. Still, it won't arise. We've emptied our bladders and we're good for several hours—or should be. And we're not venturing far off, so in case of emergency, we can come back to the Dome. We ought to leave now, Eugenia. Conditions are good outside and we should take advantage of that. Here, Marlene, let me help you with your suit."

Insigna said sharply, "Don't sound so happy."

"Why not? To tell you the truth, I would like to step out myself. The Dome can easily start to feel like a prison, you know. Maybe if we all stepped out more, our people could endure longer shifts in the Dome. There you are, Marlene, we only have to fit on the helmet, now."

Marlene hesitated. "Just a minute, Uncle Siever." She walked toward Insigna, holding out her arm, suited and bulky.

Insigna gazed at her mournfully.

"Mother," said Marlene. "Once again, *please* be calm. I love you and I wouldn't do this and cause you such anxiety just to please myself. I do it only because I know I will be fine and that you need not be anxious. And I bet you want to get into an E-suit also, so you can come out and never lose sight of me, but you mustn't."

"Why mustn't I, Marlene? How will I forgive myself if something happens to you and I'm not there to help you?"

"But nothing will happen to me. And even if something does, which it won't, what could you do about it? Besides, you're so afraid of Erythro that your mind is probably open to all kinds of abnormal effects. What if the Plague should strike you rather than me? How would you expect me to live with *that?*"

"She's right, Eugenia," said Genarr. "I'll be out there with her, and the best thing you can do is stay here and remain calm. All E-suits are equipped with radios. Marlene and I will be able to hear each other, and we will be in communication with the Dome. I promise you, if she behaves queerly in any way at all, if there is even the suspicion of oddness, I'll have her inside the Dome at once. And if I feel in any way not quite my own normal self, I will come back at once, bringing Marlene with me."

Insigna shook her head and did not look comforted as she watched the helmet being fitted first over Marlene's head, and then over Genarr's.

They were near the Dome's main airlock and Insigna watched its manipulation. She knew the lock procedure perfectly well—one could scarcely be a Settler otherwise.

There was the delicate control of air pressure to make sure that there would be a gentle transfer of air from the Dome outward, never from Erythro inward. There were computerized checks at every moment to make sure there were no leaks.

And then the inner door opened. Genarr stepped into the airlock and beckoned Marlene inward. She followed, and the door closed. The two were lost to immediate sight. Insigna distinctly felt her heart miss a beat.

She watched the controls and knew exactly when the outer door slid open and, then, when it closed again. The holoscreen sprang to life and she could see the two suited figures on it, standing on the barren soil of Erythro.

One of the engineers handed a small earplug to Insigna, who inserted it into her right ear. An equally small microphone was fitted over her head.

A voice in her ear said, "Radio contact," and at once, the familiar voice of Marlene sounded. "Can you hear me, Mother?"

"Yes, dear," said Insigna. Her voice sounded dry and abnormal in her own ear.

"We're out here and it's wonderful. It couldn't be nicer."

"Yes, dear," Insigna repeated, feeling hollow and lost and wondering whether she would ever see her daughter in her right mind again.

57.

Siever Genarr felt almost lighthearted as he stepped out upon the surface of Erythro. The sloping wall of the Dome, behind him, reached upward, but he kept his back to it, for a sight so un-Erythronian would have spoiled the savor of the world.

Savor? It was a queer word to use for Erythro, for at the moment it had no meaning. He lived behind the protection of his helmet, breathing the air of the Dome, or at least the air that had been purified and conditioned within the Dome. He could not smell the planet, or taste it, within that shelter.

And yet there was a feel to it that made him oddly happy. His boots crunched slightly upon the ground. Although Erythro's surface was not rocky, it was rather gravelly and, between the bits of gravel, there was what he could only describe as soil. There was, of course, ample water and air to break up the primordial surface rock and, perhaps, the ubiquitous prokaryotes had, in their countless trillions, added their own work patiently over the billions of years.

The soil felt soft. It had rained the day before, the soft and steady misty rain of Erythro—or at least of this portion of Erythro. The soil still felt slightly damp as a result, and Genarr imagined the bits of soil, the tiny scraps of sand and loam and clay, each with its coat of water film that had been refreshed and renewed. In that film, prokaryotic cells lived happily, basking in the energy of Nemesis, building complex proteins out of simple ones, while other prokaryotes, indifferent to solar energy, made use, instead, of the energy content of the remnants of those prokaryotes that, in their countless trillions, died during each moment of time.

Marlene was at his side. She was looking upward, and Genarr said gently, "Don't stare at Nemesis, Marlene."

Marlene's voice sounded naturally in his ear. It contained no tension or apprehension. Rather, her voice was filled with quiet joy. She said, "I'm looking at the clouds, Uncle Siever."

Genarr looked up into the dark sky where, by squinting for a while, one could detect a faint greenish-yellow gleam. Against it were the feathery fair-weather clouds that caught Nemesis' light and reflected it in orange splendor.

227

There was an eerie quiet about Erythro. There was nothing to make a sound. No form of life sang, roared, growled, bellowed, twittered, stridulated, or creaked. There were no leaves to rustle, no insects to hum. In the rare storms, there might be the rumble of thunder, or the wind might sigh against the occasional boulder—if it blew hard enough. On a peaceful, calm day, however, as this one was, it was silent.

Genarr spoke just to make sure that it *was* quiet and that he had not suddenly been struck deaf. (He couldn't have been, to be sure, for he heard the faint rasp of his own breath.)

"Are you all right, Marlene?"

"I feel wonderful. There's a brook up there." And she hastened her steps into an almost shambling run, hampered as she was by her E-suit.

He said, "Watch out, Marlene. You'll slip."

"I'll be careful." Her voice was not dimmed by increasing distance, of course, since it was a radio beam that carried it.

Eugenia Insigna's voice sounded suddenly in Genarr's ear. "Why is Marlene running, Siever?" Then, almost at once, she added, "Why are you running, Marlene?"

Marlene did not bother to answer, but Genarr said, "She just wants to look at some creek or other up ahead, Eugenia."

"Is she all right?"

"Of course she is. It's weirdly beautiful out here. After a while, it doesn't even seem barren—more like an abstract painting."

"Never mind the art criticism, Siever. Don't let her get away from you."

"Don't worry. I'm in constant contact with her. Right now, she hears what you and I are saying, and if she doesn't answer, it's because she doesn't want to be bothered by irrelevancies. Eugenia, relax. Marlene is enjoying herself. Don't spoil it."

Genarr was indeed convinced that Marlene was enjoying herself. Somehow he was, too.

Marlene was running upstream along the brook's edge. Genarr felt no great urgency to follow her. Let her enjoy herself, he thought.

The Dome itself was built on a rocky outcropping, but the region in this direction was interlaced with small gently flowing brooks that all combined into a rather large river some thirty kilometers away that, in turn, flowed into the sea.

The brooks were welcome, of course. They supplied the Dome

with its natural water supply, once the prokaryote content was removed (actually, "killed" was the better word). There had been some biologists, in the early days of the Dome, who had objected to the killing of the prokaryotes, but that was ridiculous. The tiny specks of life were so incredibly numerous on the planet, and could proliferate so rapidly to replace any shrinkage of their numbers, that no amount of ordinary killing in the process of ensuring a water supply could hurt them in any significant way. Then, once the Plague began, a vague but strong hostility to Erythro rose up, and, after that, no one cared what one did to the prokaryotes.

Of course, now that the Plague did not seem to be much of a threat any longer, humanitarian feelings (Genarr privately felt that "biotarian" was the better word) might rise again. Genarr sympathized with those feelings, but then what would the Dome do for a water supply?

Lost in thought, he was no longer looking at Marlene, and the shriek sounded deafeningly in his ear. "Marlene! Marlene! Siever, what is she *doing?*"

Now he looked up, and was about to answer with automatic reassurance that nothing was wrong, that all was well, when he caught sight of Marlene.

For a moment, he could not tell what she was doing. He just stared at her in the pink light of Nemesis.

Then he made it out. She was unhitching her helmet and was taking it off. Now she was working at removing the rest of her E-suit.

He had to stop this!

Genarr tried to call out to her, but in the horror of the emergency, he couldn't find his voice. He tried to run to her, but his legs felt leaden, and barely responded to the urgency of his feelings.

It was as though he found himself in a nightmare where dreadful things were happening, and he could do nothing to prevent them. Or, perhaps, his mind, under the stress of events, was dissociating from his body.

Is this the Plague, striking at *me?* Genarr wondered in panic. And, if so, what will happen to Marlene now, as she is baring herself to the light of Nemesis and the air of Erythro?

# TWENTY-SIX

## PLANET

### 58.

Crile Fisher had seen Igor Koropatsky only twice in the three years since he had assumed the post formerly held by Tanayama, and had become the actual—if not the titular—head of the project.

He had no trouble recognizing him, however, when the photo-entry had signaled his image. Koropatsky was still his portly, outwardly genial self. He was dressed well, with a large and fluffy cravat in the latest style.

As for Fisher, he had been relaxing through the morning and was scarcely presentable, but one did not refuse to receive Koropatsky, even when he came without warning.

Fisher signaled the tactful "Hold" image, the cartoon figure of a welcoming host (or hostess, for the sex was made conventionally ambiguous) with a hand upraised delicately in a gesture that was universally understood to mean "Just a minute" without the crassness of actually saying so.

Fisher had a few moments to comb his hair and adjust his clothes. He might have shaved, but he felt that Koropatsky would consider any further delay insulting.

The door slid aside and Koropatsky walked in. He smiled pleasantly and said, "Good morning, Fisher. I intrude upon you, I know."

"No intrusion, Director," said Fisher, making an effort to sound sincere, "but if you wish to see Dr. Wendel, she is, I'm afraid, at the ship."

Koropatsky grunted. "You know, I rather thought she might be. I have no choice, then, but to talk to you. May I sit down?"

"Yes, of course, Director," said Fisher, chagrined at not having offered Koropatsky a seat before the request was made. "Would you care for refreshment?"

"No." Koropatsky patted his abdomen. "I weigh myself every morning and that alone is sufficent to cost me my appetite—almost. Fisher, I have never had a chance to talk to you, man to man. I have wanted to."

"It is my pleasure, Director," mumbled Fisher, beginning to grow uneasy. What was this all about?

"Our planet is in debt to you."

"If you say so, Director," said Fisher.

"You were on Rotor before it left."

"That was fourteen years ago, Director."

"I know it was. You were married on Rotor and had a child."

"Yes, Director," said Fisher in a low voice.

"But you returned to Earth just before Rotor left the Solar System."

"Yes, Director."

"It was from something that was said to you—and that you repeated here—plus another suggestion you made that led to Earth's discovery of the Neighbor Star."

"Yes, Director."

"And it was you who brought Dr. Tessa Wendel from Adelia to Earth."

"Yes, Director."

"And you have made it possible for her to work here for over eight years, and kept her happy, eh?"

He chuckled deeply and Fisher felt that had Koropatsky been closer he would have dug his elbow into Fisher's side in a man-to-man fashion.

Fisher said cautiously, "We get along well, Director."

"But you have never married."

"I am already married, Director."

"And separated fourteen years. A divorce could be quickly arranged."

"I also have a daughter."

"Who would remain your daughter, even if you married again."

"It would be a meaningless formality, surely."

"Well, perhaps." Koropatsky nodded. "And perhaps it even works better this way. You know the superluminal ship is ready to move. We hope to launch it at the beginning of 2237."

"So I have been told by Dr. Wendel, Director."

"The neuronic detectors are installed and work well."

"I have been told that, too, Director."

Koropatsky held one hand in the other in his lap and nodded his large head ponderously. Then he looked up quickly at Fisher and said, "Do you know how it works?"

Fisher shook his head. "No, sir. I know nothing about the actual workings of the ship."

Koropatsky nodded his head again. "Nor I. We have to accept the word of Dr. Wendel and our engineers. One thing is still lacking, though."

"Oh?" (Cold anxiety swept over Fisher. More delay?) "What is lacking, Director?"

"Communications. I would think that if there is a device that can make a ship move much faster than light, there should also be a device that would send waves, or some other form of message-carrying device, faster than light, too. It seems to me it would be easier to send a superluminal message than drive a superluminal ship."

"I can't say, Director."

"Yet Dr. Wendel assures me that the reverse is true; that, as yet, there is no method of efficient superluminal communication. Eventually, there will be, she says, but not now, and she doesn't want to wait for such communication, which, she says, may take a long time."

"I don't want to wait either, Director."

"Yes, I'm anxious for progress and success. We've been waiting years already, and I am eager to see the ship leave and return. But it does mean that once the ship leaves, we will be out of contact."

He nodded thoughtfully, and Fisher maintained a discreet silence. (What was all this about? What was the old bear getting at?)

Koropatsky looked up at Fisher. "You know that the Neighbor Star is heading in our direction?"

"Yes, Director, I've heard of that, but it seems to be the common feeling that it will pass us at a great enough distance to leave us unaffected."

"That's the feeling we want people to have. Now the truth is, Fisher, that the Neighbor Star will pass closely enough to disturb Earth's orbital motion substantially."

Fisher paused for a moment in shock. "And destroy the planet?"

"Not physically. The climate will be sufficiently changed, however, so that Earth will no longer be habitable."

"Is that certain?" said Fisher, reluctant to believe it.

"I don't know that scientists are ever really *certain*. But they seem sufficiently close to certain to make it necessary for us to begin to take measures. We have five thousand years, and we are developing super-luminal flight—assuming the ship works."

"If Dr. Wendel says it will work, Director, I'm convinced it will."

"Let's hope your confidence is not misplaced. Nevertheless, even five thousand years with superluminal flight leaves us in a bad spot. We would have to build a hundred and thirty thousand Settlements like Rotor to carry off Earth's eight billion people plus enough plants and animals to set up viable worlds. That's twenty-six Noah's Arks a year, starting right now. That's assuming there's no increase in population over the next five thousand years."

"Perhaps," said Fisher cautiously, "we can handle an average of twenty-six a year. Our experience and expertise should increase with the centuries, and our population control has worked for decades."

"Very well. Now tell me this: If we do lift Earth's population into space in one hundred and thirty thousand Settlements, making use of Earth's full resources, plus those of the Moon, Mars, and the aster-oids, and abandon the Solar System to the gravitational mercies of the Neighbor Star, where do all these Settlements go?"

"I don't know, Director," said Fisher.

"We will have to find planets sufficiently Earth-like to accept our vast population without prohibitive requirements for terraforming. We must think of that, too, and we must think of it *now*, not five thousand years from now."

"Even if we don't find suitable planets, we can put the Settlements into orbit about suitable stars." Inevitably, Fisher made circular movements with his finger.

"My dear man, that wouldn't work."

"With all respect, Director, it *does* work right here in the Solar System."

"Not at all. There's a planet here in the Solar System that even today, despite all the Settlements, contains 99 percent of the human species. *We* are still humanity, and the Settlements are just a kind of fluff that surrounds us. Could the fluff exist by itself? We have no proof that they can, and I think not."

"You may be right, Director," said Fisher.

"*May* be? There's no doubt about it," said Koropatsky heatedly. The Settlers affect to despise us, but we fill their thoughts. We're their history. We're their model. We're the teeming source to which they return again and again for re-invigoration. Left to themselves, they would wither."

"You may be right, Director, but the experiment has never been tried. We have never had a situation in which Settlements tried to exist without a planet—"

"But we *have* had such a situation, at least in analogy. In Earth's early history, human beings settled islands and were isolated from the mainstream. The Irish settled Iceland; the Norse settled Greenland; the mutineers settled Pitcairn Island; the Polynesians settled Easter Island. Result? The colonists withered, sometimes disappeared entirely. Always stagnation. No civilization ever developed except in a continental area, or in islands in close proximity to a continental area. Humanity needs space, size, variety, a horizon, a frontier. You see?"

Fisher said, "Yes, Director." (Past a certain point, why argue?)

"So that"—and Koropatsky put his right forefinger on his left palm, didactically—"we must find a planet, at least one planet to begin with. Which brings us to Rotor."

Fisher raised his eyebrows in surprise. "To Rotor, Director?"

"Yes. In the fourteen years since they've left, what's happened to them?"

"Dr. Wendel is of the opinion that they may not have survived." (He felt a pang saying it. He always felt a pang when he thought about it.)

"I know she does. I've talked to her, and I've accepted what she has said without discussion. But I'd like your opinion."

"I don't have one, Director. I have only the earnest hope that they have survived. I have a daughter on Rotor."

"*Perhaps* you still have. Think! What was there to have destroyed them? A malfunctioning part. Rotor is not a ship, but a Settlement that for fifty years had had no serious malfunction. It traveled through empty space between here and the Neighbor Star and what can be more harmless than empty space?"

"A mini-black hole, an undetected asteroidal body—"

"What evidence? Those are just guesses and of almost zero probability, the astronomers tell me. Is it something about the inherent properties of hyperspace that may have destroyed Rotor? We've been experimenting with hyperspace for years now and there is nothing inherently dangerous in it that we can find. So we can suppose that Rotor reached the Neighbor Star safely—if that's where they went, and all seem to agree that it makes no sense to suppose they went anywhere else."

"I would like to think that they arrived safely."

"But then the question arises: If Rotor is safe at the Neighbor Star, what is it doing there?"

"Existing." (It was halfway between a statement and a question.)

"But how? Circling the Neighbor Star? A single Settlement on an endless, lonely journey about a red dwarf star? I don't think so. They would wither, and it would not take them long to realize that. I am sure they would wither fast."

"And die? Is that your conclusion, Director?"

"No. They would give up and come home. They would acknowledge defeat and come back to safety. However, they have not done so, and do you know what I've been thinking? I've been thinking they've found a habitable planet at the Neighbor Star."

"But there can't be a habitable planet circling a red dwarf star, Director. There's a shortage of energy, unless you get so close that there's too much tidal effect." He paused and muttered, shamefaced, "Dr. Wendel explained that to me."

"Yes, astronomers have explained it to me, too. But"—he shook his head—"experience has taught me that no matter how sure scientists think they are, nature has a way of surprising them. Anyway, do you understand why we are letting you go on this voyage?"

"Yes, Director. Your predecessor promised I would go in return for services rendered."

"I have a better reason than that. My predecessor, who was a great man, an admirable man, was also a sick old man at the end. His enemies thought that he had become paranoid. He believed Rotor knew of Earth's danger and had left without warning us because they wanted Earth destroyed, and that Rotor must therefore be punished. However, he is gone, and I am here. I am not old, or sick, or paranoid. Assuming Rotor is safe and is at the Neighbor Star, it is not our intention to harm them."

"I'm glad of that, but isn't this something you ought to discuss with Dr. Wendel, Director? She is to be the captain of the ship."

"Dr. Wendel is a Settler. You are a loyal Earthman."

"Dr. Wendel has worked loyally for years on the superluminal project."

"That she has been loyal to the project is beyond question. But is she loyal to Earth? Can we count on her to carry out the letter and the spirit of Earth's intentions toward Rotor?"

"May I ask, Director, just what Earth's intentions are toward Rotor? I take it that there is no longer the intention of punishing the Settlement for its failure to warn us."

"That is correct. What we want now is association, human brotherhood, only the kindliest of feelings. With friendship established, there must be a quick return with as much information as possible about Rotor and its planet."

"Surely if Dr. Wendel is told this—if she has this explained to her—she will carry it out."

Koropatsky chuckled. "One would think so, but you know how it is. She is a woman who is not in the first bloom of youth. A fine woman—I have no fault to find—but she is in her fifties."

"What of that?" (Fisher found himself offended.)

"She must know that when she comes back, with the vital experience of a successful superluminal flight, she will be more valuable to us than ever; that she will be needed to design newer, better, more advanced superluminal vessels; that she will have to train young people as superluminal pilots. She will be quite sure that she will never be allowed to venture out through hyperspace again, for she will simply be too valuable to risk. Therefore, before coming back, she may be tempted to explore further. She may not wish to abandon the thrill of seeing new stars and penetrating new horizons. But we cannot have her take one risk more than she must take to reach Rotor, gain the information, and return. We cannot afford the time lost either. Do you *understand?*" His voice had become hard.

Fisher swallowed. "Surely you have no real reason—"

"I have every reason. Dr. Wendel has always been in a delicate position here—as a Settler. You understand, I hope. Of all the people on Earth, she is the one we depend on most, and she is a Settler. She has had to be the subject of a detailed psychological profile. She has been extensively studied, with and without her knowledge, and we are quite certain that, given the chance, she will go off exploring. And she will be out of communication with us. We won't know where she is, what she is doing. We won't even know if she is alive."

"And why are you telling me all this, Director?"

"Because we know you have great influence over her. She can be guided by you—if you are firm."

"I think, perhaps, you overestimate my influence, Director."

"I am sure we don't. You, too, have been much studied, and we know exactly how bound the good doctor is to you—perhaps more than you yourself realize. We know, also, that you are a loyal son of Earth. You might have left with Rotor, stayed with your wife and daughter, but you returned to Earth at the cost of losing them. You did that, moreover, knowing that my predecessor, Director Tanayama, would consider you a failure for failing to bring information back concerning hyper-assistance, and that your career might well be ruined. That satisfies me that I can count on you to see to it that Dr. Wendel is kept under firm control and is brought back to us quickly and that you will, this time—*this* time—bring back the information we need."

"I'll try, Director," said Fisher.

"You say that dubiously," said Koropatsky. "Please understand the importance of what I am asking you to do. We *must* know just what they're doing, how strong they are, and what the planet is like. Once we know all that, we will know what *we* must do, and how strong *we* must be, and for what kind of a life *we* must be prepared. Because, Fisher, we must have a planet, and we must have it now. And we have no choice but to take Rotor's planet."

"If it exists," said Fisher hoarsely.

"It had better exist," said Koropatsky. "Earth's survival depends upon it."

# TWENTY-SEVEN

# LIFE

## 59.

Siever Genarr opened his eyes slowly and blinked at the light. He had a little trouble focusing at first and couldn't quite make out whatever filled his vision.

The image sharpened slowly and soon Genarr recognized Ranay D'Aubisson, Chief Neurophysicist of the Dome.

Genarr said in a weak voice, "Marlene?"

D'Aubisson looked grim. "She seems well. It's you I'm concerned about right now."

A pang of apprehension made its way through Genarr's vitals and he tried to drown it with his sense of black humor. He said, "I must be worse off than I thought if the Angel of the Plague is here."

Then, as D'Aubisson said nothing, Genarr asked sharply, "Am I?"

She seemed to come to life. Tall and angular, she bent over him, the fine wrinkles about her piercing blue eyes becoming more prominent as she squinted at him.

LIFE

"How do you feel?" she asked, answering no questions.

"Tired. Very tired. All right, otherwise. I think?" The rising inflection serve to repeat his earlier question.

She said, "You've been sleeping for five hours." She was still not answering.

Genarr groaned. "I'm tired anyway. *And* I have to go to the bathroom." He began to struggle into a sitting position.

At D'Aubisson's signal a young man approached rapidly. Respectfully, he placed his hand under Genarr's elbow and was indignantly shaken off.

D'Aubisson said, "Please let yourself be helped. We have made no diagnosis yet."

When Genarr was back in bed ten minutes later, he said ruefully, "No diagnosis. Have you made a brain scan?"

"Yes, of course. Instantly."

"Well?"

She shrugged. "We found nothing of importance, but you were asleep. We will take another when you're awake. And you must be observed in other ways."

"Why? Isn't the brain scan enough?"

Her gray eyebrows rose. "Do you think it is?"

"No games. What are you getting at? Say it straight out. I'm not a child."

D'Aubisson sighed. "The cases of the Plague we have had showed interesting features on brain scan, but we were never able to compare it with the pre-Plague standard because none of the sufferers had been scanned prior to onset. By the time we set up a routine and universal brain scanning program for all people in the Dome, there were no longer any unmistakable cases of the Plague. Did you know this?"

"Don't lay traps for me," said Genarr pettishly. "Of course I knew of it. Do you think my memory is gone? I deduce, then—I can still deduce, too, you know—that although you have my scan of earlier days and can compare it with the scan you just took, you found nothing of significance. Is that it?"

"You obviously do not have anything remarkably wrong, but we might have something we would consider a subclinical situation."

"If you find *nothing?*"

"We might not notice a subtle change if we're not specifically look-

239

ing for it. After all, you collapsed and you are not ordinarily given to collapsing, Commander."

"Take another scan now that I'm awake, then, and if it's something so subtle it escapes you, then I'll live with it. But tell me about Marlene. Are you *sure* she's well?"

"I said she *seems* well, Commander. Unlike you, she showed no abormality of behavior. She did not collapse."

"And is she safely inside the Dome?"

"Yes, she brought you in herself, just before you fell unconscious. Don't you remember?"

Genarr flushed, and mumbled something.

D'Aubisson's look grew sardonic. "Suppose you tell us exactly what you do remember, Commander. Tell us everything. Any of it may be important."

Genarr's discomfort increased as he tried to remember. It seemed a long time ago and the edges were blurred, very much as though it were a dream he was trying to recall.

"Marlene was taking off her E-suit." Then, weakly, "Wasn't she?"

"Quite. She came in without it and we had to send someone out there to retrieve it."

"Well, I tried to stop her, of course, when I noticed what she was doing. Dr. Insigna called out, I remember, and that alerted me. Marlene was a distance away from me, by the stream. I tried to call out, but, in the shock of the situation I couldn't manage to make a sound just at first. I tried to get to her quickly, to—to—"

"Run to her," put in D'Aubisson.

"Yes, but—but—"

"But you found you couldn't run. You were almost in a state of paralysis. Am I correct?"

Genarr nodded. "Yes. Rather. I tried to run, but—did you ever have one of those nightmares where you are pursued and somehow you can't manage to make yourself run?"

"Yes. We all have those. It usually comes when we have managed to tangle our arms or legs in the bedclothes."

"It felt like a dream. I managed to get my voice, at last, and shouted at her, but without the E-suit, she couldn't hear me, I'm sure."

"Did you feel faint?"

"Not really. Just helpless and confused. At though it were not even any use in trying to run. Then Marlene saw me and ran toward me. She must somehow have recognized I was in trouble."

240

"She didn't seem to have any trouble running. Is that right?"

"I wasn't aware that she was. She seemed to reach me. Then we— I'll be honest, Ranay. I don't remember after that."

"You came into the Dome together," said D'Aubisson calmly. "She was helping you, holding you up. And once in the Dome, you collapsed and now—here you are."

"And you think I have the Plague."

"I think you experienced something abnormal, but I can find nothing in your brain scan, and I am puzzled. There you have it."

"It was the shock of seeing Marlene in danger. Why should she be taking off her E-suit if she weren't—" He stopped abruptly.

"If she weren't succumbing to the Plague. Is that it?"

"The thought crossed my mind."

"But she seems fine. Would you like to sleep some more?"

"No. I'm awake. Take another brain scan and see to it that it comes out negative because I feel much better now that I have the story off my chest. And then I'm going about my business, you harpy."

"Even if the brain scan is apparently normal, Commander, you'll stay in bed for at least twenty-four hours. For observation, you understand."

Genarr groaned theatrically. "You can't do that. I can't lie here and stare at the ceiling for twenty-four hours."

"You won't have to. We can set up a viewing stand for you, so that you can read a book or enjoy holovision. You can even have a visitor or two."

"I suppose the visitors will be observing me, too."

"It's conceivable they may be questioned on the matter. And now we'll set up the brain scan equipment again." She turned away, then turned back with a smile that softened slightly at the edges. "It's very possible you're all right, Commander. Your reactions seem normal to me. But we must be sure, mustn't we?"

Genarr grunted, and when D'Aubisson turned again and walked away, he made a face at her straight back. That, he decided, was a normal reaction, too.

60.

When Genarr opened his eyes again, it was to see Eugenia Insigna gazing at him sadly.

He looked surprised and began to sit up. "Eugenia!"

She smiled at him, but that did not make her face look less sad.

She said, "They said I could come in, Siever. They said you were all right."

Genarr felt a wave of relief. He *knew* he was all right, but it was nice to hear that his opinion was confirmed.

He said with bravado, "Of course I am. Brain scan normal, asleep. Brain scan normal, awake. Brain scan normal, forever. But how's Marlene?"

"Her brain scan is perfectly normal, too." Even that did not lighten her mood.

"As you see," said Genarr, "I was Marlene's canary, as I had promised. I was affected by whatever it was before she was." And then his mood changed. It was no time for banter.

He said, "Eugenia, how can I excuse myself to you? I wasn't watching Marlene to begin with, and I was too paralyzed with horror to do anything afterward. I failed completely, and did so after my telling you with such confidence that I would take care of her. Honestly, I have no excuse."

Insigna was shaking her head. "No, Siever. It was in no way your fault. I'm so glad she brought you in."

"Not my fault?" Genarr felt dumbfounded. Of course it was his fault.

"Not at all. There's something much worse than Marlene foolishly removing her suit, or you being unable to act quickly. Much worse. I'm sure of it."

Genarr felt himself turning cold. What's much worse? he thought. "What are you trying to tell me?"

He swung himself out of bed and suddenly became aware of his bare legs and of the totally inadequate gown he was wearing. He hastily draped the light blanket around himself.

He said, "Please sit down and tell me. *Is* Marlene all right? Are you hiding something about her?"

Insigna sat down and looked solemnly at Genarr. "They say she's all right. The brain scan is entirely normal. Those who know about the Plague say she shows no symptoms."

"Well then, why are you sitting there as though it's the end of the world?"

"I think it is, Siever. Of *this* one."

"What does *that* mean?"

"I can't explain. I can't reason it out. You have to talk to Marlene to understand. She's going her own way, Siever. She's not upset over what she did. She insists that she cannot properly explore Erythro—*experience* Erythro is the phrase she uses—with the E-suit on and she has no intention of wearing one any longer."

"In that case, she won't go out."

"Oh, but Marlene says she will. Quite confidently. Whenever she wishes, she says. And alone. She blames herself for having let you come with her. She's not callous over what happened to you, you see. Over that, she *is* upset. And she was glad she reached you in time. Really, there were tears in her eyes when she talked about what might have happened if she hadn't walked you into the Dome in time."

"Doesn't that make *her* feel insecure."

"No. That's the oddest part of it. She's now sure that you were in danger, that anyone would have been in danger. But not she. She is so *positive*, Siever, I could—" She shook her head, then muttered, "I don't know what to do."

"She's a positive girl by nature, Eugenia. You must know that better than I do."

"Not *this* positive. It's as though she knows we can't stop her."

"Perhaps we can. I'll talk to her and if she pulls any of this 'You can't stop me,' when she talks to me, I'll just send her back to Rotor—and at once. I was on her side, but after what happened to me outside the Dome, I'm afraid I'm going to have to be tough."

"But you won't."

"Why not? Because of Pitt?"

"No. I mean you just won't."

Genarr stared at her, then laughed uneasily. "Oh come, I'm not *that* much under her spell. I may feel like a kindly uncle, Eugenia, but I'm not so kindly I'll let her walk into danger. There are limits, and you'll find that I know how to set them." He paused, and said ruefully, "We seem to have changed sides, you and I. Before today it was you who insisted on stopping her and I who said it couldn't be done. Now it's the other way around."

"That's because the incident outside has frightened you, and the experience since then has frightened me."

"What experience since then, Eugenia?"

"*I* tried to set the limits, after she was back in the Dome. I said to her, 'Young lady, don't you dare speak to me like that or, far from not being able to leave the Dome, you won't be able to leave your room.

You'll be locked in, tied up if necessary, and back to Rotor we'll go on the first rocket.' You see, I was wild enough to threaten her all the way."

"Well, what did she do? I'm willing to bet a large sum she didn't burst into tears. I suspect she gritted her teeth and defied you. Right?"

"No. I had'nt even gotten half the words out when my teeth started chattering and I couldn't speak. A wave of nausea swept over me."

Genarr said, frowning, "Are you about to tell me that you think Marlene has some strange hypnotic power that can prevent us from opposing her? Surely that's impossible. Have you ever noticed anything like that in her before this?"

"No, of course I haven't. I don't even see this in her now. She has nothing to do with it. I must have looked quite ill at the moment I was threatening her and that clearly frightened her. She was very concerned. She couldn't possibly have caused it and then reacted so. And when you two were outside the Dome and she was taking off her E-suit, she wasn't even looking at you. She had her back to you. I was watching and I know that. Yet you found you couldn't do anything to interfere with her and when she realized you were in trouble, she flew to your assistance. She couldn't have deliberately done that to you and reacted in that fashion."

"But then—"

"I'm not through. After I had threatened her, or, rather, after I had failed to threaten her, I scarcely dared say anything to her that wasn't perfectly superficial, but you can be sure I kept my eye on her and tried not to let her see I was doing that. At one point, she talked to one of your guards—you have them all over the place."

"In theory," muttered Genarr, "the Dome is a military post. The guards merely maintain order, help out when needed—"

"Yes, I dare say," said Insigna with a touch of contempt. "That's Janus Pitt making sure he has a way of keeping you all under observation and under control, but never mind. Marlene and the guard talked for quite a while, seemed to be arguing. I went to the guard afterward, after Marlene was gone, and asked him what Marlene had talked to him about. He was reluctant to say, but I squeezed it out of him. He said she wanted to arrange some sort of pass that would allow her to leave and re-enter the Dome freely.

"I said to him, 'What did you tell her?'

"He said, 'I told her that would have to be arranged at the Commander's office, but that I would try to help her.'

"I was indignant. 'What do you mean you would help her?' I said. 'How could you offer to do that?'

"He said, 'I had to do something, ma'am. Every time I tried to tell her it couldn't be done, I felt sick.' "

Genarr listened to all of this stonily. "Are you telling me that this is something Marlene does unconsciously, that anyone who dares contradict her is made ill, and that she doesn't even know that she is responsible for it?"

"No, of course not. I don't see how she can be doing anything at all. If this were an unconscious ability of hers, it would have made its appearance on Rotor, and it never happened there. And it isn't just *any* contradiction. She tried for a second helping of dessert at dinner last night, and quite forgetting that I didn't dare cross her, I said sharply, 'No, Marlene.' She looked terribly rebellious, but subsided, and I felt in perfect health, I can tell you. No, I think it's only in connection with Erythro that one can't contradict her."

"But why do you suppose that should be, Eugenia? You seem to have some notion or other about this. If I were Marlene, I would read you like a book and tell you what that notion is, but since I am not, you must tell me."

"I don't think it's Marlene at all who's doing this. It's—it's the planet itself."

"The planet!"

"Yes, Erythro! The planet. It's controlling Marlene. Why else should she be so confident that she is immune to the Plague, and that she will come to no harm? It controls the rest of us, too. You came to harm when you tried to stop her. I did. The guard did. Many people came to harm in the early days of the Dome because the planet felt it was being invaded, so it produced the Plague. Then, when it seemed you were all content to remain within the Dome, it let go, and the Plague stopped. See how it all fits in?"

"Do you think, then, that the planet wants Marlene out upon its surface?"

"Apparently."

"But why?"

"I don't know. I don't pretend to understand it. I'm just telling you how it must be."

Genarr's voice softened. "Eugenia, surely you know that the planet can't do anything. It's a lump of rock and metal. You're being mystical."

"I am not. Siever, don't slip into this trick of pretending that I'm a silly woman. I'm a first-class scientist and there's nothing mystical about my thinking. When I say the planet, I don't mean the rock and metal. I mean that there's some powerful permeating life-form upon the planet."

"It would have to be invisible, then. This is a barren world with no sign of life above the prokaryote, let alone intelligence."

"What do you know about this barren world, as you call it? Has it been properly explored? Has it been searched through and through?"

Slowly, Genarr shook his head. He said with a pleading note in his voice, "Eugenia, you're drifting off into hysteria."

"Am I, Siever? Think it out yourself and tell me if you can find an alternate explanation. I tell you the life on the planet—whatever it is —will not have us. We're doomed. And what it wants with Marlene" —her voice quavered—"I can't imagine."

# TWENTY-EIGHT

## TAKEOFF

61.

Officially, it had a very elaborate name, but it was spoken of as Station Four by those few Earthpeople who had occasion to mention it. From the name it was at once apparent there had been three such objects earlier—none of which were any longer in use, having been cannibalized, in point of fact. There was also a Station Five that had never been finished and had become derelict.

It is doubtful if the vast majority of Earth's population ever thought of the existence of Station Four, which drifted slowly around Earth in an orbit well beyond that of the Moon.

The early stations had been Earth's launching pads for the construction of the first Settlements, and then, when the Settlers themselves took over the job of building Settlements, Station Four was used for Earth's flights to Mars.

One such Martian flight was all that took place, however, for it turned out that the Settlers were far better suited, psychologically, to

247

long flights (living, as they did in worlds that were large enclosed spaceships), and Earth left it to them with a sigh of relief.

Station Four was now rarely used for any purpose and was maintained only as Earth's foothold in space, as a symbol that the Settlers were not the sole owners of the vastness beyond Earth's atmosphere.

But now Station Four had a use.

A large cargo ship had lumbered out in its direction, carrying with it the rumor (among the Settlements) that another attempt—the first in the twenty-third century—would be made to place an Earth team on Mars. Some said it was merely for exploration, some for the establishment of an Earth colony on Mars in order to bypass the few Settlements in orbit around the planet; and some for the purpose, eventually, of establishing an outpost on some sizable asteroid that no Settlement had yet claimed.

What the ship actually carried in its cargo hold was the *Superluminal* and the crew that was to propel her to the stars.

Tessa Wendel, even though she had been planetbound for eight years, took the space experience calmly, as any Settler by birth would naturally do. Spaceships were far more like Settlements in principle than they were like the planet Earth. And because of that, Crile Fisher, though he had been on many a spaceflight before, was a bit uneasy.

This time something more than the unnaturalness of space contributed to the tension onboard the cargo ship. Fisher said, "I can't endure the waiting, Tessa. It's taken us years to reach this point and the *Superluminal* is ready and we *still* wait."

Wendel regarded him thoughtfully. She had never intended to get this involved with him. She had wanted moments of relaxation to rest a mind overcome with the complexity of the project, so that it might return to work refreshed and keener. That was what she had *intended;* what she had ended up with was something much more.

Now she found herself helplessly tied to him, so that his problems had become hers. The years of his waiting would surely come to nothing, and she worried about the despair that would follow his inevitable disappointment. She had tried to dash cold water on his dreams judiciously, tried to cool down his overheated anticipation of a reunion with his daughter, but she had not succeeded. If anything, over this past year, he had grown more optimistic about the possibility for no obvious reason—at least, none he would explain to her.

Tessa was finally satisfied (and relieved) that it was not his wife

Crile was looking for, but only his daughter. To be sure, she had never understood this longing for a daughter he had last seen as an infant, but he had volunteered no explanation and she had not wanted to probe the matter. What was the use? She was certain that his daughter was not alive, that nothing on Rotor was alive. If Rotor was there near the Neighbor Star, it was a giant tomb drifting in space, wandering forever—and undetectable except by incredible co-incidence. Crile Fisher would have to be kept steady and functioning once that inevitable prospect became clearly apparent reality.

Tessa said cajolingly, "There's only a two-month wait left—at most. Since we've waited for years, another two months won't hurt."

"It's the waiting for years that makes even two months more un-bearable," muttered Fisher.

"Tell yourself otherwise, Crile," said Wendel. "Learn to bow to necessity. The Global Congress simply won't allow us to go any sooner. The Settlements have their eyes on us, and there's no way of being sure that they all accept the notion that we're heading for Mars. It would be strange if they did, considering Earth's poor record in space. If we do nothing for two months, they will assume we're hav-ing trouble—something they would readily believe, and find satisfac-tion in—and withdraw their attention."

Fisher shook his head angrily. "Who cares if they know what we're doing? We'll be off and gone and they won't duplicate superluminal flight for years—and by that time we'll have a fleet of superluminal vessels and be moving rapidly forward toward opening up the Gal-axy."

"Don't take that for granted. It's easier to imitate and overtake than it is to originate. And Earth's government, considering its dismal record in space after the Settlements reached maturity, is obviously anxious to establish unmistakable priority for psychological reasons." She shrugged. "Besides, we need the time to carry out more tests on the *Superluminal* under low-gravity conditions."

"There's never any end to tests, is there?"

"Don't be impatient. This is so new and untried a technique, and so unlike anything humanity has ever had, that it is all too easy to think of new tests, especially since we are a little uncertain as to the manner in which moving into and out of hyperspace is affected by the level of intensity of a gravitational field. Seriously, Crile, you can't blame us for being cautious. After all, as recently as a decade ago, superluminal flight was considered theoretically impossible."

"Even caution can be overdone."

"Possibly. Eventually, I will decide that we've done all we can reasonably be expected to do, and then we'll take off. I promise you, Crile, we won't wait unreasonably. I won't overdo caution."

"I hope not."

Wendel looked at him doubtfully. She *had* to ask. She said, "You know, Crile, you're not yourself lately. For the last two months you've seemed to be burning up with impatience. For a while there you had cooled down, and then you suddenly gained excitement again. Has something happened that I don't know about?"

Fisher calmed suddenly. "Nothing's happened. What can possibly have happened?"

To Wendel, it seemed he had calmed down too quickly, had wrenched himself into a most suspicious affectation of normality. She said, "I'm asking *you* what can possibly have happened. I've tried to warn you, Crile, that we are not likely to find Rotor a functioning world, or find it at all. We will not find your—we are not likely to find any of its inhabitants alive." She waited through his stubborn silence then said, "Haven't I warned you of that—possibility?"

"Often," said Fisher

"Yet you sound, now, as though you can hardly wait for what is sure to be a happy reunion. It is dangerous to have hopes that are not likely to be fulfilled, to pin everything upon them. What has suddenly produced this new attitude? Have you been talking to someone who was unjustifiably optimistic?"

Fisher flushed. "Why do I have to have been talking to someone? Why couldn't I have come to an independent conclusion concerning this, or any other matter? Just because I don't understand the theoretical physics that you do understand doesn't mean I'm subnormal or brainless."

Wendel said, "No, Crile. I never thought anything of the sort about you, nor did I mean to imply it. Tell me what *you* think about Rotor."

"Nothing terribly deep or subtle. It just seemed to me that there was nothing in empty space that is very likely to have destroyed Rotor. It's easy to say that there might only be the dead hulk of a Settlement at Rotor, if it reached the Neighbor Star at all, but what is it that would have destroyed them either on the way or once they were there? I defy you to give me a specific scenario of destruction—collisions—alien intelligences—whatever."

Wendel said earnestly, "Crile, I can't. I have no mystical visions of something having happened. It's just hyper-assistance itself. It's a tricky technique, Crile. Take my word for it. It doesn't use either space or hyperspace in a steady way, but skids along at the interface, wobbling to one side or another for short periods, and moving from space to hyperspace and then from hyperspace back to space several times a minute, perhaps. The passage from one to the other may therefore have taken place a million times or more in the course of the trip from here to the Neighbor Star."

"And so?"

"And so, it happens that the transition is far more dangerous than is level flight in either space or hyperspace. I don't know how thoroughly the Rotorians had established hyperspatial theory, but the chances are that they had done so in only a rudimentary fashion, or they would have surely developed true superluminal flight. In our project, which has worked out hyperspatial theory in great detail, we've managed to establish the effect on material objects of passing from space to hyperspace and vice versa.

"If an object is a point, there is no strain on it during the transition. If an object is not a point, however—if it is an extended bit of matter, as any ship would be—then there is always a finite period of time during which part of it is in space and part is in hyperspace. This creates a strain—the amount of strain depending on the size of the object, its physical makeup, its speed of transition, and so on. Even for an object the size of Rotor, the danger involved in a single transition—or a dozen, for that matter—is so small that it can reasonably be ignored.

"When the *Superluminal* will travel, superluminously, to the Neighbor Star, we are liable to make a dozen transitions, or possibly only as few as two. The flight will be a safe one. In a flight with hyper-assistance only, on the other hand, there may be a million transitions in the course of the same trip, you see, and the chances of fatal strain mount up."

Fisher looked appalled. "Is the chance of fatal strain certain?"

"No, nothing is certain. It's a statistical matter. A ship might undergo a million transitions—or a billion—with nothing happening. It might be destroyed, on the other hand, on the very first transition. The chances, however, increase rapidly with the number of transitions.

"I suspect, then, that Rotor embarked on its trip understanding very little about the dangers of transition. Had they known more,

251

they would never have left. There is a very good chance, then, that they experienced some sort of strain that might have been weak enough to allow them to 'limp' to the Neighbor Star or one that was strong enough to blow them completely out of existence. Therefore, we might find a hulk, or we might find nothing at all."

"Or we might find a Settlement that has survived," said Fisher rebelliously.

"Admitted," said Wendel. "Or we might ourselves be strained against the odds, be destroyed, and, for that reason, find nothing. I ask you not to be prepared for certainties but for probabilities. And remember that those who think about the matter, without some accurate knowledge of hyperspatial theory, are not likely to come to reasonable conclusions."

Fisher fell into a profound and clearly depressed silence, while Wendel watched him uneasily.

62.

Tessa Wendel found Station Four a weird environment. It was as though someone had built a small Settlement, but fitted it out to be a combination of nothing more than a laboratory, an observatory, and a launching platform. It had no farms, no homes, none of the appurtenances of a Settlement, however small. It was not even equipped with a spin that would set up an adequate pseudo-gravitational field.

It was, in fact, nothing but a spaceship with acromegaly. It was clear that, although it could be permanently occupied, provided there was a continuous drizzle of food, air, and water supplies (there was some recycling, but it wasn't efficient), no single individual could remain there for very long.

Crile Fisher made the wry comment that Station Four was like an old-fashioned space station from the early days of the Space Age that had unaccountably survived into the twenty-third century.

In one respect, though, it was unique. It presented a panoramic view of the Earth-Moon system. From the Settlements that orbited Earth, the two bodies could rarely be seen in their true relationship. From Station Four, however, Earth and Moon were never more than fifteen degrees apart, and as Station Four revolved around the center of gravity of that system (roughly equivalent to revolving about the Earth), the changing pattern of the two worlds, both in position and phase, and the changing size of the Moon (depending on whether it was on the Station's own side of Earth, or on the opposite side) was a never-ending wonder.

The Sun was blocked out automatically by the Artec device (Wendel had to ask to find out that that stood for "Artificial Eclipse" device) and only when the Sun moved too near either Earth or Moon in the station's sky was the view spoiled.

Wendel's Settlement background showed up now, for she enjoyed watching the Earth-Moon interplay, mostly (she explained) because it made it clear she was no longer on Earth.

She said as much to Fisher, who smiled dourly. He had noticed her quick glance to right and left as she said it.

He said, "I see you don't mind telling *me* that, even though I'm an Earthman and might resent it. But, never fear, I won't pass it along."

"I'd trust you with anything, Crile." She smiled at him happily. He had changed considerably since that crucial conversation when they had first reached Station Four. He was somber, yes, but sooner that than the feverish expectation of what could not be.

He said, "Do you really think they resent your being a Settler at this stage of the game?"

"Of course they do. They never forget. They're as narrow-minded as I am, and I never forget they're Earthpeople."

"You obviously forget I'm an Earthman."

"That's because you're Crile, and fall into no category other than Crile. And I'm Tessa. And that ends it."

Fisher said thoughtfully, "Does it ever bother you, Tessa, that you have worked out superluminal flight for Earth, rather than for your own Settlement, Adelia?"

"But I haven't done it for Earth, and I wouldn't have done it for Adelia in other circumstances. In both cases, I'm doing it for myself. I had a problem to solve, and I completed the job successfully. Now I'm going down in history as the inventor of superluminal flight and that's what I've done for myself. And it may sound pretentious, but I'm doing it for humanity, too. It doesn't matter on which world the discovery is made, you know. Some person or persons on Rotor invented hyper-assistance, but we have it now and so do all the Settlements. In the end, the Settlements will all have superluminal flight, too. Wherever an advance takes place, ultimately all humanity is helped."

"Earth needs it more than the Settlements do, though."

"You mean because of the approach of the Neighbor Star, which the Settlements can easily evade by leaving, if necessary, but which Earth can't. Well, I'll leave that as a problem for Earth's leaders. I've supplied the tool and they can work out methods for using it to their best advantage."

Crile said, "I understand we're taking off tomorrow."

"Yes, finally. They'll be taking holographic recordings and give us the full treatment. There's no way of telling, though, when they'll be able to release them to the general public and the Settlements."

"It can't be till after our return," said Fisher. "There'd be no sense in putting them on display if they can't be certain we'll ever come back. It's going to be an agonizing wait for them, too, since they'll have no contact with us at all. When the astronauts first landed on the Moon, they were in touch with the Earth all the way."

"True," said Wendel, "but when Columbus sailed off into the Atlantic, the Spanish monarchs never heard from him again till he returned seven months later."

Fisher said, "Earth, now, has far more at stake than Spain had seven and a half centuries ago. It is really a great pity we can't have superluminal communication, since we have superluminal flight."

"I think so, too. As does Koropatsky, who has been hammering at me to work out telecommunication. But, as I told him, I am not a marvelous supernatural force who can crank out everything anyone needs. It is one thing to push mass through hyperspace and quite another to push some sort of radiation through hyperspace. They follow different rules even in ordinary space so that Maxwell didn't work out his electromagnetic equations until two centuries after Newton worked out his gravitational equation. Well, mass and radiation follow different rules in hyperspace, too, and the rules for radiation still defeat us. Someday we'll work out superluminal communication, but we haven't yet."

"It's too bad," said Fisher thoughtfully. "It's possible that without superluminal communication, superluminal flight won't be practical."

"Why not?"

"The lack of superluminal communication cuts the umbilical cord. Could Settlements live far from Earth—far from the rest of humanity —and survive?"

Wendel frowned. "What's this new line of philosophy you've begun to track down?"

"Just a thought. Being a Settler, Tessa, and being accustomed to it, it may not occur to you that living on a Settlement is not truly natural to human beings."

"Really? It never seemed unnatural to me."

"That's because you weren't really living on one. You were living in a whole system of Settlements among which one was a large planet with billions of people on it. Might not the Rotorians, once they reach the Neighbor Star, find that living on an isolated Settlement was unsatisfactory? In that case, they would surely return to Earth, but they haven't. Might that not be because they have found a planet to live on?"

"A habitable planet circling a red dwarf star? Most unlikely."

"Nature has a way of fooling us and upsetting supposed certainties. Suppose there *is* a habitable planet there. Shouldn't it be carefully studied?"

Wendel said, "Ah, I'm beginning to get what you're driving at. You feel that the ship may come to the Neighbor Star, and find that there is some sort of planet there. We would then make a note of it, decide from a distance that it is uninhabited, and go on about our task of further exploration. You would want us to land and make a much more thorough search, so that we can at least try to find your daughter. But what if our neuronic detector finds no trace of intelligence anywhere within any planetary system the Neighbor Star may have? Must we still search the individual planets?"

Fisher hesitated. "Yes. If they show any signs of being habitable, we must study them, it seems to me. We must know all we can about any such planet. We may have to begin evacuating Earth soon, and we must know where to take our people. It's all very well for you to overlook that, since Settlements can just drift off without the necessity of evacua—"

"Crile! Don't start treating me as the enemy! Don't start suddenly thinking of me as a Settler. I'm *Tessa*. If there is a planet, we'll investigate it as much as we can, I promise you. But if there is and if the Rotorians are occupying it, then— Well, you spent some years on Rotor, Crile. You must know Janus Pitt."

"I know *of* him. I never met him, but my wi—my ex-wife worked with him. According to her, he was a very capable man, very intelligent, very forceful."

"*Very* forceful. We knew of him on other Settlements, too. And we were not generally fond of him. If it was his plan to find a place for Rotor that was hidden from the rest of humanity, he could do no better than to go to the Neighbor Star, since it was so close and since its existence was not known by anyone outside Rotor at the time. And if, for any reason, he wanted a system all to himself, he would, being Janus Pitt, fear the possibility of being followed and having his monopoly upset. If he happened to find a useful planet that could be used by Rotor, he would be even more resentful of intrusion."

"What are you getting at?" asked Fisher, who looked perturbed, as though he knew what she was getting at.

"Why, tomorrow we take off, and in not too long a time, we'll be at the Neighbor Star. And if it does have a planet, as you seem to think it might, and if we find the Rotorians are occupying it, it's not going to be a matter of just going down to the surface and saying, 'Hello! Surprise!' I'm afraid that at the first sight of us, he would give us his version of a 'Hello' and blast us into oblivion."

# TWENTY-NINE

# ENEMY

### 63.

Ranay D'Aubisson, like all the inhabitants of the Erythro Dome during their period of habitation, visited Rotor periodically. It was necessary—a touch of home, a return to the roots, a gathering of renewed strength.

This time, however, D'Aubisson, had "moved upward" (the usual phrase for passing from Erythro to Rotor) a bit earlier than her schedule had called for. She had, indeed, been summoned by Commissioner Pitt.

She sat in Janus Pitt's office, noting with her skilled eyes the small signs of aging that had accumulated since she had last seen him several years before. She did not, in the ordinary course of her work, have frequent occasions to see him, of course.

His voice, however, was as strong as ever, his eyes as sharp, and she noted no decline in mental vigor.

Pitt said, "I have received your report on the incident outside the

257

Dome, and I recognize the caution with which you approached your diagnosis of the situation. But now, off the record and unofficially, exactly what happened to Genarr? This room is shielded and you can talk freely."

D'Aubisson said dryly, "I'm afraid that my report, cautious as it was, happens to be truthful and complete. We don't really know what happened to Commander Genarr. The brain scan showed changes, but these were extraordinarily small and did not correspond to anything in our past experience. And they were reversible, since they did, in fact, quickly reverse."

"But something *did* happen to him?"

"Oh yes, but that's the point. We can't say anything more than 'something.' "

"Some form of the Plague, perhaps?"

"None of the symptoms that have been detected in the past were found in this case."

"But in the old days of the Plague, brain scanning was still comparatively primitive. You would not have detected the symptoms you have detected now in the past, so it might still be a mild form of the Plague, might it not?"

"We could say so, but we could not present real evidence to that effect, and, in any case, Genarr is now normal."

"He *seems* normal, I suppose, but we don't really know if there might not be a relapse."

"Neither is there any reason to suppose there might be."

A fleeting look of impatience crossed the Commissioner's face. "You're sparring with me, D'Aubisson. You know perfectly well that Genarr's position is one of considerable importance. The situation in the Dome is always precarious, since we never know if and when the Plague will strike again. Genarr's value was that he seemed immune to it, but we can scarcely consider him immune now. Something happened, and we must be prepared to replace him."

"That is your decision to make, Commissioner. I am not suggesting replacement as a medical necessity."

"But you'll keep him under close observation, and you'll keep the possibility of such a necessity in mind, I hope."

"I would consider that part of my medical duties."

"Good. Especially since if there is to be a replacement, I have been considering you."

"Considering *me?*" A small flash of excitement crossed her face before she could suppress it.

"Yes, why not? It's well known that I've never been enthusiastic about the project of colonizing Erythro. I have always felt it necessary to retain the mobility of humanity and not to allow ourselves to be trapped into slavery to a large planet again. Nevertheless, it would be wise if we could colonize the planet not as a place intended primarily for population but as a vast resource—rather as we treated the Moon in the old Solar System. But we can't do that if the Plague hangs over our heads, can we?"

"No, we can't, Commissioner."

"So our real task, to begin with, is to solve that problem. We never have. The Plague just died down and we have accepted that—but this latest incident shows us that the danger is not yet gone. Whether Genarr suffered a touch of the Plague or not, he certainly suffered something, and I want the matter now given top priority. You would be the natural person to head that project."

"I'd be glad to accept the responsibility. It would mean doing what I am, in any case, trying to do, but with greater authority. I hesitate at supposing that I ought to be the Erythro Dome Commander."

"As you said, that's for me to decide. I take it you would not refuse the post if it were offered to you?"

"No, Commissioner. I would be greatly honored."

"Yes, I'm sure," said Pitt dryly. "And what happened to the girl?"

For a moment, D'Aubisson seemed taken aback by the sudden change in subject. She all but stammered as she repeated, "The girl?"

"Yes, the girl who was outside the Dome with Genarr, the one who removed her protective suit."

"Marlene Fisher?"

"Yes, that's her name. What happened to her?"

D'Aubisson hesitated. "Why, nothing, Commissioner."

"So it says in the report. But *I'm* asking you now. *Nothing?*"

"Nothing detectable by brain scan or in any other way."

"You mean that at the same time that Genarr, wearing an E-suit, was struck down, the girl, this Marlene Fisher, without an E-suit, suffered nothing?"

D'Aubisson shrugged. "Nothing at all, as far as we could tell."

"Don't you consider that strange?"

"She's a strange young woman. Her brain scan—"

259

"I know about her brain scan. I know also that she has peculiar abilities. Have you noted that?"

"Oh yes. I have indeed."

"And how do her abilities strike you? Mind reading, by any chance?"

"No, Commissioner. That's impossible. The concept of telepathy is a mere fantasy. I wish it were mind reading, in fact, since that would not be so dangerous. Thoughts can be placed under control."

"What is it about her that is more dangerous?"

"Apparently, she reads body language and we can't control that. Every motion speaks." She said it with a touch of bitterness that Pitt did not fail to note.

He said, "Did you have a personal experience of that?"

"Certainly." D'Aubisson looked grim. "It is impossible to be near the young woman without experiencing some of the inconvenience of her habit of perception."

"Yes, but what happened?"

"Nothing of tremendous importance, but it was annoying." D'Aubisson flushed and, for a moment, her lips pressed together as though she were thinking of defying her interrogator. But that moment passed. She said, almost in a whisper, "After I had examined Dome Commander Genarr, Marlene asked me how he was. I told her that he was not seriously harmed and that there was every hope that he would recover completely.

"She said, 'Why does that disappoint you?'

"I was taken aback and said, 'I'm not disappointed. I'm pleased.'

"She said, 'But you *are* disappointed. That is quite clear. You're impatient.'

"It was the first time I had encountered that sort of thing directly, though I had heard about it from others, and I couldn't think of anything to do but challenge her. 'Why should I be impatient? For what?'

"She looked at me solemnly with her large, dark, and unsettling eyes. Then she said, 'It seems to be about Uncle Siever—' "

Pitt interrupted. "Uncle Siever? Is there a relationship?"

"No. I think it's only a term of affection. She said, 'It seems to be about Uncle Siever and I wonder if you want to replace him as Dome Commander.'

"At that, I just turned and walked away."

Pitt said, "How did you feel when she told you this?"

"I was furious. Naturally."

"Because she had maligned you? Or because she was correct?"

"Well, in a way—"

"No no. Don't hedge, Doctor. Was she wrong or was she right? Were you sufficiently disappointed at Genarr's recovery for the girl to notice, or was the whole thing a stroke of her peculiar imagination?"

The words seemed to force themselves out of D'Aubisson's lips. "She sensed something that was really there." She stared at Pitt defiantly. "I'm only human, and I have my impulses. And you yourself have now indicated that I might be offered the post, which would seem to mean you consider me qualified for it."

"I'm sure you are maligned in spirit—if not in fact," said Pitt, without any sign of humor. "But now consider— You have this young woman, who is peculiar, who is very strange, both as shown by the brain scan and by her behavior—and, in addition, she seems unaffected by the Plague. Clearly, there may be a connection between her neuronic pattern and her Plague resistance. Might she not be a useful tool for studying the Plague?"

"I can't say. I suppose it's conceivable."

"Shouldn't it be tested?"

"Perhaps, but how?"

Pitt said quietly, "Let her be exposed to the influence of Erythro as much as possible."

D'Aubisson said thoughtfully, "That is what she wants to do, as it happens, and Commander Genarr seems to be willing to let her."

"Good. Then you will supply the medical backing."

"I understand. And if the young woman gets the Plague?"

"We must remember that the solution of the problem is more important than the welfare of a single individual. We have a world to win, and for that we might have to pay a sad but necessary price."

"And if Marlene is destroyed and that does not help us understand or counteract the Plague?"

Pitt said, "That risk must be faced. After all, it might also be that she will remain untouched and that that untouchability, carefully studied, may give us the means of a breakthrough in understanding the Plague. In that case, we win without loss."

It was only afterward, when D'Aubisson had left for her Rotorian apartment, that Pitt's iron resolution permitted him to think of himself as Marlene Fisher's confirmed enemy. True victory would be to have Marlene destroyed and the Plague remain unsolved. At a stroke he would be rid of an inconvenient girl who might otherwise, some-day, produce young like herself; and of an inconvenient world that might otherwise, someday, produce a population as undesirable, as dependent, and as immobile as Earth's population had been.

64.

The three of them sat together in the Erythro Dome—Siever Genarr watchful, Eugenia Insigna deeply concerned, and Marlene Fisher clearly impatient.

Insigna said, "Now, remember, Marlene, do not stare at Nemesis. I know you've been warned about the infrared, but it's also a fact that Nemesis is a mild flare star. Every once in a while there's an explosion on its surface and a burst of white light. It just lasts a minute or two, but that will be enough to shock your retinas, and you can't tell when it's going to happen."

Genarr said, "Can astronomers tell when it's going to happen?"

"Not so far. It's one of the many chaotic aspects of nature. We have not yet worked out the rules underlying stellar turbulence and there are some among us who think the rules can never be worked out entirely. They are simply too complex."

"Interesting," said Genarr.

"It's not that we're not grateful to the flares. Three percent of the energy reaching Erythro from Nemesis is the result of those flares."

"That doesn't sound like much."

"It is, though. Without the flares, Erythro would be an icy world and much less easy to live on. The flares do make problems for Rotor, which has to adjust its use of sunlight quickly whenever there's a flare, and strengthen its particle-absorption field."

Marlene was looking from one to the other as they spoke, and she finally broke in with a small note of exasperation, "How long are you two going to keep this up? It's just to keep me sitting here. I can tell that very easily."

Insigna said hastily, "Where will you go when you're out there."

"Just around. To the little river, or creek, or whatever it is."

"Why?"

"Because it's interesting. Just flowing water in the open, and you can't see the ends, and you know it's not being pumped back to the beginning."

"But it is," said Insigna, "by the heat of Nemesis."

"That doesn't count. I mean human beings aren't doing it. Besides, I just want to stand there and watch it."

"Don't drink from it," said Insigna severely.

"I don't intend to. I can last an hour without drinking. If I get hungry, or thirsty—or anything else—I'll come back. You're making such a fuss over nothing."

Genarr smiled. "I suppose you want to recycle everything right here in the Dome."

"Yes, of course. Wouldn't anyone?"

Genarr's smile broadened. He said, "You know, Eugenia, I'm quite certain that living in Settlements has changed humanity permanently. The necessity of cycling is now ingrained in us. On Earth, you just threw things away, assuming it would recycle naturally, and, of course, sometimes it didn't."

"Genarr," said Insigna, "you're a dreamer. It may be possible for human beings to learn good habits under pressure, but relieve the pressure and the bad habits are back at once. Downhill is easier than uphill. It's called the second law of thermodynamics, and if we ever do colonize Erythro, I predict that we will litter it from end to end in no time at all."

"No, we won't," said Marlene.

Genarr said in a tone of polite inquiry, "Why not, dear?"

And Marlene said with impatient force, "Because we won't. Now can I go out?"

Genarr looked at Insigna and said, "We might as well let her go, Eugenia. We can't hold her back forever. Besides, for what it's worth, Ranay D'Aubisson, who just got back from Rotor, went over all the records from the start and told me yesterday that Marlene's brain scan seems so stable that she is convinced that Marlene will come to no harm on Erythro."

Marlene, who had turned toward the door, as though ready to walk to the airlock, now turned back. "Wait, Uncle Siever, I almost forgot. You must be careful of Dr. D'Aubisson."

"Why? She's an excellent neurophysicist."

"That's not what I mean. She was pleased when you were in trouble after your trip outside and pretty disappointed when you got better."

Insigna looked surprised and said automatically, "What makes you say that?"

"Because I *know*."

"But I don't understand that. Siever, don't you get along with D'Aubisson?"

"Certainly, I do. We get along very well. Never a cross word. But if Marlene says—"

"Mightn't Marlene be wrong?"

Marlene said at once, "But I'm not."

Genarr said, "I'm sure you're right, Marlene." Then, to Insigna, "D'Aubisson is an ambitious woman. If anything happens to me, she's the logical choice as my successor. She's had a great deal of experience down here and she's surely the best person to deal with the Plague if it lifts its head again. What's more, she's older than I am and may not feel there's much time to waste. I couldn't blame her if she was anxious to succeed me, and if her heart lifted a bit when I was ill. The chances are she's not even consciously aware of these feelings."

"Yes, she is," said Marlene ominously. "She knows all about it. You watch out, Uncle Siever."

"Well, I will. Are you ready now?"

"Of course I'm ready."

"Then let me walk you to the airlock. You come with us, Eugenia, and try not to look so tragic."

And so it was that Marlene stepped out onto the surface of Erythro, alone and unprotected, for the first time. It was, by Earth Standard time, 9:20 P.M., January 15, 2237. By Erythro time, it was midmorning.

# THIRTY

# TRANSITION

### 65.

Crile Fisher tried to suppress his excitement, tried to maintain the same calm expressions that the others were wearing.

He didn't know where Tessa Wendel was at the moment. She couldn't be far, since the *Superluminal* was reasonably small—though broken up so that someone in one bay might well be out of sight to someone in another.

The other three crew members were just pairs of hands to Fisher. They each had something to do and they were doing it. Only Fisher himself had nothing specific to do, except perhaps to be careful to stay out of the way of the others.

He looked at the other three (two men and one woman) almost furtively. He knew them to talk to, and had talked to them frequently. They were all young. The oldest was Chao-Li Wu, who was thirty-eight and a hyperspecialist. Then there was Henry Jarlow, who was thirty-five, and Merry Blankowitz, the baby of the team,

265

twenty-seven years old and with the ink still damp on her doctor's diploma.

Wendel, at fifty-five, was ancient by comparison, but she was the inventor, the designer, the demigoddess of the flight.

It was Fisher who was odd man out. He would be fifty on his next birthday, which was not so far off, and he had no specialized training. He had no right to be on the ship if either youth or knowledge were considered.

But he had been on Rotor once. That counted. And Wendel wanted him with her, and that counted even more. So did Tanayama and Koropatsky, which counted most of all.

The ship was making its way, lumbering through space. Fisher could tell that, even though there was no physical indication that this was so. He could feel it with the tendrils of his intestines—if they had any. He thought fiercely: I've been in space far longer than all the others put together, far more times on far more ships. I can tell there is nothing sleek about this ship just by the feel of it. They can't.

The *Superluminal* had to lack sleekness. The normal power sources that kept ordinary spaceships moving through the vacuum were cramped and cut down in the *Superluminal*. They had to be, for most of the ship was given over to the hyperspatial motors.

It was like a seabird that waddled clumsily on land because it was designed for the water.

Wendel suddenly appeared. Her hair was somewhat disheveled and she was perspiring a bit.

Fisher said, "Is everything all right, Tessa?"

"Oh yes, perfectly." She rested her rear end against one of the convenient wall depressions (very useful, considering the light pseudo-grav maintained on the ship). "No problems."

"When do we make the move into hyperspace?"

"In a few hours. We want to get into the proper coordinates with all appropriate gravitational sources twisting space precisely as calculated."

"So we can allow for it exactly?"

"That's right."

Fisher said, "That doesn't make hyperspatial flight sound very practical. What if you don't know where everything is? What if you're in a hurry and can't wait to calculate every gravitational twitch?"

266

Wendel looked up at Fisher with a sudden smile. "You've never asked anything like this before? Why do you ask it now?"

"I've never actually been on a hyperspatial flight before. The question presents itself to me with greater urgency under these conditions, you see."

"This and many other such questions have presented themselves to me with the greatest possible urgency for years. Welcome to the club."

"But answer me."

"Gladly. In the first place, there are devices that measure overall gravitational intensity, in both scalar and tensor aspects, at any point in space, whether you know the neighborhood or not. The result is not quite as accurate as it would be if you painstakingly measured each gravitational source and added them together, but it is close enough—if time is precious. And if time is still more precious and you have to push the hyperspatial button, so to speak, and trust to good fortune that gravitation is not very significant and should happen to be slightly wrong, then the transition would be accompanied by something roughly equivalent to a jar—like crossing a threshold and catching the toe of your shoe on the sill. If we can avoid that, fine, but if we don't it's not necessarily fatal. Naturally, in the first transition point, we would like it to be as smooth as possible for our psychological peace of mind—if nothing else."

"What if you're in a hurry, feel that gravitation is negligible, and it isn't?"

"You have to hope that that doesn't happen."

"You talked about strains during transition. That means our very first transition might be fatal, even if gravity is allowed for."

"*Might* be, but the odds against a fatal accident at any given transmission are enormous."

"Even if it isn't fatal, might it not be unpleasant?"

"That's harder to say because it requires a subjective judgment. Understand that there's no acceleration involved. In hyper-assistance, a ship has to work its way up to light speed, and even a little beyond at intervals, by use of a low-energy hyperspatial field. Efficiency is low, speeds are high, risks are great, and, frankly, I don't know what the discomforts may, or may not, be.

"In our kind of superluminal flight, using a high-energy hyperspatial field, we make the transition at normal speeds. We may be at a speed of a thousand kilometers per second at one instant, and at the next we are going a thousand million kilometers per second without acceleration. And since there is no acceleration, we don't feel it."

"How can there be no acceleration when you increase the speed a millionfold in an instant?"

"Because the transition is the mathematical equivalent of acceleration. However, whereas your body responds to acceleration, it does not to transition."

"But how can you tell?"

"By sending animals through hyperspace from one point to another. They are in hyperspace for only a brief fraction of a microsecond, but it's the transition between space and hyperspace that we worry about, and there is one in either direction in even the briefest possible passage through hyperspace."

"And animals were sent?"

"Of course. Once they had reached the reception point, they couldn't very well tell us how things were, but there they were, totally unhurt and calm. It was clear they hadn't been harmed in any way. We tried it on dozens of animals of all kinds. We even tried it on monkeys, all of which survived perfectly—except in one case."

"Ah. And what happened in that one case?"

"The animal was dead, grotesquely mutilated, but that was caused by a mistake in the programming. It wasn't the transition at all. And something like that can happen to us. It's not likely, but it can. It would be equivalent to stepping over a threshold, catching the toe of your shoe on the sill, tripping, falling forward, and breaking your neck. Such things have, indeed, happened, but we don't expect it to happen every time we cross a threshold. All right?"

"I guess I don't have a choice," said Fisher grimly. "All right."

Two hours and twenty-seven minutes later, the ship crossed safely into hyperspace, with no sensation whatever for anyone on board, and the first superluminal flight at speeds far beyond that of light took place.

The transition, by Earth Standard time, was at 9:20 P.M., January 15, 2237.

# THIRTY-ONE

# NAME

66.

Silence!

Marlene reveled in it—all the more so because she could break it if she wished. She stooped to pick up a pebble and tossed it against a rock. It made a small thunk, then fell to the ground and was still.

Having left the Dome with no more clothes than she would have worn on Rotor, she felt perfectly free.

She had walked straight away from the Dome toward the creek, without even watching to check the landmarks.

Her mother's last words had been a rather weak plea. "Please, Marlene, remember you said you would stay in sight of the Dome."

She had smiled briefly, but had paid no attention. She might stay in sight, but perhaps not. She did not intend to be hemmed in, regardless of what promises she had been forced to make to keep the peace. After all, she was carrying a wave-emitter. At any time, she could be located. She herself could use the receiving end of it to sense the direction of the Dome's emitter.

If she had an accident of some sort—if she fell or was somehow hurt—they could come get her.

If a meteor struck her—well, she'd be dead. There would be nothing anyone could do about that, even if she were in sight of the Dome. Even allowing for the disturbing thought of meteors, it was all so peaceful and wonderful on Erythro. On Rotor it was always noisy. Wherever you went, the air quivered and shook and battered your tired ears with sound waves. It must be even worse on Earth, with its eight billion people, and trillions of animals, and its thunderstorms and wild surges of water from the sea and sky. She had once tried to listen to a recording entitled "Noises of Earth," had winced at it, and had quickly had enough.

But here on Erythro, there was a wonderful silence.

Marlene came to the creek, and the water moved past her with a soft bubbly sound. She picked up a jagged pebble and tossed it into the water and there was a small splash. Sounds were not forbidden on Erythro; they were merely doled out as occasional adornments that served to make the surrounding silence more precious.

She stamped her foot on the soft clay at the creek's edge. She heard a small dull thump, and there was the vague impression of a footprint. She bent down, cupped some water in her hand, and tossed it over the soil in front of her. It moistened and darkened in spots, crimson showing against pink. She added more water and finally placed her right shoe on the dark spot, pressing down. When she lifted her shoe, there was a deeper footprint there.

There were occasional rocks in the creek bed and she used them as stepping-stones to cross the water.

Marlene kept on, walking vigorously, swinging her arms, taking in deep breaths of air. She knew very well that the oxygen percentage was somewhat lower than it was on Rotor. If she ran, she would quickly grow tired, but she lacked the impulse to run. If she ran, she would use up her world more rapidly.

She wanted to look at everything!

She looked back and the mound of the Dome was visible, especially the bubble that housed the astronomical instruments. That irritated her. She wanted to be far enough away so that she could turn around and see the horizon as a perfect—if irregular—circle, with no intrusion of any sign of humanity (except herself) anywhere.

(Should she call the Dome? Should she tell her mother she would
be out of sight for a little while? No, they would just argue. They
could receive her carrier wave. They would be able to tell that she
was alive, well, and moving around. If they called her, she decided,
she would ignore them. Really! They must leave her to herself.)

Her eyes were adjusting to the pinkness of Nemesis and of the land
around her in every direction. It was not merely pink; it was all in
darks and lights, in purples and oranges, almost yellows in some
places. It time, it would become a whole new palette of colors to her
heightened senses, as variegated as Rotor, but more soothing.

What would happen if someday people settled on Erythro, introduced life, built cities? Would they spoil it? Or would they have
learned from Earth and would they go about it in a different way,
taking this new untouched world and making it into something close
to their heart's desire?

Whose heart's desire?

That was the problem. Different people would have different ideas,
and they would quarrel with each other and pursue irreconcilable
ends. Would it be better to leave Erythro empty?

Would that be right when people might enjoy it so? Marlene knew
well that *she* didn't want to leave it. It warmed her, being on this
world. She didn't know quite why, but it felt more like home than
Rotor ever had.

Was it some dim atavistic memory of Earth? Was there a feeling for
a huge endless world in her genes; a longing that a small, artificial,
turning city-in-space could not fulfill? How could that be? Earth was
surely different from Erythro in every possible way but the similarity
of size. And if Earth were in her genes, why wouldn't it be in the
genes of every human being?

But there must be *some* explanation. Marlene shook her head as
though to clear it and whirled around and around as if she were in
the midst of endless space. Strange that Erythro didn't seem barren.
On Rotor, you could see acres of grain and orchards of fruit trees, and
a haze of green and amber, and the straight-line irregularity of human
structures. Here on Erythro, however, you saw only the rolling
ground, interspersed with rocks of all sizes, as though strewn care-
lessly by some giant hand—strange, brooding silent shapes, with rivulets of water, here and there, flowing around and among them. And
no life at all if you didn't count the myriads of tiny germlike cells that

271

kept the atmosphere full of oxygen, thanks to the energy supply of Nemesis' red light.

And Nemesis, like any red dwarf, would continue to pour out its careful supply of energy for a couple of hundred billion years, hoarding its energy and seeing to it that Erythro and its tiny prokaryotes were warm and comfortable through all that time. Long after Earth's Sun had died and other bright stars, born still later, had also died, Nemesis would shine on unchanged, and Erythro would roll about Megas unchanged, and the prokaryotes would live and die, also essentially unchanged.

Surely human beings would have no right to come to this unchanging world and change it. Yet if she were alone on Erythro, she would need food—and companionship.

She might return to the Dome now and then for supplies, or to refresh a need to see other people, but she could still spend most of her time alone with Erythro. But would not others follow? How could she prevent them? And with others, no matter how few, would not Eden inevitably be ruined? Wasn't it being ruined because she herself had entered Eden—only *she?*

"No!" She shouted it. She shouted it loudly in a sudden eager experiment to see if she could make the alien atmosphere tremble and force it to carry words to her ears.

She heard her own voice, but in the flat terrain there were no echoes. Her shout was gone as soon as it sounded.

She whirled again. The Dome was just a thin shadow on the horizon. It could almost be ignored, but not quite. She wished it was not visible at all. She wanted nothing in view but herself and Erythro.

She heard the faint sigh of the wind, and knew it had picked up speed. It was not strong enough to feel, and the temperature hadn't dropped, nor was it unpleasant.

It was just a faint "Ah-h-h-h."

She imitated it cheerfully: "Ah-h-h-h-h."

Marlene stared up at the sky curiously. The weather forecasters had said it would be clear that day. Was it possible for storms to blow up suddenly and unpredictably on Erythro? Would the wind rise and become uncomfortable? Would clouds whip across the sky and rain begin to fall before she could get back to the Dome?

That was silly, as silly as the meteors. Of course it rained on Erythro, but right now there were only a few wispy pink clouds above. They moved lazily against the dark and unobstructed sky. There didn't seem to be any sign of a storm.

"Ah-h-h-h-h," whispered the wind. "Ah-h-h-h-h ay-y-y-y."

It was a double sound, and Marlene frowned. What could be making that sound? Surely the wind could not make the sound by itself. It would have to pass some obstruction and whistle as it did so. But there was nothing of the sort within sight.

"Ah-h-h-h-h ay-y-y-y-y uh-h-h-h-h."

It was a triple sound now, with the stress on the second sound.

Marlene looked around, wondering. She couldn't tell where it was coming from. To make the sound, something had to be vibrating, but she saw nothing, felt nothing.

Erythro *looked* empty and silent. It could make no sound.

"Ah-h-h-h ay-y-y-y uh-h-h-h."

Again. Clearer than before. It was as though it were in her own head, and, at that thought, her heart seemed to contract and she shivered. She felt the gooseflesh rise on her arms; she didn't have to look.

Nothing could be wrong with her head. Nothing!

She was waiting to hear it again, and it came. Louder. Still clearer. Suddenly there was a ring of authority to it, as though it were practicing and growing better.

Practicing? Practicing what?

And unwillingly, entirely unwillingly, she thought: It's as though someone who can't sound consonants is trying to say my name.

As though that were a signal, or her thought had released another spasm of power, or had perhaps sharpened her imagination, she heard—

"Mah-h-h lay-y-y nuh-h-h."

Automatically, without knowing she was doing it, she lifted her hands and covered her ears.

Marlene, she thought—soundlessly.

And then came the sound, mimicking, "Mahr-lay-nuh."

It came again, almost easily, almost naturally. "Marlene."

She shuddered, and recognized the voice. It was Aurinel, Aurinel of Rotor, whom she hadn't seen since the day on Rotor when she told him that the Earth would be destroyed. She had thought of him hardly at all since then—but always achingly, when she did.

Why was she hearing his voice where he was not—or hearing any voice where all was not?

"Marlene."

And she gave up. It was the Erythro Plague that she had been so certain would not touch her.

She was running blindly, blindly, toward the Dome, not pausing to tell where it was.

She did not know that she was screaming.

### 67.

They had brought her in. They had sensed her sudden approach, at a run. Two guards in E-suits and helmets had moved out at once and they had heard her screaming.

But the screaming had stopped before they had reached her. The running had slowed and stopped, too; and that was before she seemed aware of their approach.

When they reached her, she looked at them quietly and amazed them by asking, "What's wrong?"

No one had answered. A hand reached out for her elbow and she whipped away.

"Don't touch me," she said. "I'll go to the Dome, if that's what you want, but I can walk."

And she had walked quietly back with them. She was quite self-possessed.

### 68.

Eugenia Insigna, lips dry and pale, was trying not to seem distraught. "What happened out there, Marlene?"

Marlene said, her dark eyes wide and unfathomable, "Nothing. Nothing at all."

"Don't say that. You were running and screaming."

"I may have been for a little while, but just for a little while. You see, it was quiet, so quiet, that after a while I felt as though I must be deaf. Just silence, you know. So I stamped my feet and ran just to hear the noise, and I screamed—"

"Just to hear the noise of it?" asked Insigna, frowning.

"Yes, Mother."

"Do you expect me to believe that, Marlene? Because I don't. We picked up the screams and those were not the screams of making noise. Those were screams of terror. Something had frightened you."

"I told you. The silence. The possibility of deafness."

Insigna turned to D'Aubisson. "Isn't it possible, Doctor, that if you don't hear anything, anything at all, and if you're used to hearing things all the time, then your ears might just imagine they're hearing something so they can feel useful?"

D'Aubisson forced a thin smile. "That's a colorful way of putting it, but it is true that sensory deprivation can produce hallucinations."

"That disturbed me, I suppose. But after I heard my own voice and my own footsteps, I quieted down. Ask the two guards who came to get me. I was perfectly calm when they arrived, and I followed them into the Dome with no trouble. Ask them, Uncle Siever."

Genarr nodded. "They've told me this. And we watched it happen, besides. Very well, then. That's it."

"That's not it at all," said Insigna, her face still white—from fright or anger or both. "She's not going out any more. The experiment is finished."

"No, Mother," said Marlene, outraged.

D'Aubisson raised her voice, as though to forestall any angry clash of wills between mother and daughter. She said, "The experiment is *not* finished, Dr. Insigna. Whether she goes out again or not is beside the point. We still have to deal with the consequences of what has happened."

"What do you mean?" demanded Insigna.

"I mean, it's all very well to talk about imagining voices because the ear is not accustomed to silence, but surely another possible reason for imagined voices is the onset of a certain mental instability."

Insigna looked stricken.

Marlene said loudly, "Do you mean the Erythro Plague?"

"I don't mean that particularly, Marlene," said D'Aubisson. "We don't have any evidence; only a possibility. So we need another brain scan. It's for your own good."

"No," said Marlene.

"Don't say no," said D'Aubisson. "It's a must. We have no choice. It's something we'll have to do."

Marlene looked at D'Aubisson out of her dark and brooding eyes. She said, "You're *hoping* I have the Plague. You *want* me to have the Plague."

D'Aubisson stiffened, and her voice cracked. "That's ridiculous. How dare you say such a thing?"

But it was Genarr, now, who was staring at D'Aubisson. He said, "Ranay, we've discussed this little point about Marlene, and if she says you want her to have the Plague, you must have given yourself away in some way. That is, if Marlene is serious and isn't just saying it out of fright or anger."

"I'm serious," said Marlene. "She was just bubbling with hopeful excitement."

"Well, Ranay," said Genarr a little more coldly. "Are you?"

"I see what the girl means," said D'Aubisson, frowning. "I have not studied a fresh case of advanced Plague in years. And in the days when I did, when the Dome was primitive and had just been established, I had had virtually no appropriate devices with which to study it. Professionally, I would greatly welcome a chance to make a thorough study of a case of the Plague with modern techniques and instrumentation, to find out, perhaps, the true cause, the true cure, the true prevention. It's a reason for excitment, yes. It is a professional excitement that this young woman, unable to read minds, and without experience in such things, interprets as simple joy. It isn't simple."

"It may not be simple," said Marlene, "but it's malevolent. I'm not mistaken in that."

"You *are* mistaken. The brain scan must and will take place."

"It will *not,*" said Marlene, practically shouting. "You'll have to force me or sedate me, and then it won't be valid."

Insigna said, her voice shaking, "I don't want anything done against her will."

"This is something that goes beyond what she wills or does not will—" began D'Aubisson, and then staggered back with her hand to her abdomen.

Genarr said automatically, "What's the matter?"

Then, without waiting for an answer, leaving it to Insigna to lead D'Aubisson to the nearest sofa and to persuade her to lie down, he turned to Marlene and said hurriedly, "Marlene, agree to the test."

"I don't want to. She'll say I have the Plague."

"She won't. I guarantee that. Not unless you really do."

"I don't."

"I'm sure you don't, and the brain scan will prove it. Trust me, Marlene. Please."

Marlene looked from Genarr to D'Aubisson and back again. "And I can go back out on Erythro again?"

"Of course. As often as you wish. If you're normal—and you're sure you're normal, aren't you?"

"Sure as anything."

"Then the brain scan will prove it."

"Yes, but she'll say I can't go out again."

"Your mother?"

"And the doctor."

"No, they won't dare stop you. Now, just say you'll allow the brain scan."

"All right. She can have it."

Ranay D'Aubisson struggled to her feet.

### 69.

D'Aubisson studied the computerized analysis of the brain scan carefully while Siever Genarr watched.

"A curious scan," muttered D'Aubisson.

"We knew that to begin with," said Genarr. "She's a strange young woman. The point is there's no change?"

"None," said D'Aubisson.

"You sound disappointed."

"Don't start that again, Commander. There's a certain professional disappointment. I would like to study the condition."

"How do you feel?"

"I just told you—

"I mean, physically. That was a strange collapse you had yesterday."

"It wasn't a collapse. It was nervous tension. I'm not often accused of *wanting* someone to be seriously ill—and of having it apparently *believed.*"

"What happened? An attack of indigestion?"

"Could be. Abdominal pains, in any case. And dizziness."

"Does that often happen to you, Ranay?"

"No, it doesn't," she said sharply. "Neither am I accused of unprofessional behavior often."

"Just an excitable young woman. Why did you take it so seriously?"

"Do you mind if we change the subject? She does not have any signs of brain scan change. If she was normal before, then she is still normal."

"In that case, is it your professional opinion that she may continue to explore Erythro?"

"Since she has not been affected, apparently, I have no grounds on which to forbid her."

"Are you willing to go beyond that and send her out?"

D'Aubisson's attitude grew hostile. "You know that I've been to see Commissioner Pitt." It did not sound like a question.

"Yes, I know," said Genarr quietly.

"He has asked me to head a new project designed to study the Erythro Plague, and there will be a generous appropriation toward that study."

"I think that is a good idea and that you are a thoroughly good choice to head the study."

"Thank you. However, he did not appoint me Commander in your place. Therefore, it is up to you, Commander, to decide whether Marlene Fisher can be allowed to go out on Erythro. I will confine myself to giving her a brain scan if signs of abnormality show up."

"I intend to give Marlene permission to explore Erythro freely whenever she wishes. May I have your concurrence in that?"

"Since you have my medical opinion that she does not have the Plague, I will make no attempt to stop you, but the order to do so will have to be yours alone. If anything must be put into writing, you will have to sign it yourself."

"But you won't try to stop me."

"I have no reason to."

70.

Dinner was over and soft music played in the background. Siever Genarr, who had carefully talked of other things to an uneasy Eugenia Insigna, finally said, "The words are the words of Ranay D'Aubisson, but the force behind them is that of Janus Pitt."

Insigna's look of uneasiness deepened. "Do you really think that?"

"Yes, I do—and you should. You know Janus better than I do, I think. It's too bad. Ranay is a competent doctor, has a profound mind, and is a good person, but she's ambitious—as we all are, one way or another—and she can therefore be corrupted. She really wants to go down in history as the one who defeated the Erythro Plague."

And she would be willing to risk Marlene to do it?"

"Not willing in the sense that she wants to, or is eager to, but willing in the sense of—well, if there's no other way."

"But there must be other ways. To send Marlene into danger, as an experimental device, is monstrous."

"Not from her standpoint, and certainly not from Pitt's. One mind is well lost if it rescues a world and makes it a fit human habitation for millions. It's a hard-hearted way of looking at it, but future generations might make a heroine out of Ranay for being hard-hearted, and agree with her that one mind was well lost, or a thousand—if that's what it would take."

"Yes, if it's not *their* minds."

"Of course. All through history, human beings have been ready to make sacrifices at the expense of other people. Certainly, Pitt would. Or don't you agree?"

"About Pitt. Yes, I do," said Insigna energetically. "To think that I worked with him all those years."

"Then you know that he would view this in a very moralistic sense. 'The greatest good for the greatest number,' he would say. Ranay admits that she talked to him on her recent visit to Rotor, and I'm as positive that that's what he said to her, in one form of words or another, as that I am sitting in this chair."

"And what would he say," said Insigna bitterly, "if Marlene were exposed—and destroyed—and the Plague remained untouched? What would he say if my daughter's life were uselessly reduced to vacuity? And what would Dr. D'Aubisson say?"

"The doctor would feel unhappy. I'm sure of that."

"Because she wouldn't gain the credit for the cure?"

"Of course, but she would also feel unhappy about Marlene—and, I dare say, guilty. She's not a monster. As for Pitt—"

"He *is* a monster."

"I wouldn't even say that, but he has tunnel vision. He sees only his plan for the future of Rotor. If anything goes wrong, from our standpoint, he will undoubtedly tell himself that Marlene would, in any case, have interfered with his plans, and he will consider all to have happened for the good of Rotor. It will not hang heavily on his conscience."

Insigna shook her head slightly. "I wish we were making a mistake, that Pitt and D'Aubisson were not guilty of such things."

"I, too, wish that, but I am willing to trust Marlene and her body language insights. She said that Ranay was *happy* at the possibility that she would have a chance to study the Plague. I accept Marlene's judgment in this."

"D'Aubisson said she was happy for professional reasons," Insigna said. "Actually, I can believe that, in a way. After all, I'm a scientist, too."

"Of course you are," said Genarr, his homely face crinkling into a smile. "You were willing to leave the Solar System and go on an untried trip across the light-years to gain astronomical knowledge, even though you knew it might mean the death of every person on Rotor."

"A very small chance, it seemed to me."

"Small enough to risk your one-year-old child. You might have left her with your stay-at-home husband and made sure of her safety, even though it would have meant you would never see her again. Instead, you risked her life, not even for the greater good of Rotor, but for the greater good of yourself."

Insigna said, "Stop it, Siever. That's so cruel."

"I'm just trying to show you that almost everything can be looked at from two opposing sets of views, given sufficient ingenuity. Yes, D'Aubisson calls it professional pleasure at being able to study the disease, but Marlene said the doctor was being malevolent, and again I trust Marlene's choice of words."

"Then I suppose," said Insigna, the corners of her mouth curving downward, "that she is anxious to have Marlene go out on Erythro again."

"I suspect she does, but she is cautious enough to insist that I give the order and even suggests I put it in writing. She wants to make sure that it is I, not she, who gets the blame if something goes wrong. She's beginning to think like Pitt. Our friend Janus is contagious."

"In that case, Siever, you mustn't send Marlene out. Why play into Pitt's hands?"

"On the contrary, Eugenia. It's not simple at all. We *must* send her out?"

"*What?*"

"There's no choice, Eugenia. And no danger to her. You see, I now believe you were right when you suggested there was some permeating life-form on the planet that could exert some sort of power over us. You pointed out that I was deleteriously affected, and you were, and the guard was, and always when Marlene was in any way opposed. And I just saw precisely that happen to Ranay. When Ranay tried to force a brain scan on Marlene, she doubled up. When I persuaded Marlene to accept the brain scan, Ranay immediately improved."

"Well, there you are, then, Siever. If there's a malevolent life-form on the planet—"

"Now, wait, Eugenia. I didn't say it was malevolent. Even if this life-form, whatever it might be, caused the Plague as you suggested it did, that stopped. You said it was because we seemed to be content to remain in the Dome, but if the life-form were truly malevolent, it would have wiped us out and it would not have settled for what seems to me to have been a civilized compromise."

"I don't think it's safe to try to consider the actions of a totally alien life-form and deduce from that its emotions or intentions. What it think might well be totally beyond our understanding."

"I agree, Eugenia, but it's not harming Marlene. Everything it has done has served to *protect* Marlene, to shield her from interference."

"If that's so," said Insigna, "then why was she frightened, why did she begin to run to Dome, screaming? Not for one moment do I believe her tale that the silence made her nervous and she was just trying to make some noise to break that silence."

"That *is* hard to believe. The point is, though, that the panic subsided quickly. By the time her would-be-rescuers reached her, she seem perfectly normal. I would guess that something the life-form had done had frightened Marlene—I would imagine it was as unlikely to understand our emotions, as we are to understand its—but, seeing what it had done, it proceeded to soothe her quickly. That would explain what happened and would demonstrate, once again, the humane nature of the life-form."

Insigna was frowning. "The trouble with you, Siever, is that you have this terrible compulsion to think good of everyone—and everything. I can't trust your interpretation."

"Trust or not, you will find we can in no way oppose Marlene. Whatever she wants to do, she will do, and the opposition will be left behind, gasping in pain or flat-out unconscious."

Insigna said, "But what *is* this life-form?"

"I don't know, Eugenia."

"And what frightens me more than anything, now, is: What does it want with Marlene?"

Genarr shook his head. "I don't know, Eugenia."

And they stared at each other helplessly.

# THIRTY-TWO

## LOST

### 71.

Crile Fisher watched the bright star thoughtfully.

At first, it had been too bright to watch in the ordinary sense. He had glanced at it every once in a while and would see a bright afterimage. Tessa Wendel, who was in a state of despair over developments, had scolded and spoken of retinal damage, so he had opacified the viewport and had brought the brightness of the star down to just bearable levels. That dimmed the other stars to a downcast, tarnished glitter.

The bright star was the Sun, of course.

It was farther away than any human being had ever seen it (except for the people of Rotor on *their* journey away from the Solar System). It was twice as far away as one would see it from Pluto at its farthest, so that it showed no orb and shone with the appearance of a star. Nevertheless, it was still a hundred times the brightness of the full Moon as seen from Earth, and that hundredfold brightness was condensed and compacted into one brilliant point. No wonder one still couldn't bear to turn a direct and unflinching gaze upon it through an un-opacified glass.

It made things different. The Sun, ordinarily, was nothing to wonder at. It was too bright to look at, too unrivaled in its position. The minor portion of its light that was scattered into blueness by the atmosphere was sufficient to blank out the other stars altogether, and even where the stars were not blanked out (as on the Moon, for instance) they were so overridden by the Sun that there was no thought of comparison.

Here, so far out in space, the Sun had dimmed at least to the point where comparison was possible. Wendel had said that from this vantage point, the Sun was one hundred and sixty thousand times as bright as Sirius, which was the next brightest object in the sky. It was perhaps twenty million times as bright as the dimmest stars he could see by eye. It made the Sun seem more marvelous by comparison than when it shone, uncompared, in Earth's sky.

Nor did he have much more to do than watch the sky, for the *Superluminal* was merely drifting. It had been doing that for two days —two days of drifting through space at mere rocket velocities.

At this speed it would take thirty-five thousand years to reach the Neighbor Star—*if* they had been heading in the right direction. And they weren't.

It was this that had turned Wendel, two days earlier, into a picture of white-faced despair.

Until then, there had been no trouble. When they were due to enter hyperspace, Fisher had tensed himself, fearing the possible pain, the piercing flash of agony, the sudden surge of eternal darkness.

None of that had happened. It had all been too fast to experience. They had entered into and emerged from hyperspace in the same instant. The stars had simply blinked into a different pattern with no perceptible moment in which they had lost their first pattern, yet not gained their second.

It was relief in a double sense. Not only was he still alive, but he realized that if something had gone wrong and he had died, then death would have come in such a no-time way that he could not possibly have experienced death. He would simply have been dead.

The relief was so keen that he was scarcely aware that Tessa had let out a gasp of disturbance and pain, and dashed out to the engine room with an outcry.

She came back looking disheveled—not a hair out of place, but looking *internally* disheveled. Her eyes were wild and she stared at Fisher as though she did not really recognize him.

She said, "The pattern should not have changed."

"Shouldn't it?"

"We haven't moved far enough. Or shouldn't have. Only one and a third milli-light-years. That would not have been enough to alter the star pattern to the unaided eye. However"—she drew a deep, shuddering breath—"it's not as bad as it might have been. I thought we had slipped and moved out thousands of light-years."

"Would that have been possible, Tessa?"

"Of course it would have been possible. If our passage through hyperspace weren't tightly controlled, a thousand light-years is as easy as one."

"In that case, we can as easily just go—"

Wendel anticipated the conclusion. "No, we couldn't just go back. If our controls were that slipshod, every pass we would make would be uncontrolled travel, ending at some random point, and we'd never find our way back."

Fisher frowned. The euphoria of having passed through hyperspace and back—and stayed alive—began to leak away. "But when you sent out test objects, you brought them back safely."

"They were far less massive and were sent out through far shorter distance. But, as I said, it's not too bad. It turns out we went the correct distance. The stars are in the correct pattern."

"But they changed. I saw them change."

"Because we're oriented differently. The long axis of the ship has veered through an angle of better than twenty-eight degrees. In short, we followed a curved path rather than a straight one for some reason."

The stars, as seen through the viewport, were moving now, slowly, steadily.

Wendel said, "We're turning to face the Neighbor Star again, just for the psychological value of facing in the right direction, but then we must find out why we curved in passage."

The bright star, the beacon star, the star of brilliance entered the viewport and moved across it. Fisher blinked.

"That's the Sun," said Wendel, answering Fisher's look of astonishment.

Fisher said, "Are there any reasonable explanations why the ship curved in passage? If Rotor also curved, who knows where they ended?"

"Or where we will end either. Because I don't have any reasonable explanation. Not right now." She looked at him, clearly troubled. "If our assumptions were correct, then we should have changed position but not direction. We should have moved in a straight line, a Euclidean straight line, despite the relativistic curve of space-time, because we weren't in space-time, you see. There may be a mistake in the programming of the computer—or a mistake in our assumptions. I hope the former. That can be corrected easily."

Five hours passed. Wendel came in, rubbing her eyes. Fisher looked up uncomfortably. He had been viewing a film, but had lost interest. He had then watched the stars, allowing the patterns to hypnotize him, like anesthesia.

He said, "Well, Tessa?"

"Nothing wrong with the programming, Crile."

"Then the assumptions must be wrong?"

"Yes, but in what way? There are an infinite number of assumptions we might make. Which are correct? We can't try them one after another. We'd never finish, and we'd be hopelessly lost."

Silence fell between them for a while and then Wendel said, "If it had been the programming, it would have been a stupid mistake. We would have corrected it, without learning anything, but we'd have been safe. But now, if we must go back to fundamentals, we have a chance of discovering something really important, but if we fail, we may never find our way back."

She snatched at Fisher's hand. "Do you understand, Crile? Something is wrong and if we don't find out what, there's no way—except sheer incredible accident—that will allow us to find our way home. No matter how we try, we may continue to end up in the wrong place, and find ourselves steadily wronger and wronger. Which means death eventually, when our cycling fails, or our power supply peters out, or deep despair drains away our ability to live. And it's I who've done this to you. But the real tragedy would be the loss of a dream. If we don't come back, they'll never know if the ship was successful at all. They might conclude the transition was fatal and they might never try again."

"But they must if they expect to escape from Earth."

"They may give up; they may sit cowering, waiting for the Neighbor Star to complete its approach and pass on, and dying bit by bit." She looked up, her eyes blinking rapidly, her face looking terribly tired. "And it would be the end of your dream, too, Crile."

Crile's lips tightened, and he said nothing.

Almost timidly, Wendel said, "But for years now, Crile, you've had me. If your daughter—your dream—is gone, was I enough?"

"I might ask: If superluminal flight is gone, was *I* enough?"

There seemed no easy answer on either side, but then Wendel said, "You're second-best, Crile, but it has been a good second-best. Thank you."

Fisher stirred. "You speak for me, too, Tessa, something I wouldn't have believed at the start. If I had never had a daughter, there would have only been you. I almost wish—"

"Don't wish that. Second-best is enough."

And they held hands. Quietly. And gazed out at the stars.

Until Merry Blankowitz poked her face through the doorway. "Captain Wendel, Wu has an idea. He said he had it all along, but was reluctant to mention it."

Wendel started to her feet. "Why was he reluctant?"

"He said he once suggested the possibility to you, and you told him not to be a fool."

"Did I? And what has convinced him that I'm never wrong? I'll listen to it now and if it's a good idea, I'll break his neck for not forcing it on me earlier."

And she hurried out.

### 72.

Fisher could only wait during the day and a half that followed. They all ate together as they always did, but silently. Fisher did not know if any of them slept. He slept only in snatches, and woke to renewed despair.

How long can we go on like this? he thought on the second day, as he looked at the beauty of that unattainable bright dot in the sky that, so brief a time ago, had warmed him and lighted his way on Earth.

Sooner or later, they would die. Modern space technology would prolong life. Recycling was quite efficient. Even food would last a long time if they were willing to accept the tasteless algae cake they would end up with. The micro-fusion motors would dribble out energy for a long time, too. But surely no one would want to prolong life through the full time that the ship would make possible.

With a lingering, dragging, hopeless, lonely death finally certain, the rational way out would be to use the adjustable de-metabolizers.

That was the preferred method for suicide on Earth; why should it not be onboard ship as well? You could—if you wished—adjust the dose for a full day of reasonably normal life, live it out as joyously as you could—a known last day. At the end of the day, you would grow naturally sleepy. You would yawn and release your hold on wakefulness, passing into a peaceful sleep of restful dreams. The sleep would slowly deepen, the dreams would slowly fade, and you would not wake up. No kinder death had ever been invented.

And then, Tessa, just before 5 P.M., ship-time, on the second day after the transition that had curved instead of being straight, burst into the room. Her eyes were wild and she was breathing hard. Her dark hair, which, in the last year had become liberally salted with gray, was mussed.

Fisher rose in consternation. "Bad?"

"No, good!" she said, throwing herself into a chair rather than sitting down.

Fisher wasn't sure he had heard correctly, wasn't sure that perhaps she might only have been speaking ironically. He stared at her and watched her as she visibly gathered herself together.

"Good," she repeated. "Very good! Extraordinary! Crile, you're looking at an idiot. I don't suppose I'll ever recover from this."

"Well, what happened?"

"Chao-Li Wu had the answer. He had it all along. He told me. I remember him telling me. Months ago. Maybe a year ago. I dismissed it. I didn't even listen, really." She paused to catch her breath. Her excitement had completely disoriented the natural rhythm of her speech.

She said, "The trouble was that I thought of myself as the world authority on superluminal flight, and was convinced that no one could possibly tell me anything I didn't know or hadn't thought of. And if someone did suggest something that seemed strange to me, the idea was simply wrong, and, presumably, idiotic. Do you know what I mean?"

Fisher said grimly, "I've met people like that."

"Everyone's like that, now and then," said Wendel, "given certain

287

conditions. I suppose aging scientists are particularly like that. That's why the daring young revolutionaries of science become old fossils after a few decades. Their imaginations harden with encrusted self-love and that's their end. It is now my end. . . . But enough of that. It took us over a day to really work it out, to adjust the equations, to program the computer and set up the necessary simulations, to go down blind alleys and catch ourselves. It should have taken a week, but we were all driving each other like maniacs."

Wendel paused here, as if to catch her breath. Fisher waited for her to continue, nodding encouragement as he reached out to grasp her hand.

"This is complex," she continued. "Let me try to explain. Look— We go from one point in space through hyperspace to another point in space in zero time. But there's a path we take to do that, and it's a different path each time, depending on the starting and ending points. We don't observe the path, we don't experience it, we don't actually follow it in space-time fashion. It exists in a rather incomprehensible way. It's what we call a 'virtual path.' I worked out that concept myself."

"If you don't observe it, and don't experience it, how do you know it's there?"

"Because it can be calculated by the equations we use to describe the motion through hyperspace. The equations give us the path."

"How can you possibly know that the equations are describing anything that has actual reality? If could be just—mathematics."

"It could be. I thought it was. I ignored it. It was Wu who suggested it might have significance—maybe a year ago—and like a full-grown idiot, I dismissed it. A virtual path, I said, had merely virtual existence. If it couldn't be measured, it was outside the realm of science. I was so shortsighted. I can't endure myself when I think of it."

"All right. Suppose the virtual path has some sort of existence. What then?"

"In that case, if the virtual path is drawn near a sizable body, the ship experiences gravitational effects. That was the first breathtakingly true and useful new concept—that gravitation can make itself felt along the virtual path." Wendel shook her fist angrily. "I saw that myself, in a way, but I reasoned that since a ship would be moving at many times the speed of light, gravitation would have insufficient time to make itself felt to any measurable extent. Travel would therefore be, by my assumption, in a Euclidean straight line."

"But it wasn't."

"Obviously not. And Wu explained it. Imagine that the speed of light is a zero point. All speeds less than that of light would have negative magnitude, and all speeds greater than that of light would have positive magnitude. In the ordinary Universe we live in, therefore, all speeds would be negative, by that mathematical convention, and, in fact, *must* be negative.

"Now, the Universe is built on principles of symmetry. If something as fundamental as speed of movement is always negative, then something else, just as fundamental, ought to be always positive, and Wu suggested that that something else was gravitation. In the ordinary Universe, it is always an attraction. Every object with mass attracts every other object with mass.

"However, if something goes at a superluminal speed—that is, faster than light—then its speed is positive and the other something that was positive has to become negative. At superluminal speed, in other words, gravitation is a repulsive force. Every object with mass repels every other object with mass. Wu suggested that to me a long time ago and I wouldn't listen. His words just bounced off my eardrums."

Crile said, "But what's the difference, Tessa? When we're going at enormous superluminal speeds, and gravitational attraction doesn't have time to affect our motion, neither would gravitational repulsion."

"Ah, that's not so, Crile. That's the beauty of it. That reverses, too. In the ordinary Universe of negative speeds, the faster the speed relative to an attractive body, the less gravitational attraction affects the direction of movement. In the Universe of positive speeds, hyperspace, the faster we go relative to a repulsive body, the *more* gravitational repulsion affects the direction of movement. That makes no sense to us, since we're used to the situation as it exists in the ordinary Universe, but once you are forced to change signs from plus to minus and vice versa, you find these things falling into place."

"Mathematically. But how much can you trust the equations?"

"You match your calculations against the facts. Gravitational attraction is the weakest of all the forces and so is the gravitational repulsion along the virtual paths. Within the ship and within us, every particle repels all other particles while we are in hyperspace, but that repulsion can do nothing against the other forces that hold it together and have *not* changed signs. However, our virtual path from

Station Four to here carried us close to Jupiter. Its repulsion along the virtual hyperspatial path was just as intense as its attraction would have been along a nonvirtual spatial path.

"We calculated how Jupiter's gravitational repulsion would affect our path through hyperspace, and that path curved exactly as it had been observed to do. In other words, Wu's modification of my equations not only simplifies them, but it makes them *work*."

Fisher said, "And did you break Wu's neck, Tessa, as you promised you would?"

Wendel laughed, remembering her threat. "No, I didn't. Actually, I kissed him."

"I don't blame you."

"Of course, it's more important now than ever that we get back safely, Crile. This advance in superluminal flight must be reported, and Wu must be properly honored. He built on my work, I admit, but he went on to do what I might never have thought to do. I mean, consider the consequences."

"I can see them," said Fisher.

"No, you can't," said Wendel sharply. "Now, listen to me. Rotor had no problems with gravitation because they merely skimmed the speed of light—a little below it at some times, a little above it at others—so that gravitational effects, whether positive or negative, attractive or repulsive, had immeasurably small effects on them. It was our own true superluminal flights at many times the speed of light that makes it imperative to take gravitational repulsion into account. My own equations are useless. They will get ships through hyperspace, but not in the right direction. And that's not all.

"I have always thought that there was a certain unavoidable danger in emerging from hyperspace—the second half of the transition. What if you merge into an already existing object? There would be a fantastic explosion that would destroy the ship and everything in it in a trillionth of a trillionth of a second.

"Naturally, we're not going to end up inside a star because we know where the stars are located and can avoid them. In time, we might even know where a star's planets are and avoid them, too. But there are asteroids by the tens of thousands and comets by the tens of billions in the neighborhood of every star. If we end up overlapping one of those, that would still be deadly.

"The only thing that would save us, in the situation as I had thought it to be before today, is the laws of chance. Space is so huge that the chance of striking any object larger than an atom or, at most, a grain of dust is extraordinarily small. Still, given enough trips through hyperspace, the overlapping of matter is a catastrophe just waiting to happen.

"But under conditions as we now know them to be, the chances are zero. Our ship and any sizable object would repel each other and tend to move apart. We are not likely to run afoul of anything deadly. They would all automatically move out of our path."

Fisher scratched at his forehead. "Wouldn't we move out of our path, too? Won't that upset our course unexpectedly?"

"Yes, but the small objects we are likely to encounter will alter our path in very limited fashion and we could easily make it up—a small price to pay for safety."

Wendel took a deep breath and stretched luxuriantly. "I feel great. What a sensation all this will make when we get back to Earth."

Fisher chuckled. "You know, Tessa, before you came in, I was building a morbid picture in my head of our being irretrievably lost; of our ship wandering forever, with five dead bodies aboard; of its being found someday by intelligent beings who would mourn the obvious space tragedy—"

"Well, it won't happen, you can count on that, my dear," said Wendel, smiling, and they embraced.

# THIRTY-THREE

## MIND

### 73.

Eugenia Insigna looked woebegone. "Have you really decided to go out again, Marlene?"

"Mother," said Marlene with weary patience, "you make it sound as though I've come to this decision five minutes ago after a long period of uncertainty. I've been sure for a very long time that out there on Erythro is where I intend to be. I haven't changed my mind, and I won't change it."

"I know you're convinced that you're safe and I admit that nothing has happened to you so far, but—"

Marlene said, "I feel safe on Erythro. I'm *drawn* to it. Uncle Siever understands."

Eugenia looked at her daughter, as if to object once again, but shook her head instead. Marlene's mind was made up, and she was not to be stopped.

74.

It's warmer on Erythro this time, Marlene thought, just warm enough to make the breeze welcome. The grayish clouds were scudding across the sky a bit more rapidly, and they seemed thicker.

Rain was predicted for the next day, and Marlene thought it might be nice to be out in the rain and watch what happened. It should splash in the little creek and make the rocks wet and turn any soil muddy and mushy.

She had come up to a flat rock near the creek. She brushed it with her hand, and sat down on it carefully, staring at the flowing water curling around the rocks that studded it, and thinking that the rain would feel like taking a shower.

It would be like a shower coming down from the whole sky, so that you couldn't step out of it. A thought occurred to her: Will there be trouble breathing?

No, that couldn't be. It rained on Earth all time—frequently, anyway—and she didn't hear that people drowned in it. No, it would be like a shower. You could breathe in a shower.

The rain wouldn't be hot, though, and she liked hot showers. She thought about it lazily. It was very quiet out here, and very peaceful, and she could rest and there was no one to see her, to watch her, no one whom she had to interpret. It was great not to have to interpret.

What temperature would it be? The rain, that is. Why shouldn't it be the same comfortable temperature as Nemesis itself? Of course, she would get wet, and it was always cold when you stepped out of a shower all wet. And the rain would wet her clothes, too.

But it would be silly to wear clothes in the rain. You didn't wear clothes in the shower. If it rained, you would take off your clothes. That would be the only thing that made sense.

Only—where did you put the clothes? When you showered, you put your clothes in the cleaner. Here on Erythro, maybe you could put them under a rock, or have a little house built, in which you could leave your clothes on a rainy day. After all, why wear clothes at all if it were raining?

Or if it were sunny?

You'd want to wear them if it were cold, of course. But on warm days—

But then, why did people wear clothes on Rotor, where it was always warm and clean? They didn't at swimming pools—which reminded Marlene that the young people with slim bodies and good shapes were the first ones off with their clothes—and the last ones to put them on again.

And people like Marlene just didn't take their clothes off in public. Maybe that's why people wore clothes. To hide their bodies.

Why didn't minds have shapes you could show off? Except that they did, and then people didn't like it. People liked to look at shapely bodies and turned up their noses at shapely minds. Why?

But here in Erythro with no people, she could take her clothes off whenever it was mild and be free of them. There'd be no one to point fingers or laugh at her.

In fact, she could do whatever she wanted because she had a whole comfortable world, an empty world, an all-alone world, to surround her and envelop her like a huge soft blanket enclosing her and—just silence.

She could feel herself letting go. Just silence. Her mind whispered it, so that even that would interfere as little as possible.

Silence.

And she sat upright. Silence?

But she had come out to hear the voice again. And not scream this time. Not be afraid. Where was the voice?

As though she had called it, as though she had whistled it up—

"Marlene!"

Her heart gave a little jump.

She held herself firm. She mustn't make any sign of fright or disturbance. She simply looked around, and then said, very calmly, "Where are you, please?"

"It is not—necery—necessary to vi—vibrate the air—talk."

The voice was Aurinel's, but it didn't speak like Aurinel at all. It sounded as though talking were difficult, but as though it would get better.

"It will get better," said the voice.

Marlene had not said anything. She did not say anything now. She merely thought the words— "I don't have to talk. I only need to think."

"You only need to adjust the pattern. You're doing it."

"But I hear you talk."

"I am adjusting your pattern. It is as though you hear me."

Marlene licked her lips gently. She must not allow herself to be frightened, to be anything but calm.

"There is nothing of which—whom—what to be frightened," said the voice that was not quite Aurinel's voice.

She thought, "You hear everything, don't you?"

"Does that bother you?"

"Yes, it does."

"Why?"

"I don't want you to know everything. I want some thoughts to myself." (She tried not to think that that was how others might react to her, and want to keep their feelings private, but the thought, Marlene knew, would leak out, the moment she made the effort not to think it.)

"But your pattern is unlike the others."

"My pattern?"

"The pattern of your mind. Others are—tangled—snarled. Yours is —splendid."

Marlene licked her lips again and smiled. When her mind was sensed, it could be seen to be splendid. She felt triumphant and thought with contempt of the girls who had only—outsides.

The voice in her mind said, "Is that thought private?"

Marlene almost spoke aloud. "Yes, it is."

"I can detect a distinction. I will not respond to your private thoughts."

Marlene felt herself hungering for praise. "Have you seen many patterns?"

"I have sensed many, since you hu-mans things came."

It wasn't sure of the word, Marlene thought. The voice made no response and Marlene was surprised. The surprise had been a private sensation, now that she came to think of it, but she hadn't openly marked it to herself as private. Private was private whether she thought of it or not, perhaps. The mind had said it could detect the distinction, and it clearly could. It showed in the pattern.

The voice didn't respond to that either. She would have to ask specifically, to show that it was not a private thought.

"Please, does it show in the pattern?" She didn't have to specify. The voice would know what she was talking about.

"It shows in the pattern. Everything shows in your pattern because it is so well designed."

Marlene virtually purred. She had her praise. It would only be right to return the compliment. "But your own must be well designed, too."

"It is different. My pattern stretches out. It is simple in every spot and is only complex when taken together. Yours is complex to start with. There is no simplicity in it. And yours is different from the others of your kind. The others are—snarled. It is not possible to cross-reach with them—to communicate. A rearrangement is damaging, for the pattern is fragile. I didn't know. My pattern is not fragile."

"Is my pattern fragile?"

"No. It adjusts itself."

"You tried to communicate with others, didn't you?"

"Yes."

The Erythro Plague. (There was no response. The thought was private.)

She closed her eyes, reaching out intently with her mind, trying to locate the source of the outside mind reaching her. She was doing it in some way she did not understand, perhaps doing it all wrong, perhaps not doing it at all. The mind might laugh at her clumsiness—if it did such a thing as laugh.

There was no response.

Marlene thought, "Think something."

Inevitably, the thought came back, "What shall I think?"

It did not come from anywhere. It did not come from here or there or elsewhere. It came from inside her mind.

She thought (angered at her own insufficiency), "When did you sense my mind pattern?"

"On the new container of human beings."

"On Rotor?"

"On Rotor."

She was suddenly enlightened. "You wanted me. You called me."

"Yes."

Of course. Why else had she so wanted to go to Erythro? Why else had she been looking at Erythro so longingly that day when Aurinel came to her to say her mother was looking for her?

She clenched her teeth. She must continue asking, "Where are you?"

"Everywhere."

"Are you the planet?"

"No."

"Show yourself."

"Here." And suddenly the voice had a direction.

She was staring at the creek, and she suddenly realized that while she had been communicating with the voice in her mind, the creek had been the only thing she had been sensing. She had not been aware of anything else around her. It was as though her mind had enclosed itself, in order to make it more sensitive to the one thing that had filled it.

And now the veil lifted. The water was moving along the rocks, bubbling over them, swirling in a small eddy in a space marked off by several of those bubbles. The small bubbles turned and broke, even as new ones formed, setting up a pattern that, in essence, didn't change, and in fine detail was never repeated.

Then, one by one, the bubbles broke noiselessly and the water was flat and featureless, but still turned. How could she see it turn if it were featureless?

Because it glistened very slightly in the pink light of Nemesis. It turned and she could see it turn because the shimmers formed arcs that spiraled as they turned and coalesced. Her eyes were caught in it, slowly following the turns as they collected into the caricature of a face, two dark holes for eyes, a slash for a mouth.

It grew sharper, as she watched, fascinated.

And it took on definition and became a face, staring up at her with empty eyes, yet real enough to recognize.

It was the face of Aurinel Pampas.

75.

Siever Genarr said, thoughtfully and slowly, making an effort to treat the matter calmly, "And so you left at that time."

Marlene nodded. "The time before I left when I heard Aurinel's voice. This time I left when I saw Aurinel's face."

"I don't blame you—"

"You're humoring me, Uncle Siever."

"What should I do? Kick you? Let me humor you—if it pleases me. The mind, as you call it, picked up Aurinel's voice and his face from your mind, obviously. Those things must have been very clear in your mind. How close were you to Aurinel?"

She looked at him suspiciously. "What do you mean? How close?"

"I don't mean anything terrible. Were you friendly?"

297

"Yes. Of course."

"Did you have a crush on him?"

Marlene paused and her lips pressed together. Then she said, "I suppose I did."

"You use the past tense. Don't you any more?"

"Well, what's the use? He just thinks of me as—a little girl. A kid sister, maybe."

"Not entirely an unnatural thought, under the circumstances. But you still think of him—which is why you've conjured up his voice, and then his face."

"What do you mean 'conjured up'? It was a real voice and a real face."

"Are you sure?"

"Of course I am."

"Have you told your mother any of this?"

"No. Not a word."

"Why not?"

"Oh, Uncle Siever. You know her. I couldn't stand all that—nervousness. I know. You're going to tell me it's all out of love, but that doesn't make it easier."

"You're willing to tell it to me, Marlene, and I'm certainly very fond of you."

"I know that, Uncle Siever, but you're not the excitable type. You just look at things logically."

"Shall I take that as a compliment?"

"I mean it as one."

"In that case, let's look at what you have found out, and do it logically."

"All right, Uncle Siever."

"Good. To begin with, there is something alive on this planet."

"Yes."

"And it's not the planet itself."

"No, definitely not. He denied that."

"But it's one living thing, apparently."

"I get the impression that he's one living thing. The trouble is, Uncle Siever, that what I get is not like telepathy is supposed to be. It's not like reading a mind and just getting talk. It's also impressions that come over you all at once, like looking at a whole picture instead of at the little bits of light and darkness that make it up."

"And the impression is of one living thing."

"Yes."

"And intelligent."

"Very intelligent."

"But not technological. There is nothing technological that we've ever found on the planet. This living thing that is not visible, not apparent, merely broods over the planet—thinks—reasons—but doesn't do anything. Is that it?"

Marlene hesitated. "I can't quite tell, but maybe you're right."

"And then we came. When do you suppose that it became aware that we had come?"

Marlene shook her head. "I couldn't say."

"Well, dear, it was aware of you while you were still on Rotor. It must have become aware of intelligence invading the Nemesian System when we were still quite a way off. Did you get that impression?"

"I don't think so, Uncle Siever. I *think* he didn't know about us until we landed on Erythro. That attracted his attention and then he looked around and found Rotor."

"Perhaps you're right. Then it experimented with these new minds that it sensed on Erythro. They were the first minds not its own that it may have ever sensed. How long has it lived, Marlene? Any idea?"

"Not really, Uncle Siever, but the *impression* I got is that he has lived a long time, maybe nearly as long as the planet."

"Maybe. In any case, however long it has lived, this was the first time it ever found itself immersed in many other minds, far different from its own. Does that sound right to you, Marlene?"

"Yes."

"So it experimented with these new minds and because it knew so little about them, it damaged them. That was the Erythro Plague."

"Yes," said Marlene with sudden animation. "He didn't say anything about the Plague directly, but the impression was strong. That original experimentation was the cause."

"And when it realized that it was causing damage, it stopped."

"Yes, that's why we don't have Erythro Plague now."

"And from that it would seem that this mind is benevolent, that it has a sense of ethics we can approve of, that it doesn't wish to harm other minds."

"Yes!" said Marlene with delight. "I'm sure of that."

"But what is this life-form? Is it a spirit? Something immaterial? Something beyond our senses?"

"I can't say, Uncle Siever," sighed Marlene.

Genarr said, "Well, let me repeat what it told you. Stop me if I'm wrong. It said its pattern 'stretches out'; that it is 'simple in every spot and is complex only taken together'; that it is 'not fragile.' Am I right?"

"Yes, you are."

"And the only life we have ever found on Erythro are the prokaryotes, the tiny bacterialike cells. If I don't want something that's spiritual and immaterial, I'm stuck with those prokaryotes. Is it possible that those little cells, which seem separate, are actually part of one world-girdling organism? The mind pattern would then be stretched out. It would be simple in every spot and would be complex only when taken together. And it would not be fragile, for even if large sections of it were killed, the world organism would scarcely be touched as a whole."

Marlene stared at Genarr. "You mean I've been talking to germs?"

"I can't say certainly, Marlene. It's only a hypothesis, but it fits beautifully and I can't think of anything else that would explain it as well. Besides, Marlene, if we looked at the hundred billion cells that make up your brain, each one of them, taken by itself, isn't really very much. You are an organism in which all the brain cells are clumped together. If you talk to another in which all the brain cells are separate and linked, let us say, by tiny radio waves, is that so very different?"

"I don't know," said Marlene, obviously disturbed.

"But let's ask another question, one that is very important. What does this life-form—whatever it is—want with you?"

Marlene looked startled. "He can talk to me, Uncle Siever. He can transfer ideas to me."

"Your suggestion, then, is that it just wants someone to talk to? Do you suppose that once we humans came, it realized for the first time that it was lonely?"

"I don't know."

"No impressions to that effect?"

"No."

"It could destroy us." Genarr was talking to himself now. "It could destroy us without trouble if it grew tired of you, or bored with you."

"*No*, Uncle Siever."

Genarr said, "But it definitely hurt me when I wished to get in the way of your connection with the mind of the planet. It hurt Dr. D'Aubisson, your mother, and a guard."

"Yes, but he hurt you all with only just enough force to stop you from interfering with me. He did no further damage."

"It goes to all these lengths to have you outside on the surface just so that it can talk to you, and have companionship. Somehow that doesn't seem to be enough of a reason."

Marlene said, "Perhaps the reason is something we can't understand. Perhaps he has so different a mind that he couldn't explain his reason, or, if he did, that it would make no sense to us."

"But its mind is not so different that it can't converse with you. It does receive ideas from you and transmit other ideas to you, doesn't it? You two do communicate."

"Yes."

"And it understands you well enough to try to make itself seem pleasant to you by taking on Aurinel's voice and face."

Marlene's head bent and she fixed her eyes on the floor in front of her.

Genarr said softly, "So since it understands us, we may be able to understand it, and, if so, you must find out why it wants you so. It could be very important to find that out, for who knows what it is planning? We have no way of finding out except through you, Marlene."

Marlene was trembling. "I don't know how to do that, Uncle Siever."

"Just do as you have been doing. The mind seems friendly to you, and it may explain."

Marlene looked up and studied Genarr. She said, "You're afraid, Uncle Siever."

"Of course. We're dealing with a mind far more powerful than ours. It may, if it decides it doesn't want us, do away with us all."

"I don't mean that, Uncle Siever. You're afraid for *me*."

Genarr hesitated. "Are you still sure that you're safe on Erythro, Marlene? Are you safe talking to this mind?"

Marlene rose to her feet and said, almost haughtily, "Of course I am. There is no risk. He will not hurt me."

She sounded supremely confident, but Genarr's heart sank. What she thought scarcely counted, for her mind had been adjusted by the mind of Erythro. Could he trust her now? he wondered.

After all, why should this mind built up of prokaryotes in their trillion trillion not have an agenda of its own, as, for instance, Pitt had? And why shouldn't this mind, in its anxiety to fulfill that agenda, show all the duplicity of Pitt?

In short, what if the mind were lying to Marlene for reasons of its own?

Was he right to send Marlene out to that mind under such conditions?

But did it matter whether he was right or not? Had he a choice?

# THIRTY-FOUR

# CLOSE

### 76.

"Perfect," said Tessa Wendel. "Perfect, perfect, perfect." She made a gesture as though she were nailing something to the wall, firmly and hard. "Perfect."

Crile Fisher knew what she was talking about. Twice, in two different directions, they had passed through hyperspace. Twice Crile had watched the pattern of stars change somewhat. Twice he had searched out the Sun, finding it a bit dimmer the first time, a bit brighter the second. He was beginning to feel like an old hyperspatial knockabout.

He said, "The Sun isn't bothering us, I take it."

"Oh, it is, but in a perfectly calculable way, so that the physical interference is a psychological pleasure—if you know what I mean."

Fisher said, playing the devil's advocate, "The Sun's pretty far away, you know. The gravitational effect must be pretty close to zero."

"Certainly," said Wendel, "but pretty close to zero isn't zero. The effect is measurable. Twice we passed through hyperspace, with the virtual path first approaching the Sun obliquely and then receding at another angle. Wu did the calculations beforehand, and the path we took fit those calculations to all the decimal points we could reasonably ask. The man's a genius. He weaves shortcuts into the computer program in a fashion you wouldn't believe."

"I'm sure," murmured Fisher.

"So there's no question now, Crile. We can be at the Neighbor Star by tomorrow. By today—if we're really in a hurry. Not very close, of course. We may have to coast inward toward the star for a reasonable period of time, as a precautionary measure. Besides, we don't know the mass of the Neighbor Star with sufficient precision to take too many chances on a really close approach. We don't want to be hurled off unexpectedly and have to work our way back." She shook her head admiringly, "That Wu. I'm so pleased with him, I can't begin to describe it."

Fisher said cautiously, "Are you sure you don't feel a little annoyed?"

"Annoyed? Why?" She stared at Fisher in surprise, then said, "Do you think I ought to be jealous?"

"Well, I don't know. Is there a chance that Chao-Li Wu will get the credit for working out superluminal flight—I mean, the true details of it—and that you'll be forgotten, or remembered only as a forerunner?"

"No, not at all, Crile. It's nice of you to worry on my behalf, but matters are secure. My work is recorded in full detail. The basic mathematics of superluminal flight are mine. The engineering details I have also contributed to, although others will get the major credit for designing the ship, and should. What Wu has done has been to add a correction factor to the basic equations. Highly important, of course, and we can now see that superluminal flight wouldn't be practical without it, but it's just the icing on the cake. The cake is still mine."

"Fine. If you're sure of that, I'm happy."

"As a matter of fact, Crile, I'm hoping Wu will now take the lead in developing superluminal flight. The fact is, I'm past my best years—scientifically, that is. Only scientifically, Crile."

Fisher grinned. "I know that."

"But scientifically, I am over the hill. The work I've done has been the mining of the concepts I had when I was a graduate student. It's been a matter of about twenty-five years of drawing conclusions, and I've gone about as far as I can go. What's needed are brand-new concepts, entirely new thoughts, a branching off into uncharted territory. I can't do that any more."

"Come, Tessa, don't underrate yourself."

"That's never been one of my faults, Crile. New thoughts are what we need youth for. It's not just young brains that young people have, it's *new* brains. Wu has a genome that has never appeared in humanity before. He's had experiences that are crucially his—no one else's. He *can* have new thoughts. Of course, he bases them on what I have done before him, and he owes a great deal to my teaching. He's a student of mine, Crile, a child of my intellect. All that he does well reflects well on me. Jealous of him? I glory in him. What's the matter, Crile. You don't look happy."

"I'm happy if you are, Tessa, no matter how I look. The trouble is that I have the feeling you're feeding me the *theory* of scientific advance. Weren't their cases in the history of science, as in everything else, where jealousy existed, and where teachers detested their students for surpassing them?"

"Certainly. I could quote you half a dozen notorious cases right off the top of my head, but those are rare exceptions and the fact is that I don't feel that way right now. I don't say that it isn't conceivable that I may at some time lose patience with Wu and the Universe, but it isn't happening at the moment, and I intend to savor this moment while it— Oh, now what?"

She pushed the "Receive" contact and Merry Blankowitz's young face appeared trimensionally in the transmitter.

"Captain," she said hesitantly. "We're having a discussion out here and I wonder if we can consult you."

"Is something wrong with the flight?"

"No, Captain. It's just a discussion over strategy."

"I see. Well, you needn't file in here. I'll come out to the engine room."

Wendel blanked out the face.

Fisher muttered, "Blankowitz doesn't usually sound that serious. What's bugging them, do you suppose?"

"I'm not going to speculate. I'll go out there and find out." And she motioned Fisher to follow.

77.

There were the three of them, sitting in the engine room, all of them with seats carefully on the floor, despite the fact that they were under zero-gravity at the moment. They might just as well have been sitting each on a different wall, but that would have detracted from the seriousness of the situation, and it would have shown disrespect for the office of Captain, besides. There was a complex system of etiquette that had long been developed for zero-gravity.

Wendel did not like zero-gravity and if she had wanted to push her Captain's privileges, she could have insisted on the ship being in rotation at all times to produce a centrifugal effect that would have produced *some* feeling of gravity. She knew perfectly well that computing a flight path was easier when the ship was at rest, both translationally and rotationally, with respect to the Universe as a whole, but calculating it under constant rotational velocity didn't raise the difficulty to too high a level.

Nevertheless, to insist on such motion would have been disrespectful to the person at the computer. Etiquette again.

Tessa Wendel took her seat, and Crile Fisher could not help but notice (with a secret, ingrown smile) that she lurched slightly. For all her Settlement background, she had clearly never gotten her space legs. He himself (and there was another secret smile—of satisfaction, this time), for all that he was an Earthman, could move about in zero-gravity as though he were born to it.

Chao-Li Wu took a deep breath. He had a broad face—the type that looked like it belonged with a short body, but he was taller than average, when he stood up. His hair was dark and perfectly straight and his eyes were markedly narrow.

He said softly, "Captain."

Wendel said, "What is it, Chao-Li? If you tell me some problem has developed in the programming, I may be tempted to choke you."

"No problem, Captain. No problem at all. In fact, there is such an absence of problems that it strikes me that we're through and should go back to Earth. I would like to suggest that."

"Back to Earth?" Wendel had paused before she said that, had taken the time to look a little stupefied. "Why? We haven't accomplished our task yet."

"I think we have, Captain," said Wu, his face growing expressionless. "We just didn't know what our task was, to begin with. We have worked out a practical system of superluminal flight, and we didn't have that when we left Earth."

"I know that, but what of it?"

"And we don't have any means of communication with Earth. If we go on now to the Neighbor Star and if something happens to us, if something goes wrong, Earth will not have practical superluminal flight and there is no telling when they will. This could have a serious affect on Earth's evacuation as the Neighbor Star approaches. I feel that it is important that we go back and explain what we've learned."

Wendel had listened gravely. "I see. And you, Jarlow, what are your views on this?"

Henry Jarlow was tall and blond and dour. There was a settled melancholy on his face that gave a totally wrong impression of his character, and his long fingers (which had nothing apparently delicate about them) were magic when they worked with the interior of computers or with almost any instrument on board.

He said, "I think Wu makes sense, frankly. If we had superluminal communication, we'd get the information back to Earth that way and go on. What would happen to us after that would be of no importance except to us. As it is, we can't sit on the gravitational correction."

"And you, Blankowitz?" asked Wendel quietly.

Merry Blankowitz stirred uneasily. She was a small young woman and her long dark hair was cut straight across, just over her eyebrows. Between that and the delicacy of her bone structure and her quick, nervous movements, she looked like a miniature Cleopatra.

She said, "I don't really know. I don't have very definite feelings about this, but the men seem to have talked me into it. Don't you think it's important to get the information to Earth? We've worked out crucial effects on this trip and we need more and better ships, with computers designed to take the gravitational correction into account. We'll be able to make a single transition between the Solar System and the Neighbor Star and do it under stronger gravitational intensities so that we can start closer to the Sun and end closer to the Neighbor Star and not have to spend weeks of coasting at both ends. It seems to me that Earth has to know about this."

Wendel said, "I see. The whole point seems to me to be whether it wouldn't be wise to get the information of the gravitational correction back to Earth right now. Wu, is that really as essential as you make it appear? You didn't get the idea for the correction here on the

307

ship. It seems to me that you discussed it with me months ago." She thought a moment. "Almost a year ago."

"We didn't really discuss it, Captain. You were impatient with me, as I recall, and wouldn't really listen."

"Yes, I've admitted I was mistaken. But you did write it down. I told you to make up a formal report and that I would go over it when I had time." She held up a hand. "I know I never had time to go over it, and I don't even recall if I received it, but I imagine, Wu, that you —being you—would have prepared the report in some detail, and with all the reasoning and mathematics anyone could want. Didn't you do that, Wu, and isn't that report in the records?"

Wu's lips seemed to tighten, but his tone of voice did not alter in any way. "Yes, I prepared the report, but it was just speculation, and I don't suppose anyone else will pay any attention to it—any more than you did, Captain."

"Why not? Not everyone is as stupid as I am, Wu."

"Even if they paid attention, it would still be nothing more than speculation. When we go back, we will be able to present proof."

"Once the speculation exists, *someone* will get the proof. You know how science works."

Wu said in a slow and significant tone, *"Someone."*

"Now we have the nature of your concern, Wu. You're not worried that Earth won't obtain a practical method of superluminal flight. You are worried that they will, but that the credit will not be yours. Isn't that right?"

"Captain, there's nothing wrong with that. A scientist has every right to be concerned over matters of priority."

Wendel positively smoldered. "Have you forgotten that I am the Captain of this ship and make the decisions?"

"I haven't forgotten that," said Wu, "but this is not a sailing vessel of the eighteenth century. We are all scientists, primarily, and we must make decisions in some sort of democratic fashion. If the majority wishes to return—"

"Wait," said Fisher sharply, "before this continues, do you mind if I say something? I'm the only one who hasn't spoken and if we're going to be democratic, I would like to take my turn on the floor. May I, Captain?"

"Go ahead," said Wendel, her right hand clenching and unclenching as though it just longed to grab someone by the throat.

Fisher said, "Just about seven and a half centuries ago, Christopher

Columbus sailed westward from Spain and, eventually, discovered America, though he himself never knew that that was what he had done. En route, he made the discovery that the deviation of the magnetic compass from the true north, the so-called 'magnetic declination,' changed with longitude. This was an important finding and was, in fact, the first purely scientific discovery made in the course of a sea voyage.

"Now, how many know that Columbus discovered the variation of magnetic declination? Virtually no one. How many know that Columbus discovered America? Virtually everyone. So suppose that Columbus, on discovering the variation, decided, midway, to go home and make the glad announcement to King Ferdinand and Queen Isabella, preserving his priority as the discoverer of the phenomenon? That discovery might conceivably have been greeted with interest and the monarchs might eventually have sent out another expedition headed, let us say, by Amerigo Vespucci, who would then have reached America. In that case, who would remember that Columbus had made some sort of discovery about the compass? Virtually no one. Who would remember that Vespucci had discovered America? Virtually everyone.

"So do you really want to go back? The discovery of the gravitational correction will, I assure you, be remembered by a few as a small side effect of superluminal travel. But the crew of the next expedition that will actually reach the Neighbor Star, will be hailed as the first to reach a star by superluminal flight. You three, even you, Wu, will scarcely be worth a footnote.

"You might think that, as a reward for this great discovery that Wu has made, it will be you that will be sent out on a second expedition, but I'm afraid not. You see, Igor Koropatsky, who is the Director of the Terrestrial Board of Inquiry and who is waiting for us back on Earth, is particularly interested in information on the Neighbor Star and its planetary system. He will explode like Krakatoa when he finds out that we were within reach of it and turned back. And of course, Captain Wendel will be forced to explain that you three had mutinied, which is an extremely serious offense, even if we are not an eighteenth-century sailing vessel. Far from going out on the next expedition, you will never see the inside of a laboratory again. Count on it. What you may see, despite your scientific eminence, is the inside of a jail. Don't underestimate Koropatsky's fury.

"So think about it, you three. On to the Neighbor Star? Or back home?"

There was a silence. For a while, no one said anything.

"Well," said Wendel harshly, "I think that Fisher has explained the situation very clearly. Doesn't any one have anything to say?"

Blankowitz said in a low voice, "Actually, I never thought it through. I think we ought to go on."

Jarlow grunted. "I think so, too."

Wendel said, "What about you, Chao-Li Wu?"

Wu shrugged. "I wouldn't stand against the rest."

"I'm glad to hear that. This incident is forgotten as far as the Earth authorities will be concerned, but there had better be no repetition, no further action of any kind that could be considered mutinous."

78.

Back in their own quarters, Fisher said, "You don't mind, I hope, that I interfered. I was afraid you would explode to no effect."

"No, it was good. I wouldn't have thought of the Columbus analogy, which was perfect. Thank you, Crile." She took his hand and squeezed it.

He smiled briefly. "I had to justify my presence on board ship somehow."

"You more than justified it. And you have no idea how disgusted I was, to have Wu act as he did when I had just finished telling you how happy I was over his findings, and over the credit he would get. I was feeling noble over my willingness to share credit, over the ethics of scientific research that gives to each his fair due, and then he puts his private pride ahead of the project."

"We're all human, Tessa."

"I know. And seeing that the man's interior has its ethical dark spots doesn't alter the fact that he has a scientific mind that is fearfully sharp."

"I'm afraid I'd have to admit that my own arguments were based on private desires rather than the public good, so to speak. I want to go to the Neighbor Star for reasons that have nothing to do with the project."

"I understand that. I am still grateful." It embarrassed Fisher that there were tears in her eyes and that she had to blink them away.

He kissed her.

310

### 79.

It was just a star, too faint yet to stand out in any way. In fact, Crile Fisher would have lost it were it not for the fact that he had punched in the network that zeroed in on it in concentric circles and radii.

"It looks disappointingly like a star, doesn't it?" said Fisher, his face taking on the moroseness it seemed to have when he let it fall into its natural lines.

Merry Blankowitz, who was the only one with him at the observation panel, said, "That's all it is, Crile. A star."

"I mean it *looks* like a faint star—and we're so close."

"Close in a manner of speaking. We're still a tenth of a light-year away, which is not *really* close. It's just that the Captain's cautious. I'd have dragged the *Superluminal* in a lot closer. I wish we were a lot closer right now. I can hardly wait."

"Before this last transition, you were set to go home, Merry."

"Not really. They just talked me into it. Once you made your little speech, I felt like a complete jackass. I took it for granted that if we returned, we'd all go back a second time, but, of course, you really clarified the situation. Oh, but I want to use the ND so badly."

Fisher knew what the ND was. It was the neuronic detector. He felt the stirring himself. To detect intelligence would be to know they had come upon something that was infinitely more important than all metals, rocks, ices, and vapors they could otherwise discover.

He said hesitantly, "Can you tell at this distance?"

She shook her head. "No. We'd have to be a lot closer. And we can't just coast in from this distance. It would take us about a year. Once the Captain is satisfied with what we can find out about the Neighbor Star from here, we'll make another transition. What I expect is that in two days at the most, we'll be within a couple of astronomic units of the Neighbor Star, and then I can start making observations and be useful. It's a drag feeling like a deadweight."

"Yes," said Fisher dryly, "I know."

A look of concern crossed Blankowitz's face. "I'm sorry, Crile. I wasn't referring to you."

"You might as well have been. I might not be of any use no matter how close we come to the Neighbor Star."

"You will be useful if we detect intelligence. You'll be able to talk to them. You're a Rotorian, and we'll need that."

Fisher smiled grimly. "A Rotorian for just a few years."

"That's enough isn't it?"

"We'll see." He changed the subject deliberately. "Are you sure the neuronic detector will work?"

"Absolutely sure. We could follow any Settlement in orbit just by its radiation of plexons."

"What are plexons, Merry?"

"Just a name I made up, for the photon-complex characteristic of mammalian brains. We could detect horses, you know, if we're not too far away, but we can detect human brains in masses at astronomic distances."

"Why plexons?"

"From 'complexity.' Someday—you'll see—someday they're going to be working on plexons not just to detect life but to study the intimate functioning of the brain. I've made up a name for that, too—'plexophysiology.' Or maybe 'plexoneuronics.'"

Fisher said, "Do you consider names important?"

"Yes, indeed. It gives you a way of speaking concisely. You don't have to say, 'that field of science that involves the relationship of this and that.' You just say 'plexoneuronics'—yes, that sounds better. It's a shortcut. It saves your thinking time for more important subjects. Besides—" She hesitated.

"Besides? Yes?"

The words came in a rush. "If I make up a name and it sticks, that alone would get me a footnote in the history of science. You know, 'The word "plexon" was first introduced by Merrilee Augina Blankowitz in 2237 on the occasion of the pioneer faster-than-light flight of the *Superluminal.*' I'm not likely to be mentioned anywhere else, or for any other reason, and I'll settle for that."

Fisher said, "What if you detect your plexons, Merry, and there are no human beings present?"

"You mean alien life? That would be even more exciting than detecting people. But there's not much chance, really. We've been disappointed over and over again. We thought there might be at least primitive forms of life on the Moon, on Mars, on Callisto, on Titan. It never came to anything. People have speculated on all kinds of weird life—living galaxies, living dust clouds, life on the surface of a neutron star, all sorts of things. There's no evidence for any of it. No, if I detect anything, it will be human life. I'm convinced of that."

"Wouldn't you be detecting the plexons emitted by the five people on the ship? Wouldn't we drown out anything we can spot at millions of kilometers of distance?"

"That *is* a complication, Crile. We have to balance the ND so that we five are canceled out and it has to be delicately done. Even a little leakage would wipe out anything we could detect elsewhere. Someday, Crile, automated NDs will be sent through hyperspace to all sorts of places to detect plexons. There'll be no human beings in their vicinity and that alone would make them at least a couple of orders of magnitude more sensitive than anything we can do now, with ourselves hanging around and having to be allowed for. We'll find out where intelligence exists long before we approach anyplace ourselves."

Chao-Li Wu made his appearance. He looked at Fisher with a touch of distaste and said indifferently, "How's the Neighbor Star?"

Blankowitz said, "Nothing much at this distance."

"Well, we'll probably be making another transition tomorrow or the next day, and then we'll see."

Blankowitz said, "It will be exciting, won't it?"

Wu said, "It will be—if we find the Rotorians." He glanced at Fisher. "But will we?"

If that were a question directed to Fisher, he did not respond to it. He merely stared at Wu expressionlessly.

Will we? Fisher thought.

The long wait would be over soon.

# THIRTY-FIVE

## CONVERGING

80.

As noted before, Janus Pitt did not often allow himself the luxury of self-pity. In anyone else, he would consider such a thing a despicable sign of weakness and self-indulgence. There were, however, times when he sadly rebelled at the fact that the people of Rotor were only too willing to leave all of the unpleasant decisions to him.

There was a Council, yes—duly elected, and meticulously involved in passing laws and in making decisions—all but the important ones, the ones that dealt with the future of Rotor.

*That* was left to him.

It was not even consciously left to him. The matters of importance were simply ignored, simply rendered nonexistent by mutual unspoken agreement.

Here they were in an empty system, leisurely building new Settlements, absently convinced that time stretched infinitely before them. Everywhere was the calm assumption that once they had filled this new asteroid belt (generations from now, and a matter of no immediate concern to anyone presently alive) the hyper-assistance technique would have improved to the point where it would be comparatively easy to seek out and occupy new planets.

Time existed in plenty. Time blended into eternity.

Only to Pitt himself was it left to consider the fact that time was short, that at any given moment, without warning, time might come to an end.

When would Nemesis be discovered back in the Solar System? When would some Settlement decide to follow Rotor's lead?

It had to come someday. With Nemesis inexorably moving in the direction of the Sun, it would eventually reach that point—still far distant, of course, but close enough—at which the people of the Solar System would have to be blind not to see it.

Pitt's computer, with the aid of a programmer who was convinced he was working out a problem of academic interest only, had estimated that by the end of a thousand years, the discovery of Nemesis would be inevitable, and that the Settlements would begin to disperse.

Pitt had then put the question: Would the Settlements come to Nemesis?

The answer was no. By that time, hyper-assistance would be far more efficient, far cheaper. The Settlements would know more about the nearer stars—which of them had planets, and what kind. They would not bother with a red dwarf star, but would head out for the Sun-like stars.

And that would leave Earth itself, which would be desperate. Afraid of space, clearly degenerate already, and sinking farther into slime and misery as a thousand years passed and the doom of Nemesis became apparent, what would they do? They could not undertake long trips. They were Earthpeople. Surfacebound. They would have to wait for Nemesis to get reasonably close. They could not hope to go anywhere else.

Pitt had the vision of a ramshackle world trying to find security in the more tightly held system of Nemesis, trying to find refuge in a star with a system built tightly enough together to hold in place while it was destroying that of the Sun it passed.

It was a terrible scenario, and yet inevitable.

Why could not Nemesis have been receding from the Sun? How everything would be changed. The discovery of Nemesis would have become somewhat less likely with time and, if the discovery came to pass, Nemesis would become ever less desirable—and less possible—as a place of refuge. If it were receding, Earth would not even need a refuge.

But that was not the way it was. The Earthmen would come; ragtag degenerating Earthmen of every variety of makeshift and abnormal culture, flooding in. What could the Rotorians do but destroy them while they were still in space? But would they have a Janus Pitt to show them that there was no choice but that? Would they have Janus Pitts, between now and then, to make sure that Rotor had the weapons and the resolution to prepare for this and to *do* it when the time came?

But the computer's analysis was, after all, a deceitfully optimistic one. The discovery of Nemesis by the Solar System *must* come about within a thousand years, said the computer. But how much within? What if the discovery came tomorrow? What if it had come three years ago? Might some Settlement, groping for the nearest star, knowing nothing useful about farther ones, be following in Rotor's trail *now?*

Each day, Pitt woke up wondering: Is this the day?

Why was this misery reserved for him? Why did everyone else sleep quietly in the lap of eternity, while only he himself was left to deal each day with the possibility of a kind of doom?

He had done something about it, of course. He had set up a Scanning Service throughout the asteroid belt, a body whose function it was to supervise the automated receptors that constantly swept the sky, and to detect at as great a distance as possible the copious waste-energy disposal of an approaching Settlement.

It had taken some time to set it all up properly, but for a dozen years now, every scrap of dubious information had been followed up, and, every once in a while, something seemed sufficiently questionable to be referred to Pitt. And every time it happened, it set off the clanging of an alarm bell in Pitt's head.

It turned out always to be nothing—so far—and the initial relief was always followed by a kind of rage against the Scanners. If anything was uncertain, they washed their hands of it, let it go, turned it over to Pitt. Let *him* deal with it, let *him* suffer, let *him* make the hard decisions.

It was at this point that Pitt's self-pity became lachrymose, and he

316

would begin to stir uneasily at the possibility that he might be showing weakness.

There was this one, for instance. Pitt fingered the report that his compter had uncoded, and that had inspired this mental self-pitying survey of his own continuous, unbearable, and underappreciated service to the Rotorian people.

This was the first report that had been referred to him in four months, and it seemed to him that it was of minimal importance. A suspicious energy source was approaching, but allowing for its probable distance, it was an unusually small source—a smaller source by some four orders of magnitude than one would expect of a Settlement. It was a source so small that it was all but inseparable from noise.

They might have spared him this. The report that it was of a peculiar wavelength pattern that seemed to make it of human origin was ridiculous. How could they tell anything about a source so weak—except that it was not a Settlement, and therefore could not be of human origin, whatever the wavelength pattern?

Those idiot Scanners must not annoy me in this fashion, thought Pitt.

He tossed the report aside petulantly, and picked up the latest report from Ranay D'Aubisson. That girl Marlene did not have the Plague, even yet. She madly persisted in putting herself in danger in more and more elaborate ways—and yet remained unharmed.

Pitt sighed. Perhaps it didn't matter. The girl seemed to want to remain on Erythro, and if she remained, that might be as good as having her come down with the Plague. In fact, it would force Eugenia Insigna to stay on Erythro, too, and he would be rid of both of them. To be sure, he would feel safer if D'Aubisson, rather than Genarr, were in charge of the Dome and could oversee both mother and daughter. That would have to be arranged in the near future in some way that would not make Genarr a martyr.

Would it be safe to make him Commissioner of New Rotor? That would certainly rate as a promotion and he would be unlikely to refuse the position, especially since, in theory, it would place him on an even rank with Pitt himself. Or would that give Genarr a bit too much of the reality of power in addition to the appearance? Was there an alternative?

He would have to think of it.

Ridiculous! How much easier it would all have been if that girl Marlene had only done something as simple as getting the Plague.

In a spasm of irritation at Marlene's refusal to do so, he picked up the report on the energy source again.

Look at that! A little puff of energy and they bothered him with it. He wasn't going to stand for it. He punched a memo into the computer for instant transmission. He was not to be bothered by minutiae. Keep an eye out for a Settlement!

## 81.

Onboard the *Superluminal,* the discoveries came like a series of hammer blows, one after the other.

They were still at a great distance from the Neighbor Star when it became apparent that it possessed a planet.

"A planet!" said Crile Fisher with tense triumph. "I *knew*—"

"No," said Tessa Wendel hastily, "it's not what you think. Get it through your head, Crile, that there are planets and planets. Virtually every star has some sort of planetary system or other. After all, more than half the stars in the Galaxy are multiple-star systems, and planets are just stars that are too small to *be* stars, you see. This planet we see isn't habitable. If it were habitable, we wouldn't see it at this distance, especially in the dim light of the Neighbor Star."

"You mean, it's a gas giant."

"Of course it is. I would have been more surprised if there hadn't been one than at finding out that one exists."

"But if there's a large planet, there may be small planets, too."

"Maybe," conceded Wendel, "but scarcely habitable ones. They'll either be too cold for life, or their rotation will be locked and they'll be showing only one side to the star, which would make it too warm on one side and too cold on the other. All that Rotor could do—if it were here—would be to place itself in orbit around the star, or possibly around the gas giant."

"That might be exactly what they've done."

"For all these years?" Wendel shrugged. "It's conceivable, I suppose, but you can't count on it, Crile."

82.

The next blows were more startling ones.

"A satellite?" said Tessa Wendel. "Well, why not? Jupiter has four sizable ones. Why should it be surprising that this gas giant has one?"

"It's not a satellite like any that exists in the Solar System, Captain," said Henry Jarlow. "It's roughly the size of Earth—from the measurements I've been able to make."

"Well," said Wendel, maintaining her indifference, "what follows from that?"

"Nothing, necessarily," said Jarlow, "but the satellite shows peculiar characteristics. I wish I were an astronomer."

"At the moment," said Wendel, "I wish *someone* on the ship was, but please go on. You're not completely ignorant of astronomy."

"The point is that since it revolves around the gas giant, it shows one face only to the gas giant, which means that all sides of it face the Neighbor Star in the course of its revolution around the gas giant. And the nature of the orbit is such that, as near as I can tell, the temperature of the world is in the liquid water stage. And it has an atmosphere. Now I don't have all the subtleties at my fingertips. As I said, I'm not an astronomer. Still, it seems to me that there's a good chance that the satellite is a habitable world."

Crile Fisher received the news with a wide smile. He said, "I'm not surprised. Igor Koropatsky predicted the existence of a habitable planet. He did it without any data on the subject. It was just a matter of deduction."

"Did Koropatsky do that? And when did he talk to you, I wonder?"

"Sometime before we left. He reasoned that nothing was likely to have happened to Rotor on the way to the Neighbor Star and, since they didn't return, that they must have found a planet to colonize. And there it is."

"And just why did he tell you this, Crile?"

Crile paused and considered, then said, "He was interested in making certain that the planet would be explored for possible future use by Earth, when the time came for our old planet to be evacuated."

"And why do you suppose he didn't tell *me* this? Do you have any idea?

"I suppose, Tessa," said Crile carefully, "that he thought I would

319

be the more impressionable of the two of us, more eager to urge that
the planet be explored—"

"Because of your daughter."

"He knew of the situation, Tessa."

"And why didn't *you* tell me this?"

"I wasn't sure there was anything to tell. I felt that I might as well
wait and see if Koropatsky was right. Since he was, I am now telling
you. The planet must be habitable by his reasoning."

"It's a satellite," said Wendel, obviously in a temper.

"A distinction without a difference."

Wendel said, "Look, Crile. No one seems to be considering my
position in all this. Koropatsky fills you full of nonsense in order to
have us explore this system and then, presumably, return to Earth
with the news. Wu was anxious to have us return with news even
before we reached this system. You are anxious for a reunion with
your family, regardless of any wider considerations. In all this, there
seems to be very little thought given to the fact that I'm the Captain
and that I will make the decisions."

Fisher's voice grew cajoling. "Be reasonable, Tessa. What decisions
are there to make? What are your choices? You say Koropatsky filled
me with nonsense, but he didn't. There's the planet. Or the satellite—
if you prefer. It *must* be explored. Its existence may mean life for
Earth. This may be humanity's future home. In fact, some of humanity may be there already."

"*You* be reasonable, Crile. A world can be the right size and temperature and still be uninhabitable for any of a variety of reasons. After
all, suppose it has a poisonous atmosphere, or is incredibly volcanic,
or has a high level of radioactivity. It has only a red dwarf star to light
and warm it, and it is in the immediate neighborhood of a large gas
giant. That is not a normal environment for an Earth-type world, and
how will such an abnormal environment affect it?"

"It must still be explored, even if only to find out, certainly, that it
is uninhabitable."

"For that it may not be necessary to land," said Wendel grimly.
"We'll get closer and judge better. Try, Crile, please try not to outrun
the data. I couldn't bear your disappointment."

Fisher nodded. "I'll try— Yet Koropatsky deduced a habitable
planet when everyone else told me it was totally impossible. You did,
too, Tessa. Over and over. But there it is and it *may* be habitable. So

let me hope while I can. Perhaps the people of Rotor are now on that world, and perhaps my daughter is, too."

83.

Chao-Li Wu said rather indifferently, "The Captain is really furious. The last thing she wanted was to find a planet here—a world, I mean, since she won't allow us to call it a planet—that may be habitable. It means it will have to be explored and we'll just have to go back and report. You know that's not what she wants. This is her one and only chance to be out in deep space. Once this is over, she's through for life. Others will work on superluminal techniques; others will explore space. She'll be retired to an advisory position only. She'll hate it."

"How about you, Chao-Li? Would you go out in space again, given a chance?" Blankowitz asked.

Wu didn't hesitate. "I'm not sure that I want to go wandering around in space. I don't have the exploring bug. But you know— Last night, I got the queer notion I might just like to settle down here—if it's habitable. How about you?"

"Settle down here? Of course not. I don't say I'd like to be Earth-bound forever, but I'd like to be back there for a while, anyway, before striking out again."

"I've been thinking about it. This satellite is one in—what? Ten thousand? Who would figure on a habitable world in a red dwarf system? It *should* be explored. I'm even willing to spend time on it and have someone else go back to Earth and take care of my priority on the gravitational effect. You'd protect my interests, wouldn't you, Merry?"

"Of course I would, Chao-Li. And so would Captain Wendel. She has all the data, signed and witnessed."

"So there you are. And I think the Captain is wrong to want to explore the Galaxy. She could visit a hundred stars and not see one world as unusual as this one. Why bother with quantity when you've got quality right in hand?"

"Personally," said Blankowitz. "I think that what bothers her is Fisher's kid. What if he finds her?"

"So what? He can take her back to Earth with him. What would that be to the Captain?"

"There's a wife involved, too, you know."

"Do you ever hear him mention her?"

"That wouldn't mean he—"

Her mouth closed suddenly at the sound outside, and Crile Fisher walked in and nodded at the two.

Blankowitz said quickly, as though to wipe out the previous conversation, "Has Henry finished with the spectroscopy?"

Fisher shook his head. "I can't tell. The poor fellow is nervous. He's afraid of misinterpreting the thing, I suppose."

Wu said, "Come on. It's the computer that does the interpretation. He can hide behind that."

"No, he can't!" said Blankowitz with fervor. "I like that. You theoreticians think that all we observers do is just tend a computer, give it a stroke or two, and say, 'Nice doggie,' then read off the results. It's not so. What the computer says depends on what you put into it, and I never heard a theoretician face an observation he didn't like without blaming the observer. Never once did I hear him say, 'There must be something wrong with the compu—' "

"Hold on," said Wu. "Let's not flood this place with recrimination. Have you ever heard *me* blaming observers?"

"If you didn't like Henry's observations—"

"I'd take them anyway. I don't have any theories about this world."

"And that's why you'd take whatever he gives you."

At this point Henry Jarlow walked in with Tessa Wendel close behind. He looked like a cloud making up its mind to rain.

Wendel said, "Very well, Jarlow, we're all here. Now, tell us. What does it look like?"

"The trouble is," said Jarlow, "there isn't enough ultraviolet in the light of this weakling star to raise a sunburn on an albino. I have to work with micro-waves and that tells me, at once, that there's water vapor in the world's atmosphere."

Wendel shrugged it off with an impatient lift of her shoulders. "We don't need you to tell us that. A world the size of Earth in a liquid-water range of temperature would surely have water and, therefore, water vapor. That moves it one more notch toward habitability, but only one more thoroughly expected notch."

"Oh no," said Jarlow uneasily. "It's habitable. No question."

"Because of the water vapor?"

"No. I have something better than that."

"What?"

Jarlow looked around him at the other four rather grimly, and said,

"Would you say a world was habitable if, in actual fact, it was inhabited?"

"Yes, I think I could bring myself to say that," said Wu calmly.

"Are you telling me that you can see that it's inhabited at this distance?" asked Wendel sharply.

"Yes, that's exactly what I'm saying, Captain. There's free oxygen in the atmosphere—and in quantity. Can you tell me how that can be without photosynthesis? And can you tell me how you can have photosynthesis without the presence of life? And can you tell me how a planet can be uninhabitable if it has oxygen-producing life on it?"

There was dead silence for a moment, then Wendel said, "That is *so* unlikely, Jarlow. Are you sure you didn't mess up the programming?"

And Blankowitz quietly raised her eyebrows at Wu in an unspoken: "See-e-e-e-e!"

Jarlow said stiffly, "I have never messed up, as you call it, a programming in my life, but, of course, I'm willing to stand corrected if anyone here feels he is more knowledgeable about atmospheric infrared analysis than I am. It's not my field of expertise, but I did make careful use of Blanc and Nkrumah on the subject."

Crile Fisher, who had gained considerable self-confidence since the incident involving Wu's bid to return home, did not hesitate to insert his views.

"Look," he said, "this will either be confirmed or denied as we get closer, but why don't we assume that Dr. Jarlow's analysis is correct and see where that takes us? If there is oxygen in the atmosphere of this world, might we not assume that it's been terraformed?"

All eyes turned to look at him.

"Terraformed?" said Jarlow blankly.

"Yes, terraformed. Why not? You have this world that is suitable for life, except that it has the carbon dioxide and nitrogen atmosphere that worlds without life have—like Mars and Venus—and you dump algae into the ocean and pretty soon it's 'Good-bye, carbon dioxide,' and 'Hello, oxygen.' Or maybe you do something else. I'm no expert."

They were still looking at him.

Fisher went on. "The reason I'm suggesting this is that I remember there was talk about terraforming on the farms on Rotor. I worked there. There were even some seminars on terraforming that I attended because I felt it might have something to do with the hyperassistance program. It didn't, but at least I heard about terraforming."

Finally Jarlow said, "In all you heard about terraforming, Fisher, do you by any chance recall anyone saying how long it would take?"

Fisher spread his arms. "You tell me, Dr. Jarlow. It will save time, I'm sure."

"All right. It took Rotor two years to get here—*if* it got here. That means it's been here thirteen years. If all of Rotor were solid algae and it was all dumped into the ocean and lived and grew and produced oxygen, then to get to the present level, where I estimate the oxygen content is 18 percent and carbon dioxide is present only in traces, I would imagine it would take some thousands of years. Perhaps hundreds of years—if conditions were enormously favorable. It *certainly* would take more than thirteen years. And, frankly, Earth algae are adapted to Earth conditions quite precisely. On another world, the algae might not grow, or might do so very slowly, till it adapted itself. Thirteen years wouldn't change a thing."

Fisher seemed unperturbed. "Ah, but there *is* lots of oxygen there and no carbon dioxide, so if it's not the result of Rotorian action, what is it the result of? Doesn't it strike you that we must assume there's non-Earthly life on this world?"

"It's what I *did* assume," said Jarlow.

Wendel said, "It's what we have to assume immediately. Native vegetation is photosynthesizing. It doesn't mean, for one moment, that Rotorians are on the world, or that they ever even reached this system."

Fisher looked annoyed. "Well, Captain," he said with pointed formality, "I have to say that neither does it mean that Rotorians *aren't* on the world, or that they *haven't* reach the system. If the planet has vegetation of its own, it just means that no terraforming was required and the Rotorians could move right in."

"I don't know," said Blankowitz. "I should think there would be no reasonable chance at all that vegetation evolving on a strange planet would be nourishing to human beings. I doubt that human beings could digest it, or that they could assimilate even if they could digest it. I would certainly offer high odds that it would be poisonous. And if there's plant life, there's bound to be animal life, and we don't know what that would entail."

"Even in that case," said Fisher, "it's still possible that the Rotorians would fence off a tract of land, kill the native life within it, and seed plants of their own. I imagine this alien planting—if you want to call it that—would expand with the years."

"Supposition on supposition," muttered Wendel.

"In any case," said Fisher, "it's completely useless to sit here and make up scenarios, when the logical thing is to explore the world as best we can—and from as close a view as possible. Even from its surface—if that seems feasible."

And Wu said with surprising force, "I completely agree."

Blankowitz said, "I'm a biophysicist, and if there's life on the planet, then whatever else it may have or may not have, we must explore it."

Wendel looked from one to the other and, reddening slightly, said, "I suppose we must."

### 84.

"The closer we get," said Tessa Wendel, "and the more information we gather, the more confusing it all is. Is there any question that this is apparently a dead world? There is no illumination on the night hemisphere; there are no signs of vegetation or of any form of life."

"No *gross* signs," said Wu coolly, "but *something* must be happening to keep oxygen in the air. Not being a chemist, I can't think of any chemical process that would do the trick. Can anyone?"

He scarcely waited for an answer. "In fact," he went on, "I seriously question whether a chemist could come up with a chemical explanation. If the oxygen is there, it must be a biological process that produces it. We just don't know of anything else."

Wendel said, "If we say that, then we're judging from our experience with exactly one oxygen-containing atmosphere—Earth's. Someday we may be laughed at. It may turn out that the Galaxy is littered with oxygen atmospheres that have no connection with life, and we'll be on record as having been stymied entirely because of our experience with the one planet that is a freak and has a biological source of the oxygen."

"No," said Jarlow angrily. "You can't get out of it that way, Captain. You can picture all sorts of scenarios, but you can't expect the laws of nature to change for your convenience. If you want to have a nonbiological source of an oxygen-containing atmosphere, you have to suggest a mechanism."

"But," said Wendel, "there's no sign of chlorophyll in the light reflected from the world."

"Why should there be?" said Jarlow. "The chances are that a somewhat different molecule has been evolved under the selective pressure of light from a red dwarf star. May I make a suggestion?"

"Please do," said Wendel bitterly. "It seems to me you do nothing else."

"Very well. All we can actually tell is that the land areas of the world seem to be completely denuded of life. That means nothing. Until four hundred million years ago, Earth's land areas were similarly sterile, but the planet had an oxygen atmosphere and abundant life."

"Sea life."

"Yes, Captain. There's nothing wrong with sea life. And that would include algae or the equivalent—microscopic plants that would do perfectly well as oxygen factories. The algae in Earth's seas produce 80 percent of the oxygen that pours into the atmosphere each year. Doesn't this explain everything? It explains the oxygen atmosphere and it also explains the apparent lack of land life. It also means we can safely explore the planet by landing on the sterile land surface of the world and studying the sea with what instruments we have— leaving it for a later expedition, suitably equipped, to do the detailed work."

"Yes, but human beings are land animals. If Rotor had reached this system, they would surely have attempted to colonize the land areas and of such colonization there is no hint. Is it really necessary to investigate the world further?" the Captain asked.

"Oh yes," said Wu quickly. "We can't go back with deductions only. We need some facts. There may be surprises."

"Do you expect any?" asked Wendel with a touch of anger.

"It doesn't matter whether I do or not. Can we go back to Earth and tell them that—without looking—we were sure there would be no surprises? That would not be very sensible."

"It seems to me," said Wendel, "that you've changed your mind rather drastically. *You* were ready to return without even approaching the Neighbor Star."

"As I recall," said Wu, "I had my mind changed for me. In any case, under the circumstances, we must explore. I know, Captain, that there is a certain temptation to seize the opportunity to visit a few other star systems, but now that there is an apparently habitable world in view, we must come back to Earth with maximum information on something that may be far more important to our planet in a very practical sense than any amount of catalogue-type information concerning the nearer stars. Besides"—and he pointed at the viewport with what was almost surprise on his face—"I *want* to take a closer look at that world. I have this feeling it will be completely safe."

"This feeling?" said Wendel sardonically.

"I'm allowed my intuitions, Captain."

Merry Blankowitz said in a rather husky voice, "I have my intuitions, too, Captain, and I'm worried."

Wendel looked at the young woman with sudden surprise. She said, "Are you weeping, Blankowitz?"

"No, not really, Captain. I'm just very upset."

"Why?"

"I've been using the ND."

"The neuronic detector? On that empty world? Why?"

Blankowitz said, "Because I *came* here to use it. Because that's my function."

"And the results are negative," said Wendel. "I'm sorry, Blankowitz, but if we visit other star systems, you'll have other chances."

"But that just it, Captain. The results are *not* negative. I detect intelligence on the world and that's why I'm upset. It's a ridiculous result, and I don't know what's wrong."

Jarlow said, "Perhaps the device isn't working. It's so new that it wouldn't be surprising if it weren't reliable."

"But why isn't it working? Is the neuronic detector detecting us here on the ship? Or is it simply giving a false positive? I've checked it. The shielding is in perfect order, and if I had a false positive, I ought to have it elsewhere. There are no signs of any positive responses from the gas giant, for instance, or from the Neighbor Star, or from random points in space, but every time I allow it to sweep the satellite, I get a response."

"You mean," said Wendel, "that on this world, where we can detect no life, *you* detect intelligence?"

"It's a *very* minimal response. I can just barely pick it up."

Crile Fisher said, "Actually, Captain, what about Jarlow's point? If there's life in the world's ocean and we don't detect it because the water's opaque, there might still be intelligent life, and perhaps Dr. Blankowitz detects *that*."

Wu said, "Fisher has a good point. After all, life in the sea—however intelligent—is not likely to have a technology. You can't have fire in the sea. Nontechnological life does not make itself very evident, but it may still be intelligent. And a species, however intelligent, is not to be feared without technology, especially if it can't leave the sea, and if we remain on land. It just makes things more interesting and makes it more necessary for us to investigate."

Blankowitz said in annoyance, "You all talk so quickly and so endlessly that I don't get a chance to say anything. You're all wrong. If it were intelligent sea life, I would get a positive response only from the oceans. I get it *everywhere*, just about evenly. Land as well as sea. I don't understand it at all."

"On land as well?" said Wendel, clearly incredulous. "Then there *must* be something wrong."

"But I can't find anything wrong," said Blankowitz. "That's what's so upsetting. I just don't understand this." Then, as though in extenuation, she added, "It's very feeble, of course, but it's there."

Fisher said, "I think I can explain it."

All eyes turned to him, and he grew immediately defensive. "Maybe I'm not a scientist," he said, "but that doesn't mean I can't see something that's pretty plain. There's intelligence in the sea, but we can't see it because the water hides it. All right, that makes sense. But there's intelligence on land, too. Well, that's hidden also. It's underground."

"*Underground?*" said Jarlow explosively. "Why should it be underground? There's nothing wrong with the air or with the temperature or with anything we can detect. What's here to hide from?"

"From the light, for one thing," said Fisher forcefully. "I'm talking about the Rotorians. Suppose they *did* colonize the planet. Why would they want to remain under the red light of the Neighbor Star, light in which their Rotorian plant life would not flourish, and under which they themselves would grow despondent? Underground, they could have artificial lighting and both they and their plants would be better off. Besides—"

He paused and Wendel said, "Go on. What else?"

"Well, you have to understand the Rotorians. They live on the inside of a world. It's what they're used to and what they consider normal. They wouldn't find it comfortable to cling to the outside skin of a world. They would dig underneath, as a matter of course."

Wendel said, "Then you're suggesting that Blankowitz's neuronic detector is detecting the presence of human beings under the surface of the planet."

"Yes. Why not? It's the thickness of the soil between their caverns and the surface that weakens the response the neuronic detector is measuring."

Wendel said, "But Blankowitz gets more or less the same reponse over both land and sea."

"Over the entire planet. It's very even," said Blankowitz.

"All right," said Fisher. "Native intelligence in the sea, Rotorians underground on land. Why not?"

"Wait," said Jarlow. "You get a response everywhere, Blankowitz. Right?"

"Everywhere. I've detected some slight ups and downs, but the response is so shallow I can't really be sure. Certainly, there seems to be some intelligence everywhere on the planet."

Jarlow said, "I suppose that's possible in the sea, but how is it possible on land? Do you suppose that Rotorians, in thirteen years, in *thirteen* years, have dug a network of tunnels under all the land surface of this world. If you got one area of response, or even two—small ones, taking up a tiny fraction of the world's surface—I'd consider the possibility of Rotorian burrowing. But the entire surface? Please! Tell that to my aunt Tillie."

Wu said, "Am I to take it, Henry, that you are suggesting that there is an alien intelligence underground everywhere on the land surface?"

Jarlow said, "I don't see what other conclusion we can come to unless we want to conclude that Blankowitz's device is completely meaningless."

"In that case," said Wendel, "I wonder if it's safe to go down and investigate. An alien intelligence is not necessarily a friendly intelligence, and the *Superluminal* is not equipped to make war."

Wu said, "I don't think we can give up. We must find out what kind of intelligent life is present, and how it might interfere—if at all—with any plans we may make to evacuate Earth and come here."

Blankowitz said, "There *is* one place where the response is a tiny bit more intense than it is anywhere else. Not much. Shall I try to find it again?"

Wendel said, "Go ahead. Try. We can examine the surroundings there carefully and then decide whether to descend or not."

Wu smiled blandly. "I'm sure it will be entirely safe to do so."

Wendel merely scowled unhappily.

329

85.

The peculiar thing about Saltade Leverett (in the opinion of Janus Pitt) was that he liked it out in the asteroid belt. Apparently, there were some people who truly enjoyed emptiness, who loved inanimacy.

"I don't dislike people," Leverett would explain. "I can get all I want of them on holovision—talk to them, listen to them, laugh with them. I can do everything but feel them and smell them, and who wants to do that? Besides we're building five Settlements in the asteroid belt and I can visit any one of them and get my fill of people and smell them, too, for what good that does me."

And then, when he did come to Rotor—the "metropolis," as he insisted on calling it—he would keep looking from one side to the other as though he expected people to crowd in on him.

He even looked at chairs suspiciously, and sat down on them with a sidewise slide as though hoping to wipe off the aura that the previous backside had left upon it.

Janus Pitt had always thought he was the ideal Acting Commissioner for the Asteroid Project. That position had, in effect, given him a free hand in everything that had to do with the outer rim of the Nemesian System. That included not only the Settlements in progress, but with the Scanning Service itself.

They had finished their lunch in the privacy of Pitt's quarters, for Saltade would sooner go hungry than eat in a dining room to which the general public (meaning even a third person who was unknown to him) would be admitted. Pitt, in fact, felt a certain surprise that Leverett had agreed to eat with *him*.

Pitt studied him casually. Leverett was so lean and leathery, and gave such an appearance of whipcord and gristle that he didn't look as if he had ever been young or would ever be old. His eyes were faded blue, his hair faded yellow.

Pitt said, "When was the last time you were on Rotor, Saltade?"

"Nearly two years ago, and I take it unkindly of you to put me through this, Janus."

"Why, what have I done? I certainly haven't summoned you here, though since you are here, old friend, you're welcome."

"You might as well have summoned me. What's this message you sent out to the effect that you were not to be bothered with little things. Are you getting to the point where you're so big you want only big things?"

Pitt's smile grew a trifle strained. "I don't know what you're talking about, Saltade."

"They had a report for you. They detected a small bit of radiation coming in from outside. They sent it to you and you sent back one of your special memos about how you couldn't be bothered."

"Oh, that!" (Pitt remembered. It had been that moment of self-pity and irritation. Surely he was allowed to be irritated at times.) "Well, your people are watching for Settlements. They shouldn't bother me with minor matters."

"If that's your attitude, fine. But it so happens they've found something that's not a Settlement and they don't want to report it to you. They've reported it to me, and they've requested me to pass it on to you despite your order that you are not to be bothered with minutiae. They figure it's my job to handle you, but I'd rather not, Janus. Are you becoming a cantankerous fellow in your powerful old age?"

"Don't rattle on, Saltade. What is it they've reported?" said Pitt, with more than a touch of cantankerousness about him.

"They spotted a vessel."

"What do you mean—a vessel? Not a Settlement?"

Leverett held up a gnarled paw. "Not a Settlement. I said a vessel."

"I don't understand."

"What's to understand? Do you need a computer? If so, yours is right there. A vessel is a ship making its way through space, with a crew on board."

"How large?"

"It could carry half a dozen people, I suppose."

"Then it must be one of ours."

"It isn't. Every one of ours is accounted for. This one is simply not of Rotorian manufacture. The Scanning Service may have been reluctant to talk to you about it, but they did some work on their own. No computer anywhere in the system has been involved with the construction of any ship like that vessel, and no one could have built a vessel like that without computer involvement at some stage."

"Then you conclude?"

"That it's not a Rotorian vessel. It comes from elsewhere. As long as there was the slightest chance that it might have been produced by us, my boys kept quiet and didn't disturb you, per your instructions. When it appeared, definitely, not to be one of our own, they passed it on to me and said you should be told, but that they wouldn't do it. You know, Janus, past a certain point, trampling on people is counterproductive."

"Shut up," said Pitt peevishly. "How could it be non-Rotorian? Where would it come from?"

"I suppose it had to come from the Solar System."

"Impossible! A vessel of the size you describe, with half a dozen people onboard couldn't possibly have made the trip from the Solar System. Even if they discovered hyper-assistance, and it is certainly conceivable they did, a half-dozen people at close quarters for over two years could not complete the trip alive. Maybe there are some exemplary crews, well-trained and unusually suited to the task, who could make the trip and end up at least partly sane, but nobody in the Solar System would risk it. Nothing less than a complete Settlement, a self-contained world occupied by people accustomed to it from birth, could possibly make an interstellar trip and do well."

"Nevertheless," said Leverett, "we have here a small vessel of non-Rotorian manufacture. That's a fact, and you have no choice but to accept that, I promise you. Where do *you* say it came from? The nearest star is the Sun; that's a fact, too. If it didn't come from the Solar System, then it came from some other star system and the journey was a good deal longer than two years and a bit. If two years and a bit is impossible, everything else is certainly impossible."

Pitt said, "Suppose it's not human at all. Suppose these are other forms of life, with other psychologies, that can endure long trips at close quarters."

"Or suppose they are people this big"—and Leverett held his thumb and forefinger a quarter of an inch apart—"and that the vessel *is* a Settlement for them. Well—it's not so. They're not aliens. They're not teeny-weenies. That vessel isn't Rotorian, but it *is* human. We'd expect aliens to look completely different from human beings, and they ought to build ships completely different from those of human beings. That vessel is a human vessel right down to the serial code along its side, which is in the terrestrial alphabet."

"You didn't say that!"

"I didn't think it needed saying."

Pitt said, "It could be a human ship, but it could be automated. It could have robots onboard."

"It could," said Leverett. "In that case, should we blow it out of the sky? If there are no human beings onboard, there are no ethical problems involved. You destroy property but, after all, they're trespassing."

Pitt said, "I'm considering it."

Leverett smiled broadly. "Don't! That vessel has not spent more than two years traveling through space."

"What do you mean?"

"Have you forgotten the condition Rotor was in when we arrived here? We *did* spend over two years in passage, and half of that time we were in normal space going at just under the speed of light. At that speed, the surface was abraded by collision with atoms, molecules, and dust particles. It took polishing and repairs, as I recall. Don't you remember?"

"And this ship?" said Pitt, without bothering to say whether he remembered.

"As shiny as though it had traveled no more than a few million kilometers at ordinary speeds."

"That's impossible. Don't bother me with these games."

"It's not impossible. A few million kilometers at ordinary speeds is all they passed through. The rest of the way—hyperspace."

"What are you talking about?" Pitt's patience was wearing thin.

"Superluminal flight. They've got it."

"That's theoretically impossible."

"Is it? Well, if you can think of any other way of explaining all this, go to it."

Pitt stared at him, open-mouthed. "But—"

"I know. The physicists say it's impossible, but they have it, anyway. Now let me tell you this. If they have superluminal flight, they must have superluminal communication. Then the Solar System knows they're here and it knows what's happening. If we blow the ship out of the sky, the Solar System will know that, too, and, after a while, a fleet of such vessels will come out of space, and they'll come shooting at us."

"What would you do, then?" Pitt found himself temporarily unable to think.

"What else is there to do but to greet them in friendly fashion, find out what they are, who they are, what they're doing, and what they want? Now it's my idea that they plan to land on Erythro. We'll have to land there, too, and talk to them."

"On Erythro?"

"If they're on Erythro, Janus, where do you want us to be? We've got to confront them there. We've got to take that chance."

Pitt felt his mind beginning to tick over again. He said, "Since this seems to you to be necessary, would you be willing to do it? With a ship and a crew, of course."

"You mean you won't?"

"As Commissioner? I can't come down to greet some unknown ship."

"Beneath the official dignity. I see. So I'm to face the aliens, or the teeny-weenies, or the robots, or whatever, without you."

"I'll be in constant contact, of course, Saltade. Voice and image."

"At a distance."

"Yes, but a successful mission on your part would be suitably rewarded, after all."

"Is that so? In that case—" Leverett looked at Pitt, speculatively.

Pitt waited, then said, "Are you going to name a price?"

"I am going to *suggest* a price. If you want me to meet this vessel on Erythro, then I want Erythro."

"What do you mean?"

"I want Erythro as my home. I'm tired of the asteroids. I'm tired of scanning. I'm tired of *people*. I've had enough. I want a whole empty world. I want to build nice living quarters, get food and necessaries from the Dome, have my own farm and my own animals if I can coax them to do well."

"How long have you wanted this?"

"I don't know. It's been growing on me. And since I came here and have gotten a good look at Rotor with its crowds and noise, Erythro looks better than ever to me."

Pitt frowned. "That makes two of you. You're just like that mad girl."

"What mad girl?"

"Eugenia Insigna's daughter. You know Insigna, I suppose."

"The astronomer? Of course. I haven't met her daughter."

"Completely mad. She wants to stay on Erythro."

"I don't consider that mad. I consider that very sensible. In fact, if she wants to say on Erythro, I could endure a woman—"

Pitt held up a finger. "I said 'girl.'"

"How old is she?"

"Fifteen."

"Oh? Well, she'll get older. Unfortunately, so will I."

"She's not one of your raving beauties."

"If you'll take a good look, Janus," said Leverett, "neither am I. You have my terms."

"You want it officially recorded in the computer?"

"Just as a formality, eh, Janus?"

Pitt did not smile. "Very well. We'll try to watch where that vessel lands, and we'll make you ready for Erythro."

# THIRTY-SIX

## MEETING

86.

Eugenia Insigna said in a tone that seemed to place her halfway between puzzlement and discontent, "Marlene was singing this morning. Some song about: 'Home, home in the stars, where the worlds are all swinging and free.'"

"I know the song," said Siever Genarr, nodding. "I'd sing it for you, but I can't carry a tune."

They had just finished lunch. They had lunch together every day now, something Genarr looked forward to with quiet satisfaction, even though the subject of conversation was invariably Marlene and although Genarr felt that Insigna might be turning to him only out of desperation, since to whom else could she talk freely on the subject?

He didn't care. Whatever the excuse—

"I never heard her sing before," said Insigna. "I always thought she couldn't. Actually, she has a pleasant contralto."

"It must be a sign that she's happy now—or excited—or contented

—or something good, Eugenia. My own feeling is that she's found her place in the Universe, found her unique reason for living. It's not given to all of us to find that. Most of us, Eugenia, drag onward, searching for life's personal meaning, not finding it, and ending with anything from roaring desperation to quiet resignation. I'm the quietly resigned type myself."

Insigna managed to smile. "I suspect you don't think that of me."

"You're not roaringly desperate, Eugenia, but you do tend to continue to fight lost battles."

Her eyes dropped. "Do you mean Crile?"

Genarr said, "If you think I do, then I do. But actually, I was thinking of Marlene. She's been out a dozen times. She loves it. It makes her happy, and yet you sit here fighting off terror. What is it, Eugenia, that bothers you about it?"

Insigna ruminated, pushing her fork around on her plate. Then she said, "It's the sense of loss. The unfairness of it. Crile made a choice and I lost him. Marlene has made a choice and I'm losing her—if not to the Plague, then to Erythro."

"I know." He reached for her hand, and she placed it, rather absently, in his.

She said, "Marlene is more and more eager to be out there in that absolute wilderness and less and less interested in being with us. Eventually, she will find a way of living out there and return at lengthening intervals—then be gone."

"You're probably right, but all of life is a symphony of successive losses. You lose your youth, your parents, your loves, your friends, your comforts, your health, and finally your life. To deny loss is to lose it all anyway and to lose, in addition, your self-possession and your peace of mind."

"She was never a happy child, Siever."

"Do you blame yourself for that?"

"I might have been more understanding."

"It's never too late to start. Marlene wanted a whole world and she has it. She wanted to convert what has always been a burdensome ability of hers into a method for communicating directly with another mind, and she has it. Would you force her to give that up? Would you avoid your own loss of her more or less continuous presence by inflicting on her a greater loss than you or I can conceive—the true use of her unusual brain?"

337

Insigna actually laughed a little, though her eyes were swimming with tears. "You could talk a rabbit out of its hole, Siever."

"Could I? My speech was never as effective as Crile's silences."

Insigna said, "There were other influences." She frowned. "It doesn't matter. You're here now, Siever, and you're a great comfort to me."

Genarr said ruefully, "It's the surest sign that I have reached my present age, that I am actually comforted at being a comfort to you. The fires burn low when we ask not for this or that, but for comfort."

"There's nothing wrong with that, surely."

"Nothing wrong in the world. I suspect there are many couples who have gone through the wilds of passion and the rites of ecstasy without ever finding comfort in each other and, in the end, they might have been willing to exchange it all for comfort. I don't know. The quiet victories are *so* quiet. Essential, but overlooked."

"Like you, my poor Siever?"

"Now, Eugenia, I've spent all my life trying to avoid the trap of self-pity and you mustn't tempt me into it just to watch me writhe."

"Oh, Siever, I don't want to watch you writhe."

"There, I just wanted to hear you say that. See how clever I am. But, you know, if you want a substitute for Marlene's presence, I am willing to hang around when you need comfort. Even a whole world to myself wouldn't tempt me from your side—if you didn't want me to go."

She squeezed his hand. "I don't deserve you, Siever."

"Don't use that as an excuse not to have me, Eugenia. I'm willing to waste myself on you, and you shouldn't stop me from making a supreme sacrifice."

"Have you found no one worthier?"

"I haven't looked. Nor have I sensed among the women of Rotor any great demand for me. Besides, what would I do with a worthier object? How dull it would be to offer myself as a duly deserved gift. How much more romantic to be an undeserved gift, to be bounty from the skies."

"To be godlike in your condescension to the unworthy."

Genarr nodded vigorously. "I like that. Yes. Yes. That's exactly the picture that appeals to me."

Insigna laughed again, and more freely. "You're crazy, too. You know, I never noticed that somehow."

"I have hidden depths. As you get to know me still better—taking your time, of course—"

He was interrupted by the sharp buzz of the message-receiver.

He frowned. "There you are, Eugenia. I get you to the point—I don't even remember how I did it—where you are ready to melt into my arms, and we're interrupted. Uh oh!" His voice suddenly changed completely. "It's from Saltade Leverett."

"Who's he?"

"You don't know him. Hardly anyone does. He's the nearest thing to a hermit I've ever met. He works in the asteroid belt because he likes it there. I haven't seen the old bum in years. I don't know why I say 'old,' though, because he's my age.

It's sealed, too. Sealed to my thumbprints, I see. That makes it secret enough for me to ask you to leave before I open it."

Insigna rose at once, but Genarr motioned her down. "Don't be silly, Eugenia. Secrecy is just the disease of officialdom. I pay no attention to it."

He pressed his thumb down on the sheet, then the other thumb in its appropriate place, and letters began to appear. Genarr said, "I often thought that if a person lacked thumbs—" And then he fell silent.

Still silent, he passed her the message.

"Am I allowed to read this?"

Genarr shook his head, "Of course not, but who cares? Read it."

She did so, almost at a glance, then looked up. "An alien ship? About to land *here?*"

Genarr nodded. "At least that's what it says."

Insigna said wildly, "But what about Marlene? She's out there."

"Erythro will protect her."

"How do you know? This may be a ship of aliens. Real aliens. Nonhumans. The thing on Erythro may have no power over them."

"We're aliens to Erythro, yet it can easily control us."

"I must go out there."

"What good—"

"I must be with her. Come with me. Help me. We'll bring her back into the Dome."

"If these are all-powerful and malevolent invaders, we won't be safe inside—"

"Oh, Siever, is this a time for logic? *Please.* I must be with my daughter!"

## 87

They had taken photographs and now they were studying them. Tessa Wendel shook her head. "Unbelievable. The whole world is absolutely desolate. Except this."

"Intelligence everywhere," said Merry Blankowitz, her brow furrowed. "No question about it now when we've been so close. Desolate or not, intelligence is there."

"But most intensely at that dome? Right?"

"Most intensely, Captain. Most easily noticeable. And most familiar. Outside the dome, there are slight differences, and I'm not sure what it signifies."

Wu said, "We've never tested any high intelligence other than human, so, of course—"

Wendel turned to him. "Is it your opinion the intelligence outside the dome isn't human?"

"Since we agree that human beings couldn't have burrowed everywhere underground in thirteen years, what other conclusion is it possible to come to?"

"And the dome? Is that human?"

Wu said, "That's a different thing entirely, and doesn't depend on Blankowitz's plexons. There are astronomical instruments to be seen. The dome—or part of it—is an astronomical observatory."

"Couldn't alien intelligences be astronomers as well?" asked Jarlow, a bit sardonically.

"Of course," said Wu, "but with instruments of their own. When I see what looks to me like an infrared computerized scanner of exactly the type I would see on Earth— Well, let's put it this way. Forget the nature of the intelligence. I see instruments that were either manufactured in the Solar System, or built from designs prepared in the Solar System. There is no question about that. I cannot conceive that alien intelligences, without contact with human beings, could have built such instruments."

"Very well," said Wendel. "I agree with you, Wu. Whatever there is on this world, there are, or were, human beings under that dome."

Crile Fisher said sharply, "Don't just say 'human beings,' Captain. There are Rotorians. There can be no other human beings on this world, excluding ourselves."

Wu said, "And that's unanswerable, too."

Blankowitz said, "It's such a small dome. Rotor must have had tens of thousands of people on it."

"Sixty thousand," murmured Fisher.

"They can't all fit into that dome."

"For one thing," said Fisher, "there may be other domes. We could sweep around the world a thousand times and yet miss objects of all sorts."

"There's only this one place where there seemed to be a change in the plexon type. If there were other domes like that, I would have spotted a few more of them, I'm sure," Blankowitz said.

"Or," said Fisher, "another possibility is that what we see is a tiny bit of an entire structure which, for all we know, may spread out for miles below the surface."

Wu said, "The Rotorians came in a Settlement. The Settlement may still exist. There may be many. This dome may be a mere outpost."

"We haven't seen a Settlement," said Jarlow.

"We haven't *looked*," said Wu. "We've concentrated entirely on this world."

"I haven't spotted intelligence anywhere but on this world," said Blankowitz.

"You haven't looked, either," said Wu. "We'd really have to scan the heavens to spot a Settlement or two, but once you detected plexons from this world, you looked nowhere else."

"I will if you think it's necessary."

Wendel held up her hand. "If there are Settlements, why haven't they spotted *us*? We've made no attempt to shield our energy emissions. After all, we were pretty confident that this star system was empty."

Wu said, "They may have had the same overconfidence, Captain. They haven't been looking for us, either, and so we've slipped past them. Of, if they have detected us, they may be uncertain as to who— or *what*—we are, and they're hesitating as to what action to take, just as we are. What I say, though, is that we do know one spot on the surface of this large satellite where there must be human beings, and I think we must go down and make contact with them."

"Do you think it would be safe to do so?" asked Blankowitz.

"My guess," said Wu firmly, "is that it would be. They can't shoot us out of hand. After all, they'd want to know more about us before they do so. Besides, if all we dare do is stay here in uncertainty, then we will accomplish absolutely nothing and we ought to go back home and tell them what we have discovered. Earth will send out a whole fleet of superluminal vessels, but they won't be thankful to us if we come back with only minimal information. We'll go down in history as the expedition that flinched." He smiled blandly. "You see, Captain, I've learned a few lessons from Fisher."

Wendel said, "Then you think we should now go down and make contact."

"Absolutely," said Wu.

"And you, Blankowitz?"

"I'm curious. Not about the dome, but about the possible alien life. I'd want to find out about them, too."

"Jarlow?"

"I wish we had adequate weapons, or hypercommunication. If we're wiped out, Earth will have found out nothing—absolutely nothing—as the result of our trip. Then it might be that someone else will come here as unprepared as we and just as unsure. Still, if we survive the contact, we'll be going back with important knowledge. I suppose we should chance it."

Fisher said quietly, "Are you going to ask me for my opinion, Captain?"

"I assume that you wish to land to see the Rotorians."

"Exactly, so may I suggest— Let's land as quietly as we can, and as unobtrusively, and I'll leave the ship to reconnoiter. If anything goes wrong, then take off and return to Earth, leaving me behind. I am dispensable, but the ship must return."

Wendel said at once, her face seeming to tighten, "Why you?"

Fisher said, "Because I know the Rotorians, at least, and because I—wish to go."

"I, too," said Wu. "I must be with you."

"Why risk two?" asked Fisher.

"Because two are safer than one. Because, in case of trouble, one might escape while the other holds off the threat. And most of all, because, as you say, you know the Rotorians. Your judgment may be warped."

Wendell said, "We will land, then. Fisher and Wu will leave the ship. If, at any time, Fisher and Wu disagree on procedure, Wu will be the decision-maker."

"Why?" demanded Fisher indignantly.

"Wu has said you know the Rotorians and your decisions may be warped," said Wendel, looking at Fisher firmly, "and I agree with him."

88.

Marlene was happy. She felt as if she were wrapped in gentle arms, protected, shielded. She could see the reddish light of Nemesis and feel the wind against her cheeks. She could watch the clouds obscure part or all of Nemesis' large globe, now and then, so that the light would dim and turn grayish.

But she could see as easily in the gray as in the red, and she could see in shades and tints that made fascinating patterns. And though the wind grew cooler when Nemesis' light was hidden, it never chilled her. It was as though Erythro were somehow enhancing her sight, somehow warming the air around her body when necessary, somehow caring for her in every way.

And she could talk to Erythro. She had made up her mind to think of the cells that made up the life on Erythro *as* Erythro. As the planet. Why not? What else? Individually, the cells were only cells, as primitive—much more primitive, in fact—than the individual cells of her own body. It was only all of the prokaryote cells together that made up an organism that encircled the planet in a billion trillion tiny interconnected pieces, that so filled and permeated and *grasped* the planet, that it might as well be thought of *as* the planet.

How odd, thought Marlene. This giant life-form must never, before the coming of Rotor, have known that anything live existed other than itself.

Her questions and sensations did not have to exist entirely in her mind. Erythro would rise before her sometimes, like thin gray smoke, consolidating into a wraithlike human figure wavering at the edges. There was always, about it, a flowing feeling. She could not actually see that, but she sensed, beyond doubt, that millions of invisible cells were leaving each second and immediately being replaced by others. No one prokaryote cell could exist for long out of its water film, so that each was only evanescently part of the figure, but the figure itself was as permanent as it wished to be, and never lost its identity.

Erythro did not take Aurinel's form again. It had gathered, without being told, that that was disturbing. Its appearance was neutral now, changing slightly with the vagaries of Marlene's own thought. Erythro could follow the delicate changes of her mind pattern far better, she decided, than she herself could, and the figure adjusted to that, looking more like some figure in her mind's eye at one moment, and then as she tried to focus on it and identify it, it would shift gently into something else. Occasionally, she could catch glimpses: the curve of her mother's cheek, Uncle Siever's strong nose, bits of the girls and boys she had met at school.

It was an interactive symphony. It was not so much a conversation between them as a mental ballet she could not describe, something that was infinitely soothing, infinite in variety—partly changing appearance—partly changing voice—partly changing thought.

It was a conversation in so many dimensions that the possibility of going back to communication that consisted only of speech left her feeling flat, lifeless. Her gift of sensing by body language flowered into something she had never imagined earlier. Thoughts could be exchanged far more swiftly—and deeply—than by the coarse crudeness of speech.

Erythro explained—filled her, rather—with the shock of encountering other minds. *Minds.* Plural. One more might have been grasped easily. Another world. Another mind. But to encounter *many* minds, crowding on each other, each different, overlapping in small space. Unthinkable.

The thoughts that permeated Marlene's mind as Erythro expressed itself could be expressed only distantly and unsatisfactorily in words. Behind those words, overflowing and drowning them, were the emotions, the feelings, the neuronic vibrations that shattered Erythro into a rearrangement of concepts.

It had experimented with the minds—felt them. Not felt as human beings would mean "felt," but something else entirely that could be approached very distantly by that human word and concept. And some of the minds crumpled, decayed, became unpleasant. Erythro ceased to feel minds at random, but sought out minds that would withstand the contact.

"And you found me?" said Marlene.

"I found you."

"But why? Why did you look for me?" she asked eagerly.

The figure wavered and turned smokier. "Just to find you."

It was no answer. "Why do you want me to be with you?"

The figure started to fade and the thought was a fugitive one. "Just to be with me."

And it was gone.

Only its image was gone. Marlene felt its protection still, its warm enclosure. But why had it disappeared? Had she displeased it with her questions?

She heard a sound.

On an empty world it is possible to catalogue the sounds briefly, for there aren't many. There is the noise of flowing water, and the more delicate moan of blowing air. There are the predictable noises you make yourself, whether the falling of a footstep, the rustle of clothing, or the whistle of breath.

Marlene heard something that was none of these, and turned in the direction of it. Over the rocky outcropping on her left, there appeared the head of a man.

Her first thought, of course, was that it was someone from the Dome who had come to get her, and she felt a surge of anger. Why would they still be searching for her? She would refuse to wear a wave-emitter from now on, and they would then have no way of locating her except by blind search.

But she did not recognize the face and surely she had met everyone in the Dome by now. She might not know the individual names or anything about them, but she would know, when she saw anyone from the Dome, that she had seen that face before.

She had not seen this new face anywhere in the Dome.

Those eyes were staring at her. The mouth was a little open, as if the person were panting. And then whoever it was was topping the rise and running to her.

She faced him. The protection she felt around her was strong. She was not afraid.

He stopped ten feet away, staring, leaning forward as though he had reached a barrier he could not penetrate, one that deprived him of the ability to advance farther.

Finally, he said in a strangled voice, "Roseanne!"

89.

Marlene stared at him, observing carefully. His micro-movements were eager and radiated a sense of ownership: possession, closeness, mine, mine, mine.

She took a step backward. How was that possible? Why should he—

345

A dim memory of a holoimage she had once seen when she was a little girl—

And finally, she could deny it no more. However impossible it sounded, however unimaginable—

She huddled within the protective blanket and said, "Father?"

He rushed at her as though he wanted to seize her in his arms and she stepped away again. He paused, swaying, then put one hand to his forehead as though fighting dizziness.

He said, "Marlene. I meant to say Marlene."

He pronounced it incorrectly, Marlene noticed. Two syllables. But that was right for him. How would he know?

A second man came up and stood next to him. He had straight black hair, a wide face, narrow eyes, a sallow complexion. Marlene had never seen a man who quite looked like him. She gaped a little and had to make an effort to close her mouth.

The second man said to the first in a soft incredulous voice. "Is this your *daughter*, Fisher?"

Marlene's eyes widened. Fisher! It *was* her father.

Her father didn't look at the other man. Only at her. "Yes."

The other said, even more softly, "First deal of the cards, Fisher? You come here and the first person you meet is your daughter?"

Fisher seemed to make an effort to turn his eyes from his daughter, but he failed. "I think that's it, Wu. Marlene, your last name is Fisher, isn't it? Your mother is Eugenia Insigna. Am I right? My name is Crile Fisher and I'm your father."

He held out his arms to her.

Marlene was well aware that the look of yearning on her father's face was completely real, but she stepped back yet again and said coldly, "How is it you're here?"

"I came from Earth to find you. To *find* you. After all these years."

"Why did you want to find me? You left me when I was a baby."

"I had to then, but it was always with the intention of coming back for you."

And another voice—harsh, steely—broke in, and said, "So you came back for Marlene? For nothing else?"

Eugenia Insigna was standing there, face pale, lips almost colorless, hands trembling. Behind her was Siever Genarr, looking astonished, but remaining in the background. Neither one was wearing protective clothing.

Insigna said, voice hurried, semihysterical, "I thought there would be people from some Settlement, people from the Solar System. I thought there might be some alien life-form. I went through every possibility I could think of, and in all the thoughts that crowded in on me after I was told a strange ship was landing, I never once thought it might be Crile Fisher coming back. And for Marlene!"

"I came with others on an important mission. This is Chao-Li Wu, a shipmate. And—and—"

"And we meet. Did it ever occur to you that you might encounter me? Or were your thoughts entirely on Marlene? What was your important mission? To find Marlene?"

"No. That was not the mission. Just my desire."

"And I?"

Fisher's eyes fell. "I came for Marlene."

"You came *for* her? To take her away?"

"I thought—" began Fisher, and his words stuck.

Wu watched him wonderingly. Genarr frowned in thoughtful anger.

Insigna whirled toward her daughter. "Marlene, would you go anywhere with this man?"

"I'm not going anywhere with anyone, Mother," said Marlene quietly.

Insigna said, "There's your answer, Crile. You can't leave me with my child of a year, and come back fifteen years later with a 'By the way, I'll take her over now.' And not a thought of me. She's your daughter biologically, but nothing more. She's mine by the right of fifteen years of loving and caring."

Marlene said, "There is no point in quarreling over me, Mother."

Chao-Li Wu stepped forward. "Pardon me. I have been introduced, but no one has been introduced to me. You are, madam?"

"Eugenia Insigna Fisher," She pointed at Fisher. "His wife—*once.*"

"And this is your daughter, madam?"

"Yes. This is Marlene Fisher."

Wu bowed slightly. "And this other gentleman."

Genarr said, "I'm Siever Genarr, Commander of the Dome that you see behind me on the horizon."

"Ah good. Commander, I would like to speak to you. I regret that there seems to be a family argument here, but it has nothing to do with our mission."

"And just what is your mission?" growled another new voice. Coming toward them was a white-haired figure, his mouth turned down, with something that looked very much like a weapon in his hand.

"Hello, Siever," he said as he passed Genarr.

Genarr looked startled. "Saltade. Why are you here?"

"I am representing Commissioner Janus Pitt of Rotor. I repeat my question to you, sir. What is your mission? And what is your name?"

"My name, at least," said Wu, "is easily given. It is Dr. Chao-Li Wu. And you, sir?"

"Saltade Leverett."

"Greetings. We come in peace," said Wu, eyeing the weapon.

"I hope so," said Leverett grimly. "I have six ships with me and they've got your ship in their sights."

"Indeed?" said Wu. "This small dome? With a fleet?"

"This small dome is only a tiny outpost," said Leverett. "I have the fleet. Do not count on a bluff."

"I will take your word for it," said Wu. "But our one small ship comes from Earth. It got here because it has the capacity for superluminal flight. Do you know what I mean? Faster-than-light travel."

"I know what you mean."

Genarr said suddenly, "Is Dr. Wu telling the truth, Marlene?"

"Yes, he is, Uncle Siever," said Marlene.

"Interesting," murmured Genarr.

Wu said calmly, "I am delighted to have my word confirmed by this young lady. Am I to suppose she is Rotor's expert on superluminal flight?"

"You need not suppose anything," said Leverett impatiently. "Why are you here? You have not been invited."

"No, we haven't. We didn't know that anyone was here to object to us. But I urge you not to give in, unnecessarily, to any bad temper. At any false move from you, our ship will just disappear into hyperspace."

Marlene said quickly, "He's not certain about that."

Wu frowned. "I'm certain enough. And even if you manage to destroy the ship, our home base on Earth knows where we are and is getting constant reports. If anything happens to us, the next expedition will be one of fifty superluminal battle cruisers. Don't risk it, sir."

Marlene said, "That is not so."

Genarr said, "What is not so, Marlene?"

"When he said that the home base on Earth knows where he is, that was not so, and he *knew* that was not so."

Genarr said, "That's good enough for me. Saltade, these people do not have hypercommunication."

Wu's expression did not change. "Are you relying on the speculation of a teenage girl?"

"It's not speculation. It's a certainty. Saltade, I'll explain later. Take my word for it."

Marlene said suddenly, "Ask my father. He'll tell you." She didn't quite understand how her father would know about her gift—she had surely not had it, or at least had not displayed it, when she was one year old, but his understanding was clear. It shouted itself at her, for all that others could not see it.

Fisher said, "It's no use, Wu. Marlene can see right through us."

For the first time, Wu's coolness seemed to desert him. He frowned, and said tartly, "How would you know anything at all about this girl, even if she's your daughter? You haven't seen her since she was an infant."

"I had a younger sister once," said Fisher in a low voice.

Genarr said with sudden enlightenment, "It runs in the family, then. Interesting. Well, Dr. Wu, you see we have a tool here that allows no bluffing. Let us, then, be open with each other. Why have you come to this world?"

"To save the Solar System. Ask the young lady—since she is your absolute authority—if I am telling the truth *this* time."

Marlene said, "Of course you're telling the truth, Dr. Wu. We know about the danger. My mother discovered it."

Wu said, "And we discovered it, too, little lady, without any help from your mother."

Saltade Leverett looked from one to another and said, "May I ask what you're all talking about?"

Genarr said, "Believe me, Saltade, Janus Pitt knows all about it. I'm sorry he hasn't told you, but if you get in touch with him now, he will. Tell him we are dealing with people who know how to travel faster than light and that we might be able to make a deal."

### 90.

The four of them sat in Siever Genarr's private quarters in the Dome, and Genarr tried to keep his sense of history from overwhelming him. This was the first example in human history of an interstellar negotiation. If each of the four were famous for nothing else, their names would ring down the corridors of Galactic history for this alone.

Two and two.

There, on the side of the Solar System (Earth, really, and who would have thought that decadent Earth would be representing the Solar System, that they should have developed superluminal flight rather than one of the up-to-date, live-wire Settlements) were Chao-Li Wu and Crile Fisher.

Wu was talkative and insinuating; a mathematician, but one who was clearly possessed of practical acumen. Fisher, on the other hand (and Genarr still could not accustom himself to the notion that he was actually seeing him again), sat there quietly, lost in thought and contributing little.

On his own side was Saltade Leverett, suspicious and uneasy at being in such close contact with three at once, but firm—lacking the wordy flow of Wu, yet having no trouble in making himself clear.

As for Genarr, he was as quiet as Fisher, but he was waiting for them to settle the matter—since he knew something the other three did not.

Night had fallen by now, and hours had passed. First lunch, then dinner had been served. There had been breaks to snap the tension and during one of them, Genarr had gone out to see Eugenia Insigna and Marlene.

"It's not going badly," said Genarr. "Both sides have a great deal to gain."

"What about Crile?" asked Insigna nervously. "Has he brought up the matter of Marlene?"

"Honestly, Eugenia, that is not the subject of discussion and he has not brought her up. I do think he is very unhappy about it."

"He should be," said Insigna bitterly.

Genarr hesitated. "What do you think, Marlene?"

Marlene looked at him with her dark unfathomable eyes. "I've gotten beyond that, Uncle Siever."

"A little hard-hearted," muttered Genarr.

But Insigna snapped at him. "Why shouldn't she be? Deserted in infancy."

"I'm not hard-hearted," said Marlene thoughtfully. "If I can arrange to have his mind eased, I will. But I don't belong with him, you see. Or with you, either, Mother. I'm sorry, but I belong with Erythro. Uncle Siever, you *will* tell me what's decided, won't you?"

"I promised I would."

"It's important."

"I know."

"I should be there to represent Erythro."

"I imagine that Erythro is there, but you will be part of it before it's over. Even if I didn't assure you of that, Marlene, which I do, I think that Erythro would see to it."

And then he returned to continue the discussion.

Chao-Li Wu was leaning back in his seat now, his astute face showing no signs of weariness.

"Let me summarize," he said. "In the absence of superluminal flight, this Neighbor Star—I shall call it Nemesis, as you do—is the nearest star to the Solar System, so that any ship making its way to the stars would be bound to stop here first. Once all humanity has true superluminal flight, however, distance is no longer a factor and human beings will not search out the nearest star, but the most comfortable star. The search will be on for Sun-like stars that happen to be circled by at least one Earth-like planet. Nemesis will be put to one side.

"Rotor, which has, till now, apparently made a fetish of secrecy, to keep others away and to reserve this stellar system for itself, need do so no more. Not only will this system be unwanted by other Settlements, but Rotor itself may no longer want it. It may choose, if it so desires, to search out Sun-like stars for itself. There are billions of such stars in the spiral arms of the Galaxy.

"In order for Rotor to have superluminal flight, it might occur to you that you could point a weapon at me and demand all I know. I am a mathematician, a highly theoretical one, and my information is limited. Even if you were to capture our ship itself, you would learn very little from it. What you must do is to send a deputation of scientists and engineers to Earth, where we could train you adequately.

"In return, we ask for this world, which you call Erythro. It is my understanding that you do not occupy it in any way except for the presence of this Dome, which is used for astronomical and other kinds of research. You are living in Settlements.

"Whereas the Settlements of the Solar System can wander off in search of Sun-like planets, the people of Earth cannot. There are eight billion of us who must be evacuated in a few thousand years and, as Nemesis approaches more and more closely to the Solar System, Erythro will more and more easily serve as a way station on which to place Earthpeople until such time as we can find Earth-like worlds to transfer them to.

"We will return to Earth with a Rotorian of your choosing as proof that we were really here. More ships will be built and they will return—you can be sure we will return, for we must have Erythro. We will then take back your scientists, who will learn the technique of superluminal flight, a technique we will also grant to the other Settlements. Does all this adequately summarize what we have decided?"

Leverett said, "It's not all quite that easy. Erythro will have to be terraformed if it is to support any sizable number of Earthpeople."

"Yes, I have left out details," said Wu. "These will have to be dealt with, too, but not by us."

"True, Commissioner Pitt and the Council will have to decide on Rotor's behalf."

"And the Global Congress on Earth's behalf, but with so much at stake, I don't foresee failure."

"There will have to be safeguards. How far can we trust Earth?"

"About as far as Earth can trust Rotor, I imagine. It may take a year to work out safeguards. Or five years. Or ten years. It will take years, in any case, to build an adequate supply of ships with which to begin, but we have a program that should last several thousand years, one that will end with the necessary abandonment of Earth and the beginning of the colonization of the Galaxy."

"Assuming there are no competing intelligences to be taken into account," growled Leverett.

"An assumption we can make until we are forced to abandon it. That is for the future. Will you consult your Commissioner now? Will you choose your Rotorian to accompany us and allow us to leave for Earth as soon as possible?"

Now Fisher leaned forward. "May I suggest that my daughter, Marlene, be the one—"

But Genarr did not allow the sentence to be completed. "I'm sorry, Crile. I've consulted her. She will not leave this world."

"If her mother goes with her, then—"

"No, Crile. Her mother has nothing to do with it. Even if you wanted Eugenia back, and Eugenia were to decide to go with you, Marlene would still remain on Erythro. And if you decided to stay

352

here to be with her, that would do you no good either. She is lost to you, and to her mother as well."

Fisher said angrily, "She's only a child. She can't make these decisions."

"Unfortunately for you, and for Eugenia, and for all of us here, and perhaps for all of humanity, she *can* make these decisions. In fact, I have promised that when we are through here, as I think we now are, that we will acquaint her with our decisions."

Wu said, "Surely that is not necessary."

Leverett said, "Come, Siever, we don't have to go to a little girl for permission."

Genarr said, "Please listen to me. It *is* necessary, and we *do* have to go to her. Allow me to try an experiment. I am suggesting that Marlene be brought in here so that we can tell her what we have decided. If one of you thinks that is not desirable, let him leave. Let him stand up and leave."

Leverett said, "I think you've taken leave of your senses, Siever. I have no intention of playing games with a teenager. I'm going to speak to Pitt. Where do you keep your transmitter?"

He stood up and, almost at once, staggered and fell.

Wu half-rose in alarm, "Mr. Leverett—"

Leverett rolled over and held up his arm. "Help me up, somebody."

Genarr helped him to his feet and back into the chair. "What happened?" he asked.

"I'm not sure," said Leverett. "I had this blinding headache for just a moment."

"So you were not able to leave the room." Genarr turned to Wu. "Since you don't think seeing Marlene is necessary, would you care to leave the room?"

Very carefully, eyes fixed on Genarr, Wu rose slowly from his chair, winced, and sat down again.

He said politely, "Perhaps we had better see the young woman."

Genarr said, "We must. On this world, at least, what that young woman wishes is the law."

91.

"*No!*" said Marlene so forcibly that it amounted almost to a shriek. "You can't do it!"

"Can't do what?" said Leverett, his white eyebrows drawing close to the furrowed line between.

"Use Erythro for a way station—or for anything."

Leverett stared at her angrily, and his lips drew back as if to speak, but Wu intervened. "Why not, young woman? It is an empty, unused world."

"It is *not* empty. It is *not* unused. Uncle Siever, *tell* them."

Genarr said, "What Marlene wants to say is that Erythro is occupied by innumerable prokaryote cells capable of photosynthesis. That is why there is oxygen in Erythro's atmosphere."

"Very well," said Wu. "What difference does that make?"

Genarr cleared his throat. "Individually, the cells are as primitive as life can be above the virus level, but, apparently, they cannot be treated individually. Taken all together, they form an organism of enormous complexity. It is world-girdling."

"An organism?" Wu remained polite.

"A single organism, and Marlene calls it by the name of the planet, since they are so intimately related."

Wu said, "Are you serious? How do you know about this organism?"

"Chiefly through Marlene."

"Through the young woman," said Wu, "who may be—a hysteric?"

Genarr lifted a finger. "Do not say anything seriously against her. I'm not sure that Erythro—the organism—has a sense of humor. We know *chiefly* through Marlene—not entirely. When Saltade Leverett stood up to leave, he was knocked down. When you half-rose a while ago, perhaps also to leave, you were clearly uncomfortable. Those are the reactions of Erythro. It protects Marlene by acting directly on our minds. In the early days of our existence on this world, it inadvertently caused a small epidemic of mental disease that we called the Erythro Plague. I'm afraid that, if it wishes, it can produce irrecoverable mental damage; and, if it wishes, it can kill. *Please* do not test this."

Fisher said, "You mean it is not Marlene who—"

"No, Crile. Marlene has certain abilities, but they don't extend to the point of doing harm. It is Erythro that is dangerous."

"How do we stop it from being dangerous?" asked Fisher.

"By listening politely to Marlene, to begin with. Then, too, let me be the one to talk with her. Erythro, at least, knows me. And believe me when I say that I want to save Earth. I have no desire to bring about the death of billions."

He turned to Marlene. "You understand, Marlene, don't you, that Earth is in danger? Your mother showed you that the close approach of Nemesis might destroy Earth."

"I *know* that, Uncle Siever," said Marlene in an agonized voice, "but Erythro belongs to itself."

"It might want to share, Marlene. It allows the Dome to remain here on the planet. We don't seem to disturb it."

"But there are less than a thousand people in the Dome and they *stay* in the Dome. Erythro doesn't mind the Dome because that means it can study human minds."

"It can study human minds all the more when Earthmen come here."

"Eight billion of them?"

"No, not all eight billion. They'll come here to settle down temporarily and then go off somewhere. At any one time, there'll only be a fraction of the population here."

"It will be millions. I'm sure it will be. You can't squeeze them all into a dome and supply them with food and water and all they'll need. You'll have to spread them out on Erythro and terraform it. Erythro couldn't survive it. It would have to protect itself."

"Are you sure of that?"

"It would have to. Wouldn't you?"

"It would mean the death of billions."

"I can't help that." She pressed her lips together, then said, "There's a different way."

Leverett said gruffly, "What's the girl talking about? What different way?"

Marlene glanced briefly in Leverett's direction, then turned to Genarr. "I don't know. Erythro knows. At least—at least it says that the knowledge is here, but it can't explain."

Genarr held up both arms to stop what might have been a flurry of questions. "Let *me* talk."

Then he said very quietly, "Marlene, be calm. If you're worried about Erythro, that is useless. You know it can protect itself against anything. Tell me what you mean when you say Erythro can't explain."

Marlene was breathless and gasping. "Erythro knows the knowledge is here, but it doesn't have human experience, human science, human ways of thinking. It doesn't understand."

"The knowledge is in the minds present here?"

"Yes, Uncle Siever."

"Can't it probe the minds?"

"It would hurt them. It can probe *my* mind without hurting it."

"I should hope so," said Genarr, "but do you have the knowledge?"

"No, of course not. But it can use my mind as a probe for the others here. Yours. My father's. All."

"Is that safe?"

"Erythro thinks it is, but—oh, Uncle Siever, I'm afraid."

"Surely this is madness," whispered Wu, and Genarr quickly put a finger to his lips.

Fisher was on his feet. "Marlene, you mustn't—"

Genarr waved him back furiously. "There's nothing you can do, Crile. There are billions of human beings at risk—we keep on saying it over and over again—and the organism must be allowed to do what it can. Marlene."

Marlene's eyes had turned upward. She seemed to be in a trance. "Uncle Siever," she whispered. "Hold me."

Half-stumbling, half-falling, she moved toward Genarr, who seized her and held her tightly. "Marlene— Relax— It will be all right—" He sat down carefully in his chair, still holding her rigid body.

### 92.

It was like a silent explosion of light that obliterated the world. Nothing existed beyond itself.

Genarr was not even conscious of being Genarr. The self did not exist either. Only a luminous interconnecting fog of great complexity existed, one that was expanding and separating into threads that took on the same great complexity even as they separated.

A whirling and a receding and then an expansion as it approached again. On and on, hypnotically, like something that had always existed and would always exist, without end.

Falling endlessly into an opening that widened as it approached without ever getting wider. Continuing change without alteration. Little puffs unfolding into new complexity.

On and on. No sound. No sensation. Not even vision. A consciousness of something that had the properties of light without being light. It was the mind becoming aware of itself.

And then, painfully—if there had been such a thing as pain in the Universe—and with a sob—if there had been such a thing as a sound in the Universe—it began to dim and turn and spin, faster and faster, into a point of light that flashed and was gone.

### 93.

The Universe was obtrusive in its existence.

Wu stretched and said, "Did anyone else experience that?"

Fisher nodded.

Leverett said, "Well, I'm a believer. If it's madness, we're all mad together."

But Genarr was still holding Marlene, bending over her painfully. She was breathing raggedly.

"Marlene. Marlene."

Fisher had struggled to his feet. "Is she all right?"

"I can't say," muttered Genarr. "She's alive, but that's not enough."

Her eyes opened. She was staring at Genarr, her eyes empty, unfocused.

"Marlene," whispered Genarr in despair.

"Uncle Siever," whispered Marlene in return.

Genarr let himself breathe. At least she had recognized him.

"Don't move," he said. "Wait till it's over."

"It *is* over. I'm so *glad* it's over."

"But are you all right?"

She paused, then said, "Yes, I feel all right. Erythro says I'm all right."

Wu said, "Did you find this hidden knowledge we're supposed to have?"

"Yes, Dr. Wu. I did." She passed a hand over her damp brow. "It was you, actually, who had it."

"I?" said Wu vehemently. "What was it?"

"*I* don't understand it," said Marlene. "You will, maybe, if I describe it."

"Describe what?"

"Something that's gravity pushing things away instead of pulling them toward."

357

"Gravitational repulsion, yes," said Wu. "It's part of superluminal flight." He drew a deep breath and his body straightened. "It's a discovery I made."

"Well then," said Marlene, "if you pass close by Nemesis in super-luminal flight, there's gravitational repulsion. The faster you move, the more the repulsion."

"Yes, the ship would be pushed away."

"Wouldn't Nemesis be pushed in the opposite direction?"

"Yes, in inverse ratio of mass, but Nemesis' move would be immeasurably small."

"But what if it were repeated over and over for hundreds of years?"

"Nemesis' movement would still be very small."

"But its path would be slightly changed and over the light-years the distance would mount up and Nemesis might pass Earth just far enough away so that Earth would be spared."

Wu said, "Well—"

Leverett said, "Could something of the sort be worked out?"

"We could try. An asteroid, passing by at ordinary speeds, shifting into hyperspace for a trillionth of a second and back at ordinary speed a million miles out. Asteroids in orbit around Nemesis always moving into hyperspace on the same side." For a moment, he was lost in thought. Then, defensively, "I would surely have thought of this on my own, given a little time."

Genarr said, "You may still have the credit. Marlene took it from your mind, after all."

He looked about at the other three and said, "Well, gentlemen, unless something goes terribly wrong, let's forget about using Erythro as a way station, which it wouldn't allow anyway. We needn't concern ourselves with evacuating Earth—if we can learn to make full and proper use of gravitational repulsion. I think the situation has been much improved because we brought in Marlene."

"Uncle Siever," said Marlene.

"Yes, dear."

"I'm so sleepy."

## 94.

Tessa Wendel looked at Crile Fisher gravely. "I keep saying to myself: 'You're back.' Somehow I didn't think you'd be back, once it was clear you had found the Rotorians."

"Marlene was the first person—the very first person I found."

He was staring at nothingness, and Wendel let him. He would have to think it through. They had enough to think about in other directions.

They were taking a Rotorian back with them: Ranay D'Aubisson, a neurophysicist. Twenty years before, she had worked in a hospital on Earth. There would be bound to be those who would remember and recognize her. There would be records that would serve to identify her. And she would be the living proof of what they had done.

Wu was a changed person, too. He was full of plans for making use of gravitational repulsion to nudge the movement of the Neighbor Star. (He called it Nemesis now, but if he could formulate a plan to move it ever so slightly, it might not be Earth's nemesis at all.)

And Wu had grown modest. He didn't want the credit for the discovery, which to Wendel seemed completely unbelievable. He said the project had been worked out in conference and he would say no more.

What's more, he was definitely planning to return to the Nemesian System—and not just to run the project. He wanted to *be* there. "If I have to walk," he said.

Wendel became aware that Fisher was looking at her, frowning slightly. "Why didn't you think I'd be back, Tessa?"

She decided to be matter-of-fact. "Your wife is younger than I am, Crile, and she would hold on to your daughter. I was sure of that. And, desperate as you were to have your daughter, I thought—"

"That I would stay with Eugenia because that was the only way?"

"Something like that."

Fisher shook his head. "It wouldn't have worked out that way, no matter what. I thought she was Roseanne at first—my sister. The eyes, mostly, but there was a Roseanne look about her in other ways, too. But she was far more than Roseanne. Tessa, she wasn't human, isn't human. I'll explain later. I—" He shook his head.

"Never mind, Crile," said Wendel. "Explain whenever you please."

"It hasn't been a total loss. I've seen her. She's alive. She's well. And in the end I guess I didn't want more. Somehow, after my—experience, Marlene became—just Marlene. For the rest of my life, Tessa, *you* are all I want."

"Making the best of it, Crile?"

"A very good best it is, Tessa. I'll be formally divorced. We'll be formally married. I will leave Rotor and Nemesis to Wu, and you and

I can stay on Earth, or on any Settlement you wish. We'll each have good pensions, and we can leave the Galaxy and its problems to others. We've done enough, Tessa. That is, if that's what you wish, too."

"I can hardly wait, Crile."

An hour later, they were still holding each other.

## 95.

Eugenia Insigna said, "I'm so glad I wasn't there. I keep thinking about it. Poor Marlene. She must have been so afraid."

"Yes, she was. But she did it, made it possible to save Earth. Even Pitt can do nothing about it now. In a sense, his whole life work has been made useless. Not only is there no purpose to his whole project of secretly building up a new civilization, but he has to help supervise the project for the salvation of the Earth. He *has* to. Rotor is no longer hidden. It can be reached at any time, and every bit of humanity, on and off Earth, will turn against us if we don't rejoin the human race. It couldn't have happened without Marlene."

Insigna wasn't thinking of the greater significances. She said, "But when she was frightened, really frightened, it was to *you* she turned, not to Crile."

"Yes."

"And *you* held her, not Crile."

"Yes, but Eugenia, don't make anything mystical out of it. She knew me, but she didn't know Crile."

"You're bound to explain it very sensibly, Siever. That's you. But I'm glad it was you she turned to. He didn't deserve her."

"Fair enough. He didn't deserve her. But, now—please, Eugenia, let go. Crile is leaving. He'll never be back. He's seen his daughter. He's watched her provide a way to save Earth. I don't begrudge him that, and you shouldn't either. So, if you don't mind, I am changing the subject. Do you know that Ranay D'Aubisson is leaving with them?"

"Yes. Everyone is talking about it. I won't miss her somehow. I never thought she was very sympathetic to Marlene."

"Neither were you at times, Eugenia. It's a great thing for Ranay. Once she realized the so-called Erythro Plague was not a useful field of study, her work here was shattered, but on Earth, she can introduce modern brain scanning and have a great professional life."

"All right. Good for her."

"But Wu will be back. Very bright man. It was his brain that yielded the proper finding. You know, I'm sure that when he comes back to work on the Repulsion Effect, his real desire will be to remain on Erythro. The Erythro organism has picked him as it had picked Marlene. And what's funnier still, I think it's picked Leverett, as well."

"What system do you suppose it uses, Siever?"

"Do you mean why does it take Wu and not Crile? Why does it take Leverett and not me?"

"Well, I can see that Wu must be a far more brilliant man than Crile, but, Siever, you are *much* better than Leverett. Not that I would have wanted to lose you."

"Thank you. I presume the Erythro organism has a criterion of its own. I even think I have a dim idea of what it might be."

"Really?"

"Yes. When my mind was being probed, it meant that through Marlene, the Erythro organism itself was entering us. I caught a glimpse of its thoughts, I imagine. Not consciously, of course, but when it was over I seemed to know things I didn't know before. Marlene has the strange talent that makes it possible for her to communicate with the organism and makes it also possible for it to use her brain as a probe for other brains, but I think that's just a practical advantage. It chose her for something far more unusual."

"What would that be?"

"Imagine you're a piece of string, Eugenia. How would you feel if you suddenly and unexpectedly became aware of a piece of lace? Imagine you're a circle. How would you feel if you came across a patterned sphere? Erythro had knowledge of only one kind of mind— its own. Its mind is immensely huge, but so pedestrian. It is what it is only because it is made up of trillions of trillions of cellular units, all very loosely connected.

"Then it came across human minds, in which the cellular units were comparatively few, but in which there were incredible numbers of interconnections—incredible complexity. Lace instead of string. It must have been overwhelmed by the sheer beauty of it. It must have found Marlene's mind to be the most beautiful of all. *That* was why it seized upon her. Wouldn't you—if you had a chance to acquire a real Rembrandt or a Van Gogh? That was why it protected her so avidly. Wouldn't you protect a great work of art? Yet it risked her for the sake of humanity. It was rough on Marlene, but rather noble of the organism.

"Anyway, that is what I consider the Erythro organism to be. I consider it an art connoisseur, a collector of beautiful minds."

Insigna laughed. "By that token, Wu and Leverett must have very beautiful minds."

"They probably do to Erythro. And it will continue collecting when scientists from Earth arrive. You know it will end by collecting a group of human beings different from the common run. The Erythro group. It may help them find new homes in space and, in the end, perhaps the Galaxy will have two kinds of worlds, worlds of Earthmen and worlds of more efficient pioneers, the true Spacers. I wonder how that would work out. Surely it would mean the future would lie with them. I regret that somehow."

"Don't think of that," said Insigna urgently. "Let people of the future deal with the future as it comes. Right now, you and I are human beings judging each other by human standards."

Genarr smiled joyously, his pleasantly homely face lighting up. "I'm glad of that, because I find your mind beautiful, and perhaps you find mine equally beautiful."

"Oh, Siever, I always did. Always."

Genarr's smile faded somewhat. "But there are other kinds of beauty, I know."

"Not for me any longer. You have all the kinds of beauty. Siever, we lost the morning, you and I. But there's still the afternoon."

"In that case, what more can I possibly want, Eugenia? The morning is well lost—if we can share the afternoon."

Their hands touched.

# EPILOGUE

Again, Janus Pitt sat there alone, enclosed.

The red dwarf star was no longer an engine of death. It was just a red dwarf star to be pushed to one side by an ever more arrogant humanity, growing yet further in power.

But Nemesis still existed, though it was no longer the star.

For billions of years, life on Earth had been isolated, performing its separate experiment, rising and sinking, flourishing and undergoing vast extinctions. Perhaps there were other worlds on which life existed, each one isolated for billions of years.

All experiments—all, or almost all, failures in the long run. One or perhaps two that were successes and worth all the rest.

But that was only if the Universe were large enough to isolate all the experiments. If Rotor—their Ark—had been isolated as Earth and the Solar System had been, it might have been the one to work.

But now—

He clenched his fists in fury—and desperation. For he knew that humanity would run from star to star as easily as it had run from continent to continent and before that from region to region. There would be no isolation, no self-contained experiments. *His* grand experiment had been discovered, and doomed.

The same anarchy, the same degeneration, the same thoughtless short-term thinking, all the same cultural and social disparities would continue to prevail—Galaxy-wide.

What would there be now? Galactic empires? All the sins and follies graduated from one world to millions? Every woe and every difficulty horribly magnified?

Who would be able to make sense out of a Galaxy, when no one had ever made sense out of a single world? Who would learn to read the trends and foresee the future in a whole Galaxy teeming with humanity?

Nemesis had indeed come.